"YOU'RE AS BEAUTIFUL AS JACE DESCRIBED YOU."

Jake's deep voice had taken on a seductive tone, and incredibly, started a spiral of fire deep in Vanessa's stomach.

"If you came here looking for Jace," he went on, smiling, "I'd be happy to stand in."

"No, thank you," she bit out hoarsely.

"But you're hungry, Vanessa," he half-whispered, in a voice so like Jace's she could have screamed. He ran a hand lightly down her bare arm. "Why so hungry?"

She was too shaken to answer. When he bent and kissed her lips the spiral spread its sensuous burning languor through her.

Suddenly Vanessa was filled with a deep consummate longing in which every gray day of every year she had been deprived of a man's passion was outlined against the roaring fire that was ignited in her now....

ALEXANDRA SELLERS

is also the author of

SUPERROMANCE #13

CAPTIVE OF DESIRE

Laddy Penreith was seventeen the night she met Soviet writer Mischa Busnetsky. Surrounded by a watchful crowd, neither could reveal the searing passion that flared between them.

Eight years later—years Mischa had spent in prison for his writing—that flame still burned for Laddy. When Mischa was suddenly released, she flew to him. His touch told her he had forgotten nothing.

Until an act of betrayal drove Mischa so far away that Laddy felt the brief golden hours of their lovemaking had been all in vain....

ALEXANDRA SELLERS

FIRE IN THE WIND

To Terry Fox,
in salute

Published December 1982

First printing October 1982

ISBN 0-373-70042-3

Printed in Canada

Love in absence is like fire in
the wind: the small is extinguished,
the great inflamed.

Comte de Bussy-Rabutin

Prologue

He couldn't have said exactly how he knew her, from such a distance. It wasn't really by the color of her hair, though he had thought it unique then and he knew it unique now: in the long intervening years there had been few women in his life with hair that shade, though for a long time he had actively sought them out. Nor was the spark of recognition entirely touched off by that somehow distinctive line of her back, which he had known so briefly in those distant days that suddenly, now, seemed sharper than the memory of yesterday.

It was her attitude of intense interest, he pinpointed it suddenly—the angle of her head, cocked just that way when she was listening to someone; and although he was behind her he knew with an almost disconcerting clarity just how the half-smile and the dark, slightly narrowed gaze would give her face a look of passionate inquiry that could keep a man talking for hours.

The man's own eyes narrowed then, and he smiled a slightly crooked smile, as though the muscles on one side of his face did not respond as easily to the dictates of his nerves as those on the other side. It gave him a faintly cynical look—but then, he was a cynical man.

He was also rather cruel emotionally, or so he had been told. His eyes narrowed even more and the smile became more satirical. Perhaps he *was* cruel. He had been told by women that he took pleasure in the emotional hurt he caused them, but that wasn't true: mostly he had been indifferent to it. He was not indifferent now, however. He gazed at the gracefully curving back across the room and felt the deep slow thud of anticipation begin in his brain and his stomach.

This heart he was going to enjoy breaking.

CHAPTER ONE

"YOU SURPRISE ME," the man who told her he had arranged the show said with a smile. "Most New Yorkers—especially in the fashion industry—seem to think that Montreal and Toronto are the only cities in Canada."

"Do they?" asked Vanessa. "There was a time when I thought Vancouver was going to be my home. I nearly immigrated here."

Gary Smeaton blinked at her. He was young and seemed almost too self-effacing to have sold Vancouver to the trade organization as a location for the fall show. But then—Vanessa glanced around the moderately crowded room where manufacturers, models, buyers and designers were talking and drinking and introducing themselves—perhaps Canadians were, as a nation, more low-key than she was used to. This introductory cocktail evening was certainly proceeding quietly enough, without any of the hoopla, the wheeling and dealing, the loud voices that she was used to.

"Oh?" His voice called her back. "So you must know the city well. I had the impression this was your first visit." He looked hurt; he had just been telling her about certain attractions in the city that she must not miss. Some of them she had heard of before, a long time ago, from Jace. Funny how memory could be so tricky—let you forget the name of a person you'd met yesterday, but remember names like Grouse Mountain, Stanley Park, Gastown and Galiano Island—places you'd only dreamed of seeing—for nearly ten years.

"It is my first visit," Vanessa said. "It's the first time I've ever been to Canada."

She had got here at last, if not in the way she had imagined, nine and a half years ago. She had come on business, on the strength of her own talents, and the knowledge gave her a quiet satisfaction that was stronger than the bittersweet memory. Vanessa sipped her drink and smiled at Gary's faint bewilderment. "Haven't you ever fallen in love with a place you've never seen?" she asked.

He laughed. "Really?" he queried. "You fell in love with Vancouver way over there in New York? How did you happen to do that, or is it a long story?"

Her face slowly lost its smile. *It's a short story,* she was thinking. *I fell in love with a man who told me to dream of Vancouver, and I've never been able to stop. And that's all there is.*

She had let a silence fall between them, and she realized that Gary was watching her with an air of puzzled interest. Vanessa forced herself to smile.

"Yes, it's a long story," she agreed. "Tell me what it's like to organize a week-long trade fashion show."

He finished off his drink and looked around absently for a place to set his glass. "I didn't actually organize the show," he said. There was nowhere to set the glass, so he continued to hold it. "I work for Concorp, the company that owns this hotel. Concorp also owns a ladies'-wear manufacturing company, Designwear. My boss, who owns Concorp, never misses a trick. I started working three years ago on bringing this trade show to Vancouver and to this hotel. That's really all I did."

"Your boss sounds like—" Vanessa broke off when Gary coughed significantly and interrupted her with "Hi, Jake. What do you think?" She turned, and the man behind her was so close they were almost touching, so he must have heard what she said. Vanessa's cheeks pinkened, though all she had been going to say was, "Your boss sounds like a pretty smart businessman."

"Looks good, Gary," the man was saying in a deep voice, but when she looked up his dark eyes were on her.

"H-hello," Vanessa said softly, disconcerted to find him staring at her like that, like someone who saw something he wanted and didn't care who knew it. He was a dark man, with thick black hair curling slightly down over his forehead, and skin bronzed with tan. He was tallish—just over six feet, she thought—and of a lean muscularity more like a tennis player or a rodeo rider than a weight lifter.

He exuded power. He did not need the pretty curvaceous blonde clinging to his arm as a symbol of his influence, not this man. Nor, Vanessa was suddenly thinking, as a sign of his sexual power. Or perhaps men didn't pick up on the strong masculine tension in him, a tension that was attracting her and making her wary all at once.

"Hello," Jake returned in a deep rich voice that was sending her more than just a message of greeting.

"Vanessa Standish, meet Jake—"

"And Louisa," Jake said at the same time.

Louisa seemed a vapid little beauty, but she was not slow where her own interests lay, and her greenish eyes told Vanessa in no uncertain terms that she knew what effect Jake's nearness was having on Vanessa and that Vanessa could just forget it. Vanessa wanted to laugh. It had been a long time since a woman had challenged her as openly as this, but she had no desire whatsoever to poach on Louisa's preserves. She wasn't interested in any week-long affair. She tried to communicate this with an open smile, but Louisa's face remained closed and hard and unconvinced. "We've met, haven't we?" Vanessa asked then, and she was close enough to Jake to sense the odd fact that he tensed when she spoke. "Aren't you modeling with us—TopMarx?"

"Oh! Oh, yes," said Louisa coolly, her eyes running almost insolently over the other woman's face.

Vanessa was striking. Her high broad forehead tapered to a firm jawline and delicate chin, and her brown eyes had a way of darkening whenever she was interested so that, like a black hole in space, they seemed to absorb everything. People didn't usually forget her.

But Louisa was looking at her as though she could not quite remember ever having seen Vanessa before. The meeting had been brief, and Tom and Martita had done all the talking to the three local models they had hired, so perhaps it wasn't surprising that Louisa hadn't recognized her, Vanessa thought. But as Louisa turned deliberately to Jake then, drawing his and Gary's attention back to herself with a soft comment, the message she was sending Vanessa was much stronger than mere nonrecognition. *You are an outsider here,* she was saying. *You are not important enough to remember.*

Neither of the two men was excluding her, though, and Vanessa stayed. The three-way conversation allowed her to study the man Louisa was being so possessive about. Jake had a lean narrow face with thick eyebrows, dark eyes and a prominent nose. His mouth was wide and well cut, with a slightly crooked smile that would have been charming were it not for the look in his hooded eyes. He was impatient, and he didn't mind letting it show. There was something he wanted, and he wasn't getting it, and Vanessa tilted her head curiously and watched to see what it was and how Jake would go about getting it.

Suddenly, it seemed to her, because she had not been attending to the conversation, Gary was moving off in the direction of the bar with Louisa on his arm. Vanessa looked blankly after them and caught a look of such venomous anger from Louisa that she gasped.

Then, realizing, she went still, turning slowly to gaze up into Jake's dark face.

It was there in his eyes. What he wanted was *her.*

A silence fell between them.

"How do you like Vancouver?" he asked her finally, but there was another conversation going on behind his eyes, and Vanessa was abruptly nervous.

"It's very beautiful," she said, though she hadn't seen much of it yet, just a vision of mountains and ocean from the air this afternoon and what she could see out of the taxi window.

"Your first trip?" he asked.

"Yes, how did you know?"

Jake shrugged. "It seemed likely," he replied, lifting his arm for a drink from the glass he was holding.

"Did it?" she asked curiously. "Why?"

She remembered what Gary had said about east-coast Americans not being familiar with Vancouver and wondered if that was the reason.

"I think," Jake said meaningly, "I'd have known if you'd come before."

She breathed. "My goodness, and they told me Canadians weren't aggressive," she said lightly, fighting the little inward flutter his words had caused. She had never been laid siege to quite like this. "You think we were destined to become acquainted?"

In the act of raising his glass for a drink he paused and looked at her for a long, long moment. Then, astoundingly, he threw back his head and laughed. "Yes," he said. "Yes, I do. Let's get acquainted, Vanessa."

He finished off the liquid in his glass and glanced at the nearly empty one she was holding. He slid an arm across her back and they began to move across the room toward the bar. "Tell me," he said, "why is a woman like you wasting her time in the modeling game?"

"The *modeling* game?" Vanessa repeated, almost choking on her indignation. "I'm not in the modeling game. I'm a designer, a fashion designer!" She wondered suddenly if this was what had made him think he could make such an obvious play for her. "Do I *look* like a model?"

She was slim and tall, and her russet-colored hair was a shining asset, but her face was not a model's face. It had a great deal too much character to be able to take on the bland self-effacement of a woman whose brain is less important than her beauty and whose beauty is less important than the garment she is wearing. Jake looked at her, taking in the details of her gold-flecked dark eyes, her hollow cheeks and her wide full mouth with an intensity that disturbed her.

"No," he said after a moment. "You're far too beautiful to be a model."

Vanessa swallowed. He was too good at this. He had made that sound not like the easy practiced compliment it was but as though the admission had been torn from him. Vanessa wasn't beautiful; she had never been beautiful, but looking into his eyes she could almost believe that Jake thought her so.

On their journey across to the bar he had neatly evaded several people who were trying to catch his attention, but now there was one man who wasn't taking the hint. As Jake waited for their drinks the man elbowed up beside him.

"Say, Conrad, I've been trying to get past your secretary for a week—" he began, but the rest of the conversation was lost on Vanessa as a pinwheel of stars went off in her head.

"What did he call you?" she asked distantly when Jake finished with the man and returned to hand her her drink.

Jake raised his eyebrows. "Did he call me something?"

"A name," she said. "I mean, your name. What is your name?"

He looked down at her, still, unmoving. "Conrad," he told her. "My name is Jake Conrad."

She would not have believed it would affect her like this, just the sound of that name making her tremble inside. Vanessa gazed into the pale liquid in her glass, trying to collect herself. "How extraordinary," she said, wondering if her voice sounded as high to his ears as it did to her own. "I knew a Conrad once, a long time ago. Jason Conrad. He was from Vancouver. I wonder if you know him?"

"Jason Conrad is my name," he said slowly above her head.

"It is?" she squeaked. It shook her; she looked up at the dark face, the hooded eyes more closely, as though for some evidence she might have missed. "The thing is, you do look...your eyes...." She faltered and trailed off, and began again. "There is something about you that reminds me of Jace," she said with a laugh. "I don't suppose you're related to him?"

"Jace," he repeated thoughtfully. "It's been a long time—" He broke off. "How long ago did you know him?"

"Nearly ten years ago," answered Vanessa. "In New York."

"That's a long time between visits," he said, and for the first time his odd crooked smile was directed at her. "What caused you suddenly to come searching for an old lover like this, I wonder?"

"What makes you think he's an old lover?"

"Your eyes, Vanessa. They give you away." He smiled more broadly, but his gaze was dark. "They also intrigue me. So full of mystery. Why are you coming for Jace Conrad now?"

He knows something, she thought uneasily, looking up at him. What did he know?

"I'm not coming for him!" she retorted crossly. "I'm here in Vancouver for the fashion show. Some of my designs are being shown. And it just crossed my mind that I might look him up."

Jake's eyes glinted down at her. "And what will your husband think of that?" he asked; she felt as though some other question were being asked, too. But she did not know what question.

Vanessa ran her thumb across the protective gold band she still wore. "My husband is dead," she told him quietly.

His eyes hardened, and she knew she had answered the unspoken question, too. "Ah," he breathed slowly. "A widow. Poor old Jace. He missed it. The beautiful widow Vanessa came for him and he missed it."

This was unaccountable hostility. Vanessa looked up at him in perplexity. "You talk as though you know him," she said tentatively. She could think of no other reason for his attitude; he must know the other Jason Conrad, and he must know what she had done to him. "Do you know him?" she prompted. She felt oddly confused; if he had told her then that *he* was the Jason Conrad she had known she might almost have believed him.

"Yes, I knew him," said Jake, his eyes suddenly very heavy lidded, his expression unreadable. "We were related: Jason Conrad was my cousin. We had the same name."

Vanessa breathed a dismayed gasp at his use of the past tense.

"Was?" she whispered.

He blinked pityingly down at her. "Jace Conrad is dead, too, Vanessa," he said. "Looks like you lost them both."

Without warning the world went black.

"COME ON, DRINK THIS," said the deep commanding voice above her head, and there was a strong scent of brandy under her nose. Vanessa pushed at the glass and the hand holding it. She was lying on something soft.

"I don't need that," she said, struggling to sit up. "I'm all right."

Jake Conrad helped her to sit up. "Are you?" he asked.

She had a splitting headache; that was all. She watched as Jake set the glass down on a table beside her and sank into a chair nearby. She looked around. They were in some kind of private lounge, and she remembered that Gary had told her this was Jake's hotel.

"I'm fine," she repeated, putting her hand to the

back of her head. "My head aches. What happened?"

"You fainted," Jake Conrad said briefly. "When did you eat last?"

"Oh," she said, remembering. She looked at him. "You're Jace's cousin. You told me that he's dead." She wondered why she had fainted; it had all been so long ago. She hadn't been in love with Jace for years.

"And you fainted," Jake Conrad repeated. "I'm curious: did you faint when your husband died, Vanessa?"

That was a brutal thing to ask, but she was too shaken to be angry. She squeezed her dark eyes shut, then opened them. Her head ached abominably. She wondered if she had struck it when she fell. "My husband was terminally ill for some time before he died," she said. "I knew it was coming."

"You knew Jace well," he said matter-of-factly. He was watching her closely, one ankle across the other knee, the heavy crystal glass in his hand warm with the glow of amber liquid.

"Yes," she said softly. "Pretty well." Well enough to have loved him, but now he was dead. She touched her forehead. "Did I hit my head when I fell?" she asked. She had never had a headache like this—except once, she remembered, on her wedding day.

"You didn't fall," said Jake Conrad. "You collapsed against me and I caught you before you went any farther." He glanced toward the other end of the sofa she was sitting on and she looked to see the jacket of his beige suit lying there, a dark damp patch on the front where she must have spilled her drink.

"Thank you," she said mechanically. The pain in her head was all Jace, then. Well, she had tried. She had tried to forget him.

"What was it?" Jake asked suddenly, as though he couldn't help himself. "A summer romance?"

She thought of the Christmas tree in Rockefeller Plaza, of snow falling thickly on dark nights, of the laughter of ice skaters floating in the afternoon air....

"No," she said dully. "Not exactly."

There was silence between them for a long moment, and then Vanessa found the courage to ask, "How did he die?"

He paused. "Of complications following an accident," he said.

Vanessa sat up and said breathlessly, feeling as though her heart had been clenched in a fist, "*When?* It wasn't—it couldn't have been the accident he had nine and a half years ago, could it?"

Jake blinked. "Yes, that's right," he said briefly.

"*Complications?* But he was all right; he was perfectly all right!" Vanessa protested helplessly. "What went wrong?"

"I honestly don't remember at this distance in time," said Jake. "It was nearly ten years ago, as you say."

And she had not known. All these years she had imagined him alive somewhere, marrying, raising children, settling into a life that took him farther and farther away from her—and all the time he had been dead. Vital, laughing Jace had been dead practically since the night of their last goodbye, the night whose memory had never left her, for all her attempts to banish it....

She had been doing volunteer work at the hospital a few hours a week while attending the design course at college. Jace Conrad had been brought in late one afternoon after a traffic accident, with several broken bones and a face cut to ribbons. He was a Canadian, he was in New York alone, there was no one to visit him. His eyes were swollen shut; he was bored and lonely and very irritable.

"I don't need sympathetic visits from little do-gooders!" he had stormed at Vanessa the first time she had tentatively suggested that he might like her to visit with him or read to him. Vanessa was young and vulnerable, so she had retired into hurt silence, and after that she had spoken to him as little as possible, quietly and unobtrusively bringing him the coffee he asked for.

"Dammit," he said suddenly one day, "can't a man have one show of temper without wounding you forever? You used to laugh and chatter, and now when you come in here I feel as though I'm on death row."

"How do you know it's me?" she asked in astonishment, gazing at the bandaged face with its swollen unseeing eyes.

"Well, of course I know!" he exclaimed impatiently, as though that was explanation enough. She felt an odd little flutter in her stomach, as though he had said something very significant.

She was as good as engaged to her childhood sweetheart, Larry, but she was not wearing a ring. In a very short time she was coming to the hospital every day to visit Jace, and by the time the stitches had been removed from his disfigured face they were in love.

He was released from hospital just as she began her college Christmas break, and then they spent all day, every day together. Sight-seeing, window-shopping, walking through an early thick snowfall, warming themselves over coffee, singing carols—everything they did was magical, bathed in the glow of their love. He loved New York City, and he showed Vanessa her own city in a way she had never seen it, the tourists' New York. She copied his accent, not so very different from her own, saying "oot" and "aboot" instead of "out" and "about." He told her she sounded like a demented Scotswoman, not a Canadian, but, laughing, she insisted that she sounded just like him. One day a waitress paused to talk to them about Canada and told Vanessa how much she admired her country and wanted to visit. With a straight face Vanessa urged her to do so, telling her in her atrocious mock accent that Vancouver was the most beautiful city in the world.

"I told you so!" she crowed when the waitress had gone. Jace shook his head, smiling.

"After this I'll believe anything," he said.

He had to return home. His face needed surgery, and his work wouldn't wait forever, even though he was in his father's business. She promised to go and visit him at her Easter break, and it was unspoken between them that he would ask her to marry him then and she would say yes.

Jace was scheduled to leave on the afternoon of Christmas Eve. On their last night together he took her to a very special restaurant, and then they walked through cold streets white with a fresh snow that hadn't yet turned to gray slush, and then, unable to part, they had gone back to his hotel room.

His body was battered, bandaged and sore, but he wanted her; like a soldier going to war he wanted the memory of her to take with him, like a promise.

She wanted to give him that promise; he was her first lover, and she loved him more than anything in the world. "But you'll start bleeding again!" she protested, half-laughing.

"I bleed every time I look at you," Jace said hoarsely, reaching for her, and her smile died on her lips when she saw the look in his eyes.

She was nervous and afraid, being undressed by a man for the first time. He was clumsily one-handed, his other wrist in plaster, his arm in a sling, but the intensity of his gaze as he looked at her breasts and her body for the first time stilled her fears, made her want to weep for joy. This was why her breasts were full and rounded, she learned, so that Jace's eyes would close helplessly when he saw them; this was the reason her waist narrowed in just that way above her hips, so that his hand would tremble as it followed the curve to her thigh.

He told her it was so. "I've never loved anyone in the world but you, Vanessa," he said, clenching his jaw as though the love he felt was almost a torment. "Do you believe that? I've never loved one person in all the world before. And I love you enough for a thousand lifetimes. I must have been saving all my love for you; I must have known."

His hoarse voice started a fire in her, and he saw the look in her eyes and smiled in triumphant intensity. "Help me take off my clothes," he commanded urgently then. "I want to feel your skin touching mine."

He was bandaged at ribs, knees, shoulder, arm, shin and ankle, and they had laughed as she undressed him, because it seemed as though she hardly undressed him at all.

But she was shaken to the core when she saw what power she had over him, and her laughter died in her throat. She was suddenly desperate for his touch, desperate for him to take what he needed from her body.

Jace knew it, and he lay back against the pillows, his eyes burning into hers. "Come here, Vanessa," he whispered, and she lay beside him and rested her head on his bandaged shoulder while his one good hand stroked her with a gentle magical passion.

"Give yourself to me," he said softly. "I need to feel your pleasure, Vanessa. I need it."

Because of his need, of the heat of his love, because in that moment she trusted him completely, she let go, allowing him to give her the shuddering pleasure he wanted to give her. She understood that her need to have him take what he wanted from her body had enclosed the seeds of another need: to be given the pleasure she suddenly needed from his. And she learned that there was no greater joy in the world than this sweet wild commingling of giving and receiving.

When, unable to stop herself, she cried out her surprised joy to him, Jace looked down into her eyes with a triumphant possessiveness.

"You're mine," he said hoarsely. "There'll never be another woman in the world for me, Vanessa, and there'll never be another man for you! Tell me!" he commanded. "Say it!"

"There'll never be another man for me," she promised wildly, and beside the blinding truth of it, everything else was shadow.

He kissed her until she was breathless, and the next day he caught his plane for Vancouver, promising to wire her a ticket in time for her Easter break....

Vanessa, not sure how many of her memories she had communicated to Jake Conrad, lapsed into silence, letting her thoughts wander.

"Are you telling me," Jake's voice broke in on her, "that you were waiting for him to send for you, and you simply never heard from him again?"

"What?" Vanessa asked absently, breaking out of her reverie. "Oh—no. No, I sent him a Dear John letter and married Larry a few weeks later."

CHAPTER TWO

TopMarx, the manufacturing house Vanessa worked for, was third on the list at the afternoon showing of ladies' suits, but when her first model appeared Vanessa's thoughts were far from gauging how the trade in Canada would like her simple lightweight wool suit with the softly pleated skirt. Designing a women's medium-priced ready-to-wear line need not have been the constant unhappy grind that the past three years had been, but Tom Marx was committed to giving as little value for the money as he could, and that meant constant battles between them on the subject of quality. Battles that Vanessa, in a process that she felt was finally eating away her soul, invariably lost.

The suit as she had conceived it had a jaunty English school-miss flavor, as though the school miss had grown up and become office manager. But the perkiness in the line had disappeared with the few inches of fabric that Tom had insisted could be saved on the skirt. Vanessa always kept the needs of middle-income, self-supporting women at the forefront of her mind when she designed. But she knew that once a design had been through Tom's "process," a woman looking at it in Eaton's or Simpsons, the big Canadian department stores, would first think, *yes,* and then, trying it on, *well, maybe if I can't find what I really want*. But thinking of it was futile, and Vanessa's mind had wandered....

It wasn't that she had expected anything to come of a meeting with Jace even if she *had* found him after ten years. She had not imagined him single and waiting for her. He would have been thirty-three, after all. No, she had thought of him as being happily settled, competently running his father's business—what had it been, a trucking firm—but devoting most of his time and attention to his family. She had imagined going to visit him in a pretty townhouse or perhaps a house in the suburbs with all the neighborhood children shrieking happily around the pool, a house that her designer's eye would have found pleasing and tastefully done....

She would have worn one of her own designs—not one of the ready-made, skimped-on models, of course; for her own wear, Vanessa always made her designs up individually—and his wife would have admired it and Jace would have congratulated her on making a career for herself. And then, in a quiet moment, when his wife had left them alone, she would have explained why she'd married Larry, why she'd written him that letter without explaining anything...and then Jace would have understood and forgiven her, would have told her how happy he was without her, and she could have gone on with her life without the guilt and perhaps with a little less bitterness for her ten lost years.

Her worst nightmare had been that she would find

him unhappy, cheating on his wife and yelling at his kids. She would have hated that. She wondered now if the fear of it would have kept her, in the end, from dialing the phone. . . .

But her fears and imaginings had been for nothing. Jace was dead. If she had looked up Jason Conrad in the Vancouver directory she would have reached the cynical Jake.

Jake. When she had told him about the Dear John letter and marrying Larry, he stood up to refill his glass with an awkward abruptness that made her pause. The story wasn't unfamiliar to him, she was convinced of that. He had known.

"Were you close to your cousin, Jake?" she asked tentatively.

"Pretty close," he said shortly, his back to her, taking a sip of Scotch.

"Did. . .did he get my letter?" Vanessa swallowed over the lump that was in her throat. Perhaps he had died without knowing.

"Oh, yes, he got it," Jake said in a firm voice, turning around to face her. "He got it when he was lying in hospital awaiting surgery. He didn't wake up from the anesthetic. I've always thought it was your letter that killed him."

She felt as though she'd been shot in the stomach at close range. She actually made a small animal grunt, wrapping her arms across her stomach, hugging the pain to her. "No," she whispered hoarsely, begging. "No."

"I found the letter on his bedside table when I was clearing out his things," the voice that was suddenly so like Jace's went on inexorably. "I kept it. I think I've still got it somewhere. I give it a prize for the most concentrated cruelty in the most innocent schoolgirlish handwriting I ever expect to see."

Vanessa remembered her misery as she had written the letter, the torment of her mind. "Cruel..." she repeated. "Was it cruel?"

"It was, if I remember, a very bald statement of the fact of your preference for another man, written almost on the eve of your wedding. By the time he got the letter you were already married."

"Oh, God," she whispered. She was incapable of saying anything else. She hadn't meant to be abrupt or cold in the letter. She had wanted to beg, but she hadn't known how.... Suddenly, remembering, she sat up with a small helpless laugh.

Jake Conrad's eyes narrowed and the muscles of his face tightened till he looked like a carved wooden mask. The muscles pulled differently on one side of his face, so that the straight harsh line of his mouth was pulled down on one side, giving him an even crueler look.

"Enjoying your victory?" he asked grimly.

Vanessa sat up straight. "No," she said, "no, please don't think... I was just thinking about fate. I just remembered that all the time, I was half expecting Jace to turn up and stop the wedding. Even right at the last minute I was hoping he might be there and stand up—you know, when they say, 'Speak now or forever hold your peace.' And when he didn't come, I thought...." Vanessa set down the brandy glass and stood up. "And now you tell me the damn letter never even got to him till the wedding was over." She laughed once, harshly, feeling light-headed with pain.

The most incredible animal look passed over Jake Conrad's features, and he moved to her in a couple of quick steps and grasped her shoulders. "You were *hoping*?" he demanded harshly. "You were standing in church marrying another man hoping that...that my cousin would come and stop the wedding? Why were you marrying him, for God's sake, if you still loved Jace?"

He was looking at her with an angry hatred and she realized that he hadn't said what he'd said just to shock her. He must truly believe that her letter had caused his cousin's death, and he must hate her for it. But there was no point in making explanations. No amount of explanation would change the facts.

"I loved Larry, too," she said simply.

His hands on her shoulders shook her a little. "But you didn't want to marry him?" he insisted.

Vanessa sighed. It was all so long ago, and none of it was important anymore. Jace was dead, she was alive, and life had to go on.

"I'm tired," she said, pulling against the harsh grip of his powerful bronzed hands. "I'm going to go to my room and get some sleep."

He didn't let her go. His grip tightened and his eyes glinted down at her. He said, "You came looking for Jace Conrad for a reason, little widow. Were you maybe hoping for a brief nostalgic affair, just for old time's sake? Was that it?"

Vanessa moved her shoulders uncomfortably under his hands. "No, of course not," she said.

"Sure now?" he asked. "Because you're very beautiful—just as beautiful as Jace described you. In fact, even more beautiful now; women like you improve with age." His deep voice had taken on a seductive tone and, incredibly, started a spiral of fire deep in her stomach. She gasped in astonished protest at her own feelings.

"If that *was* what you were looking for, I'd be happy to stand in for Jace," he went on. "I like beautiful women." He bent and kissed her lips, and the spiral spread its sensuous burning languor through her body. It was a response she hadn't felt in her body for a long time, perhaps not since Jace had last kissed her. Larry's lovemaking had been sometimes gentle, sometimes passionate, and she had enjoyed his touch, but for him she had never felt a consuming passion that threatened to engulf her, as she had felt with Jace, as she was unaccountably feeling now, for Jace's cousin....

She pushed him away and stared at him coldly, her heart pounding in her chest and temples. "No, thank you," she bit out.

Jake threw back his head and looked down at her out of slitted glittering eyes. "No?" he queried. "But you're hungry, little widow," he half whispered in a seductive voice so like Jace's she could have screamed. "I tasted hunger on your lips." He ran a hand lightly down her bare arm. "Why so hungry?" he asked.

She was shaken enough to answer, "I told you my husband was very ill for several years before he died," She wanted him to believe that was the reason, not wanting him to know the hunger had been for him because he reminded her of Jace.

"For several *years*?" he asked, astonished. "And you never cheated on your sick husband, little widow?"

"Of course not!" she snapped. The gold in her dark eyes flickered into flame now with her anger.

"There's no 'of course' about it, Vanessa," he said. "In this day and age not many women would remain sexually faithful to a dying man, no matter how loyal they otherwise were."

Yes, many men had told her that, particularly Tom Marx, who had never stopped trying to start an affair with her. But Vanessa hadn't been able to give in to their reasoning or their demands.

"In any case, he's been dead for a year," Jake Conrad said cynically. "In all that time has no one tried to efface the memory of your beloved Larry?"

Yes, they had tried. But she merely shook her head at him, wondering what would have happened if Tom had ever kissed her the way this man had just kissed her. A man she had met only a couple of hours ago!

He said slowly, "I begin to see why you came looking for Jace. It was for more than just a nostalgic affair, wasn't it? You wanted him to release you from the memory of your husband. You thought you could give in to him because he'd made love to you once before, isn't that it? And then you'd be free of Larry's memory."

Only it wasn't Larry's memory she'd needed to be freed from; it was Jace's. She understood that now.

She'd needed to see him irrevocably tied to another woman so that she could try to find her happiness without him.... *That* was why she'd dreaded finding him unhappily married, because if Jace had still wanted her after all this time, if he'd wanted her on any terms at all, she couldn't have refused him.

"When we were kids," that caressing voice was suddenly saying, "everybody thought Jace and I were twins. You almost thought I was Jace yourself."

But that hadn't been because of his looks. Jace's face had been so disfigured by the scars of the accident, still fresh and angry when he had left her to go home, that physically she might not have recognized him now. It wasn't the fact that this man looked like his cousin that caught at her throat, it was the little things: his eyes when he was laughing, his voice, his hands. In other ways, Jace and his cousin were quite different. Jace had been thinner, more wiry. His cousin had a lean muscular build and was at least an inch or two taller than Jace had been.

"You could tell yourself that I was Jace and get the cure from me," the voice finished. "I'd play the game."

Vanessa gasped in outrage. "How dare you?" she snapped.

"It isn't I who will need to be daring," said Jake. "But you look like a woman who's never lacked for courage."

She had left him then without a word, pushing coldly past him, her mind an angry race of emotions she hadn't dared to examine too closely. It had been hours before she had fallen asleep last night, and now she was paying for it, her mind slow, unable to concentrate on the show.

She was sitting in the last row of seats in the showroom, and when the show broke for coffee, Jake Conrad was standing behind her. In the sudden hubbub of sound in the room he bent down to speak into her ear.

"Can I take you to dinner tonight?" he asked her, his voice a half-whisper, and Vanessa jerked back from his lips as though he had bitten her: she was unprepared for the sensations that shot along her skin at his near touch.

Tom, getting to his feet beside her, threw her a look and then one at Jake, but he said nothing. In a moment he was moving along the row in the wake of a woman buyer from Toronto he had met last night.

"What for?" Vanessa demanded coldly, all the more hostile because she felt so threatened by his close presence. "More of the same? I had enough last night, thank you."

"So that I can apologize," Jake said firmly, fixing her with a look that she couldn't break.

"You're sorry, are you?" she asked sarcastically, raising one eyebrow and, except for the tingling sensation his nearness had caused in her neck and breast and arm, feeling much more like herself and in control than she had been last night.

"Yes," he said. "Of course I am."

"So apologize now," she returned with a snap. "I don't need food to make me susceptible to apology for ugly behavior."

Other people in the row were having trouble getting out past her, and he took her arm over the chair backs and led her to the aisle.

"Ah," he said, "but I need good food to drown out the flavor of the crow I'm going to be eating." He smiled his slightly crooked smile at her, and his eyes for a brief moment held the dark intensity of Jace's gaze. "Humor me," he said quietly. "I want to see you."

She found that she simply could not say no. However much her reason told her to stay away from this man who obviously had an ax to grind with her, her emotions did not want to obey. Talking to Jake was a bittersweet reminder of Jace that she could not leave alone. She looked him in the eye, tasting this new sensation of logic losing the battle to emotion.

"I've heard that British Columbia salmon is a taste not to be missed," she smiled with a sudden exhilarating feeling of devil-may-care.

He gave her an admiring smile for the manner of her capitulation. "Nine-thirty?" he asked.

This evening's showing of day dresses was scheduled to end at eight-thirty, but it would be later than that before she could get away to her room to change. He had judged it nicely. Vanessa nodded, and in answer to an imperative wave from a friend across the room she moved away, uncomfortably aware that she didn't want to.

Colin James was a designer with whom she had studied at school; now he designed medium-priced sweaters for a New York firm. They had remained friendly over the years, following the changes in each other's careers, talking shop over innumerable coffees in the little greasy spoon that was midway between their two places of work.

"Super stuff, darling!" Colin said now, kissing her cheek. "I especially liked the last two numbers. Tell me how you squeezed them by the Philistine."

They always called their current employer the Philistine because, to a greater or lesser extent, the age-old conflict between business and art was always present between manufacturer and designer. Colin's eye was excellent. He had unerringly picked the designs she had had to wage a battle royal with Tom to get included in the fall line. Vanessa smiled delightedly.

"They'll be the better sellers, won't they?" she said. "But it was a battle. I only half convinced him to go for fall colors. Tom's convinced that if they buy blue in New York they'll buy blue everywhere."

It was a fact of fashion that generally Canadian women preferred the soft warm beiges, reds and browns of fall to the colder blues their sisters south of the border liked to wear, but Tom, attempting to break into the Canadian market for the first time with this trade show, didn't like change, and he didn't like to be told. Only the two outfits that he did not like were being offered in the full range of those autumn colors, and Tom confidently expected that those designs would be ignored by the major Canadian buyers. Vanessa was aware that Tom had finally given way to her ideas only because in some odd way he *wanted* her to fail.

"You're going to fall flat on your face, Vanessa,"

he had said at last, capitulating. "Flat on your face." And the tone in his voice had told her Tom would like the taste of that.

"Good for you," said Colin, who had given her this pointer on the Canadian market. Colin's firm had been marketing in Canada for some time. "Am I going to see you tomorrow afternoon?"

"For the sweater show?" she asked, and at his nod, "I'll be there. Are you coming tonight?"

In the push of the crowd they moved closer to the bar, and, deep in their shoptalk, obtained coffee. When they had moved away to a more open space by a wall, Colin interrupted himself suddenly to say, "Who's the eagle-eyed admirer, darling?"

"What?" Vanessa asked stupidly.

"The moody corsair over there who can't take his eyes off you," said Colin, who had a knack for labeling people. "The one you were talking to earlier."

"Can't take his eyes off me!" she repeated in amazement. "Who...?" She turned her head in the direction Colin was looking and caught Jake Conrad's gaze head-on, getting the full emotional content of it in one stunning blast before he disguised it. Vanessa sucked in her breath in audible dismay—because the look was one of brooding fiery anger, an anger whose heat she could almost feel.

Jason Conrad didn't look like a man who intended to apologize to her for anything at all.

THE EVENING SHOWING of day dresses was little short of disaster for TopMarx. The order of the showing of the dresses got mixed up; several of the accessories were almost garishly wrong, and Vanessa's best design came out on the wrong model, who was a size too small for it and who looked like a frump in it. To Vanessa it all looked very bad indeed, and Colin, who was a perfectionist in all matters of dress and style and who sat beside her for the show, did not help. In a steady stream of muttered asides he unerringly picked out every mismatched accessory, every single thing that went wrong. When the frail Louisa came out in the too large wool shirtwaist that was the pride of Vanessa's heart he groaned and shut his eyes.

"Navy shoes and a russet tent," he muttered. "A bit girl scoutish, isn't it, darling?"

The thing was that Colin took what he called sartorial solecisms personally, so that even walking down Fifth Avenue with him was often an exercise in torment. He was an avid clothes watcher and he would tear a passing pedestrian to pieces in a few choice phrases, always in a scathing undertone that only Vanessa could hear. But this was the first time she had been personally subjected to his systematic biting sarcasm. The fact that he was attacking not her designs but the presentation really only made it worse. When her company's parade mercifully concluded, Vanessa, with Colin in tow, stormed out to the dressing rooms and through the door marked TopMarx.

The first thing she saw was the reflection in the large lighted mirror that ran above the makeup table all along one wall. The mirror showed her Louisa's white naked back, crossed at the bottom by very tiny, very frilly bikini underwear and held at the curving waist by two large bronzed hands of the man to whom she was passionately clinging. The second thing she saw, turning her eyes from the mirror to the actual figures in the center of the room, was that the bronzed hands and the dark hair above Louisa's fairness belonged to Jake Conrad.

For a reason Vanessa couldn't define, it was the ultimate outrage. Her anger threatened to swamp her. In a voice of chipped ice she said to Jake Conrad, who was just lifting his eyes to hers, "Do you think you could make love to my models on *their* time, please?"

Louisa, who had been oblivious to everything except Jake's embrace, gasped and whirled, covering her breasts with her arms. All at once Vanessa realized most of the mistakes in tonight's show had involved Louisa, and certainly the worst ones had been her fault. Vanessa felt an almost overwhelming urge to slap the pretty, vapid face.

"You could at least knock," Louisa protested sullenly, at which Vanessa looked at her so witheringly the model's gaze dropped, and she turned mutely to reach for the bright turquoise robe that was draped half on a chair, half on the floor behind her.

Vanessa held the door wide, aware that Jake Conrad was looking at her through hooded calculating eyes, a crooked half-smile on his wide lips. "Would you get out please?" she demanded coolly.

Before he could respond, Louisa said in her high voice, slipping on the robe, "It's his hotel, you know!" Her tone was childishly triumphant, as though this was a telling blow in a close battle. Vanessa gazed at her, her anger sharpening at this evidence that Louisa was showing no professional remorse over the way she had botched the show. She wondered suddenly if Louisa had been trying to get back at her for last night, when she had lost Jake to Vanessa at the party.

"I'm sure that gives Mr. Conrad special rights with *you*," Vanessa said silkily, in a voice whose sheer female bitchery surprised her, "but he can hardly expect it to work with everyone. Mr. Conrad?" she finished, indicating the still open door.

"Vanessa," he returned politely, inclining his head as though at a greeting. His voice was soft, but his dark eyes took in everything. He took the door knob from her clasp and closed the door softly as he went out.

Vanessa ripped into Louisa with the ferocity of an avenging angel. As soon as the door closed behind Jake Conrad she began coldly listing the mistakes the model had made that evening, outfit by outfit, counting them off on her fingers with a catalog's accuracy. When she got to the issue of the size of the russet dress each word came out like a small shard of ice.

"That dress," she said hardly, "is for the sophisticated white-collar working woman who has some sense of style. You looked like a charity patient at Bellevue Hospital. It was supposed to be worn by Martita, who came out instead in the navy A-line. You were supposed to show that. Now just what the hell was going on here tonight?"

Colin was leaning negligently against the door saying nothing, but Vanessa was wishing she had asked him to leave, too. Louisa's sullen pretty mouth was setting into a mulish line and it was probably a mistake to have taken her to task in front of an audience. Angrily she wondered where Tom was. He should have been here, too, or was his fashion eye so bad that he hadn't seen what had happened?

"It didn't look that bad," Louisa said. "It's a shirtwaist—and anyway, I pulled it in at the waist and rolled up the cuffs."

"Why were you wearing it?" Vanessa demanded.

"Because I was busy talking and Martita was nagging me to put on the navy because I was going to be late and finally I just told her to put it on herself, and she did, so I put on hers."

Vanessa closed her eyes and thanked God for the Martitas of the world, who felt some sense of responsibility to the job. Martita was a regular TopMarx model who had traveled with them from New York. Louisa and two other local models had been hired on their arrival in Vancouver for the duration of the show. Vanessa wondered what kind of evening Martita had had, trying to organize not only herself but Louisa, too.

"Where are Martita and the others now?" she asked.

"Alison and Jenny are over at the West Coast Sportswear dressing room." Most of the local models worked for more than one manufacturer at these shows. "And I don't know where Martita is." Her tone added, *and I don't care!*

Vanessa took a breath, the anger somehow drained

out of her. "All right, you won't be needed here anymore. You may as well take your things with you when you leave tonight."

Louisa's mouth opened. "But the show goes on for three more days!" she protested.

"We'll be getting someone else in," Vanessa said. Tom wouldn't argue this decision. If necessary three girls could do the show.

"But this is my first job," she wailed, like a child being robbed of a promised treat.

"Well, watch out it isn't your last," Vanessa said unfeelingly, making a mental note to tear a strip off the woman at the modeling agency. "If you don't act like a professional you won't be hired as one."

Louisa's eyes narrowed and glinted green as she gazed insolently back at Vanessa. "Well, anyway, I don't care," she said. "Jake's taking me out to dinner tonight, and I won't need a job after that. Jake'll look after me. He's always wanted to look after me, and tonight I'll tell him he can."

CHAPTER THREE

AT TEN O'CLOCK that night Vanessa lay in bed thinking very unkind thoughts indeed about Louisa Hayward. She had gone to bed early in the hopes of catching up on last night's missed sleep, but so far she hadn't even bothered to put out the bedside lamp; she knew her mind was too busy to let her sleep.

She had been looking forward to dinner with Jake Conrad, damn him. How dare he suddenly decide to take out another woman, just like that? Men! Vanessa sat up and punched her pillow angrily. What did they *see* in all that vapid beauty?

She was hungry, she realized with increasing irritation. Famished, in fact. Suddenly she was no longer counting up Louisa's sins, but Jake Conrad's. She was hungry because she'd deliberately not eaten since lunch in order to be able to do justice to B.C. salmon! He could at least have *told* her! Damn all the pretty, frail blondes in the world, anyway, and all the cruel dark men with Jace's eyes....

She heard the quiet knock on her door with welcome relief. Someone to take her mind off her troubles, that was what she needed, and this could only be Colin, since Tom was entertaining the buyer from

Toronto tonight. Vanessa had wanted to point out that the woman was buyer for only a small chain of Toronto-area stores and that he'd be better advised to entertain the buyer from Eaton's or Simpsons, whose chains extended right across the country. But she didn't. If Tom wanted to put pleasure before business that was his affair.

The knock sounded again as she was pulling her bathrobe from the hanger, and she sang out, "Coming!" as she slipped into its black terrycloth folds and tied it around her. Vanessa was naked; otherwise she wouldn't have bothered with a robe. She would have greeted Colin in pajamas without even thinking about it. In her first year of college she and Colin had shared an apartment platonically, and he was used to seeing her in just about every state of undress.

But a moment later she was glad of the robe. It wasn't Colin James at her door, but Jake Conrad.

"Hello!" She blinked, her hand going to her loose cloudy hair in self-conscious surprise. "What are you doing here?"

He smiled slowly at her. "You're a little late," he said tolerantly, as though that was what he expected from a woman. "I thought I'd just check to make sure you hadn't locked yourself in or something. May I come in?" he asked, doing so. He paused beside her, looking down. Suddenly his eyes narrowed.

The only light in the room was the lamp by the bed, and he seemed to catch sight of the rumpled sheets and take in her lack of makeup and the black robe all at once.

"Are you in *bed*?" he demanded in surprised concern. "What's wrong? Are you sick?"

Just in time she remembered how angry with him she was. "Yes, I am. Sick of you. What happened—Louisa pass out already?" Vanessa returned waspishly.

He had taken the door out of her hands and closed it, and he turned his dark head now and eyed her in mute surprise. After a moment he said slowly, "Let me get this straight. You were going to stand me up tonight because you saw a naked girl clinging to me?"

"I. . .I. . . ."

"Which is it—prudery or jealousy?"

"It isn't either, and you know it!" Vanessa exploded. "Now will you please get out of my room?"

For an answer he leaned his shoulders back against the door and looked at her lazily in the half-light. "Lady," he said softly, "you had a date with me tonight, and you did not do me the courtesy of informing me that you had changed your mind, or why. Suppose you give me a reason now?"

His body, in that casual posture, seemed dangerously lithe, and Vanessa most uncharacteristically lost her head.

"I said, *get out!*" she hissed, flinging herself at him as though she might be able to push him bodily out of the room. His arms, which had been linked across his chest, unwrapped with a speed that shocked her, and in a moment she was pressed up against his body, his arms securely around her.

"I want a reason, spitfire," he said, his eyes unreadable as he looked down at her, "and an apology. And—" as an afterthought "—a forfeit." His look seemed suddenly angry as his arms tightened around her. "I think I'll have the forfeit first."

He bent his head and kissed her, a slow expert kiss in which each teasing motion of his mouth created a need for the next until her lips were stretched wide in passionate acceptance of the tormenting thrust of his tongue. Vanessa was filled with a deep consummate longing in which every gray day of every year she had been deprived of a man's passion was limned against the roaring fire that was ignited in her now. Her desire shocked her and at the same time dulled her reason, so that, like a distant spectator, part of her was thinking, *I shouldn't let him kiss me like this.* But she made no effort to stop him. Instead, if her arms had not been clamped to her sides by his hold, she would have clung to him.

Jake lifted one hand to stroke her throat, then his mouth left hers to follow the trail his hand had blazed over neck and throat, down the deep V of her robe to the valley between her breasts.

Vanessa moaned, lifting her free hand to his dark hair, dropping her head back to expose her milky throat, pressing him to her. The hot wetness of his mouth caressed the fullness of one pale breast along the edge of her black robe and then, as his long fingers drew the material back, sought and found the nipple.

She moved into a region of no conscious thought. There was nothing she would not give him, nothing she did not want from him.

"Jace," she whispered hoarsely, and the sound of that name on her lips immediately jerked her into cold awareness. The magic was gone. With a gasp she pushed at him, trying to cover her exposed breast with the robe against the pressure of the long fingers that held it.

Jake held his hand against the swell of her breast and raised his head to look into her horrified eyes. "Don't think about it," he murmured. "Jace or Jake, what difference does it make?"

She pushed his hand away, stepped back out of his arms. "No," she said flatly.

He smiled unkindly. "Little hypocrite," he said softly. "Who are you trying to kid—me or yourself?"

Vanessa straightened and stared at him, feeling her skin stretch tightly over the thin bones of her face. "I wouldn't expect you to understand," she said in cold anger. "You—"

"Oh, I understand." His knowing smile glinted at her. "If Jace were alive now, he could enjoy what you so obviously want to offer, not because you want him any more than you want me—and you do want me—but because you could pretend that it *meant* something. And you'd conveniently forget—"

Vanessa pulled the robe closely over her breasts like a schoolgirl and interrupted, "I do not want you."

Jake Conrad laughed. "No? Who do you want, then?"

She mustered her dignity. "Would you please lea—"

"Because you want someone, lady, believe me, you do," he breathed, and reached for her again.

She was fire and gold under his hands, and he was right. This had never happened to her before, a man charging her skin with electricity like this, so that she moaned helplessly the first moment he touched her, and it must be him she wanted, but how could that be, she was thinking dimly, as his expert hands and insinuating mouth turned her thoughts to clouds. Because he reminded her of Jace?

His strong arms were tightly around her and his lips moved under her ear and down her neck and she was aghast at her response.

"Stop," she whispered hoarsely, and then loudly, *"Stop!"*

He let her go again. "All right," he said in faint contempt. "We'll follow your rules." He looked at his watch. "You expressed a desire for British Columbia salmon. Can you be ready in ten minutes?"

Vanessa was breathless, lost. She blinked, trying to marshal her thoughts. "I. . .uh. . . ."

"Try," said Jake Conrad briefly. "I'll be back at ten-thirty." He smiled crookedly down at her. "If you decide not to get dressed, I'll assume you're expressing a desire for something else." His dark gaze locked with hers for one long moment as he touched her cheek with strong sensitive fingers, and then he was gone.

"Do YOU WANT your apology with the hors d'oeuvre or with the entrée?" Jake Conrad set down his drink and smiled crookedly at her, looking just like Jace.

Startled, she remembered why he had invited her to dinner.

"Oh, fire when ready," she said lightly.

He breathed once, then reached out and touched her fingers where they lay on the thick white damask cloth. The restaurant he had brought her to was as elegant as it was expensive, and the soft lighting and the gentle sounds of a piano encouraged its patrons to take their time. Vanessa looked into Jake's eyes and involuntarily remembered an Automat just off Fifth Avenue and a cold December afternoon when she had had a hole in her glove.

Jace had looked up from his cardboard cheese sandwich and smiled endearingly at her through his scars. "The coffee's good," he had said. "The coffee's always good in New York, it seems to me."

"Is it?" she had asked in surprise, liking the sound of it. "You should give that idea to the tourist board," she'd said; and together they'd visualized posters saying, "We may be broke, but we can always afford the price of a cup of coffee!" or "Promise her anything, but take her for coffee in New York...."

"I know where I want to take you," Jace had said, sobering. "A restaurant called Skookum Chuck's out on English Bay near the park. It looks out over the water, and you can see the lights of all the oceangoing ships out in the distance.... I'll take you there someday."

That promise would never be fulfilled now. But Vanessa, slipping into the present, looked out past Jake's shoulder to the lights of distant ocean vessels and asked hoarsely, interrupting him just as he was beginning to speak, "What's the name of this restaurant?" knowing before he said it what answer she would hear.

"Skookum Chuck's," he said briefly, his voice expressionless, his eyes losing their warm approval and narrowing into calculation. He looked as though he were waiting for something, but that must be her imagination.

"Jace promised to bring me here once," she said softly, still in her memories. "Funny that you should pick it—it's the first restaurant I've been to in Vancouver, outside the hotel."

"I told you I'd make a good stand-in," Jake said, moving aside his drink for the arrival of the avocado-with-crab-meat concoction that was their hors d'oeuvre.

"Yes, you did," Vanessa agreed mildly, "and unless I'm mistaken, that was what you were going to apologize for."

"Is that what you thought?" he returned with a half-smile. "But how could I apologize for thinking you beautiful and desirable and wanting you on almost any terms?"

To her annoyance, Vanessa felt herself blushing. With as calm an air as she could muster she averted her gaze, picked up her dry vodka martini and finished the last of it.

"Well, what *were* you going to apologize for, then?" she asked coolly.

"For saying—for telling you it was your fault that. . . Jace died," Jake said slowly and hesitantly as though he were fighting against a strong emotion. Vanessa set down her glass and looked at him.

She said bluntly, "Are you apologizing because you don't think it's true or only because you feel you shouldn't have said it?"

Jake didn't answer. "I see," she said softly. He looked suddenly dark and demon ridden, and she added, "You were very close to your cousin, weren't you?"

"What?" Jake said, startled, and then, "Oh—yes, I suppose, in a way."

So that wasn't it, she thought. He wasn't looking at her like that because she had murdered his best friend. She wondered if perhaps a woman had hurt him once, in a similar way, and he was somehow taking it out on her because she had done the same to Jace....

"You've been hurt by a woman, too," she said softly, thinking aloud, and immediately a shutter went down behind his eyes, and he smiled and shook his head.

"That is women's romantic fantasy," he said sardonically. "All women get it, sooner or later, and they all, sooner or later, offer to bind the wounds." His eyes were darkly cruel. "If you want to offer to bind my wounds, however, I'll take you up on it. I'm sure I can dredge up a scar or two for you to weep over."

He spoke lightly, cynically, but he was trying to hurt her. Vanessa looked at him without speaking. *We all have our own Keep Off signs,* she thought. *And this is yours, and you are lying to me. Someone has hurt you—and you want to take it out on me.*

Nervously Vanessa lifted her small silver spoon and tasted the avocado's crab-meat filling. It was delicious.

"Do you really own the hotel, or was that another of Louisa's little flights of fancy tonight?" she asked him, though she knew the answer, and she was rewarded when Jake relaxed.

"Does Louisa have flights of fancy? Yes, Conrad Corporation owns controlling interest in the hotel."

"And Designwear, too?" That was the name of the fashion company Gary had told her Jake owned.

"That, too."

"Then what do you actually do for a living?" she queried curiously. She had never met anyone before with a diversity of interests like this.

Jake laughed. "I make money."

"Jace worked for his father's trucking company, didn't he?" she observed. "How did you start?"

He paused. "After the operation—after Jace's death, I bought out my uncle in the trucking firm. He wasn't very imaginative and he wasn't ambitious. The trucking firm made him a nice little income and he would have been satisfied with that."

"I suppose after Jace's death there didn't seem much reason to work hard," she said. Jace had been an only child, she knew, and his mother had left him and his father when he was only a child. It had scarred Jace; she had known that, though he would not talk about it. Perhaps it had scarred his father, too.

"I suppose not," Jake agreed. "After that I bought a trucking firm in Seattle and then a chip-barge outfit in Campbell River.... I was lucky a lot of the time. I've got very diversified interests now."

"Any gold mines?" she asked with a little laugh. Jace had wanted to own a gold mine one day. She looked up, finishing the last of the avocado with a delicately appreciative flick of her tongue over her lips. He was staring at her, and he was suddenly demon ridden again.

"God, you're just like a cat!" He dragged in a ragged breath. "I've never seen a woman eat the way you do."

His sudden intensity took her aback. "What do you mean?" she faltered.

He said, "Has no man ever told you that you are completely sensuous? Why do you think I can't keep my hands off you?"

"Oh...I...." Vanessa blinked.

"Did you ask if I own any gold mines?" he continued harshly. "I own two, in Northern Ontario—small but promising. Do you want one? I'll give you one if you'll come to bed with me."

The little silver spoon clattered delicately against china, and then an electric silence settled between them. Jake Conrad's dark eyes watched her intently, unnerving her. Vanessa lost all power of breath and speech. Finally she shook herself and straightened her shoulders.

"You look as though you expect me to consider that suggestion seriously," she said with a faint, catty little laugh she was surprised she could produce.

Jake Conrad drew a breath and his eyes lost some

of their intensity. But he still watched her. "And won't you?" he queried. "Most women would."

"Most women would *what*?" she snapped.

His lips twitched. "Would consider the proposition seriously," he said slowly, as though he were talking to a child or a half-wit.

A slow anger burned in Vanessa. She wasn't going to take this. She took a deep breath.

"Look," she said, "I know what you want, and I think I know why. But it's nothing to do with me, so kindly keep your personal demons to yourself. If there was a woman once who thought money was more important than you, then I am sorry for you, but it is manifestly not my fault."

She would have stopped there, but he was looking arrogantly, cynically amused, and unaccountably she wanted to break through his defenses, to reach his real emotions, even if only his answering anger.

"However, having seen the kind of women you seem to choose, I must say I'm not surprised. I've never seen anyone more likely than Louisa Hayward to be the kind of woman to choose money over love."

She did not break through. Jake Conrad's face took on a cynical smile, and his voice when he spoke was triumphant, as though they were debating and she had just lost a point. "The kind of woman you are, in fact?" he said.

"I *beg* your pardon?" Vanessa's anger burned faster.

"Larry Standish was from a very wealthy family, wasn't he? Isn't that why you married him? Jace's father's trucking firm couldn't stand up against the Standish millions."

At that precise moment the quiet waiter appeared at her shoulder with their poached salmon. Biting back her response was so difficult it was painful. Vanessa clenched her jaw and her hands and breathed deeply, as tears started in her eyes. After what seemed an age, the tuxedoed waiter had arranged everything to his satisfaction and disappeared as silently as he had come.

"How dare you!" she hissed at Jake. "How *dare* you!" It was all she could say. She wanted to laugh and cry at the same time. Giving up Jace to marry Larry had been the cruelest sacrifice ever asked of her. To be accused now of having had mercenary motives was almost more than she could bear.

"Isn't that true?" he asked. "It's easy to see you've got more money to spend than the average working girl. That dress you're wearing now has most of the women in the room gnashing their teeth in envy. You didn't get that on your salary, now, did you?"

"This dress is of my design and my execution!" she said hotly, angry because she was making explanations. "As are all the clothes I wear. And the clothes I wear are not enough justification for the hideous accusation you just made to me! Who the devil do you think you are?"

"It's not true?" he asked intently, a startled look coming into his eyes. "I...that's what Jace thought."

"What *Jace* thought? How do you know what Jace thought?" she demanded.

"He told me what he thought," Jake said.

Vanessa stared at him, her eyes wide. "When?" she insisted.

"In the hospital. Before he went in for his operation," Jake replied. "He told me about La—"

She interrupted fiercely, "What's going on here? You told me you found out about my letter after he was dead, when you cleared his belongings out of his hospital room!"

He blinked as though he had lost his bearings for a moment. Then he said hesitantly, "No, I...he didn't show me the letter. He told me you had married someone else. Larry. And he told me why. Later I found the letter."

Vanessa eyed him for a long moment. She was sure he had said...but she couldn't remember the conversation well. She had been too emotionally shaken. It seemed she was always being shaken emotionally while this man was around. She breathed deeply in an effort to calm herself.

"I can't believe that's what he thought," she said quietly, all her anger suddenly dispelled. "Oh, God, I can't believe he died thinking that about me!"

Tears pricked her eyes and she looked down. The sight of the damask cloth brought to her mind suddenly the long dining hall at the Standishes, glittering with silver and crystal under a magnificent chandelier.

She wanted to clear herself of the accusation of having sold out to that, she wanted to go back in time and tell Jace it wasn't true...but there was no Jace to tell, only Jake. And it wasn't his fault if he believed what his cousin had told him on his deathbed.

She said, "I never took money from them. I always made my own way. After I married Larry I stayed in college even though they said no matter what happened I'd never have to work again. When Larry got really ill they paid all his hospital and medical fees, but I never took money from them." She looked up at Jake, her eyes unconsciously pleading.

She thought, *let him tell me he lied. Let him tell me Jace never thought that....* "Is that what he believed, really believed, about me?" she asked.

His voice was harsh. "Jace probably thought a hundred different things. What difference does it make whether he had the right reason or not? The hard fact was that you jilted him without a word of explanation. What do you care what explanation he dreamed up for himself? What difference does it make to you?"

"It makes a difference," Vanessa said doggedly. "I didn't tell him the reason because he didn't ask. If he'd—"

She broke off because Jake was laughing, a mirthless incredulous laugh. "He didn't ask? What room did you give him to ask?" he demanded harshly. "I told you, you were already married by the time—" He broke off. "You're a woman who demands a lot from a man, obviously. You want a man to keep coming at you while you're saying no, is that it? Is that what I should have done tonight? Taken you in spite of yourself?"

She gasped under the force of his attack. "No!" she said angrily.

"No, eh?" He looked unconvinced. "Well, I'm glad to hear it. Because I don't like shrinking violets and I don't much care for rape. When you come to my bed I want you willing—just remember that. The blame for any wasted time will be at your door, not mine."

Vanessa sat stunned. "You must be out of your mind," she said coldly. "Believe me, I will not be coming to your bed, willingly or otherwise." And in that moment she believed it.

Jake shrugged lightly. "Fine," he said. "Nobody wins them all. Let's eat this salmon before it gets cold." He changed the subject then with admirable ease. His voice was cool, uninterested, as though she were no more to him than a casual conquest he could easily do without. But his eyes held another expression, one she could not read—and she knew that somehow, somewhere, Jake Conrad was lying to her.

HE DROVE HER through Stanley Park before taking her back to the hotel, and the magic stillness of the tall Douglas firs enveloped them in the quietly purring car till she could hardly believe she was in a city.

"It's beautiful," she whispered, and Jake pulled the car over and stopped.

"Would you like to walk for a few minutes?" he asked. "There's a very pretty pond just over there."

"At one in the morning?" she asked in surprise. "Is it safe?"

He laughed. "This is Vancouver, Vanessa. The population is barely one million. No one's going to jump us. Come on." He climbed out of the car and walked around toward her door, but she got out by herself and joined him. She breathed deeply in the night air, reveling in the stillness, the peace that surrounded them.

Brrrh, brrrh.

Vanessa jumped and reached instinctively for Jake's strong arm. "What was that?" she whispered hoarsely.

He laughed down at her. "Relax," he said. "It was a frog over on Lost Lagoon. Where we are heading." Suddenly there was a chorus of frog noises so loud it made her laugh. She took Jake's arm, feeling perfectly easy. After he had forgotten his demons tonight, he had been a fascinating companion. She had forgotten her anger.

"What a serenade!" she exclaimed. "I'm glad I'm not a lady frog expected to fall for that racket!"

"If you were a lady frog," he said softly, "You'd be swooning and falling off your lily pad right now."

"The croaking is that good?" she asked, smiling.

"I'm no expert on the quality of the croaking," Jake replied. "But there's no reason to think you'd be less responsive as a lady frog than you are as a woman."

Her stomach fluttered at the tone in his voice. The night was too softly cool, the stars too bright, the setting too romantic. She wanted to ask him why he was so sure she was responsive, but that way lay danger. She searched her brain for a safe subject.

"Lost Lagoon," he said, as the path emerged from the thick trees at the edge of a small lake, still and perfect in the night. Vanessa sighed in delight.

"There's a paved path around the circumference," Jake said. "It would take about twenty minutes to walk it. How are your shoes?"

"Not up to it, I'm afraid," Vanessa said regretfully, lifting a delicately strapped foot for his view. She would have liked the walk. "It's very beautiful, Jake. I wish...." She stopped.

"It's much more prosaic by daylight," Jake said. "But perhaps you'd like to come back on the weekend when the trade show's finished? It's quite a famous bird sanctuary."

Vanessa bit her lip. She would have liked that, too. "I'm flying home first thing Saturday morning," she said.

His arm tightened for a moment around her waist. "Well, then, let's walk a little now. Who knows when you'll get another chance to see it?" Any regret in his voice was impersonal, so she must have mistaken that momentary tightening of his fingers.

They were passed by a pair of midnight joggers, sex indeterminate in the darkness, and this evidence of the park's safety bemused her.

"Canada's a very safe country, isn't it?" she asked. "Jace always said so."

"No country is as peaceful or as safe from vandals as it was ten years ago," he said quietly. "But we fare pretty well."

"Is it because of your gun-control laws?"

"Partly, I suppose," he replied. "A lot of the reason is historical. We didn't have the lawless opening of the West that you had south of the border. In Canada the settlers moved west accompanied by the

Royal Canadian Mounted Police—in those days they were called the Northwest Mounted Police. They were pretty impressive in maintaining law and order. We didn't massacre our Indians or fight wars with them. We made treaties instead. That doesn't mean they weren't ripped off," he said parenthetically. "Just that it was done in a peaceful lawful manner."

"And you think that makes a difference today?" she asked in surprise. "The way the West was settled?"

"Canadians had different heroes," Jake said. "In the States you were glorifying the Fastest Gun in the West, the rugged individual who didn't knuckle under to anything or anyone, including the law. Canadians, on the other hand, had heroes like Sergeant Preston of the Yukon, who kept drunken prospectors in line, whose great deed was the victory of law and order over lawlessness."

Vanessa found herself charmed by this insight. "Was Sergeant Preston of the Yukon *your* hero?" she asked.

"I had the best collection of Sergeant Preston comic books in three blocks," he said laughing. "Instead of practicing my quick draw I used to practice saying, 'Well, King, looks like this case is... *closed*,' in what I thought was a suitably heroic voice."

She gurgled into laughter. "Did Sergeant Preston say that very much?"

"He said it in the last panel of every story. King, of course, was his enormously intelligent husky, who could be counted on to bite the bad men at just the right moment."

Vanessa stopped and leaned against the large trunk of a Douglas fir, and gazed out over the lagoon to the lights of the tall buildings in the distance. The guardedness with which she walked through every moment of her life in the much larger, much faster-paced, much more exciting city of her birth slipped a little. She felt rather than saw the presence of the mountains that surrounded the city. Vancouver seemed to have a different sort of excitement, one that was threaded through with peace.

"If I'd come to Jace back then, I'd know this city very well, wouldn't I?" she remarked quietly.

"I guess you would," Jake agreed.

"Canada's like an island in the storm of the world," she said.

"Is it?"

"Look at the Middle East, look at Africa, look at Britain, look at us," she said. "You're always reading horrible things in the papers, but never about Canada."

"Give us time." In the starlight she saw one eyebrow raised over his crooked smile.

"You're cynical," she protested. "But I'm telling you Canada's different." She raised her arms. "Thank you, Sergeant Preston. I'm standing in the middle of—what is this, Stanley Park? I'm standing in the middle of a huge park in the middle of a large industrial city wearing a dress and a pair of shoes that wouldn't let me outrun a snail and I don't have to worry about someone grabbing me and—"

Jake interrupted her, placing his hands on her waist and pulling her against him. "Don't you?" he asked, and kissed her.

She was wearing her russet hair loose, and he threaded his hand in its silken cloudiness and cradled her head in his lean palm.

In the darkness he was more like Jace than ever, and that was dangerous. But her defenses were down, and she wrapped her bare arms up around his neck and opened her mouth to his seeking lips. They were firm and sure, knowing what they wanted. She could trust herself to this man's mouth, to his strong embrace....

He was holding her away from him, breathing deeply. "Let's get back," he said.

Vanessa felt drugged; she had wanted the kiss to go on. "Why?" she whispered.

"Because safe as Stanley Park may be, I am not going to make love to you on the edge of Lost Lagoon." Vanessa caught her breath at this evidence of her power over him. "Come on," Jake said, giving her arm a little jerk to get her moving.

They walked back to the car in silence while Vanessa came to her senses and wondered how the mood and her own feelings could have changed so drastically in the space of a minute. She looked at Jake's profile as he started the engine and realized with a sickening thump that somehow she had no armor against him. A lot of men had kissed her or tried to kiss her in the years since Larry had become really ill, and particularly in the year since he had died. She had never had the least difficulty in controlling whatever feelings their kisses had aroused in her, in keeping them at arm's length.

This man was different. He was too much like Jace, and her memories of Jace were suddenly too sweet and too close for her to control the feelings Jake raised in her.

The car slid to a halt in the drive of the hotel and a uniformed man opened the door to her.

"Park it for the night, Jerry." She heard Jake's voice behind her and turned to see another uniformed man sliding in behind the wheel of the elegant car. Her eyes caught Jake's over the top and she stared at him as the car slid away from between them.

"I'm not spending the night with you," she said in an undertone as they crossed into the lobby.

He looked at her. "Why not?" he asked calmly, just a little as though she were out of her mind.

The question flummoxed her. "Because...because you're too much like Jace and I don't want to make love to a ghost," she stammered unhappily.

"I told you it didn't bother me," he said, shepherding her across the lobby and through a door into the same private lounge she had been taken to on Monday night by him.

"Well, it bothers me!" she protested, pulling out of his guiding arm as the door closed behind them. "So what are we doing here?"

"I am offering you a nightcap," he said placidly. "The hotel bar is closed."

He crossed to a cabinet and pulled it open to reveal a shelf of bottles and a fridge. "What'll you have?"

"Perrier and lime, please," she requested primly,

half-expecting him to protest, to try to persuade her to have something more potent, but he merely pulled open the fridge.

"It will have to be Montclair," he said, examining the interior while he massaged a dark green lime between fingers and thumb. "No Perrier in here."

Vanessa laughed. "Don't tell me you have an interest in Montclair, too!"

"No," he replied absently. "What I expect I have is a patriotic-minded staff. Montclair is a Canadian mineral water."

He handed her a full glass and settled in the chair opposite hers as though they would be there for some time. But Vanessa finished her drink quickly, hardly hearing the idle conversation he began. Uncomfortably she set down her glass.

"I should go. I've got a full day tomorrow."

"Tomorrow?" He looked up. "Tomorrow is lingerie in the morning, knitwear and blouses in the afternoon and then cocktail dresses. Do you mean to say you've got designs in all of them?"

In fact, she didn't design in any of those areas. "No," she said sheepishly, feeling a fool, "but I promised Colin to sit with him for the sweater...." She broke off in confusion as he leaned over and took her hand.

"What are you running from, Vanessa?" he asked. She stopped breathing.

"I'm not running," she protested.

He was holding her left hand, and he fingered the broad gold band of her wedding ring. "Aren't you?" he asked. "Why are you still wearing Larry's ring?"

"Because Larry...I'm a widow," she protested. "Not divorced."

"Larry had nine good years of your life, and from what I hear, the last few at least weren't very happy. You aren't keeping men off for Larry's sake anymore. It's for some other reason, Vanessa."

Jace. It was Jace. Without knowing it she had somehow been remaining loyal not to Larry's memory but to Jace. And now Jace was dead, and she should stop wearing a wedding ring like a talisman to ward off evil.

Vanessa gazed down at the gold band, wondering what would have rested on her finger if she had refused to marry Larry and had married Jace instead....

"Someday I'm going to bring you here and buy you a diamond so big you'll need a crane to lift your hand," Jace had promised one cold crisp day as they stood in front of Cartier's. He had taken her inside, insisting that she pick the ring she would want when he was rich enough to buy her anything at all. They had been politely ignored by the staff, who knew to a nicety the difference between those who could and those who could not buy. Over Vanessa's protests that she didn't care about precious stones he had brashly made her look at everything in sight. No one in the luxuriously appointed rooms had spoken to them.

When they had gained the street again he had smiled at her. "They ignored us today," he had said with a laugh. "They didn't recognize the multimillionaire Jason Conrad behind all these scars." Then he had sobered. "Next time, they won't ignore me. Next time I take you in there, they'll say, 'Good day, Mr. Conrad. How are you today?' And I'll be able to buy you anything in the place. I'll do that on our tenth anniversary, Vanessa."

The ring blurred before her eyes. The last nine and a half years had been very different than she had envisioned in that moment, and Jace had been dead for nearly all that time. . . .

Jake's voice above her said, "Remembering Cartier's?" and she snapped her head up in amazement.

"How on earth do you know about Cartier's?" she demanded, a chill creeping down her spine.

"Haven't you guessed yet?" he asked dryly. "I know because Jace told me. Jace told me everything there was to know about you before he died. He told me so much I fell in love with you myself."

CHAPTER FOUR

"IN LOVE WITH ME!" Vanessa repeated in breathless surprise. Jake laughed.

"Don't panic, I got over it," he said. "But Jace was very persuasive. And you are very beautiful."

"You—but you hadn't seen me," she protested.

Jake paused. "Jace showed me your picture."

"Jace never had a picture of me!" she began. "At least—" She broke off. Nine and a half years was a long time. *Had* he had her picture?

Jake's eyes narrowed. "Well, he showed me one," he said positively. "It was a Polaroid shot, I think—the kind they charge tourists five dollars for on Fifth Avenue."

It sounded like the sort of thing they'd have done—get their picture taken like yokels. Funny she couldn't remember it. She thought she'd remembered everything about Jace, that wonderful week with Jace.

"Do you still have it?" she asked. "I'd like to see it, if I could."

Jake blinked. "Oh—I...I probably threw it out later when I came to my senses."

"But you saved the letter," Vanessa pointed out. Then she caught her breath. If he'd seen her picture,

Jake must have recognized her on Monday night at the cocktail party. Or at the very least when she mentioned Jace that must have sparked his memory. Why hadn't he told her that he knew who she was?

"I might have kept it, now that I think of it," Jake said. "If I get time I'll have a look for it." And suddenly he was saying good-night and ushering her out the door so expertly that she couldn't ask him any of the questions that were whirling around in her brain. *Had* he loved her, she wondered—or had he only hated her for what she had done to Jace?

VANESSA WAS DOWN early for breakfast. She had meant to sleep late, but her body was still on New York time: she woke just before eight with a guilty start, feeling it must be nearly eleven. Once awake, her mind began to pick over the thoughts and worries that had lain dormant all night, and she knew there wasn't any point trying to get back to sleep.

She showered and dressed, looking out her windows over the bustling city, the water and the mountains beyond. Vancouver, she had learned, was built on a large peninsula created by an inlet to the north and a river to the south. The main downtown area, where Jake's hotel was, was situated on a smaller peninsula that jutted out from the large one into the inlet. The tip of this small peninsula was given over entirely to the thickly forested Stanley Park she had visited last night, so that the park was almost surrounded by water, meeting the city only at one narrow edge. Vancouver itself was also nearly surrounded by water—the Fraser River to the south, the

Strait of Georgia and the Pacific Ocean on the west, Burrard Inlet to the north, and had nowhere to go but up—up in skyscrapers and up the side of the mountains.

Looking north now across Burrard Inlet, Vanessa could see how the city, like a raging forest fire, had jumped the strip of water and had climbed as high as was possible up the low mountains on the other side. She wondered what it would be like to live high on the mountain and gaze down on the Pacific and the distant skyscrapers of the city center.

She breathed deeply. Jace had been right. Vancouver was the most beautiful city she had ever seen, with its own pace and its own enveloping peace. People were relaxed, casual and often unbusinesslike. She thought of Louisa Hayward last night and her resistance to the New York type of pressure to do everything absolutely right, absolutely on time, and she remembered her own violent irritation when the girl hadn't apologized for her unprofessionalism. There was a slower pace here that was just beginning to get to her.

What would she be like now, if Jace had lived and she had come here to marry him? Perhaps she would have finished her education at a Canadian university—there were two respected universities right in and near Vancouver. Perhaps she would have attended one. And she might have gone into a job in fashion design, casually, without trying to claw her way to the top or carve out a career for herself. She might have had a baby and brought her to work every day, the way a lot of Canadian women seemed to do.

There had been a pretty little baby in one of the dressing rooms each day of the show so far. His mother was either a model or a designer; Vanessa hadn't worked it out. He had played in a corner quite happily, and once she had seen him wandering from chair to chair as the models made up before the show, watching them with concentrated fascination.

Vanessa, standing at the window looking down on the city, had a sudden painful vision of a young child with Jace's eyes—the child she should have borne. She felt tears prickle the back of her eyes, and then the thought flashed through her mind: *Jake has Jace's eyes.*

It was a dimly formed, irrelevant thought. She pushed it away almost before she had grasped it, and instead deliberately made herself laugh by imagining Tom's face if he should walk into the design office one day and find her changing her baby's diaper on a design-strewn tabletop....

Tom was up early, too. She saw him, breakfasting with the buyer from Toronto, as soon as she walked into the restaurant. He caught her eye as she paused by the door, and she crossed to the table for two.

"Good morning." If Tom had been writing out a companion-wanted ad he would have described himself as a "young forty." He dressed five years younger than that and was in fact five years older, and the heartbreak of his life hadn't been his wife's leaving him six years ago, but his receding hairline.

He was dressed casually this morning, his shirt-front open over the gold chains around his neck, his Levi's fitting snugly around hips and thighs that were just a little too fleshy. In contrast, the woman with him was almost severely businesslike in a black linen suit and masculine white shirt.

Clawing out a career for herself, just like me, Vanessa sized her up at once and smiled. "Good morning."

"Have you two met?" Tom put his hand on the woman's arm in the way that a man touches a woman when he wants everyone to know he has just spent the night with her, and he looked up at Vanessa with a triumphant little smile.

He wanted to see if she would be jealous, Vanessa knew. She wondered how he could imagine that she, having turned him down herself, would still want to keep other women away from him.

"Margaret, Vanessa."

Margaret lifted her hand to shake Vanessa's and smiled up at her. "We've said hello," she said, "if we haven't actually met."

"Monday night," Vanessa agreed.

"How come you're up so early?" Tom inquired, as though he did not want the women to get chatty with each other. "Thinking you might start a lingerie line?"

The morning showing was of lingerie, in which TopMarx didn't carry a line.

"No, I'm going to do some sight-seeing this morning, I think, if we can get a replacement model fast enough."

Tom snapped his fingers. "I forgot, you fired that

girl last night, didn't you? Can you get another one in before tomorrow night?"

Typical of him to expect her to find the replacement, as though Vanessa had fired Louisa for some petty personal reason and not because it was good business to have TopMarx's designs shown to their best advantage.

"Tom..." she began, and then stopped. If she tried a showdown now, in front of a woman he obviously wanted to impress, Tom would get ugly and then Vanessa would be irritated for the whole morning. And then she wouldn't know whether he had got a replacement till half an hour before the show. She had enough on her mind without a fruitless argument with Tom.

"Is that one of your own designs?" Margaret was eyeing the summery green cotton pants with the intriguing tied waistband as though she hadn't noticed the slight tension in the air. Vanessa turned to her gratefully.

"Yes, they are. Not the top, of course." Her top was a simple T-shirt in matching green that she had picked up at Macy's.

"*Very* chic," said Margaret. "Are we seeing something like that tomorrow night?" Thursday night skirts and slacks were being shown, but although Vanessa had designed a pair similar to these in wool, Tom had axed them from the fall line as being too expensive in both material and production time.

Tom was shaking his head. "Too bulky in wool," he said shortly. "Made 'em look fat."

The woman's professional eye was not fooled; but she said only, "Pity. They'd go over big here in a lightweight wool. Toronto's a cold damp city in the winter, and with a coordinated jacket those could look very smart in the office."

Just about exactly what Vanessa had said to Tom six weeks ago, but she didn't show the rather bitchy triumph she felt now. She smiled her thanks at Margaret, saying to Tom, "I'll let you know when I've got a model." The waiter arrived then with their breakfast, and Vanessa moved away to a table by the window.

It was a beautiful early summer day and the restaurant window faced in the same direction as her bedroom, looking across Burrard Inlet toward Grouse Mountain. There was a cable lift up the mountain, she knew, and she was suddenly wishing she hadn't promised to watch this afternoon's showing of blouses and sweaters with Colin. She could have had the whole day free, and most of Thursday, since TopMarx had nothing showing until tomorrow night's slacks and skirts. She could have rented a car and spent the two days sight-seeing.

She ate her breakfast quickly, because she did not like eating alone. She was half expecting to see Jake Conrad appear, since she was sure he had spent the night in the hotel. But by the time she had finished her last cup of coffee he hadn't appeared, and she realized with irritation that she had spent the entire meal watching the door for him and thinking over what had happened the night before.

There was something very confusing about Jake

Conrad, something she couldn't understand. Had he really ever loved her, or had he merely told her that he had for some reason of his own? She had never been more confused by a man in her life.

Tom and Margaret had had a leisurely breakfast. Vanessa was just waiting for the waiter to bring her change when Tom crossed to her table.

"I forgot to tell you—I'll be taking one of the buyers out to dinner tonight. I'd like you to come along. If you're going out will you be sure to be back by eight-thirty? I'll meet you in the hospitality suite."

He was gone without waiting for her to say yes or no, but what did it matter? She wasn't likely to be doing anything else tonight. If Jake asked her out, she knew she would have had to refuse anyway. There was no sense courting trouble, and Jake, however adept he sometimes was at disguising it, was trouble.

THE WOMAN AT the modeling agency listened to the litany of Louisa Hayward's sins with a placid lack of horror that secretly drove Vanessa up the wall. *It's a clash of cultures,* she reminded herself, gritting her teeth and gripping the receiver so tightly she thought her hand would break.

"She didn't come up to scratch, eh?" The woman clicked her tongue. "Poor Louisa. She doesn't understand yet that modeling is hard work. She thinks it should be glamorous."

Culture clash or no culture clash, Vanessa had had enough.

"You seem to suffer from a little of that same naiveté yourself," she said coolly and unmistakably. "I would like you to understand that you sent us a girl under the guise of a professional model who refused to go onstage in the middle of a trade show because she was *talking* and who single-handedly destroyed the showing with a collection of tricks I wouldn't expect from a *child*. Now I am telling you that we are not paying you for Louisa's services and you should consider yourself lucky if we don't sue you for lost business. I was going to ask you for a replacement, but from now on we'll deal with someone else!"

"Listen," the woman began earnestly, and Vanessa had the satisfaction of knowing that at last she had got through to her. She listened while the overdue apology and concern were expressed, but steadfastly refused to allow the agency to send a replacement model.

As soon as she hung up she kicked herself for a fool. Now she was stuck with finding another agency and she knew nothing about the Vancouver agencies. Nor did Tom, evidently. He had probably pulled this one out of the phone book, when with a couple of phone calls he could have got their New York agency to recommend one here.

She looked at the phone. It was nine-thirty on a beautiful morning and she had to be back at two-thirty for the sweater show. She could easily waste an hour trying to find a model, and they didn't need anyone till Thursday night's slacks and skirt showing.

To hell with it. Martita and the two girls they already had could cover if they had to. She would worry about the model later. It was Tom's problem as much as hers and *he* wasn't wasting the day worrying.

Vanessa picked up her bag and the loose green cotton jacket that matched her slacks, let herself out of her room and went down to the tourist desk in the lobby.

"You've missed the tour bus," the young girl said sadly. "It just left a couple of minutes ago. The next one's not till eleven-thirty, and it wouldn't get you back in time for two-thirty. You could rent a car, but I don't know what you could see in a few hours. There's the Grouse Mountain cable car and the Capilano Suspension Bridge, you could do that. That's across in North Vancouver. Or you could—"

"Or you could let me show you the sights," said the deep male voice she had been unconsciously waiting to hear all morning, and Vanessa turned and involuntarily smiled at Jake Conrad.

"Jake!" she said, not quite aware of what her smiling face told him.

"Good morning, Mr. Conrad," said the pretty blond tour advisor in a shy voice, and Vanessa turned in time to catch the look of teenage adoration in the soft eyes. She smiled tolerantly at the girl, not realizing that the look in her own eyes had not, for that fleeting second, been so very different.

"Good morning, Cathy, how's it going?" He smiled, and there was no trace of cynicism in the crooked grin when he looked at the girl, Vanessa saw enviously.

"A bit slow," said Cathy in a tone that strove for businesslike maturity, "but the season's just beginning, isn't it?"

He was wearing blue jeans and a blue plaid shirt rolled up at the cuffs, and he looked attractive and unpretentious. He did not wear gold chains around his neck, Vanessa thought inconsequentially, as, at last and almost unwillingly, he turned to her. "How much time have you got?" he asked. It crossed her mind that he was in two minds about wanting to take her anywhere.

"I don't have to be back until two-thirty," she said, feeling as though somehow she was courting danger. But if Jake didn't want to show her the sights he would have to say so. Something had happened to her since last night. She felt different with Jake this morning: she wanted to be with him.

"Have you got a pair of tennis shoes with you?" he asked.

In the middle of nodding yes, her cheeks suddenly flamed, and she felt the hot blood rush into her face until she knew she was blushing fiery red. Jake's attention, not unnaturally, was instantly caught, and she turned away as fast she she could, muttering a stifled, "I'll get them. Wait here."

She half walked, half ran to the elevators, one hand pressing her cheeks to try to cool them. She knew now what had happened between last night and this morning to change her feelings for Jake: last night she had dreamed that he had made love to her.

The dream jumbled around in her memory as she rode up in the elevator and walked to her room.

He had been fierce and tender, angry and loving, by turns. It was a dream that seemed confusing now, but had made perfect wonderful sense while it was happening. Afterward she had flown, exultant in the dark sky, the lights of the city below her. Jake had been at her side, as naked and free as she, his face sometimes smooth, sometimes angry with scars....

Not Jake. Jace. Vanessa bit her lip. Even in her dreams she was confusing them. Even deep inside her unconscious she was trying to find Jace again in Jake.

Vanessa dragged her suitcase open and snatched out her tennis sneakers, then left the room, her thoughts in turmoil.

In all her confusion, one thing stood out clearly: it would be asking for heartache to become Jake Conrad's lover when she could think only of Jace—and Jake could think only of his demons.

When he heard her step he turned away from Cathy's adoring gaze and stood looking at her with an expressionless face. "That was quick," he said in a tone of voice that irritated her. She raised an eyebrow at him.

"If you've changed your mind you've only got to say so," she said levelly. What the devil did the man want? For an answer he took her arm and escorted her across to the huge glass-fronted main entrance, where his long silver car sat by the curb.

"Do you like sailing?" he asked as the car purred out the drive and onto the street.

"I haven't sailed for years," she confessed with longing in her voice.

"No?" Jake asked, as though he had caught her in a lie. "Don't the Standishes sail?"

She glared at him in silence until he glanced over at her. Then she said coldly, "Yes, the Standishes sail, and yes, I learned to sail with them. But I have not been sailing since the second year of my marriage."

She remembered the first summer they had spent every weekend in the city, Larry answering the phone to his mother every Thursday to tell her calmly that no, this weekend they would be too busy.... He had been so angry, so hurt, he'd wanted nothing from them ever again. Later he had had to accept their help, he had even forgiven them, but by then sailing was only a horrid reminder of his increasing disability....

"Well, then," said Jake, "I'll have the pleasure of giving you something your—" He broke off. "Would you like to sail?"

He couldn't possibly have been going to say, *something your husband couldn't give you,* because that would have been ridiculous, but then what...? Vanessa nodded mutely, and before long the car was speeding along the shore road around English Bay and into a small park. She could see boats moored in the distance and a sign saying Royal Vancouver Yacht Club.

One didn't have to be in Canada very long to know that anything with Royal in the title was going to be pretty exclusive, Vanessa thought. Jake parked the car near the clubhouse and pulled a duffel bag out of the back seat while she changed her high-heeled shoes for tennis sneakers.

Near the end of a long dock he pointed out a beautiful sloop-rigged sailboat with a furled jib in deep burgundy. As they drew closer she saw that the boat, thirty-five or forty feet long and painted gleaming white, was trimmed with a long racing stripe in the same burgundy. Underneath the stripe on the bow was the name, *Skookum Sail*. The canopy over the cockpit was also burgundy.

As she clambered aboard after him, she asked, "That word Skookum. It was in the restaurant name. What does it mean?"

He was unlocking the padlocks on the main hatch and all the storage lockers in the cockpit. He moved around the boat with an easy economy that showed her how much at home he was on a boat.

" 'Skookum' is an Indian word meaning big," he explained. " 'Chuck' means a body of water. The ocean is sometimes called the 'salt chuck,' meaning, of course, body of salt water; and sometimes 'skookum chuck,' meaning big body of water."

The explanation delighted her. "So the name of your boat is *Big Sail*," she said. "And another name for Skookum Chuck's would be Pacific Ocean." She laughed. "And I thought it was named after a man named Charles."

"It is," said Jake. "It's owned by an old ex-fishing guide, ex-member of provincial parliament named Charles Catfish. Chuck is a very big man, and somewhere back in history he picked up the name Skookum Chuck."

Jake pushed open the cabin and threw the duffel bag down inside.

"If you want to change, you'll find something in the forward locker," he said, and stood to one side to let her climb down into the cabin.

It was beautiful, and it had everything. There was a small galley, a bathroom with a shower, two large lounges that obviously converted into sleeping quarters at night—and quantities of teak paneling and trim. She found the locker without difficulty and sorted out a navy jersey and a pair of worn blue jeans that were large for her around the waist, but not too bad around the hips. They were obviously men's jeans and quite possibly Jake's, since he was slim hipped for his height, and she had to roll them up at the cuffs. There didn't seem to be anything feminine anywhere in sight, even in the bathroom. Perhaps Louisa did not like to sail?

The engine had started while she was changing, and when she climbed back up on deck they were moving out between rows of parked sail and motor craft toward the open water of what she now knew was English Bay.

Jake looked up with a smile as she came through the hatch, and then his jaw tightened and his eyes went so dark she gasped; it was as though she had hit him.

"What's the matter?" she demanded, and Jake drew his brows impatiently together.

"Matter? Nothing's the matter," he said.

But she wasn't going to be put off. "What were you thinking of just now, when you looked at me?" she asked.

"What?" he asked irritatedly, bending over the rope he was holding.

"What were you just thinking of?" she persisted.

He replied coolly, "I was thinking that I like seeing you wearing my clothes—hardly a tragic thought."

No, she thought. *It isn't. So why were you looking at me as though you wanted to kill me?*

When he shut off the engine, the silence of the ocean enveloped them, broken only by the luffing of the wine red jib and the calling of some distant gulls.

"Good day for sailing," Jake said quietly as his lithe body moved to adjust ropes and cleats, and Vanessa stood stock-still and gazed until the mainsail was at its full height and the jib was hauled close and beautiful against the wind.

"Jake, it's wonderful," she breathed. "I'd forgotten how much I love to sail."

The sun was glinting on the curls that the wind was stirring up in his dark hair and he was smiling, his eyes narrowed against the light sparking off the water. He looked perfectly at home. It was an almost physical pleasure to watch the Vancouver skyline shrink behind his still, lithe figure.

"Do me a favor," Jake said briefly, glancing up at the sails and then to his compass. They were running straight out, away from the city toward the distant shapes of tree-covered islands dark against the clear blue sky.

"What?" she asked, expecting to be asked to adjust a rope or to get him something from the cabin.

"Take your hair down," he said. "I'd like to see it blowing in the wind."

It sent an odd little thrill through her, as though he had made verbal love to her. With hands that weren't quite steady Vanessa pulled out the clip and the pins that held her hair and slid them into the back pocket of the jeans she wore. Her hair tumbled down of its own weight, clouding around her shoulders in the soft silent breeze that caressed her face and forehead. With hands that were suddenly self-conscious she shook it loose, not daring to look at Jake Conrad.

"Did anyone ever tell you your hair is an absolutely unique color?" he asked softly.

Many people had, but Jace was the one who had loved it. "All those days of not being able to see a thing," he had said. "And the first thing I saw when my eyes finally opened enough to let the light in was sunlight on your hair. I thought I was hallucinating."

"Jace told me about your hair," Jake said then, watching the memory steal over her face. "He said there's not a sight more beautiful in the world than your hair spread out on a pillow." He looked at her. "And I believe him," said Jake Conrad.

COLIN'S OFFERING at the knitwear showing that afternoon was somehow lacking. Vanessa couldn't quite place what was wrong, but the entire collection was uninspired. It was the first time she had been unimpressed by his work, and at first she didn't want to tell him so. Then she remembered Colin's own knack for dishing out the brutal truth and knew that he would not thank her for a comforting lie. They had been friends for far too long.

"What happened to the Colin James flair?" she whispered to him as a model whom she recognized as Alison disappeared through the curtains wearing the last sweater suit in Colin's line and they were moving out to the lounge.

"The Philistine loves them, every one," Colin returned sotto voce, with every appearance of not giving a damn. "Just like television," he went on bitingly. "Pap for the mindless millions. Nobody has any taste anymore."

Since Vanessa enjoyed quite a number of shows on television, she wasn't in entire agreement with this stricture, but she was used to sweeping sarcasm from Colin and put it down to his irritation at having had his Philistine in control of the designs. This lot looked as though it had been designed by a computer.

"Colin," she said when they had ordered coffee, "sometimes I hate your stuff and sometimes I love it. But I almost always know it's your design. I wouldn't have known today. What happened?"

Colin drank some coffee and said bluntly, "What happened is that I am sick of the Philistine and I'm going to quit. On Monday, as a matter of fact."

"Colin!" She was surprised. "Where are you going? Who will you be working for?"

"Myself, darling," said Colin. "I'm going to open up my own business. Want to join me? I am serious."

"What?"

"You heard me, Vanessa."

"Colin, what would you want with two designers?

You need an administrator. And what are you going to finance this with?"

"Darling, I have a wealthy friend," he said calmly. "I put a proposition to him and he thought it looked good. He knows I'm wasted on what I'm doing. That's why I had no time to argue over the Philistine's pronouncements. I've been planning this."

"What are you planning? Fabrics?" she asked. Colin's first love was fabric design.

"You got it," he agreed. "All kinds of fabric, from painted leather to crinkled cotton. In some instances I shall merely sell the design to the trade, but for some I will have the cloth made up. This is where you would come in. While I am designing the fabric, you might design the items that are going to be made from the fabric. You know we would work extremely well together. What do you say?"

She was flabbergasted. "Good God, Colin," she stammered. "I'd need notice of that. I mean, what would I be—a partner, an employee? I couldn't contribute any backing—"

"What about the Standishes?" Colin asked. "They'd back you fast enough."

There was no arguing that. Colin knew probably better than anyone how often the Standish family had tried to press money on her. "If it was a question of a *loan*, Vanessa, I thought you might feel differently about it. A business loan, to be paid back."

She bit her lip. "I'd have to think it over, Colin," she said, shaking her head.

They spent the afternoon and early evening discussing it. Colin was more enthused than she had seen him since college days, and by the time she left him to dress for dinner with Tom and the important buyer, Vanessa was almost as excited as he was.

She dressed in the simple black dress she had worn on Monday night, and noticed as she made up that her face had picked up some color from her morning on the *Skookum Sail*.

Jake had asked her out for dinner tonight, giving her an uneasy suspicion that he had decided to rush her. It had been almost with relief that she had explained about the business dinner with Tom.

"It won't run late, then, will it?" Jake had asked. "Call me when you come in, and come for a nightcap."

She had found herself weakly agreeing that if it wasn't too late she would see him, but she knew she'd be a fool if she did so.

And yet—she stood back from the mirror and looked at herself. The black dress, with its shoestring straps and fitted bodice curving low over her breasts and leaving her shoulders and arms bare, was perhaps the sexiest item in her wardrobe and wasn't what she had planned to wear tonight. And her hair was dressed in a way she rarely wore it, held back tightly at the sides with combs, but cascading down her back in a cluster of curls.

She was dressing for Jake, she realized with dismay. Damn him, damn him. Here she was telling herself that she wouldn't call him when she got in, and at the same time unconsciously dressing in a way she knew would entice him! What a fool she was. She would have no one to blame but herself if she got hurt. Jake was not pretending to be in love with her now. He had told her what he wanted from her on day one. And somehow she knew that, for some reason known only to himself, Jake Conrad was determined to get it.

THE DINNER WAS NOT a great success. That the important chain-store buyer was well used to being entertained by manufacturers trying to curry favor was evident, as was the fact that she didn't appreciate being in a party consisting of three women and one man. For Tom, who was more smitten than Vanessa had ever seen him, unless this was some elaborate act, had brought Margaret along, too. And he was paying altogether too much attention to her.

When the conversation veered to politics in the desperate way that conversations in danger of flagging often do, Vanessa nearly despaired. The Canadians she had met always seemed to be much more knowledgeable about American politics than she was about Canadian politics, and she was sure that Tom's lecture on the swing to the Right in America could only bore these women, in whose country they were, after all, guests. Surely she could think of *something* to ward off Tom's imminent lecture?

"Tell me," she heard herself saying to the disgruntled buyer, "do you think that the way the West was opened in Canada has an effect now on the level of crime you have here, compared to the States?"

"How do you mean?" asked the buyer, her eyes showing a glint of real interest for the first time that evening. With a silent salute to Jake Conrad,

Vanessa presented the theory he had outlined to her last night, complete with the Northwest Mounted Police and (hoping she had the name right) Sergeant Preston of the Yukon and his dog, King.

"Sergeant Preston of the Yukon!" exclaimed the buyer, beginning to laugh. "Wherever did you hear of him? My God, it must be thirty years since I heard that name!"

Tom was looking at her in surprise, but the discussion of crime and law and order in Canada lasted for the rest of the meal and launched the important buyer and Margaret into a political discussion that kept the buyer happy, even if Tom and Vanessa didn't understand a word of it.

It was only eleven o'clock when she said good-night to them in the lobby and headed toward the elevators. She had made up her mind. She wasn't going to call Jake tonight. She knew he would read a message into it if she did; she knew she would be walking into the lion's den.

Vanessa stepped off the elevator on her floor and walked slowly down the hall and opened the door to her room. There was a soft light burning beside the bed and the draperies were open. The lights on Grouse Mountain and Hollyburn Mountain twinkled in the surrounding blackness. Vanessa opened the window and breathed in the sweet sea-scented air.

Pity. She would have liked to tell him about how Sergeant Preston of the Yukon had won another battle tonight. She knew she could make him laugh with that and with an imitation of Tom's self-important lecturing. She would have liked to thank him for telling her about Sergeant Preston and the Royal Northwest Mounted Police, if that was their name. She might even have liked to tell him about Colin's offer, just to see what he thought of it....

With a short self-deprecatory sigh, Vanessa dropped her hand from the drapery and turned back to the room. Then she crossed the room to the bed and picked up the phone receiver. "Mr. Conrad's suite, please," she told the switchboard operator.

"Hi," she said softly when the male voice answered. "Does the offer of a nightcap still hold?"

CHAPTER FIVE

SHE HAD EXPECTED to be going down to the private lounge off the lobby, where she had been twice before, but instead Jake had told her to come to the top floor of the hotel.

When she stepped out of the elevator there were only four numbered doors opening onto the small lobby, and she gasped when she realized how big each of the four suites must be. These could only be the presidential suites, where royalty and foreign dignitaries stayed. Each of the four doors was a large and ornate double door, and one stood open onto a softly lighted interior. With a gentle tap on the panels Vanessa slipped into the room.

It was a huge room, deeply carpeted, luxuriously furnished, and Vanessa leaned her back against the door as she closed it and gazed around. There were several lamps shedding soft light around the room, but the light was still low enough for the room to be dominated by the view out of the far wall. It was all glass, at least twenty-five feet long and ten feet high, and beyond the glass there seemed to be a very large expanse of grass and shrub and even trees on the roof balcony. Beyond that was the city, and then the broad black expanse of the ocean.

Jake was standing by the window, a glass in his hand, staring out as though completely absorbed in his thoughts. He hadn't heard her; he didn't know she was there. For a moment Vanessa enjoyed the luxury of watching him without being seen.

He was wearing dark pants and a cream shirt open at the neck and rolled up at the sleeves. His hair was ruffled and curling as though he had been running his hands through it, and when her glance moved farther she perceived the reason.

A beautiful antique desk lighted by a soft yellow glow, as well as a long coffee table and the couch behind it, were strewn with business papers. It looked as though he had been working between the desk and the couch, which were several yards apart across the room. It seemed like an awful lot of paper for one man to be considering at once.

"Hello," she said softly, dismayed by the caressing note she heard in her own voice. Jake turned his head and then his body, put down his glass and moved smilingly across the room toward her.

"Hello," he responded when he reached her, just as softly, just as caressingly. He took her hands and gently pulled her into his arms. "Thank you for coming," he said. "I needed you." Then he bent his head and his mouth gently found hers.

It was what she had been waiting for all day, without knowing it, ever since she had awakened from that dream of perfect communion. For the first few moments the touch of his lips filled her with perfect peace, with solace, soothed her after a day of turmoil. Then her heart started to beat in heavy, slow thuds and a thin flame licked through her body, setting her alight. She lifted her arms up around his neck and felt his hands grip her back responsively.

Her lips parted in unconscious invitation, and his seeking tongue came in with a teasing exploration that she felt down to her toes. Vanessa pulled her lips away from his to gasp in a breath, and then they were smiling into each other's eyes, and there was no tension, no pressure, nothing but the perfect communion of her dream.

"Come and sit down," said Jake, releasing her to lead her over to a large stuffed chair. "Talk to me."

"What shall I talk about?" she asked, smiling.

Crossing the room to open the door of a drinks cabinet much like the one in the lounge many floors beneath them, he said, "Anything. Anything at all that will take my mind off my work. Mineral water and lime again, or would you prefer something stronger? Brandy, liqueur?"

"Brandy would be nice," she said. "It will help me sleep." And then she could have kicked herself.

"Will it?" was all he said, and he looked over his shoulder at her for only a moment, but the effect this had on her was profound. Suddenly there was more than just desire in the air between them—there was desire and the promise of fulfillment.

"What have you been working on?" Vanessa asked abruptly, in the most matter-of-fact voice she could muster.

"A reverse takeover bid, but I don't think it's going to come off this time."

"What's a reverse takeover bid?"

"It's what happens when I want to take over a company that's too big for me to buy out. I sell them my corporation first, and then with the money they pay me for it, I buy back controlling interest in the corporation that now includes the target company and my corporation."

He handed her a thick carved glass that might have been Waterford crystal in which the brandy glowed with a dark fire. He sank down on the couch that was at an angle to her chair, cleared a few papers from the couch to the table in one motion, and taking a sip from his glass slung his feet up into the middle of the document-strewn coffee table.

"Goodness!" Vanessa exclaimed. "Does it work?" She was rather surprised that he would discuss such a plan with her so openly.

"Oh, yes. In this case everyone concerned would agree to the thing beforehand. It doesn't depend on sleight-of-hand, just politicking and hard work." He threw back his head and rubbed his hand in his hair, making it stand even more violently on end. "Sometimes too much work. And that's how it seems to me tonight. Like too much work. What have you been doing today?"

"Tonight I was, predictably, helping entertain some buyers. This afternoon...." She took a sip of the brandy and wondered about outlining Colin's plans to someone who owned a competitive firm, then decided to go ahead. "This afternoon I most unpredictably received an offer to start up in business with a friend."

"Did you?" Jake grunted. "Difficult time to be starting up in business."

"Yes, I suppose you're right. But—oh, I don't know, it was all very sudden. I'm not even sure I believe he's serious," said Vanessa, her indecision and worry sounding in her voice.

"Care to tell me about it?" he offered.

Jake listened without comment and with only a few questions till she had told him the idea as Colin had presented it to her. Then the two of them discussed the pros and cons, with Jake giving her the benefit of his obviously large experience of the business world.

"What attracts you most about the proposition?" he asked eventually.

"Artistic freedom," she said unhesitatingly. "The chance to produce what I think will sell on the market. I've been thinking about making a move for some time now. But this is not the best time to be looking for a job."

He asked what she meant by artistic freedom, and suddenly she was telling him all her ideas for what working women wanted in clothes, about how they wanted to look businesslike without sacrificing femininity, about simplicity.

"It sounds as though Colin's dream and your own dream don't quite coincide," Jake said at last.

"What do you mean?"

"You won't have much room for your own ideas if you're turning his fabric into garments, will you? And the kind of setup he's talking about sounds as though he means to appeal to a very different market group than the one you feel committed to."

"Do you think so?" She had had her doubts about the number of times Colin had used the word "exclusive" this afternoon, but....

"You did mention that he planned to be designing exclusive fabric design for individual customers as well as for the trade."

"Yes, but that was to be later, if we caught on."

"Well, correct me if I'm wrong, but fashion rarely goes from the masses upward. It usually happens first with the upper classes or the wealthy and then filters down, am I right?"

"Yes," she agreed, impressed but no longer surprised by the scope of his knowledge.

"Then it stands to reason his target group is going to be the wealthier women right from the start. When it's caught on with them and is in full bloom, *then* it will be ready for mass-market delivery. But unless he's planning a very big operation indeed someone else will be doing that."

Of course that was exactly what Colin was planning. There was nothing wrong with it—it could be a brilliant success. But was it *her* dream? Was it something she wanted to spend her life—or the next few years of her life—doing?

Vanessa looked at Jake Conrad and made a moue of disappointment. "You're right," she said. "I guess the thought of getting away from Tom Marx was so attractive I just started to think anything would do. But I can't make this decision without a lot of thought."

"Do you have a lot of trouble with Tom Marx?" Jake asked, and she laughed.

"Don't you have arguments with your designers?" she asked lightly.

"No, I don't. Should I?"

"You mean you don't scream when they want to use two inches more fabric than is absolutely necessary in a skirt? Or fabric-covered buttons instead of plastic ones? Or a stronger thread?"

He looked apologetic. "Is that what it's like? I don't have much to do with the actual running of the company. There's a manager who does that."

"Well, you can take it from me he makes the designer's life hell," she said with a grimace.

"You don't sound very happy," he observed.

Vanessa shook her head. "I'm sick of always offering the cheapest possible execution of a design, when a few cents more per item would make all the difference. I'll never understand what's wrong with producing a well-made product for a little less than the ultimate profit. It just makes me—" She broke off abruptly and self-consciously. "Don't get me started." She laughed. "I make boring speeches on this subject."

Jake didn't answer. He was looking at her consideringly. "Everyone has a weak spot," he said slowly, as if he were thinking aloud. His eyes were somehow distant; he seemed not to see her.

It made her uncomfortable. "What?" she asked, tilting her head at him inquiringly, and immediately his eyes were focused on her again.

"Tom Marx," he said. "His weak spot is that he wants to get something for nothing. The less he gives his customers for their money the happier he is. That's why you can't fight it. It's not really the profit he's after—it's the psychological kick."

That was certainly interesting, but Vanessa was uncomfortably certain that the "weak spot" Jake Conrad had been thinking about wasn't Tom Marx's, but her own. Her sexual weak spot, perhaps?

Suddenly she wondered if all this conversation was really nothing more than Jake Conrad's way of getting her into bed, if in fact he was only pretending to be interested, pretending to take her seriously. He had looked right through her just now, as though... she might just as well, Vanessa thought irritatedly, have been Louisa Hayward. He'd listen to her woebegone little life story with exactly the same flattering attention.... Vanessa leaned forward and carefully set down her glass.

"I must go," she said. "My body clock is still on New York time, and I'm dropping." It wasn't true. She felt wide awake...and regretful. She had wanted to tell him about how Sergeant Preston of the Yukon had saved the day again.

Jake's eyes were intent on her, and he was as still as a cat. "Be careful, Vanessa," he said softly as she stood up. "When you're always running there's always a risk that you'll trip."

He walked with her to the door, and she could still sense the stillness in him. He wasn't angry, as men so often were when she refused them. He wasn't even insulted. He was merely...watchful. He was like a chess player. His opponent's queen had moved out of danger, but the game was not over.

SHE SUCCEEDED AT LAST in sleeping late and was awakened at ten by a knock on the door. Outside was a waiter pushing a damask-covered table laden with an elaborate breakfast.

"I think there's been a mistake," she said, involuntarily stepping back as the table came through the door. "I didn't order this."

The waiter stopped, plucked a cardboard check from the tabletop, glanced at it, glanced up at the number on the door. The numbers obviously matched, and the man, who appeared to be of Italian descent, cocked an eyebrow and turned the check over.

"Mrs. Standish?" he queried, reading the name scrawled at the top, and Vanessa nodded, perplexed. The little man shot her a look. "Perhaps someone else ordered it for you," he suggested, with just a trace of romantic innuendo in his voice that was designed to let her know that *he* did not disapprove of whatever she had done last night to warrant this.

She smiled coolly, refusing to acknowledge the unstated assumption. "Yes, perhaps," she said tonelessly, standing back again and holding the black robe close over her naked body. "Please bring it in."

It took him five minutes to lay out the meal to his satisfaction, during which time Vanessa stood at the window gazing out. She didn't care to see any more sly glances. There was a mist on Grouse Mountain this morning, and the sky was overcast. Her balcony looked wet; it must have rained during the night.

"Bon appetit, madame," said the waiter and she turned to smile her thanks as he let himself out.

"Oh, just a moment," she said, recollecting herself and reaching for her handbag. The waiter held up one pudgy hand to stop her.

"No, thank you, *madame*." He smiled. "Everything has been taken care of." He inclined his head and closed the door after himself.

He had laid two places, she noted with wry amusement. Did he imagine she had someone skulking in the bathroom?

The meal looked delicious. There were covered dishes filled with Canadian bacon and scrambled eggs and sausages; there was buttered toast and pots of honey and jam and Scottish marmalade; there was a basket of fresh fruit and a huge steaming pot of coffee.

There was also a little white envelope in one of the coffee cups. Inside on the little white card was a black angular full-looped scrawl: *Spend the day with me? Jake.*

So she had been right last night: it was a game to him, and Jake was still playing it. What was it he wanted from her? What did it mean to him to become her lover for what—and she realized this with a confusing stab of regret—could only be a very brief time? Why were one or two nights so important to him?

She looked down at the breakfast table, and involuntarily she remembered Jace. Jace had ordered breakfast to the room after the night they had spent together—a breakfast like this, hearty and appetizing. But she had looked into Jace's eyes and loved him with all her heart, and what she ate was nectar and ambrosia.

"They say a woman never forgets her first lover," Jace had said, his voice roughened with emotion. "Don't forget me, Vanessa. Don't ever forget me."

"Never," she had promised, tears in her eyes, knowing that soon he would be leaving her. "I promise."

Did Jake know that, too? He seemed to know everything. After last night's setback, was this his new gambit, perhaps—if he couldn't succeed as Jake, to try as Jace?

Into her thoughts came the sound of a knock, and Vanessa stood still in the center of the room, biting her lip. She might pretend to Jake, but there was nothing to be gained by pretending to herself. She was in danger from Jake Conrad, and she didn't know whether that was because he reminded her of Jace or because she was falling for Jake himself.

And Jake wanted her, but was that because he was falling for her or was it for some other unfathomable reason?

This situation, she suddenly saw very clearly, could get very complicated—and someone just might get hurt. Slowly, slowly, Vanessa went to open the door.

Jake walked in, smiling, cool and confident, wearing casual pants and an open-necked shirt.

"Good morning," he said, closing the door and taking in the details of her tousled appearance in a glinting admiration that tingled over her body like a touch.

"You haven't brushed your hair this morning," he said, following her over to the table. "If you'd been in my bed looking like this I wouldn't have let you get up." He cupped her head in his hand and bent and kissed her, and just as her body burst into a flame of need he gently lifted his lips from hers.

"Very nice," he said, looking down at the table, so that she wasn't sure whether he meant the kiss or the meal.

"Shall we relive that special breakfast, Vanessa?" he asked softly, and she knew she had been right. Jake Conrad was going to stop at nothing to—

"My God, Jake," she whispered to cover her thoughts. "Did he tell you everything?"

He looked at her distantly for a moment. "Everything," he said softly, and she felt herself blushing for the second time in as many days. She hadn't blushed for years, but Jake Conrad seemed to have the knack.

"I can't believe Jace would have talked about such private things," she said, feeling that Jace had somehow betrayed her by this. "How could he have told you all that?" When she thought of the intimacy they had shared, she could have wept.

"I should have told you," Jake said. "Jace was on powerful drugs for a while before the operation. Sometimes he was raving. I was with him almost constantly, but he didn't always know I was there. Sometimes he thought he was talking to you. Sometimes he thought he was holding you. After he got your letter he spoke to you a great deal in his ravings. He pleaded with you, and once he. . . spent some time reminding you of how you had responded to his touch, to his lovemaking. He said it was because you loved him. But I remember thinking how highly sexed a woman you must be."

"No," she protested weakly, her eyes on the floor, memory and heartbreak flooding over her. "No, I'm not. It *was* because. . .because I was so in love with him. I guess every woman is highly sexed with the man she truly loves. I realized that later, after—"

She was startled to hear the rasp of his indrawn breath. "You mean, you didn't have that with your husband? You weren't like that with him?" he demanded in a voice harsh with suppressed emotion.

Her silence gave him his answer. "Then why did you marry him, Vanessa? Why? If it wasn't for money and it wasn't for love, what the hell was the reason?" He grasped her arms as though he wanted to shake her, and his eyes blazed.

There was a long tension-filled pause while her thoughts swirled in confusion. Why was it so important to him? Out of loyalty to Larry she had never told anyone, but it seemed so important to Jake, and Larry was dead. . . .

"Vanessa, I want to know!" His voice was low but commanding, and suddenly she was afraid of what power the knowledge might give him over her.

"Jake," she said, "it had nothing whatever to do with you. Larry is dead, and so are my reasons for marrying him." She sat down nervously in the large easy chair the waiter had pulled up to the table, but it was too low for the height of the table. She sank down until her plate was at chin level. After the overloaded emotion of the past few moments the humor of the situation was a welcome relief, and she giggled. "I feel like a five-year-old." She began to laugh in earnest, half-hysterically, uncontrollably. Well, it was better than crying. She leaned over on one arm of the chair, the laughter that shook her making her weak.

"Vanessa!" Jake was standing over her, gripping her arm with an almost painful clasp, his jaw set. "Enough." Obediently she stopped laughing. "Sit in the other chair," he said.

That was the one she'd wanted to sit in, she thought, giggling as she stood. But she would have had to push by Jake to get to it, and she'd had a funny feeling that wouldn't have been healthy. She sat down on the straight-backed chair and watched as he threw some pillows from the bed into the stuffed chair and sat down opposite her. She hiccuped on a giggle and then sobered.

"I think the chair was trying to tell me something," she said. "I think I'm out of my depth with you."

Jake smiled his half-smile and raised an eyebrow. "You're not even in the water yet," he said. "Stop worrying." That crooked half-smile could pack an enormous wallop when he chose. Vanessa wondered how consciously he used it, even while it relaxed her.

"What would you like to do today?" he asked as they began to eat.

"I don't know, do I?" she said, wondering why it was she wasn't trying harder to say no. "I don't know what there is to see and do."

"How about the cable car up Grouse Mountain? We can have lunch at the top." He paused, chewing. "If you had more time I'd like to take you up into the interior, but it would be too much of a rush trying to do it in a day."

"What's in the interior?" she asked.

"Mountains," he said. "The canyon of the Fraser

River, the Squamish Valley—B.C. has extremely varied scenery. Some people say you can find any kind of scenery you want here. It's worth seeing."

She sighed unconsciously. She would love to spend more time in this province. . . .

"I've got a ranch up in the Fraser Valley," he said. "I'll be flying up there this weekend." He was pouring coffee, speaking almost too casually. "If you'd like to come along—"

She cut in, "I'm flying home Saturday morning."

"Flight bookings can be changed."

"No," she said, fighting the knowledge that she wanted to stay. "I have to get back."

Jake shrugged casually. "All right," he said. "You'll have to be satisfied with Grouse Mountain, then."

THERE WAS SNOW on Grouse Mountain. As the cable car moved slowly up the mountainside, Vancouver became visible below and beyond them, but finally a thick gray mist enveloped them and all Vanessa could see was evergreens and snow. Jake had told her to bring a warm jacket, but the best she could do was a sweater. When he had returned to pick her up after she had dressed he had brought her a bomber jacket to wear. Vanessa was glad of its comforting warmth as they stepped off the red cable car into the decidedly nippy air of the mountaintop.

"Thank you for the loan of the jacket," she said as he led her through the arrival lodge, which housed several restaurants and tourist shops. When they were in the cold again she snuggled into its folds.

He smiled. "I told you I like seeing you wear my clothes."

"So you did. Does this mean I have carte blanche on your closet?"

"How about starting in my bureau?" He was smiling, but she could not follow his train of thought.

"Your bureau? Why, what's in your bureau?"

He looked sideways at her. "My pajamas," he said softly. "Now, you would look very good in those."

She caught her breath, and his eyes glinted with the victory, but she wasn't letting him win as easily as that. "Pajamas?" she drawled. "I'm surprised to hear that a man as sexual as you are sleeps in pajamas."

His eyelids dropped, giving him a sleepy dangerous look. "Don't worry," he said. "When I have you in my bed, I shall not be wearing pajamas."

Her heart kicked against her ribs. "What makes you imagine you'll ever have me in your bed?" she asked, fighting for calm.

They were tramping on the snow up toward the skiing area, but now he stopped and turned her ever so gently toward him. "Shall I show you?" he asked lazily, his eyes still hooded.

Vanessa drew a deep breath, realizing that she had deliberately provoked this sort of conversation because she wanted just what he was offering now: she wanted him to kiss her. The knowledge shocked her rigid. If she wasn't careful, she would soon be out of control with this man. "No," she said briefly, turning away from him. "Can we eat now? I'm starving."

Since they had eaten the large breakfast only three hours ago this was not strictly true. Jake made no comment on it until she added feebly, "Cold air makes me hungry."

Then he laughed. "If a few minutes on Grouse Mountain has made you hungry it's lucky you don't live in northern Saskatchewan. You'd be as fat as an egg."

"Is northern Saskatchewan cold?" she asked with interest. Nine and a half years ago Jace had disabused her mind of the idea that everything north of the forty-ninth parallel was Eskimo country, and certainly Vancouver's climate was milder than New York's. But still this country extended well into the Arctic and owned islands running right to the north pole, so *some* of the myth had to be fact.

"In the winter it is," Jake said succinctly. "Too bloody cold."

"Have you been there?"

"A few months ago, in the dead of winter," Jake said wryly. "I went to have a look at some land I wanted to acquire an oil lease on. Couldn't see any land, of course; it was under six feet of snow."

"Is there oil in Saskatchewan?"

"Could be." He shrugged. "More likely not."

"But you bought the oil lease?"

He shrugged again. "It's easier to be wrong than right."

Vanessa looked around. They seemed to be right on top of the mountain, and she wrinkled her forehead, puzzled. "Is this Jasper?" she asked him.

He looked down at her with a little smile. "No,"

he said. "Jasper is about five hundred miles northeast of here, in Alberta."

She said, "There are trees-all over the place. But when Jace told me about the Rockies, I thought they went way above the tree line. Jace told me—"

"That the Empire State Building only proved how puny all man's achievements were compared with nature," Jake finished for her, and she smiled at the sudden memory....

"Oh, Jace, nobody goes to the top of the Empire State Building," she had protested laughing.

Jace had replied, "My darling Vanessa, hundreds of people go up every day, and it's time *you* did. I'll bet you haven't seen it since your public-school class outing, and how long ago was that?"

So she had put on her Canadian accent and allowed herself to be dragged to the top of what had been the world's tallest building for so long. She had been surprised to find herself impressed, gazing at the city in all directions. She had felt as though she were standing on the bridge of an enormous ship that was Manhattan.

"Someday I'll take you to Jasper," he had said when they were on the ground again, warming their chilled hands over a cup of coffee deep inside the building. "Right in the heart of the Rockies. That is truly something to see." And then he had said the words Jake had just quoted....

"The Rockies do rise above the tree line," Jake was saying. "These are more like very distant foothills of the Rockies."

"Could I fly to Jasper?" she asked.

"I imagine there's a flight by one of the small airlines," Jake mused. "You might get there and back tomorrow and have a few hours in Jasper. It's a pity you're leaving Saturday. I could take you up on the weekend in the company plane."

"Could you?" she breathed, suddenly desperately wanting to see what Jace had wanted to show her.

A dark flame leaped in Jake's eyes, and he pulled her irresistibly to him and bent to kiss her. In the cold air his lips were warm against hers, and she surrendered completely to the kiss. His mouth was gentle and she was hungry for the indescribable comfort he could give her.

After a long still moment, Jake drew back and touched a gloved finger to her pink cheek. "Stay the weekend, Vanessa," he said softly.

But she knew what he was really asking, and she wasn't prepared to make that commitment, especially not when her brain was so fuddled by his kiss that she wanted to shout out, "Yes!" and hear it echoing down the valley.

She drew out of his arms. "I can't," she said. He smiled at her as though she were a charming coward, and she added defensively, "You're wrong."

His eyes were black. "What am I wrong about?"

She faltered. "You think I want to become your lover and I'm too afr—"

His eyes darkened and he pulled her closer in his arms. "You do," he said. "Don't try to deny it, Vanessa. It's in your eyes, every time you look at me. It has been right from the beginning."

"No," she said levelly.

He gave a crack of laughter. "No?" he asked, his eyes blazing at her. "You think not? Then you don't know yourself, lady. Because if I started to kiss you now we'd be making love in that snowdrift behind you in five minutes. And believe me, you would make no protest."

She gasped in a breath of cold air and tried to step back out of his arms. "Let me go," she demanded.

He didn't move. "If I'm wrong," he suggested softly, "kiss me now. Let me kiss you the way you need to be kissed, and then, if you want me to, I'll let you go."

Hypnotized by his eyes, by his seductive voice, she swallowed.

"Kiss me," he repeated in a whisper, and there was black flame behind his eyes and she knew if she made the smallest move toward his chiseled lips he would let loose the passion she saw in him.... She closed her eyes against the pleasure the thought gave her, then turned her head to the large snowdrift behind her that cut them off from the view of the lodge and the few tourists in the distance.

He was watching every thought play across her face. "I do not want to kiss you," she said coldly. "Let go of me."

With only the briefest convulsive tightening of his arms around her, he complied. The dark flame left his eyes. "Let's go get a meal," said Jake. "That's one appetite you don't deny, isn't it?"

Over the adequate but by no means ideal lunch they were served in the lodge's main dining room, Jake talked lightly about a variety of things. He was as calm as if he had forgotten what had just happened between them, and Vanessa fought for a similar degree of calm.

She asked him about Canada's political background, and he explained to her the difference between Canada's parliamentary democracy and the American democratic republic.

Jake was obviously well-read and he explained things clearly and understandably. But he was politically cynical, and he could not help imparting his idea of things along with the recital of facts she had requested. Although he did not care which of the three major political parties formed the government, he did not like the present prime minister, and he was passionate on the subject of police powers and the erosion of civil liberties in the country that seemed to her as free as her own.

"The laws are there," he told her. "If the police invoked all the laws half the country could be in prison tomorrow."

Vanessa could neither believe what he said nor believe that he was lying. "Well," she said consideringly, thinking of the locks on the door of her mid-Manhattan apartment, "I know *I* feel freer here, Jake. I mean, think how free we were in Stanley Park the other night."

He shrugged. "True. No doubt I'm biased at the moment because the government ruled a couple of weeks ago that if Conrad Corporation went through with a takeover of Carvers Cartage it would have to divest itself of Conrad Trucking. As well as losing a sizable chunk of money on the deal I now have to sit back and watch a takeover of Carvers by a foreign firm."

"The reverse takeover you were looking at last night," she queried, "was that a Canadian company or a foreign one?"

"A British Columbia firm, as it happens," Jake said. "Fraser Valley Helicopter has the largest fleet of helicopters in the world. They do everything from helicopter logging to ferrying workers to offshore oil rigs."

"Does that mean I should run out and buy shares in Fraser Valley Helicopter?" she asked lightly.

Jake smiled crookedly. "You should buy shares in Conrad Corporation," he said meaningly, and his eyes locked with hers, and Vanessa's heart skipped a beat.

At the foot of Grouse Mountain it was possible to rent a helicopter for a five-minute overflight of the mountain and the city, and as they crossed the parking lot after leaving the cable car on the downward trip, Vanessa stopped and gazed across at the helicopter landing pad and the sign announcing the ride.

"I'd like to do that, I think," she said to Jake.

"Do what? Oh." He followed the direction of her gaze. "You won't get much of a thrill in five minutes," he said. "If you're free tomorrow morning I'll take you up in the company helicopter instead. All right?"

As it happened she was free all day Friday. The showing of accessories—bags, shoes and hats—was scheduled for the afternoon, and that was the last show. The evening was given over to another cocktail party that would close the week's events.

"I'd enjoy that very much." Vanessa smiled, moving again in the direction of the car. "If it's not going to be too much trouble." Jake had been spending a lot of time with her, and he must be a very busy man.

"It's not going to be too much trouble," Jake said, smiling down into her eyes, and just then there was a flicker of something behind his eyes—some depth of purpose far beyond anything she could have imagined him feeling—so intense and so brief that in the moment she opened her lips in a gasp, it was already gone.

VANESSA STAYED BACKSTAGE for the skirt and slacks showing that night. Although she had managed to get a replacement for Louisa, who had worked the show for a lingerie manufacturer and who was therefore probably experienced, she didn't feel confident enough to sit in the audience.

In the dressing room an extra pair of hands was usually welcome, though with four models working, no one was ever very rushed. Vanessa became indispensable, however, by virtue of being there. So she brushed lint off skirts and adjusted clasps on earrings and handed the models their accessories and inspected makeup, on command. And when Alison put a large run in her pantyhose and a panicky search around the dressing room did not bring to light the box of spares, Vanessa sat down and calmly stripped off her stockings and passed them over.

After the show she went around to the TopMarx

hospitality suite, where the buyers had a chance to look at the garments again and place their orders.

Tom was sitting alone, looking glum. "You know," he said, "I've been wondering why we didn't book to go home tomorrow. We may as well have. I was nickeled and dimed to death this morning. The big orders come in after the show or not at all." Vanessa recognized this as a disguise for the worry he felt after every show that there would be no orders.

She said, "They're just having a drink, Tom. They'll be along." She moved over to the racks to straighten a few of the model garments.

"Speaking of flying home," she said abruptly after a moment, "I'm staying in Vancouver over the weekend and flying back Monday. I'll be back in the office Tuesday." Inwardly she was amazed and apprehensive. When had she decided on this, she wondered—and what other decision might she have made without knowing it?

"Yeah? Why?" Tom asked. He seemed taken aback by her directness and Vanessa felt a little thrill of power. Why on earth hadn't she taken this assertive attitude with him ages ago, instead of asking for permission all the time like a junior filing clerk?

"This is a very beautiful country, Tom. I want to see something of it, now that I'm here."

"Yeah?" Tom shuddered. "I wish you luck." Tom hated everything foreign and didn't care who knew it.

But Vanessa didn't intend to argue with him. Instead she asked, "What are the orders like?"

Tom pulled out a notebook in which he had noted

down style numbers and running totals. They were good without being overwhelming and after she had looked them over Vanessa picked up the folder of the actual order forms and glanced quickly but expertly through them.

There was absolutely no doubt that the Canadian buyers went for the beiges, browns, soft pinks, russets and reds. In some cases, she noted, Tom had taken large orders for items in colors that he hadn't planned on offering at all. Vanessa flipped back and forth through the orders, calculating.

"You realize we haven't got any wool-mix tweed in russet on order for the bomber suit?" she asked. "And what's this order for 6703 in the dusty-rose wool blend? We've only ordered that for the 5203 skirt and the jacket trim. And the same—"

It was the same for half a dozen fabrics in colors that Tom had refused to believe would sell. Tom had the grace to look uncomfortable.

"Yeah, well, that can be fixed."

Vanessa looked back through the file. "You've got some pretty early delivery dates for some of these large orders. Aren't you worried about not getting the fabric on time?" If the fabric manufacturers didn't have on hand the colors Tom hadn't previously ordered there might be a long delay while they made them up.

"Ah, we'll be okay," said Tom with a dismissing wave of his hand.

It was obvious that the orders vindicated her on the issue of color, and only a little less on style. The items that Tom had included in the fall line only because of

Vanessa's arguments had gone down well with many of the large buyers—and almost without exception with the small buyers, she noted with wry amusement. Tom would not be exactly thrilled over that, but Vanessa was. The small stores had to compete very hard to survive beside the large chain stores. Every item in stock had to be chosen with an eye to its power to take away a sale from the chain stores.

In her room shortly afterward Vanessa took her airline ticket out of her purse and stood looking down at the phone a long time.

It's only a simple decision, she told herself. *It doesn't mean anything except what I told Tom—that I want to see some of the country before I go back.* But as she reached for the receiver she could hear Jake's cynical voice saying, *little hypocrite.*

Tom would not be happy to be left to fly home alone. Air Canada was the only airline that flew between Vancouver and New York without a change of planes, and she had induced him to fly on the country's national carrier much against his will. Tom was as unadventurous in travel as he was in business and he was afraid of things foreign. But Vanessa had wanted to experience as much as she could of the country that had so nearly been her adopted home, and so they had flown on the big red-black-and-white Air Canada jet.

"What the hell language is that?" Tom had demanded irritably when, after the stewardess had welcomed them in English over the public-address system, she obviously began to say the same thing in another language.

"Oh, Tom, it's French," Vanessa had said, suddenly thrilling to the strangeness of it. She had been on many business trips with Tom, but all of them had been in the continental United States. Although she was greatly attracted to the thought of foreign travel, her marriage to Larry and his long demanding illness had prevented her doing anything about it. They had honeymooned in Puerto Rico and that was her one and only trip abroad. Until this one.

"*French?* What the hell are they speaking French for?" Tom had looked threatened, as though he expected to be pounced on at any minute. "It's an English country, isn't it? Besides, we're still in New York!"

"Tom, it's a bilingual country," she'd said. "They speak French, too. Haven't you ever heard of Quebec?"

"Yes, I've heard of it," Tom said. "I still don't know why they want to speak French. English is a perfectly good language. What do they need with two?"

Since Vanessa hadn't known the answer to this she'd fallen silent and then become aware that the man on the other side of her in the aisle seat was laughing silently.

Sitting on her bed beside the phone remembering now, Vanessa laughed, too. They must have sounded like a comedy duo, she and Tom. "Who's on third?" "No, Who's on first." "I dunno...."

When the man had stopped laughing he had admitted to being Canadian and had answered her questions about his country. "Why do I see Spanish on signs in New York?" he asked, and Tom had answered for her that there were a lot of Puerto Ricans in New York. "Well, the stewardess speaks French because there are a lot of French-speaking people in Canada," the man had explained calmly, "not because everyone speaks two languages. In fact, the French are French and the English are English and rarely do the twain ever meet."

She'd heard a lot in recent years about the twain not meeting. Many people in the province of Quebec wanted to separate and form their own country, she knew that. "Where did the French come from?" she asked the stranger, whose name was Bill and who was a teacher in a remote school in northern British Columbia, the province to which they were going.

He told her that the French had come from France to settle the New World, just as the English had, and that there had been many battles between the two countries for supremacy in the colonies. Finally, in 1759, the Battle of the Plains of Abraham had given supremacy in North America to the British. But for many years after that another battle had raged, a political one: what to do about the French settlers. Some people had wanted to stamp out the French language and law and Roman Catholicism; others had not. Then, when the thirteen colonies to the south had begun to show disaffection, it was decided that Britain needed a loyal stronghold on the continent. All the rights that had been taken away from the French after 1759 were given back in 1774, and the French were given sovereignty over a vast tract of land that extended right into the Ohio Valley.

The move failed. Not only did it fail to win the loyalty of the French settlers, but it further disaffected the thirteen colonies, with what results every American knew, Bill said. But the principle of allowing the French to maintain their own language, religion and laws persisted under attack until it was enshrined in the Canadian constitution—known as the British North America Act—about a hundred years later. The descendants of those early settlers still spoke the language of their ancestors, just as did the English of both Canada and the States.

Vanessa had never before realized that the history of the two countries was so connected. As she sat on her bed now, waiting for Air Canada to answer the phone, it occurred to her that it was no wonder they were so similar. Both countries had had the same parents, the same early influence.

When the quiet-voiced Air Canada agent answered the phone, Vanessa changed her flight booking from Saturday to Monday morning.

She hadn't heard the last of this from Tom, she knew. But it wasn't Tom's reaction she was thinking of now, but Jake's, when he learned she was staying over the weekend as he had asked.

IN THE MORNING Vanessa waited for Jake in the coffee shop, as agreed, lingering over her breakfast and a second cup of coffee that was doing nothing to calm her nervousness. In spite of almost ten years of marriage she was far too inexperienced with men. How could she tell him she was staying over the weekend without having him think she was agreeing to become his lover? Did she even know whether or not she was agreeing to that?

It was a relief when he came striding through the doors and over to her, wearing a gray three-piece summer suit that made him look very dark in contrast and very businesslike.

He was preoccupied. With little more than a nod to her he pulled out a chair and sank into it, signaling a distant waiter in sign language for a cup of coffee.

"Where's the helicopter?" she joked. "On the hotel roof?"

He looked at her, startled. "Oh," he said, "the helicopter. I forgot. I want to talk to you."

He waited while the waiter filled his cup and her own, then took a quick sip of coffee; Vanessa would have sworn he was nervous.

"I've got a proposition for you," he said abruptly, setting his cup down and looking at her intently. "How would you like to come and work for me?"

CHAPTER SIX

VANESSA CHOKED on her drink. "What?" she asked incredulously, setting down her cup and reaching for the napkin in her lap. She coughed into the napkin, staring over it into Jake's steady gaze. "What?" she repeated when she could.

"I would like you to come and work for me." Now, suddenly, he was very calm, like a psychiatrist working with an autistic child.

Vanessa laughed shortly. "What as?" she asked with real curiosity; there was no saying what he might have in his mind.

"What *as*? As a designer of women's clothing! What else?"

Elbow on the table, Vanessa cupped her chin in her hand. "You had me wondering," she said with a half-smile. She was leaning half over the table toward him as though he were a magnet that drew her physically. When she realized that she was wishing that he would lean over, too, and kiss her mouth, she drew hastily back.

"Do you want to hire me at Designwear?" she asked, frowning in thought. "Is somebody leaving?"

Jake set his drink down on the table. "I want you," he said calmly, "to design a line of women's ready-to-wear I will be backing. You would have complete artistic control. You would be answerable only to me, and to me you would be answerable only in terms of profit." He paused. "Although of course you would be free to consult with me should you wish."

It took her breath away. It was everything she had ever wanted in her career, the chance to put all her ideas to work. Vanessa stared at him.

"Are you serious?" she whispered.

"Yes," said Jake evenly, watching her.

"I could do what I liked as far as design and production go?"

"As long as you're showing a profit you may do whatever you like."

"What happens if I don't show a profit?"

"You get fired."

Well, that was straightforward enough. Vanessa took a deep breath and felt her confidence in her own ideas waver.

"I...I'm very inexperienced with the business end of things," she said, thinking frantically that she didn't know one end of a profit-and-loss statement from the other. Jake sat looking at her, not speaking, and suddenly she was disgusted with herself for being so feeble. Everything she wanted was being offered to her on a silver platter! Suddenly, like a coal that had been smoldering unseen, the idea caught fire in her. "I can really run it however I want?" she asked him, her eyes alight.

He nodded. He was watching her closely, as though he had missed nothing of her progress from fear to conviction.

"When would you want me to begin?" she demanded.

Jake paused. "As soon as possible. As soon as you're ready."

Ideas were bubbling over inside her head as though the lid had suddenly come off a pressure cooker, and Vanessa tried to curb her excitement. "There are a lot of things we would have to discuss before I could make up my mind," she said slowly.

Jake smiled as though at a secret thought. He pushed back his chair, "Of course," he said. "I'd like you to come with me to the office now and talk to my accountant. I'd like to have your answer before you leave tomorrow."

She wasn't leaving tomorrow; she wasn't leaving till Monday, but for some reason Vanessa was more nervous now than ever about telling him so. "That's not a lot of time, Jake," she protested. "Why so soon?"

"Well, all right," he said. "Shall we say a week today?" His tone was faintly patronizing, as though she were being too cautious and cowardly, and she wondered if someone with more confidence would have jumped at this, when privately she felt that even a week was scarcely enough time to decide.

She shifted uncomfortably. "Yes, that would be all right."

Jake initialed the bill with a casual scrawl and rose. "Ready?" he said, and she wasn't ready; she would have liked a few more minutes just to sit there and absorb the idea. But it was obvious that in business Jake didn't waste any time, and so she got up and followed him out of the coffee shop.

"Are we going to your office now?" she asked, catching up with him outside the door. Jake nodded. "I'm not dressed for it," Vanessa said, indicating the blue jeans and sneakers she had put on in anticipation of the helicopter ride.

"Never mind that," Jake said impatiently. "It doesn't matter."

But here she had the strength to put her foot down. "It does to me," she insisted. "I won't be ten minutes."

She changed as fast as she could, somehow infected by Jake's impatient hurry, suddenly afraid of irritating him with delay. She pulled on stockings and a light gray suit and blouse and threw the contents of her large navy shoulder bag into a smaller smarter gray bag that matched her shoes.

"If it weren't for the slow elevators in your hotel," she smiled at Jake as she stopped beside him, "I'd have made it in five."

But he didn't get the joke. "Eight minutes is fine," he said, glancing at his watch, then guided her out to the car waiting at the curb.

Conrad Corporation was in downtown Vancouver, not far from the hotel, in a large modern office building. According to the building directory Concorp took up the top seven floors, and in the elevator Jake pushed the indicator button for the top floor.

It was obvious from the rich decor that this was the executive floor, the face Conrad Corporation showed to the public. Jake nodded to the receptionist and led Vanessa around a corner and down a hallway. "Morning, Jean," he said to a woman sitting behind a desk. "Would you tell Robert we're ready for him?"

Then he opened a carved walnut door and ushered Vanessa into his office. She sank down into one of the stuffed leather chairs he indicated in front of his desk, feeling as though Jake's rate of doing business was going to put her into a spin. In the car he had driven fast and competently, filling her ears with fact after fact about the business she would be expected to run.

When Robert Dawe, who turned out to be an accountant, arrived, it was more of the same. He was carrying lists of hastily devised figures, which he explained to her with a flattering assumption of her quick comprehension.

Vanessa's I.Q. was good; it wasn't that she did not understand the figures and facts she was being given, just that she wanted time to absorb the implications and ask questions. But it was all so exciting, so completely thrilling that finally she forgot caution and felt herself get caught up in the excitement of a new venture—small potatoes to Robert Dawe and Jake Conrad, perhaps, but her biggest opportunity yet.

The next time she looked at her watch it was two o'clock, and Jake was saying, "Good enough. Let's get some lunch."

Robert declined to join them, and in a few minutes Vanessa and Jake were out on the street. The sun was shining now, though earlier there had been a very light rain. "Let's walk," said Jake.

"Slowly," Vanessa added with a smile. "I'm beginning to feel like a whirligig."

"Slowly," agreed Jake, suiting his pace to the words and giving her the benefit of that slow crooked smile.

Conrad Corporation's offices were not far from the Granville Mall, a street, Jake told her, that had been closed to all traffic except for buses in an effort to make the downtown core more pleasant for pedestrians.

"This is great," she said. "I wish New York would do this to Fifth Avenue. You know," she confided as Jake pulled open a door and led her into a quiet restaurant, "when you're in New York it's hard to believe you could live without that incredible pace, where everyone around you is constantly running. But Vancouver's starting to get to me. I'm slowing down. I think I'm going to like it here."

He led her to a table by the window and looked at her as they sat. "Are you?" he asked with a meaningful smile.

She blinked. "Yes, I. . . oh!" she exclaimed in surprise, lifting a hand to her mouth. *I'm going to like it here,* she had said, not *I could get to*. . . . So unconsciously she must already have decided to take the job.

Consciously she was still overwhelmed, still undecided. But deep down, something in her had weighed the pros and cons and come up with a decision. Vanessa admitted all this with a self-deprecating laugh. "If only I were sure I could trust my unconscious decision-making process," she said ruefully.

"Always trust your instincts," said Jake softly.

"Do you always trust yours?" she asked curiously.

"Let's say I trust them without always obeying their dictates."

Vanessa laughed. "Oh, well, there has to be such a thing as civilized restraint. What do you do when you can't obey your instincts?"

"I bide my time," Jake said quietly, and the tone of his voice caused a sudden hollow in the pit of her stomach. Her gaze locked with his and a small flame puffed into life between them. When the tension in the air was almost unbearable he broke it by asking, "Are you going to follow your instincts?"

She wished she could be sure which instincts he was referring to. Resolutely Vanessa moved her eyes from his and said softly, "It's a very exciting chance for me. And it seems as though the risk is all on your side—"

She was startled by the sound of the sharp intake of his breath. "On *my* side!" he repeated, amazed.

Vanessa reminded him, "You're supplying all the backing. I'll just be an employee, but I'll be getting a share of the company if I make it a success. I don't even have to start making a profit for one year." It was what they had decided in this morning's meeting, so he could hardly have forgotten.

Jake blinked and relaxed. "Oh—yes," he said. "Well, for you the risk is quitting a secure job in an uncertain economic climate and moving to a city and a country you don't know well. If it doesn't work out for you you'll have to look for another job. For me it'll just be a tax write-off."

Vanessa sat up straighter. "Is that what you want?" she demanded in sudden suspicion.

"Is what what I want?"

"Are you setting me up to fail? Do you hope I'll make a mess of it so you can have a tax write-off for Conrad Corporation?"

"No," said Jake dryly. "If that was what I wanted I'd invest in Canadian movies. But I don't begin anything in the expectation of failure."

She smiled at him, suddenly wondering if that had a double meaning. She decided not. Jake was a different person when it came to business, it seemed. A shutter seemed to have come down over the private Jake, and when he had looked at her this morning in his office it was as though he had forgotten that anything personal had ever passed between them. She was a commodity, a talent.

And she had nearly made up her mind to spend the weekend with him at his ranch. She had nearly decided that Jake Conrad was the man she... well, she was glad he'd offered her the job before she'd told him of her changed flight booking. Now there was no reason to rush into anything. She would be coming back to Vancouver, and there would be lots of time to make the decision about Jake as a lover.

There was no reason now to stay over the weekend and every reason to return home tomorrow as she'd originally planned.

"Is there an Air Canada ticket office nearby, Jake?"

He was tearing a roll between his dark fingers, and the sight gave her an odd pleasure. The sudden return of his dark intent look startled her. "Why?" he demanded. "Are you going to stay the weekend after all?"

She'd spoken without thinking, and now she babbled, "No, no, I'm definitely going home tomorrow, it's just...."

He was still, watching her. "It's just what?"

This was ridiculous. "I'd thought of staying over to see a bit of the country, but now that's not nec—"

He grasped her wrist in a strong hand. "Are you telling me you've changed your flight booking?"

He looked angry, really angry. "Well, yes," she said uncomfortably, "but I—"

Suddenly he was laughing, an angry self-mocking laughter. "When did you decide that—last night?" he asked. She nodded. "And before you had a chance to tell me I was telling you about the job." Another mirthless bark of laughter escaped him; there was something here she did not understand, and she shifted in her seat.

"Look," she said, feeling as gauche as a teenager. "I hadn't made up my mind to—I wanted to see more of the country, that's all, but now it doesn't matter, because I'll be coming back."

Jake dropped her wrist. "Yeah," he said. "Be sure you do. When are you going to start?"

They had not decided this morning whether the new company should begin with a spring line or a summer. A spring line would mean Vanessa would have to start very soon; for a summer start she needn't be back in Vancouver till the end of August. Jake had told her the decision would be hers.

Now they began to discuss the pros and cons of a spring versus a summer start, with Jake taking it absolutely for granted that Vanessa no longer needed the week she had asked for to make up her mind about taking the job: now it was simply a question of when.

"I'd like to have a spring line as a goal," Vanessa heard herself saying after a while. "You have to generate excitement in the fashion business—a fast start would be much better than a slow one. The staff needs to get that feeling of working together under pressure...."

She really was committed. After her earlier hesitation, confidence flowed through her while she outlined her ideas under Jake's flattering interest. He was right: there was no way back now. She was drunk on the thrill of challenge. By the time they had finished their meal Vanessa had promised Jake that she would give serious consideration to starting up the company in time for a spring line and returning to Vancouver for that purpose by July first.

July second, in fact, because July first was a holiday. It was Canada Day, the anniversary of the country's independence. It seemed symbolic to Vanessa that she might make this enormous change in her life on a date that was of such significance to the country that would be her new home. In her eagerness she hardly noticed the fact that July first was scarcely three weeks away.

JAKE LEFT HER outside the restaurant to go back to the office. He said goodbye casually, as though he would be seeing her later, but this was her last night in Vancouver and he didn't ask her to save her evening for him.

She wandered till she found a travel agency, but her original flight back to New York was fully booked now. If this afternoon Jake had said anything more about wanting her to stay, Vanessa realized, she might have looked on this as a sign that she should stay. But she had felt oddly chilled by his preoccupation with business, and she allowed the travel agent to book her on a Canadian Pacific Airlines' flight to Toronto Saturday morning and a connecting flight through to La Guardia. When it was done and she was back in the bright warm sunlight again, she felt oddly desolate. Was it possible that Jake Conrad had wanted her only until he knew she wanted him?

She wandered along Granville Mall toward the water of Burrard Inlet and then, following the directions the travel agent had given her, cut across a few streets till cobbled streets and a sign informed her she was in Gastown.

Gastown, Gary Smeaton had told her Monday night, was an area of town several blocks long that, in the sixties, had been like Toronto's Yorkville district or—when she had looked blank—San Francisco's Haight-Ashbury. Now it was filled with trendy boutiques and cafés and was a major tourist attraction. Vanessa browsed through the shops, then drank capuccino outside a small café, watching the world pass and imagining that someday this would be old and familiar to her, that one day she would know Vancouver as well as she now knew Manhattan. She looked across the road at a small women's boutique and thought that if she did decide to come back in July, by next March that shop would be stocking her designs. Her heart beat faster as she imagined a small hanging tag reading something like Vanessa Fashions, and suddenly she could feel it, could taste it.

The air smelled softly of the sea, and people moved slowly along the streets, laughing and chatting, no one rushing. It was all just as Jace had described it to her nine and a half years ago, and even without him, Vancouver was still the right place for her to be. She had fallen in love with Jace's city, just as he had promised.

THE FAREWELL COCKTAIL PARTY that night was an anticlimax. Most of the buyers and manufacturers had left after the accessories show in the afternoon, and the few still around seemed to have evening flights to catch. Vanessa stayed at the party for two hours, feeling unaccountably restless. Jake Conrad did not come at all.

She listened to a Montreal manufacturer with half an ear as she thought about the decisions ahead of her: whether to give up her Manhattan apartment or merely sublet it, whether to sell or ship her furniture. But he was talking about Canada's unstable economic climate and gradually he won her full fascinated attention. Things, after all, were not so very different in the States.

The man was talking about high interest rates and the way Canadians who had to renew their mortgages were now losing their homes, and she heard him say, "Life gets less secure with every day," and suddenly that resonated.

"Do you realize I've only got your word for it that you'll fire me only if I don't make a profit?" she said with a smile on her lips when Jake Conrad opened the door of his penthouse suite in answer to her knock.

Jake slid his hands into the pockets of his loose casual pants and gazed down at her. "Have you?" he asked. "And do I take it that my word isn't worth much in your opinion?"

"Well...." She hesitated, a little taken aback. "You...you could—"

Jake stepped back and opened the door wider. "Why don't you come in? I see that you've discovered I'm not the only one at risk in this enterprise." There was an odd quality to his voice that made her look at him as she passed through into the large comfortable room.

But his face showed nothing but amused interest. He moved to the drinks cabinet. "Can I offer you something?"

"Sherry?" she asked. She didn't like cocktails much as a rule, though she had enjoyed the vodka martini he had ordered for her at Skookum Chuck's the other night. Afterward they had gone walking in the park and his kiss had gone straight to her head. Vanessa felt safer sticking to sherry.

"So, you want to back out of the job?" Jake asked when he had handed her a glass of dry sherry and was settling on the couch near the thick leather armchair she had sunk into.

Vanessa looked up, her dark eyes startled. Was there something in his voice that sounded as though he would be relieved if she made that decision? "No," Vanessa stated with decision. "No, that's not it at all. It's just—I'd like a contract, Jake. A management contract."

His eyes were hooded when he looked at her; he took a thoughtful sip of his drink. "And what do you want in the contract?"

She had a strong feeling that there was something happening at an entirely different level from the one they seemed to be speaking on. It was as though every word had a deeper significance that Jake understood, while she did not. And because she did not, she was operating at a disadvantage.

"Well, something that prevents you from arbitrarily firing me or folding the company during the first year; and guarantees my position as long as the company makes a profit after that; and something that guarantees my being able to buy into the company. Things like that," she said. "I haven't thought it all through, but I'd like to talk it over with my lawyer in New York and get him to draw up a contract."

"Bring your lawyer into this and you won't be starting before Christmas," Jake observed, and in her mind the suspicion flickered to life that there was more to this than Jake's wishing to start a new company. Then he said, "I'll get one of the company lawyers to talk to you tomorrow and draw something up for you to show to your own lawyer next week."

"I'm leaving for New York tomorrow," Vanessa said. "I changed my reservation again."

He looked at her. "Let's stop fooling ourselves," he said roughly. "Why don't you stay the weekend and forget the job? It would would be a lot easier on both of us." And he was looking at her, oddly, as though she were a danger to him.

Vanessa stared at him in surprised shock. "What do you mean?" she asked. She couldn't understand him, didn't want to understand. Had it all been a joke?

Jake laughed the self-mocking laughter she had heard him use before. "Forget it," he said, reaching for the phone. "What time does your flight leave?"

"Eleven o'clock."

He dialed a number. "Shelley," he said. "Jake. Is Howard home?" Then, after a moment, "Howie, Jake here. Are you free for an hour tomorrow morning?"

Within a few minutes it was arranged that the lawyer would see her in the morning to discuss the contract, and then Jake hung up and sat looking at her. "Well, now that's out of the way," he said softly. "We can get down to the real business of your visit."

Vanessa sat up straight, but his gaze had caught and locked with hers, and she couldn't break it. "What do you mean?" she demanded, but she was already breathless, and he knew it.

He stared at her, and her heartbeat quickened.

"What made you into a coward, Vanessa?" he asked after a long moment. "You were braver than this at nineteen, from all I've heard."

And he had heard it all. His gaze on her was frighteningly compelling and she knew that he wanted her complete capitulation, that he would not make a move toward her until she admitted that was what she wanted.

It *was* what she wanted, and she knew with a suddenly stinging insight that this was the reason she had come here tonight, the reason she had stayed at the cocktail get-together for two long hours. Abruptly she looked around the suite. There were no papers tonight. She looked at him. He was in shirt sleeves rolled up, the same clothing he had been wearing earlier today. On the coffee table were an empty coffee cup and a used glass.

He had been waiting. He had deliberately not come downstairs to find her, because he had wanted to force her to come to him.

Vanessa looked into his dark intent gaze, his waiting face. "What do you want?" she questioned in angry fear, her voice low. "What are you trying to prove?"

Jake's gaze narrowed as, still watching her, he took a sip of whiskey. In a flash, as he looked at her, his demons were back with frightening intensity. "You know what I want," he said hoarsely. "I want you willing—I want you demanding."

You want me begging. She heard the words in her own head with crystal clarity. A chill settled on her heart then, a chill of fear. *And you're the man I'd beg for*, she was thinking. *But if you want me begging, is it for any other reason than to give your demons the chance to refuse what I ask?*

She set down her glass and stood up, and it took all her strength not to run to him, to ask for his mouth on her lips. *If I went to you now,* she thought, *if you saw me begging, it might tear down your defenses, I might reach you the way I want to. And I might not. If I didn't—if I didn't, if you stayed cold and distant, the way you are right now*—she looked at his chiseled sensuous mouth and saw it pressed against her breast with an anguished need that tore at her determination—*you would destroy me. And I'm afraid that's what you want.*

Vanessa caught her breath on a little sob, unable to break their locked gaze. *Don't make me ask,* she willed him silently, thinking of his hands on her flesh, the burning thrust of his tongue. *Come to me, Jake, meet me more than halfway....*

In the moment before his hands clenched on the chair arm she dropped her eyes and turned. "Good night," said a cool voice that could only be her own. She walked to the door then, afraid to look back, afraid of his cold compelling anger, which had so nearly won.

But the cold anger was gone from Jake's face. In the moment when she dropped her eyes he stood, and now he stared after her, his face filled with a blazing need. Unseeing and afraid of the power her need would give him over her, Vanessa almost ran to the door.

THE NEXT MORNING she met Howie Spiegel in Jake's suite as arranged, but Jake did not stay after she arrived. Howie put any fears she had had to rest. Young, bright and honest, he was simply not the sort to be capable of dishonesty on a personal scale. Vanessa could imagine that Fraser Valley Helicopter ought to go over any contracts he drew up very carefully, but this morning Jake had briefed him on the sort of arrangement he and Robert had discussed with her, and Howie seemed intent on making her future with the new company as secure as possible.

"You aren't expected to *lose* money the first year," he cautioned. "What this clause will give you is the right to pare your prices to the bone if you want to in order to establish yourself in the market. Do you follow?" She nodded. "You will, in addition, have access to another fifty to a hundred thou for advertising in that first year, which cost will be underwritten by Conrad Corporation directly. This means, in effect, that you will be incurring a loss. It just won't go on the books as such."

"Oh!" Vanessa made a surprised face. Robert certainly hadn't mentioned this; nor had Jake.

"It will give you some extra leeway, Vanessa, so you should be able to come on the market with quite a little bang. What's your trademark going to be?"

Vanessa began to laugh. Never in her life had events moved so fast around her. What was her *trademark*? Yesterday when she'd got up she'd had about as much idea of starting her own company as she had of flying to the moon! And now—

"I haven't given that much thought yet," she confessed dryly. "This whole thing has been very sudden."

"Really?" Howie Spiegel raised a curious eyebrow. "That doesn't sound like Jake."

"It doesn't?" faltered Vanessa. "But...what do you mean?"

"Just that Jake's usually pretty thorough." Howie shrugged it off. "But it's not my business."

Of course, there wasn't anything to say that Jake hadn't been thinking of this for a long time, she thought uneasily. And when the right person had come along....

"Now, you'll have profit sharing of fifty percent, once Concorp has made its designated return on investment," Howie was saying. "From the second year you're entitled to take back shares in the company to the value of your share of the profits. We'll establish a share value that's mutually agreeable."

He was making notes on a yellow legal pad on which he had already scrawled a great many indecipherable notes while Jake had been briefing him. He referred to them now. "Now," he said, "Jake usually has a three-to-five-year restraint of trade clause as standard in his management contracts. He says he wants five with you because he expects your work to be very individualistic."

That would mean she couldn't set up in competition with her own company. "That's okay," she said. "I'm going to be buying into this company. I don't intend to quit."

She didn't have one complaint about the terms they discussed; there was nothing she had to argue for, nowhere she had to compromise. It was so ideal it was almost frightening. She was being given complete control; all the decisions would be hers. It was just as Jake said: all she had to do was earn a profit.

She discovered that the venture was being financed not by Jake personally but by Conrad Corporation, which was taking a debenture to secure its investment, whatever that meant.

"That looks like it," Howard Spiegel said finally, bringing his briefcase up onto the small table between them and throwing the yellow pad of his notes inside. They were in the lounge of Jake's suite. She had not been in the suite before in the daytime, but today rain and low-lying clouds obscured the view of the city and the ocean.

As they stood to leave, the door opened and Jake walked in. Vanessa somehow hadn't expected to see him again before she left, and she smiled at him, feeling a little bubble of pleasure in spite of herself.

"Hi!" she said happily.

Jake took in the smile through narrowed eyes for one disconcerting second and then smiled back.

"Hi," he returned. "How did you get on?"

"Very well," said Howie Spiegel.

At the same time Vanessa said, "I have to let Howie tell you about it. I've got a plane to catch."

"Don't rush off," Jake said in a slow caressing voice as he reached out a hand to detain her. "I'll take you to the airport."

Vanessa stopped as though his voice were her hypnotic control. "All right, thank you," she replied softly. Jake was already looking inquiringly at Howie, but he did not take his hand from her arm.

"Tie everything up?" he asked.

"It's a pretty tight contract," Howie replied. "Concorp's taking a debenture, of course, which will entail a separate agreement, but I think Vanessa's own contract is quite satisfactory."

"Oh, yes," interjected Vanessa with a smile.

"There's a problem, of course, anytime you try to guarantee employment. We eventually settled on a monetary penalty clause in the case of dismissal without just cause."

"Mmm-hmm," said Jake, eyeing him. "What kind of penalty?"

Howie hesitated. "A quarter mil," he said, flicking a glance at Vanessa. "And the only—"

"A quarter million?" Jake repeated with an incredulous laugh. "For God's sake, Howie, did you tell her I was made of gold?" He flicked a glance at Vanessa, the light of angry laughter in his eyes.

The lawyer breathed deeply. "Well, Jake, you promised not to fire her for any reason other than not turning a profit. But you know that's not contractually enforceable. She'd have a difficult time in court." He cleared his throat. "The only feasible protection was a penalty. And we've defined 'just cause' as being limited to financial mismanagement. It would be a lot easier for Vanessa to win a case this way than any other. And the penalty has to be sizable enough to dissuade you, or there's no point. Anyway," he said with a slightly questioning smile, "there's no question of its ever being paid, is there?"

It was a statement, not a question. "In the six years I've been with Concorp I've never known you to dismiss anyone who was turning a profit."

"No, there's no question of its ever being paid," Jake agreed flatly. "All right, thanks, Howie. Send me the contract Monday or Tuesday so I can sign it and get it to Vanessa in New York by Friday, will you?"

Howie hesitated. "Jake, you know I'm working flat out on the Fraser Helicopter bid?"

"Damn," Jake responded without emphasis. "Well, never mind, Howie. Just get this out of the way as fast as you can. The Fraser bid will just have to suffer."

The lawyer's face gazed impassively at Jake. "Yeah. Yeah, sure," he said in a voice devoid of emotion.

"Thanks for giving me your time this morning," Jake said. "I won't keep you any longer now. I'm sure you want to get back home."

"Okay," said Howie. "Bye, Vanessa, I'll be seeing you. I wish you the best of luck and I'm sure you'll succeed. Not many people get a squawk of protest out of Jake their first time out." He looked back at Jake. "She's pretty tough," he said with a grin, and a moment later he was gone.

There was a short silence as the door closed after him. Then Vanessa said, "It's late. I have to get to the airport."

"On Saturday morning it'll only take fifteen minutes," Jake said. "Are you packed and ready to go?"

Vanessa nodded.

"There's plenty of time, then," he said. "Sit down and have a coffee while I make a phone call."

Ten minutes later they were driving through heavy rainfall to the airport.

"This rain seems to be getting worse," Vanessa observed. "Or does it just seem that way because we're out in a car?"

Jake didn't seem to hear. He was watching the road, his eyebrows coming together in a frown of concentration as he drove. She lapsed into silence.

"How did you and Howie settle on the figure of two hundred and fifty thousand dollars?" Jake asked suddenly.

A car roared past them, sending up a wave of water that sprayed the windshield and thrummed loudly on the metal body of the car. Vanessa felt as though she were enclosed in a little world with Jake, a warm safe world.

When she spoke her voice was soft. "I'm not quite sure how we arrived at it. Howie explained to me that a penalty would be more practical than a simple guarantee, and I said that the penalty would have to be a real deterrent, and I think I asked what amount of money would really deter you."

And that had been the moment when she truly realized that she was in the "big time," though she did not tell Jake so. When Howie had answered her question with a casual, "Oh, a quarter to a half million, I guess," she had stared at him in speechless incredulity, but Howie hadn't seemed to notice. And somehow they had settled on the figure of, as Howie put it, "a quarter mil."

"Mmm-hmm," murmured Jack thoughtfully. "Well, Howie knows his business. That will certainly deter me." He laughed shortly.

"But it can't matter," Vanessa pointed out mildly. "He said you never fire anyone who's making a profit, and I intend to make a profit, Jake. And if I don't, you can fire me with impunity."

"Mmm-hmm," Jake responded again, "and just supposing a quarter of a million dollars in ready cash is more attractive to you than slugging it out in the hard world of business?"

She looked over at him, noticing as she did so that the rain had increased: the world was very gray indeed.

"My flight's going to be delayed, I'll bet," she observed. "This is halfway to a monsoon. Does it rain like this all the time?"

"It rains one hell of a lot," he said tersely. "Didn't Jace tell you?" His quick glance caught hers. "You didn't answer the question."

"Because I don't know what you mean."

"Suppose you deliberately foul up in the first year—when I can't fire you for not making a profit? Suppose I've got a choice of kissing a million dollars goodbye or firing you and cutting my losses with a mere quarter million?"

"We defined 'just cause' as financial mismanagement, Jake, not failure to make a profit. So under those circumstances you could fire me."

"So I could," he agreed softly. "You're pretty bright, aren't you, Vanessa?"

"Didn't Jace tell you?" she countered in response to an uncontrollable impulse.

"You've improved with time," he said.

"I want to know something," Vanessa stated suddenly, as a host of tiny suspicions suddenly formed a group picture inside her head. She turned on the seat to face him. "There are just too many contradictions in your story, Jake. Sometimes you talk to me as though you've met me before, seen me before. You know so much about me. And it just doesn't make sense that you got all that just from talking to Jace, no matter how delirious he was."

Jake's eyebrow went up, and his face looked suddenly stark and drawn in the gray light. "No?" he asked.

"No," she said. Her mental vision was quite clear now. "So what I want to know is—after Jace died, did you by any chance come looking for me? Did you come to New York and watch me or even meet me, something like that? You've told me that you loved me, and you've told me that you blamed and hated me for Jace's death. And either of those...." She paused.

"And either of those would be sufficient motive to go looking for you, is that what you want to say?" Jake finished for her in a hard voice.

She dropped her eyes in silent agreement. For a long moment the only sounds in the car were the low roar of rain on metal and the steady *swish-click* of the windshield wipers. Then Jake took an audible deep breath.

"After Jace died I...about six months afterward I had to go to New York on business again. I did look you up, Vanessa. I followed you around a bit. I even danced with you once.''

''Are you serious?'' she whispered.

''Yes, I'm serious,'' he said flatly. ''I was nearly obsessed with you, Vanessa. I can't say exactly why. In one way I suppose I hoped that if I saw you a. . . it would be a cure, that I'd be able to forget you. After you danced with me, you danced with your husband. I wanted to kill him. It was an almost ungovernable thing. It scared me. I left then, and I never saw you again.''

She couldn't look at him. ''So there *was* no photograph,'' she stated softly.

''No,'' said Jake.

''Jake, why have you offered me this job? Howie says you're acting out of character.''

Jake's eyes were hooded. ''Howie will be lucky if he's still got a job Monday morning,'' he muttered. ''Why did I offer you this job, is that what you want to know? Aside from expecting you to make me a profit, you mean?'' He flicked a look at her, and his eyes under his hooded lids seemed almost black with an emotion she couldn't read. He said slowly, ''I offered you the job because I want you, Vanessa. Because I have a ghost to exorcise just as you do. The difference is that I know how that ghost can be exorcised, and you haven't accepted it yet. I want to be around when you do.'' Jake's voice dropped to harshness. ''Because you will, Vanessa, whether you know it or not. You will.'' The car slid to a stop in front of the airport terminal building and Jake killed the engine. The drumming of the rain on the roof suddenly seemed deafening, as though it hammered inside her skull. Wordlessly Vanessa watched as Jake lifted one lean brown hand to her hair.

"We are going to be lovers, Vanessa," he said softly. "You know that, but you're fighting the knowledge. One day you'll stop fighting." Mesmerized, she gazed into his eyes as his hand cupped her head and he drew her gently to him, and his faintly smiling mouth lowered toward hers. When he stopped smiling and his eyes narrowed she closed her own against the sight. Then his passionate lips covered hers, and she trembled under his touch like the new green leaves of the trees outside that were trembling under the lash of the rain.

CHAPTER SEVEN

WORK BEGAN THE MOMENT she arrived in her Manhattan apartment Saturday night. Although she would not resign from TopMarx until she had seen the signed management contract from Jake, she would have to begin making arrangements to sublet the apartment and ship her belongings immediately if she intended to be back in Vancouver by July first.

Vanessa's furniture consisted mostly of antiques lovingly obtained over the years, and when she stood in the middle of her apartment and looked around her after her arrival, she knew that she couldn't leave it behind. She would have to take it along into her new life. Suddenly the realization of all that would have to be done in three short weeks fell on her like a cloak, and she grimaced and mentally staggered under the weight of it. Moving to the kitchen to make a cup of coffee she wondered if she should put off the move till August. If she didn't produce a spring line after all, what difference would it make? If she did, she would be rushing through the next three weeks at breakneck speed, with hardly a moment's thinking space.

When the coffee was ready she sank into a chair and lazily dialed Colin's number.

"Guess what?" she said without preamble when he answered the phone.

She needed no introduction; Colin always recognized her voice—and her mood.

"You've strangled the Philistine and are now a free agent," Colin said promptly with a laugh in his voice. But he was only half-joking; he knew the "what" was something big.

Vanessa laughed. Suddenly, at his use of the word, she *felt* free. Totally, marvelously free, as though she could suddenly fly. She gazed out of a window onto the dull brown brick of the building beside hers and thought of English Bay and Grouse Mountain and Stanley Park. Yes, she was a free agent, and soon she'd be flying to a new life, in a new city, with a new—she brought her thoughts up short. She had been going to think, *with a new man,* but for the moment she had better restrict her thoughts to the city and the job.

"It wasn't necessary to strangle Tom, however," she replied, excitement bubbling through her voice.

"My dear," said Colin, and his tone became ever so slightly guarded, "do I take it that you have burned your bridges?"

Oh, Lord, he thought she meant to go and work with *him*. In all the sudden pressure and excitement of the past two days, she had forgotten Colin's offer.

"Yes," she said slowly, "but I'm not coming in with you after all, Colin. I'm going to be starting a business in Vancouver for Jake Conrad."

"What?" asked Colin blankly.

She told him all about it. He was one of the few

people she could tell right now, before the contract was signed and she could feel it was definite. Colin was one friend who would keep the news quiet and wouldn't commiserate too deeply if the thing fell through next week. He would understand the vagaries of fortune.

"Well, darling, what can I say?" he asked at last. "I'm shattered. I was sure you were going to throw in your lot with me."

"Well...." she began.

"But of course I'm delighted for you, Vanessa. I know it's the kind of thing you wanted."

"Yes."

The irrepressible though lighthearted sarcasm that was Colin's trademark and that she had subconsciously been waiting for finally crept into his tone. "Though why you would want to bury yourself in that little backwater on the *west coast* is more than I can imagine," he said, managing to make the west coast sound like the other side of the moon. "And in *Canada*, too, darling, which—"

Vanessa laughed protestingly. "Now, Colin, Vancouver is a very modern cosmopolitan city. Just because people move more slowly—"

"Well, I can see you're unregenerate, my dear. Still, this has its potential silver lining. You can be my first client, Vanessa. I shall design some sort of signature fabric for you."

Vanessa blinked at the receiver in her hand, then put it back to her ear. It was becoming real too fast. In a very short time, decisions like that would be the order of her day. She would be choosing a trademark, a logo, a line of clothing, and her word would be law. For a moment she sat stunned as the reality sank in: from now on, she would rise or fall entirely on the strength of her own talents.

"My God, Colin," she breathed suddenly. "Am I being crazy to think I can do this?"

"What are you worried about, darling?" he responded calmly. "It's an ideal situation. If you don't make it, Conrad takes the loss, not you. You just get yourself another job. There's no risk at all on your side. . . ."

No risk. "I'm not the only one at risk in this situation," Jake Conrad had said. But Colin was right—financially, Jake *was* the only one at risk. And Jake certainly knew that. One failed enterprise wouldn't blight her career forever.

But he had implied that she was as much at risk as he was. And he had meant it.

What had he meant? In what way was she at risk?

THE CONTRACT ARRIVED at her apartment by courier on Thursday evening. Vanessa read it as carefully as she could; to her layman's ears it seemed straightforward, the terms set out exactly as she and Howard Spiegel had discussed them.

But two things nagged at her: Jake Conrad had told her he wanted to be her lover, and he had said that she was at risk. And so the sight of his black full-looped signature on the last page did little to quell the nagging disquiet she had been feeling all week long.

On Friday morning she dropped in to see Louis Standish, Larry's brother, at his legal offices. "I need an immediate opinion, Lou," she said after she had told him about it. "I may want to hand in my resignation today if you think the contract looks all right."

The lawyer eyed her curiously without saying anything for a moment. Then he shook his head and sighed. "I suppose it's no good telling you to wait and give me enough time to do an investigation so my opinion is worth something?"

"Well, Lou, I'd really like. . . ."

"To get things settled," he finished for her dryly. With another sigh he picked up his horn-rimmed glasses and settled them on his nose and picked up the contract. Then he dropped it again and looked at her.

"Vanessa," he said, "I don't think that, for the most part, I am an interfering man. In fact, I rarely advise you about anything, even though sometimes I've wanted to shake you for your impulsiveness. But sometimes one has to offer advice even though one knows there's not much chance of being heard. Now, I want you to look at me, Vanessa, and remember while I'm talking that this is the man who told you not to marry my brother ten years ago."

"Lou—" she began.

Lou leaned back in his chair and raised a palm toward her. "Please," he said. "That is the only time I've offered you advice without being asked, and I bring it up now because I was right then and I'm probably right now. And I'm telling you—" he tapped the documents on his desk with one firm finger "—to let me give this a good solid appraisal and to wait until next week before making any final commitment."

Bring a lawyer into this, she heard Jake's voice, *and you won't be starting before Christmas.* She admired Lou; he was a more than competent lawyer, but he was also cautious. And suddenly she did not want to wait till Christmas—or even next week!

Lou saw it in her eyes. "Vanessa," he said before she could answer. "If the man wants you to run his company for him, one extra week—an extra month—is not going to change his mind. On the other hand, if he's rushing you into the decision, you should have a long look at it."

"He isn't rushing me," Vanessa objected. "I'm the one who wants to start immediately."

"Why?" asked Lou reasonably.

"Well, I. . . ." She hesitated. "Because I'm fed up with TopMarx and—and because I'd like to start out with a spring line with the new company."

Louis Standish was a Rhodes scholar and a graduate of Harvard Law School and sometimes when he looked at her, her own perfectly competent I.Q. seemed sadly puny under the piercing examination of his own. Ten years ago, when he had harshly told her not to marry Larry, his look had been just as piercing, but it had made her uncomfortable in a different way.

Lou took off his glasses and threw them down lightly on his desk. Resting his head against the high back of his plush black leather chair he lowered his eyes to the desk and then looked back to her. In the transition his gaze had become hooded.

"I am not by nature altruistic," Lou said conversationally. "But ten years ago I wanted you and I didn't lift a hand to get you. I had no children then; divorce would have been easy for me. I wanted to divorce Marjorie and marry you more than I've ever wanted anything in my life."

Vanessa gasped a faint breath through parted lips and gazed at him in wordless astonishment.

"I didn't do anything about it, Vanessa. I was thirty-two and you were nineteen, and you were in love with my brother. So like a fool I decided I couldn't soil the bloom of young love.

"When it became obvious that you were falling in love with someone else I could cheerfully have killed you first and then myself. But too late is too late and you still had a right to young love."

She had never heard anything of this. She had never suspected the least hint of it. Vanessa couldn't say a word.

"And the next I knew there was this business with Larry, and my mother's harebrained scheme to get you to marry him in spite of everything."

She said finally, "Why are you—"

He raised a hand. "Please listen," he said quietly. "I told you not to marry Larry then for your sake, not for my own, but because of the way I felt about you I couldn't fight. I might have tried much harder to prevent the marriage if I hadn't been so damned aware that it would suit me royally to have you single and with a little experience behind you. I didn't try harder, and you married Larry, to the eternal shame of the Standish family."

He took a deep breath, and so, suddenly, did Vanessa, feeling as though she had forgotten to breathe while he had been speaking.

"Well, I've got the same problem with my motives today—except that now I've really only got the memory of having loved you. Love doesn't survive what I've done to it, I've discovered. In fact, it sometimes feels as though not much of anything survives.

"If you want me to look at this damn thing, I'll do it. There's not much I could refuse you. And I'll do it today if you insist. But my real advice to you is to get another lawyer, Vanessa. Because my legal advice will be clouded by the fact that I don't want you to leave town."

"But that'll take—"

"That'll take time. God." He shook his head. "Where the hell does all this youthful eagerness come from? You're twenty-nine years old and you still make me feel the way you did when you were nineteen: old." He let out a bark of self-deprecating laughter. "In my more sanguine moments I used to tell myself that that enthusiasm for life would rub off on me." Lou breathed deeply and sighed. "All right, Vanessa. Leave it with me. Come back and pick me up for lunch and I'll tell you what I think."

She went through the rest of the morning in a daze, listening to Tom trying to blackmail and wheedle the fabric salesmen into increasing his orders on the colors he had ordered too lightly for the sales he had made in Vancouver. She felt completely detached from everything around her—the truly pressing reality was in her head.

Lou Standish was the second oldest of the four Standish sons. He had got married at twenty-seven shortly after opening his own legal practice and now, at forty-two, wore three-piece navy suits and well-cut hair and kept in shape at his club. Larry had never been very close to him and as a result nor had Vanessa. That ten years ago he had been thinking of divorcing Marjorie to marry herself astounded Vanessa. If it was true, he had never let her see the slightest sign of it. He had driven her home from a party once, she remembered suddenly, on a night when the Standish family had all been together in their parents' house and Larry had drunk a lot. Lou had behaved to her like an elder brother on the way home, listening with polite attention while she babbled her excitement about just beginning college to study fashion design.

"No, you said I could increase my order anytime up to July for immediate delivery," Tom was saying in a hectoring voice, and Vanessa surfaced briefly to watch the blond, blow-dried young salesman try to appease a lying unreasonable customer who was obviously trying to pull a fast one but who could not be told so.

"Ah, now, Tom, you know I can't guarantee. . . ."

Vanessa shut his voice out, her restless spirit feeling caged. While not looking anything like him, the salesman reminded her of Lou Standish. Of course he hadn't told her how he felt, ten years ago. He was afraid. Afraid of life, afraid of taking events into his own hands.

So he had looked around, not for an opportunity but for a convenient excuse to run away from whatever threatened his orderly life. Nineteen and thirty-two were not such disparate ages. Lou had lied to himself.

Involuntarily her thoughts flew to Jake Conrad, and a small laugh escaped her. He at least was a man who saw what he wanted and tried to get it! He had tried just about every way there was to get her into bed with him—from sweet seduction to outright bribery! And he made no bones about it.

Tom and the salesman were looking at her expectantly, probably because of the laugh. Vanessa reached out for her coffee cup and patted her chest lightly.

"Sorry, something in my throat," she apologized, wondering how they would look at her if she told them, *I was just remembering that a man offered me a small but promising gold mine if I would sleep with him!*

When she spoke her voice came out perfectly clearly with no hint of anything in her throat, and she wanted to laugh again at the wonderful stupidity of life. The expression on their faces had moved from expectancy to blankness to, now, polite wariness. It wasn't the laugh, she perceived suddenly. They must have been talking to her.

"Sorry," she said again. "Did you say something? I'd wandered."

Tom's be-ringed hand caressed the gold chains and amulets around his throat.

"Brian's suggesting the wool-polyester blend as a substitute for the 077 line," he said. "We can get delivery next week. What do you think?"

Vanessa reached out to pick up the yard-square sample of coffee-colored fabric lying uppermost on the desk. She shrugged lightly.

"Tom, it's the same stuff we decided against in the spring. It's got too hard a hand and too much of a gloss. You won't be able to sub this without asking your customers first, and that would take two or three weeks with the Canadian buyers. There's no point in talking delivery next week."

"Excuse me—"

They looked up to see the receptionist at the door of Tom's office. "There's a long-distance call for you, Vanessa. Do you want to take it? Line three."

Conferences were interrupted for long-distance calls because otherwise it meant calling the client back on TopMarx money. With a quick nod to Susan, Vanessa reached out across the desk and picked up the receiver while Tom pushed down the lighted button for her.

"Vanessa here," she said, and suddenly there *was* something in her throat, because the voice on the other end of the wire was Jake Conrad's.

"How's the rat race?" he asked, and just at that moment a siren shrieked along Seventh Avenue, ululating over the general hubbub of horns and engines that until now she had been blanking out of her hearing.

There was no doubt about it, there had to be a better way to live.

"There has to be a better way to live," she said with a smile in her voice.

"Oh, yes," Jake said softly, and just for a split second she imagined that that was somehow a threat.

She pushed the idea aside. "Did you get the contract?" he asked.

"Last night," she said. All the excitement of her new future surged up in her again and she wanted to laugh.

"And is it signed and on its way back to me?"

She laughed. "Not yet!" she protested. "I'm having a...a friend look at it for me." She swallowed convulsively. She had almost said "a lawyer," forgetting that Tom was listening to the conversation, forgetting everything except that....

"And what does your friend think?"

She wished she could get off this subject. Tom was not stupid. In a moment he would realize it was not a client she was talking to.

"Well, they're very attractive designs and he thinks you've got potential, but he doesn't advise dropping everything too quickly. He thinks he'd be able to advise better next week...."

"What did I tell you about lawyers?" said Jake, correctly interpreting the coded message. "Is your boss listening to this?"

"I can't really go into it now," she said apologetically. "I'm just in the middle of a meeting, but if you'd like to...."

Tom had realized it was no customer she was talking to, and he had no intention of letting his employee's time and his own be taken up discussing the possible talents of a would-be designer.

"Get them to call you at home," he said impatiently, loudly enough for whomever was at the other end of the phone to hear.

"Jake, listen, I—"

"Domineering son, isn't he?" Jake said mildly. "Do you have to put up with that kind of rudeness a lot?"

"On paid time," she agreed.

"The hell with paid time," responded Jake. "Paying a wage doesn't entitle one human to be rude to another."

Tom had picked up the wool-polyester swatch and now he began to talk in a loud, deliberately carrying voice to the young salesman.

"Suppose we take a few hundred yards of this to keep us going till you can fill our order on the worsted?" he demanded. "How soon could. . . ?"

Jake was speaking again and Vanessa plugged her other ear to shut out Tom's voice. "Pardon?" she said.

"I said, doesn't that kind of behavior make you angry? You might be talking to someone very important to you. For all he knows, you could be talking to an old lover whom you desperately want to see again." His voice dropped. "Or a brand new lover whom you'd like to impress. Aren't you a little annoyed?"

He was right; it *was* making her angry, although normally she took Tom in her stride. She could feel adrenaline pumping into her bloodstream, making her heart beat fast in the ancient anticipation of battle.

"Yes," she said, "I am."

"I've got the perfect cure," said Jake.

She thought she knew what that was. "Really?" she said, laughing a little. "What is it?"

"You look at him and you say, 'Tom,' clearly and firmly," directed Jake.

More adrenaline chased through her heart and brain.

"I. . . ."

"Just say it. 'Tom,' " he directed.

An imp of irresponsibility took charge of her brain. *Well, why not,* it demanded. *What the hell!*

"Tom," she said, clearly and firmly, and again, "Tom."

Silence fell in the little office whose walls were crowded with hanging garments of every shape and color. Tom and the salesman looked at her, Tom's mouth still open on an interrupted word. Jake heard the silence at the other end.

"Now say, 'Tom, I quit,' " he directed calmly.

Vanessa opened her mouth on a faint stifled gasp and froze.

"I guarantee you he'll never be rude to you again," said that low voice. A tone of persuasiveness might have made her wary, made her think, but Jake Conrad sounded detached, businesslike, like a doctor telling her to soak in warm water. " 'Tom, I quit.' That's all it will take. You'll enjoy it."

The imp considered it with delight.

"Tom, I quit," said Vanessa.

Tom's jaw, which had been on the point of closing, fell farther open, so that he looked like a fish gasping for oxygen. Vanessa stifled an insane desire to giggle. Jake was right: this was fun. She looked at Tom and knew he would never have any power over her again.

"What in God's name—?" began Tom angrily.

"Does he look like a fish?" Jake asked with calm curiosity, and then he laughed as though he could no longer contain it. Vanessa bit her lip against the need to join in.

The young salesman diplomatically stood up and disappeared out the door. "Tell him you're renouncing the fleshpots forever and—" Jake began.

"I'm immigrating to Canada," Vanessa told Tom firmly. "I'll be leaving in two weeks."

"Ah, Vanessa," said Jake's approving voice in her ear. "There isn't a woman in the world to match you."

Not for stupidity, that was for sure, Vanessa thought, suddenly calm. A little thrill of dismayed fear rushed up her spine. Well, she had burned her boats this time, and no mistake.

"I'll talk to you later," she said briefly, and hung up the phone.

Tom shouted angrily, "What the hell are you talking about, Vanessa?"

CHAPTER EIGHT

LOU CAST HER a fulminating glance over his Perrier and lime. "Resigned already?" he repeated. "My God, Vanessa, what for? Why didn't you wait?"

An explanation of the why would leave him thinking her even more witless than he plainly already did. Vanessa shrugged. "I let myself get cornered, Lou," she said. The irritation that she felt both for her own silly rashness and for Jake Conrad colored her tone.

"Oh, well, it's done now," Lou said. He seemed perfectly willing to imagine that it was Tom Marx who had cornered her and forced her into resigning, and Vanessa wondered if that was what made the difference between a criminal lawyer and a corporate lawyer: the instinct, or the lack of it, for querying human motives.

"Is there going to be a problem with the contract?" she asked.

Lou leaned back to allow the waiter to set down a crisp salad in front of him. Then there followed a pause while he eyed her curiously. "Funny," he said musingly.

"What?"

"Funny how often one misses what's right under one's nose. I've always thought of you as having more than average intelligence and more than average talent. Now I have to take a good long look and wonder whether I shouldn't revise that estimate to brilliant."

"What?" Oddly enough, her heart began to beat hard, as though some message of fear had been transmitted to her body.

"It's a pretty good contract, Vanessa," Lou said, reaching into his inside breast pocket and pulling the document out. "I don't think I could have drawn one up better if I'd been doing it for you myself."

Vanessa breathed a shaky laugh and felt an unbearable tension she hadn't been aware of leave her body.

"Congratulations, Vanessa—someone wants you very badly and they're willing to pay to get you." Vanessa stifled a laugh. *Yes, indeed,* she thought dryly. *If you only knew how right you are!*

He went through the contract clause by clause, discussing each one with her and pausing long enough after each to take in a few forkfuls of food. "The debenture comes under a separate agreement, which you ought to have a look at. Send me a copy if you can't sort it out, but I imagine it's quite straightforward. Now, about this five-year restraint of trade. Are you satisfied with that?"

"Well, my market area is going to be Vancouver and environs," she said. "So it wouldn't be much of a restraint. Anyway, Lou, I'll be buying into the company. I won't want to quit."

"That won't be for a while," he nodded. "When it does come along, try to remember that you are frequently too impulsive for your own good, and get advice on it. Vanessa, are you listening?"

She smiled. "Yes, I'm listening, Lou, but please don't try to tell me not to invest in my own company when the chance comes along."

"There, you see? You've made up your mind already! Now, Vanessa—" His voice was too reasoned and calm, and it grated on her own bubbling delight.

She said, marveling, "Lou, how do you live without ever letting excitement get to you? You're sitting there now trying to calculate and plan and predict something new and exciting out of existence!" She bubbled into irrepressible laughter, laying her hand on his arm. "Isn't there a law somewhere against killing anticipation with common sense?"

Lou looked at her, shaking his head a little in wonder. "You amaze me," he said slowly. "You never cease to amaze me. You're twenty-nine years old and you're off to a new country, a new life, and the kind of business challenge that is more of a risk these days than it's ever been. Aren't you afraid at all?"

Vanessa laughed again. "Lou, what is there to be afraid of? If I fail at this I'll get another dream. I'm not going to die. Anyway, I'm not going to fail. I'm going to succeed. I'm not insanely ambitious, you know. I don't want to be Yves St. Laurent or Coco Chanel. I want to make a small comfortable name for myself in a small comfortable pond. I'll be happy if middle-income women in ordinary shops learn to look for my tag on a garment and feel they can trust it."

Lou smiled reluctantly, still watching her intently. "I wonder," he said quietly, "if I had gone after you and married you when I wanted to, would you have changed me, or would I have changed you?"

Vanessa's eyes became hooded and dropped to her plate. *Oh, Lou, grow up,* she thought in irritated exasperation.

They had no dessert; Lou's health and fitness regime was very strict. Over coffee, which Lou drank decaffeinated, he handed her back the contract. He seemed to be looking at her with a new respect, and Vanessa wondered with idle amusement whether that was because of her intrepidity or because Jake Conrad had put a quarter-of-a-million-dollar price tag on her head. For no reason that she could think of, she suddenly wanted to describe this scene to Jake Conrad. *He* would understand, he would laugh with her, she felt, not knowing why.

"If you ever need any legal advice," Lou was saying as they stood to go, "give me a call and I'll find someone out there for you. Don't just go to some fresh-faced, hole-in-the-wall kid. Remember that you'll be taking on a corporation that can pay for the best talent around."

I'll be taking on Jake Conrad, Vanessa thought involuntarily, and discovered that the thought gave her pleasure.

SHE ARRIVED IN VANCOUVER on Dominion Day, and she learned with a little shock that the country was barely fourteen years past its hundredth birthday. The colonies north of the forty-ninth parallel hadn't stood up to Great Britain's control until the time of the American Civil War—nearly a hundred years after their sisters to the south had made their rebellious stand. Vanessa wondered what had caused this enormous division in loyalties in the colonies, allowing one half of the continent to remain so loyal to the mother country that, although independent, it was still in the British Commonwealth two hundred years later, and the other half to sever all ties.

Oddly, on such a day, every flag she saw on the way to the city was at half-mast. After the car had passed the fourth one, Vanessa leaned forward and said to the chauffeur, whom Jake had sent to meet her, "Why are all the flags at half-mast?"

"Terry died on Sunday, ma'am," he said. "They're flying like that all over the country."

The only Terry Vanessa had ever heard of was the actress Ellen Terry, and she doubted very much if Ellen Terry had died on Sunday. Feeling more than usually awkward about her ignorance of this country, she said softly, "I'm sorry, I don't recognize the name. Who was Mr. Terry?"

"Not Mr. Terry," said the chauffeur. "That's his first name. Terry Fox, his name is, but I guess everybody in the country called him Terry. Sometimes the newspapers call him Mr. Fox."

Vanessa wrinkled her brow, beginning to imagine that she had heard the name somewhere. An ex-prime minister, perhaps?

"He was a young kid who got cancer in his leg—they had to amputate at mid-thigh. He was just an ordinary kid, about twenty, you know; they say there wasn't anything special about him. But he didn't like the idea that he was supposed to give up on life, that cancer was supposed to take the stuffing out of him. And he said he was going to run right across Canada—5,000 miles—on an artificial leg to raise money for cancer research. He trained for months out here; he was a Port Coquitlam boy, you know; that's not far from Vancouver—and then he flew to the east coast and dipped that artificial leg of his into the Atlantic Ocean and set off running."

"Goodness," she breathed.

"At first no one gave him a blind bit of notice. No one gave a damn. Here was this kid on an artificial leg running across the country at a rate of twenty-six miles each and every day, and he was lucky to make page ten."

"Twenty-six miles a day?" repeated Vanessa. "But that's—that's the distance of the Boston marathon, isn't it?"

"You bet," said the driver. His voice had an odd quality that was a mixture of pride, anger, sorrow and something else she could not pinpoint but which might have been a kind of exaltation. "You bet. He ran a marathon every damn day for weeks without anybody caring. Even the Canadian Cancer Society wasn't too keen on what he was doing, by all reports. And he was doing it for them—his goal was a million dollars.

"Well, he got in around Toronto there, and all of a sudden the country started to sit up and take notice. And the next thing any of us knew, we had us a real live Canadian hero who was making us feel as though we had something after all. He was big news, he was everybody's brother or son, he was the gutsiest person this country has seen for a long, long time. Here we all were, whining about separatism and the domestic price of oil and the economy and feeling as though we were hardly a country at all. And this young kid with no special gifts was out there fighting cancer in a way nobody in history ever fought it.

"Maybe it doesn't make sense to an outsider, I don't know. But I'm telling you that the whole nation fell in love with that boy, and because of that, we felt united for once.

"And then, just as the country was building up to a real excited frenzy of hero worship, we turned on our TV sets one day to see Terry on a stretcher, swallowing hard and telling the country that the cancer had reappeared in his lungs. He'd run just halfway across the country."

"Oh, my God," whispered Vanessa sympathetically.

"Yeah. Well, that was last September, and we've been waiting and watching and hoping...the whole country. People wrote songs and poems about him, and school kids wrote essays on 'Heroism' and 'Terry Fox' and every other title you can think of, I guess—but mostly we felt angry that cancer was going to beat Terry Fox after all. It just didn't seem fair.

"Well, as I said, that was last September, and so far Terry's Marathon of Hope has raised nearly twenty-five million dollars for cancer—over a dollar for every man, woman and child in Canada. In your country that'd be the equivalent of about two hundred and fifty million dollars."

"An enormous achievement," agreed Vanessa quietly.

"Well, he died on Sunday, though he must have had more people praying for him than anyone else in the world in this decade. Twenty-two, he was. And just about everybody in the country feels as though he's lost his nearest and dearest." He paused, and coughed a little. "I guess it doesn't sound much in the telling; it seems strange even to me that so many people could love a stranger like that, and I guess you think it's kind of odd. . . ."

"It's a very moving story," Vanessa replied.

"Well, better you know what it's about," said the driver, regaining a matter-of-fact tone in his voice, "or you'll be wondering what's wrong with us—he's in the papers and on TV so much I guess World War III might displace him, but not much else. The funeral's tomorrow. You won't hear anything except the story of Terry till it's over. Here we are now."

The car pulled up in front of Jake Conrad's hotel, and Vanessa looked out at its beautiful glass entrance with a feeling of something like homecoming.

Was Jake somewhere behind those walls, waiting for her? Was he going to welcome her to her new country, her new home?

Her new country. Vanessa was not yet a landed immigrant in Canada, but knowing the trouble that foreigners experienced immigrating to the States, she marveled at how quickly and easily Canada had accepted her. Three weeks had not been enough time for her to go through the regular immigration channels, but a request for rush handling from Conrad Corporation to the Canadian immigration authorities in New York had resulted in her being granted a six-month temporary employment authorization. Now, at her leisure during that time, she would be able to drop down to Seattle or another American city and apply at the embassy there to reenter Canada as a landed immigrant.

Vanessa felt as though she had taken a giant step, and as she stood in the bright warm sunshine and looked around, she badly wanted a friendly familiar face to come and say, "Welcome to Canada."

"So you came," abruptly said a deep voice behind her with a hint of surprised antagonism that startled her. "I wondered if you would." She whirled.

Of course, the only face that was really familiar to her in Vancouver was Jake Conrad's, so it must have been his she wanted to see. If at this moment he didn't seem entirely friendly and wasn't saying the words she'd imagined, still, her heart beating with a sudden surge of happy surprise, Vanessa told herself, *it'll do.*

She smiled unselfconsciously up at Jake. "But I told you I was coming," she protested mildly. "Just yesterday."

He shrugged. "You don't exactly have a history of keeping your word," he said.

Vanessa sucked in a hurt breath. He was referring to her promise to visit his cousin at Easter all those years ago, and that was unfair. She felt as though a cloud had passed across the sun.

"Look," she said. "Let's get something straight between us." She glanced around, but the chauffeur was on his way into the building with her bags; they were alone. "I made a mistake ten years ago, and I spent ten years paying for it. But Jace—"

A harshly intent look came into his eyes. "Ten years paying?" he repeated hoarsely. "Damn you, you keep saying things like that. What the devil do you mean?"

Coolly she ignored the interruption. "But Jace made some mistakes, too, and so, I guess, did fate. And I don't—"

"What mistakes did Jace make?"

Vanessa took a breath. "He should never have left me behind," she said softly. "He should have taken me with him then, when he came home at Christmas. I would have come—I was waiting for him to ask. Later, it was easy to believe he hadn't loved me as much as he'd said, that it was just a wild kind of dream."

"That's pretty harsh," said Jake in a voice that was tight with strain. "He was still banged up from the accident; he might have been disfigured for life, for all he knew."

"Well, so what?" asked Vanessa rudely, the pain of not being asked ten years ago suddenly swamping her again. "He couldn't have thought that would matter to me."

"I—"

She raised a protesting hand to cut him off. "Jake, it's ancient history. And it has, forgive me, nothing whatever to do with you. And I just don't want to be constantly reminded of Jace like this. Can't you understand? I loved him. I've carried him around in my heart for ten years, but he's dead! He's dead, and I want to forget him!" To her surprise her voice broke and hot tears suddenly pricked her eyes. Just as Jake reached for her, she turned away to hide her eyes; his arm fell to his side.

"Vanessa, listen, I—"

"Your room's ready for you, Mrs. Standish. They've got your key at the desk." The chauffeur had come back through the doors and with a brief nod to both of them was moving toward the car.

"Thank you," Vanessa said, so faintly that he could not have heard it. With an effort she raised her voice and called more firmly, "Thank you."

As the car pulled away a pair of taxis pulled up, and Vanessa and Jake were suddenly engulfed in a small chattering crowd. As the tourists moved into the hotel lobby, Vanessa and Jake followed silently in their wake.

"Did you have lunch on the plane?" Jake asked after she had checked in, and when she looked at him there was no sign of any emotion aroused by the conversation they had had outside.

"Yes," she said. It was a lie; she had been too tense with expectation to have anything more than a glass of tomato juice on the plane. But she didn't want to have to eat lunch with Jake Conrad. She wanted to get away from him.

"Good," he responded. "Why don't you go to your room to freshen up a bit and meet me in my suite in about half an hour?"

Oh, damn. Her imp prompted her to say something like, "Isn't this a holiday in Canada? And aren't I a new Canadian?" but common sense prevailed. He was her financial backer now, not Jace's cousin, and it couldn't hurt to impress him with her eagerness to get started on this new enterprise. That was no lie; she was eager. She just didn't want any more of Jake Conrad's disturbing company at the moment.

And when, half an hour later, she dutifully presented herself at the door of his suite, she got a strong impression that Jake didn't really want to see her, either. He answered the door with his white shirt sleeves rolled up, his hair ruffled and on end and a sheaf of papers in his hand. He had forgotten her existence, and the sight of her now was unwelcome: Vanessa knew that as though she had been told.

If she had said then, "Why don't we leave this till tomorrow?" she was quite sure he would have agreed, but perversely, Vanessa suddenly wanted to be in his company, to make him notice her.

She said instead, "You look busy. What are you working on this time?" and moved past him into the room as he automatically stepped to one side.

There were papers everywhere; he must be one of the untidiest businessmen she had ever met. On the sofa there was room for only one person to sit; on both sides of this clear space was paperwork, and paper was littered along the length of the coffee table in front of it. A glass of whiskey sat atop a pile of what might have been company reports. Vanessa eyed the room in amusement.

"Ever been married, Jake?" she asked lightly.

"No," he answered briefly, moving over to his drinks cabinet. "Drink?"

"Sherry, please," she said. "Your secretary must be a brave woman."

"Must she?" He spoke coolly, almost rudely; for some reason he was nettled by her—by her mere presence or by her attitude, she couldn't tell. But she knew she wanted to continue to nettle him.

"I'll bet you're the sort of man who demands that someone find a file that turns out to have been sitting on his own desk the whole time." Smiling, she lifted some papers out of the armchair that sat at right angles to the sofa, placed them on the floor and sank into it.

Jake Conrad was in no mood for her lightly mocking humor. With cool hooded eyes he handed her a glass of sherry, then slid his hands into his pockets and stood looking down at her. "Whatever the virtues and qualities of my employees, they have at least one thing in common," he said quite matter-of-factly. "They do not engage in character assassination to my face."

Vanessa blinked. That was pretty strong. She couldn't tell whether he was joking or not, but instinctively she felt that he was really trying to cow her. She had no intention of being cowed her first day—at any time, in fact—and the sooner Jake Conrad learned that, the better.

"But then, I'm not, strictly speaking, one of your employees, am I?" she pointed out reasonably. "My contract is with Conrad Corporation—to start and operate a business...without taking orders from anyone."

Her heart was beating in frightening thuds, as it always did when she was faced with this kind of challenge. The last time it had beaten like this was when she had said to Tom Marx, "I quit."

She looked up at Jake now and remembered how he had engineered that unnecessary bridge-burning confrontation, and suddenly she was afraid. Perhaps, after all, the contract wasn't as sound as she'd thought. Since she'd given Lou very little time to judge, it was possible there was some loophole he had missed. Perhaps Jake Conrad could fire her with impunity, for something as ridiculous as insubordination....

"Which reminds me," she added before he could speak, "my lawyer says I should have a look at the debenture agreement under which the corporation is putting up the capital."

The unreadable tension went out of Jake's body as he turned easily to move around the coffee table to his seat on the sofa among the papers, and Vanessa thought that he must have been joking when he challenged her on character assassination. She found herself relaxing by degrees.

"You'd better speak to Howard about that," Jake said carelessly, throwing the sheaf of papers he'd been carrying down beside him. "He's handling all the minor legal details."

A smile played involuntarily over her lips as all the tense wariness left her body. Of course there were no loopholes, she thought. He wouldn't be reacting like this if there were. But the fear of the unknown was bound to manifest itself in odd unaccountable ways, and everything about her future was unknown right now.

"Are we going to drink to the success of Modish Operandi?" she asked then, raising her glass.

Jake picked up his glass and leaned back against the sofa. "Is that the name of the new line?" he asked with interest.

"It's one of the finalists," she admitted. "I haven't made up my mind yet."

"Mmm-hmm," said Jake. "You've been working already, I see. What else have you been doing?"

"Well, not too much. I asked Robert to commission a market research report for me from a local company and to look around for a production manager, because I'm going to need a good one."

Jake was watching her, a slight smile playing on his sensual, strongly drawn mouth. But his eyes were narrowed consideringly. "Very good," he said. "And what else?"

"Mostly I've been designing a spring line. I was afraid I'd be so wrapped up in business details from the moment I got here that my creativity would go out the window."

Jake's look now was one of glinting admiration. "Now, how did you find time to start designing a spring line?" he demanded. "You only had—"

"Well, really, it was more a question of getting some ideas down on paper before I lost them," Vanessa explained.

"On Tom Marx's time?"

"Oh, no. No, I left TopMarx the day I resigned. The day you phoned. So I had two free weeks to get organized."

He cocked an eyebrow at this, in a way that indicated he was prepared to be amused. "I can imagine."

She didn't smile at him; the scene with Tom had not been pleasant, though it might be amusing now in its retelling to someone as willing to be cynical as Jake. Tom had been angry and hurt and outraged and had adopted a tone almost identical to the one he'd used when she had refused to go to bed with him. Vanessa hadn't realized that until later, when, it was true, she had suddenly found it amusing.

He'd begun with, "But what'll I *do*, Vanessa?" But within a very few minutes that plea had degenerated into a surly variation on the theme, "You're not nearly as good as you think, kid, and believe me, I'm not the one who's going to regret this."

Without really meaning to, she was telling Jake about it—for the reason, she realized when she asked herself, that she liked his eyes when they twinkled with amusement. He was never more like Jace than when his eyes were laughing.

"My God," he said when she had finished, "is that the way men react when a beautiful woman turns them down?"

"I should think it's the way they react when any woman turns them down," Vanessa answered, because she wasn't beautiful. "Why, how do *you* react?"

Jake hesitated perceptibly, and Vanessa burst into

laughter. "What's the matter?" she demanded, unable this time to repress the imp. "Haven't you ever been turned down?"

She could almost believe it. Jake, although lean of build, had the sort of powerful virility that most women might find difficult to walk away from.

He said dryly, "Every man in this culture learns rejection practically in the cradle. If I seemed at a loss it was because you should know better than I how I react—you turned me down yourself not so long ago."

Suddenly she felt on dangerous ground. This was a stupid provocative topic to get involved in with someone like Jake Conrad. And this time she couldn't blame him—it was she, not he, who had made the conversation personal. Did he never get rejected, indeed! That was waving a red flag.

"Well, but—" she stammered.

"In fact, far from being instantly welcome in any woman's bed, if I recall correctly," Jake pressed on, "even the addition of a gold mine couldn't make me an attractive proposition."

Before she could stop herself, Vanessa was saying, "On the other hand, maybe it was the addition of the gold mine that made the proposition unattractive."

"Think so?" said Jake, with an arrested light in his eyes. "Do I take it that Larry Standish put you off love for money?"

She felt as if she had been stabbed. There was a sharp hard pain somewhere inside and Vanessa realized that for some reason Jake Conrad could hurt her more than anyone she knew. It was particularly painful because a moment ago they had been joking; a moment ago she had as good as told him that if he hadn't insulted her with the gold mine she would have become his lover.

"That's unforgivable," Vanessa said in a low voice, and dropped her head. "That's not fair."

" 'All's fair in love and war,' " Jake quoted softly, watching the afternoon sun create a halo of the fine hairs that escaped from her loosely piled russet hair. It glowed like dark fire.

Vanessa breathed deeply and raised her head to look straight into his unwary eyes. "And which is this?" she asked bluntly.

Jake raised an inquiring eyebrow.

" 'All's fair,' you said, 'in love and war,' " Vanessa pressed in measured tones. "And it behooves me to know, since I'll be working for you, just exactly which this is—love or war."

Jake raised his glass to his lips, his eyes never leaving hers, and took a sip of whiskey.

"My dear Vanessa," he said slowly, and a half-smile was on his lips but not in his dark eyes. "My dear Vanessa, if only I knew the answer to that one."

CHAPTER NINE

"THE BIG THING," Robert said, "is that you're going to have to make an enormous adjustment. The Canadian market is very, very different from what you're used to."

It was Thursday morning, and Vanessa was already at work with Robert in his office at Conrad Corporation. The wiser course might have been to spend the next few days looking for an apartment, but common sense had stood no chance against the excited enthusiasm that churned in her stomach. She would not believe in this adventure until she had embarked on it.

"I know it's going to be smaller," Vanessa said. "I know the population of Canada is only a tenth of the States'."

"It's also very spread out," Robert said. He reached out an arm to pick up a thickish wad of typewritten pages that were bound with a spiral of black plastic and a red cardboard cover. "We asked Berringer and Hare to do the marketing report you asked me to get, and while it won't be ready for another week or two, it turned out they had done a similar report for an American company two years ago. That company abandoned plans to move into the Canadian market, and Ben Hare let me have a copy of that report so we'd have something to look at while we're waiting. I've read it." Robert dropped his eyes to the report on his desk and absently rifled the pages. "I think you should," he said, looking at her, his eyes ever so slightly veiled. Vanessa felt the faintest tinge of alarm.

"What does it say?" she asked abruptly.

"Well, it's pretty discouraging. On the other hand, it was written up for the economic climate of two years ago."

"Has the economic climate in Canada improved from two years ago?" Vanessa asked quietly, her excitement abruptly subdued by the tone of Robert's voice.

"No..." said Robert, drawing out the vowel thoughtfully, and Vanessa smiled a half-smile. Of course it hadn't. There could hardly be a country in the world whose economic climate had improved during the past two years. A little breath of panic touched Vanessa. Had she been a fool to make such a profound change in her life with so little investigation? Was this project doomed to failure before she'd even begun?

"On the other hand, Vanessa," Robert was saying, "Jake hasn't backed many losers since I've known him. Jake likes to make money. And his decisions often run directly counter to prevailing opinion. So while you're reading this—" he passed the bound report across the desk to her "—remember that he picked you because he thinks you've got the talent and drive to make a success."

"Right," she returned quietly, knowing, however much he tried to hide it, that Robert had a lot of doubts.

"Right," repeated Robert, picking up a pen to make a small tick on a paper in front of him. "Now, next on the agenda: I've located a company in the fashion trade in Vancouver that's gone insolvent. Their factory is vacant and available, and best of all it seems to be equipped for the kind of operation you're going to want to set up. I suggest we go out there and have a look at it tomorrow. It could save you a lot of money—and time—to buy the place as it stands if it's suitable."

"All right," Vanessa nodded.

"I've set up an appointment with the trustee's representative at ten in the morning. That suit you?"

It suited her, and Robert made a notation on the agenda.

"Oh, yes, then there's the question of me," he said, raising his head. "Jake has asked me if I'd be willing to be seconded to you for the first six months while the thing gets started. I'm quite willing to do that if you, uh, if you want me to."

He was pulling awkwardly on his ear and Vanessa felt a little burst of amused warmth for this odd quality of apology she had noticed among Canadians. In New York a man of Robert's ability—he was, after all, a top accountant in a large corporation—would not have put the suggestion to her in that way. He would more likely have made it very clear that she was the recipient of a very large favor. She wondered if Canadians weren't a little like the Japanese, with their constant polite apology for the humbleness of their station, talents and possessions. With this difference—that Canadians really believed their own poor publicity.

Vanessa, however, did not believe it. One didn't need to be long in Robert's company to realize that he was financially very astute. Vanessa felt a weight lift from her shoulders. She wanted to be designing, not drawing up profit-and-loss statements, and she knew she could depend on Robert's business acumen. She smiled delightedly.

"Robert, thank you! I'm saying yes before you change your mind!"

A good deal of Robert's charm lay in his slow shy smile, and he gave her the benefit of it now. "All right, we'll take that as settled, shall we?"

"You bet." Vanessa smiled, and thought what a strange contradiction Jake Conrad was, giving her everything in business and nothing at all where it really counted—in their personal relationship.

THE TELEVISION COVERAGE of the funeral of young Terry Fox was just beginning as Vanessa walked into the Concorp staff room later in the day, and people were crowded around a television set that sat against one wall of the room. Vanessa poured herself a cup of coffee from the urn and moved down to watch first the moving funeral service and then, more and more absorbed by that courageous young face, a documentary of the extraordinary mission of Terry Fox.

Again, during the film clips of his speeches, she

noticed that odd quality of apology, of self-effacement. He had run not for himself but to show all those suffering from cancer, particularly the children, that the human spirit could triumph. "I am ordinary," his message seemed to say, "but I can rise above this because I have to. You can, too."

Then came the film of the moment Jake's chauffeur had mentioned, of the moment when Terry Fox, lying on a stretcher, told the Canadian nation that the cancer had reappeared in his lungs.

Tears choked her. Vanessa blinked them away, but her throat ached with her need to weep for this extraordinary, brave young man.

My God, she thought wonderingly a few minutes later as the documentary came to an end and she was released from the hypnotic hold of the story. People around her had unashamedly wet cheeks and a kind of glow behind their faces. *My God, and they think he's ordinary! They think he's an ordinary man, like them, turned into a hero! They think they're ordinary, too!* Vanessa gazed in startled wonder at the Canadian faces around her, so like and yet so different from their American counterparts. *I can understand the ordinary being called extraordinary,* she thought. *What kind of a nation calls the extraordinary ordinary?*

THERE WAS ONE CANADIAN, however, who was neither apologetic nor self-denigrating, and Vanessa bumped into him in a corridor shortly afterward. She was wearing her coat and carrying her handbag and the market report Robert had given her. Jake raised a startled eyebrow and smiled at her.

"Starting work already?" he asked. "I didn't expect to see you today. Are you looking for Robert or me?"

"Neither, at the moment," Vanessa replied with an odd little burst of pride because she had surprised him. "I've just spent most of the morning with Robert, and I'm on my way home to read this." She indicated the market report she was holding. She had already read some of it and what she had read was disturbing. "But I'd certainly appreciate the chance to talk to you when I've read it."

Jake looked at her consideringly. "What is it?"

"It's a market report that was done a couple of years ago," Vanessa said. "I've only started it, but it's pretty depressing."

"So depressing it made you cry?" asked Jake.

"What? Of course not!" Vanessa almost snorted in derision. *Cry* over a market report? What on earth did he think of her?

Jake lifted an eyebrow. "Your mascara has run," he explained softly.

"Well, it wasn't running because of any market report, I assure you!" Vanessa said, outraged. She looked at him balefully, then recollected herself. "If you do have any time to spare," she said more calmly, "I'd appreciate being able to discuss this report with you."

His heavy lids dropped over his dark eyes, hiding their expression from her. "But of course," Jake said urbanely. "My secretary will call you with an appointment."

She hated it when he retreated behind that coldly

businesslike exterior. She felt left out, an outsider, no different to him than any of the countless other people who worked for him and with him.

She was suddenly burning with the need to shake this indifferent attitude of his that said there was nothing between them except a management contract each had signed. She felt the desperation for his recognition claw at her stomach with a ferocity like nothing she had experienced before.

Damn the man, what was he doing to her? This was lunacy. Vanessa looked up into the cold, tightly drawn mask of his face and opened her mouth to speak. For a moment she felt just a little apprehensive about what man would emerge if she did succeed in shattering that mask, but she was driven by an urgency beyond her control.

"Considering that I never did anything to hurt you, you're the most unforgiving man I've ever met," she breathed shakily.

"What?" demanded Jake in a deep hoarse voice.

"You punish me far more than Jace would have. Jace would have understood and forgiven me ages ago."

"Would he?" Jake's eyes glinted as he began to laugh harshly. "You may be right. Jace always was a damned trusting fool."

"And you're just a damned fool!" she snapped angrily.

He laughed then in real, if cynical, amusement, as though at a private joke. She was out in the cold again.

"You're right," he said softly. "The big difference

between me and Jace is that he was trusting and I am not. And that, Vanessa, whether you know it or not, is what makes you angry. You keep thinking you're going to be able to pull the wool over my eyes the way you did la—the way you did with Jace and God knows how many others. And when you don't succeed—"

She wished now she had left him behind his mask. Bitterly, she interrupted, "You've really got a sense of mission, haven't you? You're as good as the Reverend Ian Paisley—you could be out causing a war somewhere instead of wasting yourself on business!"

She pushed by him and stalked up the corridor, and if he meant to call after her he was forestalled by the appearance of a group of his employees emerging just then from the elevator.

ON FRIDAY MORNING she went with Robert to view the factory without having discussed with Jake the contents of the market-research report she had read.

The full report had more than lived up to the disturbing inferences she had drawn from her first quick glance through it. Vanessa hadn't slept well after reading it and this morning in the car she had to force herself to concentrate on what Robert and the trustee's assistant were saying about the factory they were going to see.

"Here we are," announced Robert as the assistant, a quiet-looking woman named Moira, pulled the car to a stop in front of a three-story gray brick building that looked about fifty years old.

Vanessa stood assessing the exterior as Moira produced a key, and then they all trooped inside. The factory itself was on the ground floor; the sewing machines and irons and hanging rails were all still in place. Vanessa drew in a long slow breath, glad that the market report had in some way prepared her for this.

"Is this the entire factory floor?" she asked quietly.

"That's right," said Moira. "The offices and design rooms are—"

"There can't be more than thirty or forty machines in here."

Moira consulted her clipboard. "Thirty-eight sewing machines and six ironing stations," she said. "However, there's lots of room for expansion, Mrs. Standish. There are two tenants on the second floor of the building. Both are on five-year leases that expire in three years. And the whole third floor is empty at present."

It was cleaner and brighter than a lot of factories Vanessa had seen, and all the walls and ceilings were painted the same light gray as the outside of the building. Odd bits of bright summery fabric and thread were littered on the floor and tables, a rather sad reminder that not so long ago this factory had been a bustling enterprise and that what they were presiding over was something like a funeral. Vanessa shivered. Could she build a success on the bones of so recent a failure?

Moira took them through the shipping and receiving areas and the cutting room. Everything was on the same small scale as the factory.

Off the small reception area where they had come in was a flight of stairs by which Moira led them to the second floor.

"Now here," she said, "are the administrative offices, design office and showroom. . . ."

It took them two hours to go over the premises to Vanessa's satisfaction, and even so she was aware of holes in her own knowledge that made it difficult for her to assess the building.

Back in Robert's office at Conrad Corporation they discussed the drawbacks and advantages. There were not many disadvantages. The space truly seemed almost ideal for their purposes.

"Robert," Vanessa said at last, tossing her notebook and pen down and leaning back, "did you check into why the company that had this space went bankrupt?"

Robert sat up and pulled a folder from a drawer in his desk. "Mostly it was because they were undercapitalized. They tried to do too much with too little. Also—" he pushed his glasses up on the bridge of his nose and consulted the papers in the folder "—they weren't careful enough with their credit. We don't have the first problem, and I'll make sure we don't run into the other two." He smiled.

"Do you think we should go for this, Robert?"

It was a complicated decision. Since the bankrupt company had owned the building Vanessa had the choice of merely buying up all the machinery and equipment and finding factory space elsewhere or buying the building, as well. The former course involved minimal risk, the latter much more.

"Not unless we can guarantee ourselves some tenants on the third floor, in any case," Robert said.

"Could we do that?"

Robert looked thoughtful. "We could, if we lease them to companies in Conrad Corporation."

"Oh!" Vanessa blinked. For some reason that gave her an odd feeling of being part of a family.

"If I'm not mistaken," Robert continued, "there are one or two companies in buildings not owned by Concorp whose leases are coming up for renewal. I'll look into that. In fact...." He paused, and a smile lighted his eyes. Vanessa wasn't experienced enough to recognize it as the smile of an accountant who has discovered something Absolutely Risk-Free; she only knew that it made her lean forward in curious expectation. "In fact, if we're lucky, Conrad Corporation just might buy the building for us. Then *they* could have the leasing headaches, and we would lease only the space we need...." Vanessa was fascinated to see how quickly Conrad Corporation had become "them" to Robert, and the new company "we." He had, after all, agreed to be seconded to this enterprise only yesterday.

"I'll run it by Jake and see what he thinks," Robert continued, and her heart fell. Vanessa already regretted the stupid argument she had thrust on Jake in the corridor yesterday, but she would regret it a whole lot more if he were to let his angry feelings get in the way of a business decision and refuse to let Concorp buy the building.

But she said nothing to warn Robert of his possible reception by Jake, and the conversation moved on to the question of the machinery and equipment.

"I wish we'd hired a production manager before this decision came up," Vanessa sighed after a long discussion of pros and cons. A good production manager would recognize faster than she would any major drawbacks in the machinery and, for that matter, in the factory space.

"Look, we don't have to decide today," said Robert in a calm voice. "It's Friday afternoon. Why don't you go home, relax and have a nice weekend? Don't think about this at all this weekend. We'll take a fresh look at it on Monday and see what we think."

"I can't think about it this weekend. I've got to look for an apartment," she said, feeling relieved.

"Good God," said Robert. "Well, I don't envy you that task. This city must be one of the tightest housing markets there are."

"Don't encourage me," said Vanessa wryly.

"Look, my wife and I are having a small dinner party Saturday night. Would you like to come? Nothing very strenuous—but you'll need to unwind after a day's apartment hunting."

"I'd love to," Vanessa replied instantly, with an alacrity that made them both laugh. Vanessa was an outgoing person; she had a lot of friends in New York. She was going to miss them badly until she met new people here. Robert probably had a wife just as nice as he was; he seemed the sort of man who would. It would be lovely to think she had found friends so soon.

"Do you have any friends in Vancouver?" he was asking now.

"No one at all," Vanessa said cheerfully. No one but Jake Conrad, and he wasn't exactly a friend. "But it seems like a friendly city."

"Oh, it is," Robert agreed. "Casual and friendly. Vancouver's nothing like the east. You won't have any trouble settling in."

HIS WORDS SEEMED PROPHETIC when, late the next afternoon, Vanessa found an apartment. It was on the second floor of a large and ramshackle duplex near English Bay and Stanley Park, and Vanessa loved it on sight. It was light and airy, with large rooms, big ill-fitting windows and uneven, unpainted wooden floors, and it was costing a fortune, but to Vanessa it had a marvelous magical feel that was worth nearly anything. She could move in the first of August.

She dressed for the dinner party that night feeling a delightful sense of exhilaration and well-being. Anyone who said Vancouver was a tight housing market had never hunted for an apartment in New York City!

She put on a dress of her own design, a deep green watered-silk taffeta with a very full skirt, a self-ruffle that swept from the hem on the left to the waist on the right, and a ruched bodice with shoestring straps. Around her neck she snapped a small double ruffle in the same fabric, which made the dress seem less formal and more a rather marvelously rich but subdued costume.

She swept her russet hair up in a very loose casual style from which tendrils escaped to catch the light, creating a kind of halo around her head.

As she was spraying her cologne gently onto the skirt of the dress so that its scent would be wafted into the air when she moved, the phone rang.

"Did I understand Robert to say you were going to his dinner party tonight?" asked Jake's deep voice.

Her stomach clenched like a fist. She had wanted this, all day she had wanted this, she realized, looking at the cologne bottle in her hand. Smiling, she bit her lip.

"Yes, I am. Are you?" she asked in a voice that was remarkably calm considering that she wanted to laugh with excitement.

"Shall I pick you up?" he said by way of answer.

"Yes, please. I'll be ready in two minutes."

"All right," said Jake, putting the phone down.

She spent the two minutes perfecting her hair and makeup in a haze of perfume and anticipation. She draped a black silk coat over her shoulders and snatched up a matching black silk evening bag and, putting out the light, pulled open the door.

Jake Conrad was standing there with his fist raised to knock and the unexpected sight of him made her gasp.

He was dressed in black with a white frilled shirt, his hair curled damply from the shower, and he was smiling his crooked quizzical smile.

"You...you startled me!" she said with a little laugh.

"Were you running out on me?"

He must be mad. "I was going downstairs to wait for you," she said.

"You don't have to wait for me," he said. "I'll come and get you. I'll always come and get you."

There was a look in his eyes that flustered her and she ignored the comment, saying, "How do I look?" in a voice that was not as cool as she meant it to sound.

"Like an angelic choir boy," Jake answered. "A spurious impression on both counts."

"Pardon?"

"You are not angelic and you are not a boy," he said quietly, reaching behind her to close the door. He tucked her hand through his arm and smiled meaningfully down at her.

What on earth was the matter with her? She was as weak-kneed as if she'd drunk a whole bottle of brandy. How could the same man make her mad enough to kill one day and ready to faint with desire two days later?

Because it *was* desire; she felt it even as he tucked her skirt into the car and closed the door. She had sublimated an awful lot in the past few years since Larry had got really ill, so much so that she'd sometimes thought, of her cool response when men were making passes at her, that she wouldn't have known sexual desire if it came up and bit her on the ankle.

But when Jake sank into the seat beside her she felt an electric tension prickle along her left side and through her body, as though she were exposed to some strange power source.

She looked over at him as he reached to turn the starter, and at the same moment Jake looked at her; and it was there in his eyes.

He meant to make love to her. It was a dark, possessive look, and he was not asking anymore. He was telling her, and if she didn't break the look now, she was accepting it and all that it meant. When he reached for her tonight, there would be no more decisions to make. She was giving him his answer now.

Her blood hammered in her temples but no muscle obeyed her frantic summons to move, and the look between them went on while Jake's dark eyes smashed the resistance in hers, smashed it and then ferreted out every scrap of it and destroyed it, until finally she herself, responding to a turmoil inside her she had never known before, felt her own acquiescence in her eyes. She knew that he saw it. Then he smiled a small meaningful smile and moved his hand, and the car engine roared into life.

Over the delicious dinner that Robert and Maria, his wife, had prepared, Vanessa tried to make herself believe she had imagined that moment in the car, tried to forget it had happened. But Jake did not allow her to forget it. Every glance, every caress of his voice, every slightest touch as he sat beside her reminded Vanessa that she had made him a promise, and that he would take what she had promised.

The dinner party was a great success. There were four couples besides Robert and Maria, and everyone except Vanessa knew each other well. They laughed and talked and sometimes shouted good-naturedly at one another, and they all liked Vanessa. Since she was the fresh face they focused on her after dinner, making her talk, finding out all about her; and under the smiling, watchful, possessive eyes of Jake Conrad she kept them entertained for a while with stories of the rag trade and with imitations of Colin delivering some of his scathing criticisms of the fashion sense of certain famous people, from presidents' wives on down.

She surprised herself. She was normally friendly and amusing, but rarely took the center of the stage so obviously. Her close friends sometimes saw this side of her, but strangers seldom did.

It was as if Jake could make her drunk just by looking at her, but she was on the verge of becoming frantic. Vanessa took a deep breath and while they were all laughing at her last sally she asked Maria a question and quietly passed over the conversationl ball.

After that the talk became general, and all too soon it was time to go. Maria led her upstairs to find her coat and sat on the bed chatting as Vanessa tidied her makeup and hair.

"It's been a super party," Vanessa said. "It was kind of Robert to invite me at the last moment, when I must have thrown your plans out." In fact, she had expected to be the odd woman out. It had been a pleasant surprise to find the numbers even.

"No, you didn't," said Maria easily. She was a dark-haired and dark-eyed young woman of twenty-three or -four whose Italian heritage was obvious. "We were going to invite another man to make the numbers even, but then Jake's date got sick, so that made everything easy."

"Yes," said Vanessa slowly. "It made everything very easy, didn't it?" and laughter was bright in her blood.

"WHAT POOR GIRL did I unwittingly cut out tonight?" she asked Jake in the quiet of the car as they crossed the bridge over the narrows and entered the rich darkness of Stanley Park.

A short laugh escaped him but he didn't deny that he had canceled a date in order to be able to take her instead.

"Her name is Marigold," Jake said.

"Did she mind?"

"She screamed blue murder." Jake sounded almost appreciative.

"I wonder she dared," Vanessa said wryly. "Are you going to make it up to her?"

"Never mind Marigold." His voice was low and caressing as he reached for her in the darkness. His long fingers closed on her wrist and he brought her hand up and pressed his mouth hungrily against her palm.

It sent shock waves through her body. Vanessa drew in a breath through parted lips as the wave reached her throat, and the sound electrified the air between them.

His hold on her wrist tightened convulsively and his eyes gleamed at her for a second in the gloom, and a second shock wave went through her at the expression in them.

"Take your hair down," he said in soft command. Vanessa's eyes widened as her hand went involuntarily to her head.

"What?" she breathed.

"Take it down," he repeated the command in a voice that tingled along her veins. "You look too damned elusive. I want to know you're within reach."

His voice was hoarse with need and she was nearly fainting.

"I'm within your reach," she said before she could stop herself, and she saw his hands clench on the wheel and waited to hear it break under the pressure of that white-knuckled grip.

Beyond the car everything was black, the thick luxuriant black of forest at night. As Vanessa watched out the window, the car emerged from the trees and she saw the lights of the city and stars reflected in the stillness of the lagoon. She rolled down her window and the lush summer air with all its rich scents filled her nostrils.

"Do it," said Jake.

She was trembling, she noted distantly as her hands moved hesitantly to her hair's softness.

She opened her black silk bag, whose touch now was a sensual torment under her fingers, and one by one she dropped into it the pins and combs that held her hair. It fell in a weighty cloud around her shoulders and caressed her bare back with a touch like satin.

They were out of the park now, traveling more slowly through the streets toward the hotel. Jake reached out and his hand caressed her soft hair for a moment. Then his fingers pushed their way through to her scalp and his hand closed almost painfully in her hair. He forced her to look at him then, and in the glow of streetlights his eyes were dark with need.

"I want you," he said softly, but his jaw was tight

and determined and she saw with a sudden agonizing clarity that he wished he did not.

She smiled then, a slow sensual smile that twisted in him like a knife.

I love you, she thought. *That's why I'm out of control. It's why you're out of control, too—because you love me. But you don't know it yet. I wonder how long you'll torture yourself before you accept it.*

CHAPTER TEN

JAKE CLOSED THE DOOR to his suite and leaned against it, staring at her across the room. He seemed dark; everything about him was dark. His keys jangled as he slipped them casually into his pocket, not taking his eyes from her, in a way he had probably done many times before, with other women.

"Take off your coat," he said.

This time was different, she thought, though he did not know it. He only knew that for the first time his need tortured him. And the sight of that tortured need in his face set up a clamor in her blood that was almost terrifying, and she knew his casual posture was a lie. Vanessa slid the black coat off her shoulders and dropped it on the couch, then stood waiting, watching.

"Now take off your dress," he commanded softly. But she could hear a restraint in his voice like steel hawsers clamping a roaring need, and she knew as though she had heard him confess it aloud that he was afraid of what would happen when he let himself touch her.

Her head dropped back under the intensity of sensuality that stirred in her, and she knew that she wanted to see his need unleashed.

"No," she challenged softly, and Jake cursed and moved toward her with a look like death on his face. His hands shook as they found the snaps on the ruffle around her neck and removed it, and then he grasped her by the shoulders and pulled her body into his as he bent his mouth to the hollow of her throat.

It seared her flesh like a brand and Vanessa moaned aloud as his arms encircled her. She lifted her arms up around his back and clung, and felt Jake's strong searching fingers find the zipper of her dress.

His mouth moved along her throat and into the hollows of her shoulders, trailing a smoky fire that stopped her breath, while the zipper slid down her back under the pressure of his fingers. With the first release the thin straps brushed off her shoulders and whispered down the roundness of her upper arms. A cry escaped her, a cry that was nearly a scream of aching desire. Her breasts were naked under the dark green taffeta, and his mouth kissed the full swell of them, searching for the still-hidden tips. Vanessa strained against him, wanting him, needing desperately the tormenting caress of his hungry lips.

The zipper caught and stopped with a sudden pull at her waist, and Jake's breath rasped like a wild animal whose prey is taken away. Through the mists of desire that clouded her mind, Vanessa felt the snap of the enormous control he had been keeping on himself, and her breath hissed between her teeth.

He jerked the zip once. It did not move. Then his hands moved and clenched in the small of her back, and then they parted.

The taffeta tore under his hands with a long, high, silken shriek like a cry of animal passion, electrifying her and sending a blinding throb of blood into her temples.

He ripped again and stood back from her, and the dress came away in his hands.

Jake looked at her nearly naked body, then down at the beautiful fabric crushed between his hands. Then slowly he raised his dark eyes to hers.

"Damn you," he said softly, bitterly. "Damn you to hell."

She was wearing only a thin wisp of underwear, and nylon stockings that clung to her firm slim thighs with their own elastic. Jake's face was planes and angles as he took in the sight of her, the muscles drawn tight across his forehead and cheekbones. For a second they were both motionless, staring at each other, and then with a hoarsely muttered oath he threw the torn silk from him and reached for her.

The bedroom was dark, and when he laid her down on the bed the coverlet was cool under her back. She heard the quiet rustle as he undressed near her and knew by the sound that he was fighting for control.

She wanted to tell him that she loved him, to let him share in that private perfect knowledge that made his anguish unnecessary. But she was afraid to. There were demons tearing at him. She had known that about Jake from the beginning; she knew it as if she saw them in the air around him.

But what demons she did not know. She only knew, with a distant foreboding, that if she told him that she loved him now she might destroy him.

Her eyes grew accustomed to the darkness and as he stood for a silent moment staring down at her on the bed she saw his naked body faintly brushed with moonlight. It carved out shadowy hollows along his temple, his cheek, the muscles of his chest and his flat stomach, and for one moment of stillness, it was like looking at a statue.

Except for his eyes. Even in that room of shadows his eyes somehow seemed darker than the night as they gazed at her; even though she could not see them, she felt their hungry possessive touch along her trembling waiting body.

When at last he sank down beside her on the bed she could only turn to him, feeling the heat of his need in every pore, feeling the answering pulse of her own desire as first his mouth and then his arms found her.

She loved him. Her body ached for his, physically and emotionally, and she had been waiting for this moment all her life.

She kept nothing back. She gave herself freely, willingly, opening like a flower to the demands of his mouth and his body. When he sought to destroy her with pleasure she responded with an innocent delight that shook him. When he set out to make her beg she begged instantly and without shame, so that he was robbed of the triumph he had sought.

She gave him her surrender as a gift, a gift of love; he had no one to battle but himself—and his demons. He warred with the demons on the battlefield of her body for long minutes while she moaned and clung to him and cried out her small cries of gratitude, and with each one his breathing grew more ragged and desperate.

Then from the darkest well of her self came a response that drew her whole being up into the burning blinding light of passion and offered it all to him; and then she cried out with a howling intensity that tore down every defense behind his dark eyes and rushed through him like a flame. He cried out his release and his surprise in a voice that was all she had ever wanted to hear. She clung to him as tightly as if they were one being, and his shuddering protesting cry somehow made her weep for joy.

WHEN DAWN PINKENED the sky and crept through the slatted blind to find their bed, they had slipped into sleep. Under the light covering of the sheet Vanessa lay curled against Jake's chest, her breath easy, a small smile on her swollen lips. But Jake's sleep was not easy. His hand clenched and unclenched in the tangled sweep of her hair, and even in the cool of morning sweat was beaded on his brow.

"GOOD MORNING," VANESSA SMILED as she emerged from the bathroom wrapped in a white terry-cloth bathrobe that she had found hanging on the door.

"Good morning," responded Jake from a deep chair by the windows, looking up from his newspaper smiling and urbane, as though in the night just past he had not tried to destroy her with passion and been himself destroyed.

His bathrobe was navy, falling open over the dark hair crinkling on his chest. She knew the scent and feel of that hair intimately, and the memory made her smile and drop her eyes.

"Shall we order some brunch?" Jake asked, his voice politely friendly, and Vanessa knew he was back in control again. Although last night he had been hers and hers alone, this, now, was the man that Marigold and Louisa and probably many other women had known.

Vanessa looked at the calm face that said there was nothing between them except a certain physical satisfaction they had given each other and wondered how any woman could bear to have as a lover a man so cool and unmoved. For she would always feel the need to disturb him on the deepest level, and if she could not have that, nothing less would do....

"Sounds lovely," she said with a smile, as friendly and well-bred as he.

Over brunch Jake relaxed and unwound, treating her less and less like just another pretty face he had slept with last night, and more like the woman whose talent and drive he admired and who was running his newest business. Sometimes she caught a look of faint surprise on his face, as though he wasn't used to this kind of conversation over Sunday brunch.

"My secretary tried to reach you Friday," he said over coffee. "Do you still want to discuss that market report with me?"

She said, "That market report is a nightmare. If you'd read it first you'd never have offered me this job!"

"No?" said Jake, raising his eyebrows interestedly.

"First of all," she began, "it says that Vancouver is not a good city to be manufacturing clothing in, because there's almost no labor pool here and I'll have to pay above the market rate to steal them away from competitors. To get a good production manager Robert thinks we'll probably even have to go to Montreal or Toronto, where the majority of clothing manufacturing is done in Canada and there's a large labor pool."

"Hmm," grunted Jake.

"The second thing," she continued, taking a sip of her coffee, "and by far the more terrifying, is the fact that my experience in New York—everything I've picked up over the years—is going to be absolutely useless to me. The difference between the Canadian and American markets is so vast that I'm on the level of a novice. Worse than a novice."

Jake was watching her with an arrested look in his eyes. "Really?" he inquired.

She wondered what kind of reports he'd been reading when he dreamed up this venture.

"Jake, I have to sell across five thousand miles of Canada to get the same market size I have in a few miles' radius of New York! I can't believe it. Do you know how many small towns there are in five thousand miles?" If she hadn't known much about Canadian geography before, the market report had been a crash course. She had been amazed to discover that there were only three cities in Canada with a population of over a million.

"And what were you expecting?"

"I was expecting to be able to restrict my operations to the area around Vancouver for the first few years, the way we did in New York," she said. "But to do that, I'd have to go for a very small exclusive designer-model business—which is exactly what I don't want to do."

"Well, then," Jake pointed out reasonably, "you won't be doing that. So you're stuck with selling to the entire country. Other than the need for salespeople in the various regions, what problems does this raise?"

He made it sound so easy, as though a few minor adjustments would make everything right. But this was going to take more than minor adjustments.

"That's only the distribution problem, which can obviously be solved the way every other manufacturer in Canada solves it," Vanessa said. "There's also a production problem, and worse, a design problem. From a design point of view, the facts are—" she was ticking things off on her fingers now "—one: women in Canada apparently are more conservative and quality conscious in their tastes than their American counterparts. Even in the larger centers.

"Two: as far as clothing tastes go, women in smaller centers—the small towns and villages—are always much more conservative than big-city women. There are lots of reasons for this, good reasons, too, but the fact remains that if I stole an exclusive Paris design and modified it for mass production and had it out in the stores in a month, practically no one would want it.

"Jake, it means that the one thing I dreamed of doing is the one thing I'm not going to be able to do in this country—give middle-income women top-quality clothing with style and flair for their money."

"I disagree," said Jake, shaking his head. "Your feeling, as you told it to me a few weeks ago, was that middle-income women aren't being given the product they really want. That's still true, but you're going to have to adjust your ideas about just what it is they want. That's all. And even that's a minor adjustment, if you choose to look at it that way—you can still give quality in line and fit and materials, but you'll have to compromise as far as fashion trends are concerned."

"Compromise!" exclaimed Vanessa with a vexed laugh. "You don't understand! I'm always going to be working on designs that are at least a year behind the fashion!"

"On the other hand," Jake pointed out, "weren't some of the designs you fought so hard to have included in TopMarx's fall showing very classical models? And you said they sold well here. It seems to me you might have a natural feeling for the Canadian market."

"Yes, but—" Vanessa sighed. "It's hard to explain. A lot of the *excitement* is knowing what's going to happen before it happens—getting a mass-market model of a couturier design in the stores almost before it's on the runway. Now the competitive spur will be missing. There'll be competition for a piece of the market, of course, but that's not the kind of thing that keeps me going."

It was a bad blow. At least Tom had always produced the latest designs, however cheaply they were made. A good part of the satisfaction of her job had been the constant jumping to keep on top of what was happening.

"I wanted a quieter life," Vanessa said ruefully, feeling a sudden sense of loss that surprised her. "I didn't expect it to be *this* quiet."

"Well, hell," said Jake. "Can't you design two lines? One for the major cities and one for the smaller centers?"

"Can you afford to give me two factories?" she responded dryly. She shook her head. "It wouldn't be practical, Jake. A production line has to be set up.... No, I'll just have to be satisfied with including a few of the more exciting designs in the line each season and papering my walls with the rest."

And at that moment, suddenly, she was resigned. Life was a series of changes, after all. There would be plenty of learning to do here, plenty to make her new life exciting. She had to face what came along, not try to wish it away.

"Does that mean you've decided to stay?" Jake asked, leaning over to pour another cup of coffee for her.

She laughed. "I guess I have. I guess I decided to stay yesterday when I signed the lease on an apartment. It must have been the apartment that decided me; it's so beautiful."

Jake smiled.

"Anyway," she confided, "there's a lot of satisfaction in being a technician, too. I enjoy making a really good fit. I never seemed to have time for that with Tom."

He nodded, still saying nothing, and she was briefly angry because she wanted him to be glad that she was staying, as glad as she was to be here. She said, "I can't understand why you didn't know all this before you offered me the job."

Jake's crooked smile flashed. "What makes you think I didn't?"

"Well, I—but of course! You own Designwear, so you must have known about the labor problems here, at the very least."

"Designwear functions entirely without my supervision," said Jake.

"Well, there you are!" said Vanessa. "If you'd known the facts you'd never have decided to start this business in Vancouver, and you'd never have hired an American to run it—not against such drawbacks. In fact I can't understand why you want to start this kind of business at all—the economy's so bad. If it weren't for Robert's telling me you always make money I'd be a lot more scared than I am now."

"Of course, Robert doesn't know everything about me. What he should have told you is that I usually get what I want. Maybe this time I want to lose money. Maybe I need a tax write-off."

He was smiling; it was a joke. He had told her before he didn't want a tax write-off.

"Well, you won't get what you want, then." Vanessa laughed. "Because I'm going to make you good money on this."

"I thought you'd feel like that," said Jake, his eyes glinting with approval and satisfaction.

To hide her leaping response to his approval Vanessa stood with her coffee cup and moved over to sit in one of the deep chairs in front of the windows. When she looked up again Jake was refilling his cup.

"I've been meaning to ask you," she said, "whether you own Fraser Valley Helicopter now. Did the reverse takeover go through?"

"You've got a good memory," Jake observed, moving over to the chair beside her. "We ran into a hitch with Fraser Valley, but we may give it another try."

"Oh," she said, struck by a sudden thought. "You wouldn't be interested in buying a building in the meantime, would you?"

No sooner were the words out of her mouth than she regretted them. This wasn't the time or the place. Vanessa wanted to bite off her impulsive tongue.

"What building?" Jake asked, his dark eyes already considering.

What a fool she was. "Oh, it...never mind. Robert was going to ask you about something...."

"You ask me," Jake said, and behind his smile there was a tone of irresistible command.

"It...we looked at a building on Friday, one that was owned by a ladies'-wear manufacturer that has gone bankrupt...."

She told him about it in a neatly businesslike tone, making the best she could of a very bad job.

"I really shouldn't have brought it up," she apologized. "Robert is going to be asking you about it. It just popped into my mind."

"And why not?" asked Jake urbanely. "It may be

indiscreet, but at least it's more original than a diamond bracelet."

"More original than a diamond bracelet?" she repeated stupidly.

"That's what I'm most commonly asked for over Sunday brunch," he said with a smile that was like a kick in the stomach.

"Jake, for God's sake!" she whispered, pleading.

"A building," he mused. "A three-story brick building near Gastown, about fifty years old. Well, why not? At a cost of a couple of dozen diamond bracelets, of course, but then, as you proved last night, you are far from ordinary yourself."

"Jake, stop it!" Vanessa said angrily. "You know damned well I didn't. . . didn't—"

"No?" he interrupted, in the manner of one sparing the blushes of someone who hadn't blushed for years. "Then why did you, my pretty?"

She had not been going to tell him; it was a mistake to tell him so soon. But it would be a far worse mistake to let him go on thinking what he was thinking now—or pretending to think. Vanessa could not be certain.

"I love you, Jake," she said quietly.

He laughed. He threw back his head and laughed; it was not a pretty sound. And she knew she was right, that once he had been badly hurt by love. She sat through it with a clenched jaw; when he had sobered, he said, "You forget that I've heard that one before."

"Not from me."

He looked fleetingly surprised, then his expression became hooded.

"No," he said in a flat voice. "Not from you." She wondered what ugly memory was tearing at him and wished she had not had to speak. "And such selfless love ought to be rewarded," he suggested. "Of course with love to offer as well as all the rest—" he eyed her warmly up and down "—I do see why you feel you are worth so much more than a paltry diamond bracelet."

Vanessa stood up abruptly, thrusting her hands into the deep pockets of the robe. "Will you shut up about the building?" she demanded harshly.

Jake smiled. "But of course, my love. When Robert mentions it to me on Monday, shall I tell him no?"

Vanessa bit her lip and turned to stare out the window. It was another beautiful sunny day, though she had been told it rained almost constantly in Vancouver.

Behind her Jake was laughing softly. When she turned his crooked smile was cynical, cruel, and his dark eyes were filled with angry contempt.

"Poor Larry," he said softly. "I could almost believe Jace got the better deal. Do I take it you do want the building after all?"

Vanessa held onto emotional calm with an effort. "What I would like is for you to listen to Robert and decide on the merits," she said, "the same way you would have done if I hadn't mentioned this to you today."

Finally he stopped smiling that cruel damned smile. "Well, I might have decided on the merits," Jake said. "On the other hand, if you hadn't slept with me last night, I might have bought the building to offer you as an inducement. The gold mine didn't work very well, if I remember. Or do you consider that I owe you that, too?"

This was beyond endurance.

"What I consider you owe me," Vanessa said furiously, "is an apology. You don't strike me as the sort of man who would have to pay a woman to come to his bed, but no doubt you know yourself better than I do. Nevertheless, you are *not* going to pay me. If you can't accept that I wanted to make love to you last night, then you will have to assume that I felt sorry for you," she said, and if she had caught sight of herself in a mirror at that moment she would have been appalled by the cruel smile that now curled her own lips. She moved across to the bedroom door and stopped, turning to look at him over her shoulder. Her eyes glinted with leashed anger, though her mouth was still smiling. "Call it charity," she said softly, and left him.

Her clothes were on the bed where she had put them before the waiter had brought the brunch. Vanessa slipped on her stockings, shoes and underwear with an angry silent speed and then put on the black silk coat and buttoned it. She threw the torn dress over her arm and picked up the neck ruffle and her evening bag and caught sight of herself in the mirror. She looked like just what she was: a woman who had not been home after an evening out.

She felt like hurling the torn dress into his wastepaper basket and letting *him* run the gauntlet of his staff's curious eyes, but common sense stopped her: the dress was a favorite of hers, and she might be able to repair it.

She wondered fleetingly whether in the future the dress would ever be free of the memory of last night. Vanessa doubted it. Even through her fury she could feel a churning inside her when she thought of Jake Conrad's hands as he tore the dress off her; his hands and his eyes....

He was not there when she emerged from the bedroom, the dress flung defiantly over her arm. Nor did she look for him. She walked straight across the room without pausing and did not even slam the door as she went out.

ON MONDAY VANESSA FOUND she had been assigned a temporary office in the Concorp building on the floor below the one where Robert's—and Jake's—offices were.

"No one in the corporation except Mr. Conrad has a private secretary," the office manager told her as she opened the door into Vanessa's temporary home. It was a smallish office, but it had a large window and a large desk, and that was all Vanessa needed to begin designing: light and space. The carpet wasn't as thick as in the executive offices upstairs, but to Vanessa, remembering the paper and clothing and fabric-strewn barracks at TopMarx, it was a kind of luxury.

Unfortunately it was also as sterile as a hermetically sealed syringe, and Vanessa wondered how anyone could be creative—even about money—in an environment like this.

"Of course, you should be upstairs in the senior-executive offices, Mrs. Standish," the office manager was saying apologetically. "But all those offices are full, and Mr. Dawe said as this was only going to be a temporary arrangement it would be better to give you an office that was available rather than shuffle everyone around into new ones."

"Of course," said Vanessa, dropping her bag and design portfolio onto an armchair and moving into the room. She wondered how the hierarchy at Concorp worked—by the amount of money Jake was investing in you, perhaps—and how many people would have been bumped down the line into a less prestigious office if her stay had been permanent.

"Oh, yes," the office manager said, "about the secretaries: in this office we work on the pool concept—all the secretaries, including the senior-executive secretaries, work out of a pool. It's much more Efficient, of course," said the office manager, a rather handsome woman somewhere between forty and fifty who looked as though she always said efficient with a capital E. "When you need secretarial work done, bring it to me and I'll assign it out to whoever is available."

"I understand," said Vanessa, gazing rather fascinatedly at the office manager's dress.

It had suddenly occurred to her that this woman was part of her target group—the kind of woman she would be designing for. In all her life Vanessa had never worked in an ordinary business office, had never seen the women she designed for against their working environment, however often she had seen them in restaurants.

The office manager was wearing a dress in navy

linen with three-quarter sleeves, a narrow self belt and a pencil skirt. The neckline was covered with a navy-and-white printed silk scarf that was tied and pinned with a gold brooch.

It could have been designed anytime between 1955 and the present. Vanessa's heart fell. The woman was no dowd. Her hair was short and smartly cut and styled, and her makeup was faultless. She looked well dressed, even elegant. Just very, very conservative.

"I'm sorry," Vanessa said abruptly and smiled, because the woman had paused in what she was saying and was looking just a little indignant. "Was I staring? I was looking at your dress. I haven't designed for Canadian women before, and they tell me it's going to be quite different."

That interested the office manager. "Really?" she asked. "I would have thought we were very much like the Americans. Not quite such *loud* dressers, perhaps," she added parenthetically, as though assailed by a sudden memory. "I admire what you're wearing very much," she said with a nod at Vanessa's rather Gypsyish concoction of scarves. "It's what you younger ones are wearing, I suppose. I know my daughter would love it. But, of course, it wouldn't do for the office, would it?"

She recollected herself and grew flustered. "Oh, but I mean—you're a creative person, you're a designer. It's different for you, isn't it? I know in the advertising department—their offices are on the other side of this floor—there was a terrible fuss with all the art-department people until Mr. Conrad came down and said the artists and copywriters could wear what they liked and do what they liked. . . ."

Vanessa laughed and the woman smiled appreciatively. Although they had been introduced on Thursday, Vanessa was trying in vain to remember her name. If they talked much longer the woman was bound to notice, and that would be embarrassing.

"You wouldn't think a pair of blue jeans would cause such a fuss, would you?" she went on. "But there was a lot of talk about creative freedom and the like, and Mr. Conrad said he didn't care what anybody wore to the office. They could come naked for all he cared, he said, as long as they did their work. And the next time something as insignificant as that required his executive decision he'd be looking for someone to fire. Now, of course, blue jeans are the least of it. If that was all we saw we'd be lucky!"

The two women laughed appreciatively for a moment, and then the office manager showed her the location of the photocopy room, the staff lunchroom and the ladies'.

"Please call me Vanessa," Vanessa said the next time she was called Mrs. Standish, hoping they hadn't been introduced by their first names.

But the office manager smiled and said, "My first name is Celeste. My mother was a francophile."

Vanessa blinked. "I'm sorry, a what?" she asked.

"She loved all things French," Celeste explained. "My brother changed Pierre to Peter when he was twelve, but what can you do with Celeste?"

"But it's a lovely name," protested Vanessa.

"Unfortunately it didn't sit too well with Meadows

when I was single and it doesn't sit too well now with B—"

"Mrs. Boyd, you're wanted on the telephone," a young woman called, and with a brief apology Celeste Boyd left her.

Vanessa wandered back to her new little office and spent the rest of the morning absorbed in designs for a spring line. She had no idea how much time had passed when the phone rang but was not surprised to see her watch saying nearly one o'clock. She was used to time disappearing when she was working.

"Busy?" asked Robert's voice in her ear.

"Yes, but I can stop," she said.

"No, don't stop," he answered. "I'll be quick: I just wanted you to know that Jake has agreed to have Concorp buy that building and lease us the space."

It was hard not to be delighted by that, in spite of everything. But after a few minutes Vanessa asked casually, because she had to know, "Was it a good business proposition for him, Robert?"

"Oh, well, it was neither here nor there, really, as far as Concorp is concerned." He chuckled. "Jake said he'd do it purely for the sake of your fine eyes."

CHAPTER ELEVEN

VANESSA FLUNG DOWN her felt-marker pen with such violence that the fat black smear it made cut right across the elegant, penciled face of the model she was sketching. She leaned back in the ridiculous leather executive chair they had given her and cursed Jake Conrad with a peculiarly comforting fluency.

After a few minutes her rage subsided, and Vanessa's eyes narrowed as she began to think constructively. She was not going to let him get away with it. She felt determination clench her spine like a fist. Jake Conrad had slapped her face and she was damned well going to slap his. Metaphorically.

How? She had neither the money nor the power to—oh, she wished she had the money to buy Fraser Valley Helicopter and throw it casually down in front of him! That would feel good! That would probably be worth a few diamond bracelets, all right!

Diamonds. . . the *nerve* of him comparing her to the kind of woman who would ask for jewelry on Sunday morning! *Diamonds!* As if she—how would *he* feel if a woman handed over a little velvet box the morning after with a couple of garish jeweled cuff links in it?

How, indeed?

A slow delicious smile curved Vanessa's mouth and angry delight sparkled in her eyes. She licked her lips as though she could already taste her revenge and it was sweet.

"I'M AFRAID HE's very busy, Mrs. Standish," Jake's secretary said with apologetic firmness an hour and a half later. "He's leaving this afternoon for—"

Vanessa nodded. "That's quite all right." She laid the small box, elegantly wrapped in jeweler's paper, on the center of the secretary's desk. "Would you just see that he gets that before he leaves, please? It's very important. He is expecting it."

"Of course," said Jean, taking unsurprised charge of the box in the calmly competent manner of one who can be counted on, and Vanessa left her knowing that sometime today Jake would be opening that box....

In the end she had settled on a ring. A gold ring with six small diamonds set in a circle. It was the sort of thing that Tom Marx wore on his little finger, though less flashy. But Jake Conrad wasn't Tom Marx. He didn't wear jewelry of any sort that she had ever seen, and Vanessa knew that men who didn't wear jewelry often despised men who did. She hoped that the ring, which was really quite beautiful—he couldn't fault her on taste, whatever he would think of her intention—would nevertheless insult him.

"Thank you for a wonderful night," she had written on the little card inside and had signed it, "V."

Laughter bubbled inside her when she thought of

it, but it had been an expensive revenge. It had cost her just over half of the money she had brought with her, the combination of her savings and the money she had got subletting her New York apartment.

It meant her new apartment would not be decorated as beautifully as she had planned, not right away. And it meant she would have only her paycheck to fall back on in an emergency. Speaking relatively, it meant she had spent much more on his ring than Jake had spent on her building, she thought, and he would know it. She would have loved to see his face when he opened it.

She didn't see his face. Nor, it turned out, was she likely to, for some time to come. At the end of that week, when Vanessa finally cracked and phoned Jake's secretary to find out when he would be back in town, the answer was, not for several weeks. He was going to be in England and in Saudi Arabia and the Lord only knew how many countries in between, and there was no certainty when he would be back. Yes, he had been given the little package before he left—but though he was in regular telephone communication with his secretary, there had never been any mention of a message for Mrs. Standish.

THERE WERE TIMES when Vanessa thought she was packing more work into July than she usually did in a year. She left the hotel well before eight every morning and often did not get back until after nine or ten at night.

And she was working on all fronts: designing the spring collection was only one part of her day. Usually the day began with a meeting with Robert, followed by meetings with what seemed dozens of other people: sewers and finishers, union representatives, fabric salespeople, pattern makers, cutters, design assistants and a whirl of others.

In between, she was constantly on the phone or studying sales brochures. Her first priorities had been to try to hire a production manager and an office manager so that much of the work could be delegated to them. Although after the first week there were several excellent applicants to choose from for an office manager, not one likely prospect turned up for the post of production manager.

"Robert, we're not offering a big enough salary," Vanessa said again one morning, for this was their biggest area of disagreement. Robert was in charge of cost, and he liked to Keep Cost Down.

He said, "We're offering the going market rate, Vanessa. If you go above what your competitors are paying on salary your cost per item goes up and your price goes up, and then you're not competitive. Believe me, you've got a very low profit margin already in this business."

If there was one thing she knew from her time with TopMarx it was that there was a very low profit margin in ladies' ready-to-wear.

Vanessa sighed. "Robert," she said wearily, "I don't know anything about production. You don't know anything about production. We have got to have a very good production manager, and ideally we should have someone from Vancouver. That means we have to steal from a competitor. It would be nice if we could find someone who's unhappy and already wants a change, but, Robert, they aren't answering the ads. Whoever is out there is not going to come without some real inducement."

"Let's give it another day or two," said Robert, and Vanessa shook her head helplessly. They had had nearly the same conversation two days before.

"Two more days and that's *all*," she said. "Robert, I'm snowed under with work the production manager should be doing. We have got to get that factory set up and ready to go—"

"All right, two more days," he agreed.

She tried to save her afternoons for designing the spring line, though most often she didn't manage to settle to that till four or five in the evening, when her phone stopped ringing. Then she worked right through supper and on into the evening. The hotel staff had come to recognize her, and when she didn't get in till nine or ten for dinner, they would cluck their tongues at her and say she would wear herself to the bone. Sometimes, if the restaurant was closed by the time she got in, she would find that the night staff in the kitchen had saved her a meal.

It was an exciting and rewarding time, and she felt that everyone around her wanted her to succeed. From time to time the secretaries of Concorp came in to admire the sketches, which by now were covering the walls of the once sterile little office, and they freely offered advice and information and their opinions about whether they would or wouldn't buy some design she had just conceived.

For at least an hour every day Vanessa "browsed."

That meant that, rain and shine, she walked the streets of Vancouver's downtown core, studying the window displays in clothing stores, watching women in the streets, browsing item by item through women's departments in department and clothing stores. She was opening herself to suggestion, nuance, getting a crash course in the "feeling" of Canadian design.

Their bid on the factory equipment and machinery was accepted, and without much ado Concorp purchased the gray brick building that housed the bankrupt factory.

But there was no one to move into it. She didn't have even half the sewers she needed, and the response to the ads for cutters and pressers and the other people needed remained obstinately and depressingly low.

"Robert," she said finally, "if you don't let me offer at least four thousand a year more than the market rate for a production manager *tomorrow*, we may as well declare bankruptcy right now. We've got to give somewhere along the line, and *I want a good production manager*!"

After that things smoothed out. The production manager they had been waiting for was quite willing to run the risk of starting with a new company for what turned out to be a raise of thirty-five hundred dollars a year for him.

Ted Loomis had twenty years of experience and he knew the town well. He knew whom to approach and what to offer them, and by the last week of July the labor problem was solved.

"I've found you a prize," Robert said one morning shortly before they were due to shift base to the gray brick building that would be their new home.

"I know you have," Vanessa replied with feeling. "Ted told me yesterday that he's got us another cutter, and that means—"

"I wasn't talking about Ted," Robert said. "This is another prize."

"Yes?" encouraged Vanessa, her ears pricking up.

"I have just talked to a dynamite salesman named Gilles Dufour who seems willing to take on your line in Montreal."

"Great!" said Vanessa.

Robert raised a hand. "That isn't the whole story. Gilles has some very good connections with buyers. He mentioned to me the possibility of being able to bring with him a contract for a standard cut of women's slacks that one of the big chains—he hasn't said which—will market under their own label. There would also be the possibility of a contract for a jacket of your own design."

"Robert, I don't want to start off being a production house for someone else's label," she began. "That's for—"

"Don't want it?" he repeated incredulously. "Are you crazy?"

"Robert, you don't understand," she began. "A contract like—"

He said, "I understand that a contract like this right now—" his forefinger most uncharacteristically was tapping his desk top in his urgency to make a point "—would allow our whole production line to start up immediately. While you're involved with a few people in turning out samples for the spring line, the factory can be in full operation. It's a bread-and-butter proposition, Vanessa, and we're not so plump in the pocket that we can afford to turn down bread and butter. And it would help pay Ted's wages," he muttered in an aside.

She leaned forward over the desk. "Robert, it is a favorite ploy of large retail organizations to give big contracts to small manufacturers and encourage them to expand their operation on the expectations."

"Well?" he asked aggressively. He was disappointed; he had expected her to be thrilled.

"And then one year there's no big contract, and the overextended manufacturer goes bankrupt, and who buys out the firm lock, stock and barrel?"

"The retail organization," Robert said. "All right, Vanessa, but—"

"And with no heartache or elbow grease whatsoever the retailer has a nice cheap little factory that will churn out nothing but wretched undershirts or pajamas under the store's label. That may be bread and butter, Robert, but if so it's poisoned."

"Vanessa, we are not going to overextend ourselves—"

"This year," she interjected in a mutter.

"And we aren't going to expand. What I'm hoping we'll be able to do is go for a piece of the action just big enough for us to handle. There's no reason for us to get into difficulties with it."

This argument she lost. Gilles Dufour signed on as salesman in Quebec and within a week produced the order for wool-polyester slacks to be manufactured under the label of Fairway, one of the big chain stores.

FEELING LIKE an overworked juggler, Vanessa found another brightly colored ball added to those that hovered mercilessly in the air above her: on the first weekend of August she had to move into her apartment.

She set aside the whole weekend for the move, planning to spend Saturday getting the furniture in and unpacking and Sunday doing all the little odd jobs that make a place home. But the furniture, which was due from New York on Saturday morning, did not arrive on schedule. Vanessa and Maria Dawe, Robert's wife, waited all day in the empty apartment, sitting on the bare uneven floorboards, playing cards and reading newspapers and phoning the moving company in New York at intervals. Finally, at four in the afternoon, after five calls to New York, the information finally emerged that the furniture would arrive Sunday.

"Well, that's really rotten!" exclaimed Maria, lying on the floor now in a jumble of very thoroughly read Saturday papers, lazily patting Vanessa's neighbor's cat, who had formed his own welcoming committee. "Why couldn't they have told you that this morning?"

"It's in *Vancouver*!" Vanessa shrieked, raising her arms heavenward. "All this time I've been phoning New York and the furniture has been in storage in Vancouver for a whole month!"

"What?" Maria sat up and abruptly dislodged the beautiful furry cat, who stalked off indignantly. "How the hell can that be? It's supposed to have been in transit from New York for three days!"

"When they asked me where I wanted it stored, I said New York," Vanessa explained. "But now it seems that someone marked it for storage here in Vancouver. So all the time they've been reassuring me that it was on its way, they actually didn't have any idea where it was. They found it twenty minutes ago. Here in Vancouver. But they can't send it till tomorrow because it's too late to start loading and their drivers have all been scheduled elsewhere for today."

"Give me that phone," Maria said in minatory tones. "Where's the number?"

It was as Italian as opera. Maria snorted and yelled and shook her fist and even cursed in Italian. "I've never been to Italy in my life except the summer I was sixteen," she giggled parenthetically to Vanessa during a pause in the electrifying conversation she was carrying on with the hapless dispatcher at the other end of the line. Her black curls seemed to spark with electricity.

The dispatcher was no match for her, and with a new respect Vanessa began to understand where Robert got his skill in vigorous debate: he practiced at home.

"It'll be here by seven-thirty," Maria said as, after twenty minutes of nearly nonstop argument, she hung up the phone.

"I'm not surprised," Vanessa laughed. "No wonder I lost the argument about those wretched slacks."

"What?"

Vanessa explained, to shouted laughter from Maria. But after a moment Maria's black eyes sobered and she asked, "Vanessa, is Jake Conrad in love with you?"

Vanessa was caught very much off guard. "I—uh, in love with me? I—no. I don't know, Maria. Why do you ask?"

"Robert will kill me if I tell you, but it's so fascinating. And a little bit worrying. Robert says Jake's gone crazy with this company of yours. He's doing all kinds of things he'd never normally do."

Unreasoning fear clutched at Vanessa's heart for a moment, then she shook herself to calm. "Such as?" she asked.

"Well, such as—you know Gilles Dufour?"

"Yes, he's our—"

"He's your Montreal salesman. I know. Did you also know that he's what Robert calls 'Jake's tame salesman'?"

"What?" Vanessa whispered.

"The company whose line Gilles dropped to pick up yours was Designwear. Designwear is—"

"It's Jake's." Vanessa's heart was beating with a combination of fear and excitement. Fear because it was so strange, excitement because...because surely it was a sign that he loved her?

"Well, and Robert says Gilles is an excellent, hard-working salesman, but the kind of pull that got you the Fairway contract he doesn't have."

"What? But then how...?"

Maria waved her finger admonishingly. "Jake, that's how. Robert says Jake went to school with the guy who's the western-district manager of Fairway's, and if anyone used pull, it's Jake, not Gilles."

"Well—"

"And then there's the business of Robert. Not that Robert didn't want to work with you, Vanessa, it's just that...." She trailed off.

Just that Robert's talents were far above what he was doing for her. But Maria diplomatically didn't say so.

"Jake's not like that," she said instead. "He never calls a favor like that, Vanessa. But he's calling them now, you better believe it. If Jake's in love with you, honey, you've got it made. If he's not in love with you, why is he doing it?"

VANESSA WAS AT LEISURE to consider that question all day Sunday while she pottered in her apartment alone, straightening, polishing, hanging and rearranging.

The furniture had arrived Saturday night at eight, and it had been midnight before all the unpacking and arranging was finished and she and Maria had had a last cup of coffee.

"Is it home?" Maria demanded as they sank exhausted into chairs and waited for the water to boil. "Does it feel like home?"

Of course it did. It had been home right from the beginning. Vanessa nodded. "Home," she said.

"Good. If that water ever boils, I'm going to drink a cup of coffee and go home to my husband."

"Maria, thank you so—"

"You're welcome," Maria had interrupted. "Please don't thank me, you're welcome. I like you, Vanessa. I wanted to see you properly settled in."

Vanessa smiled now, thinking of it. It had cost her to leave all her friends in New York and come in search of a dream, and perhaps if she'd thought about it longer, she wouldn't have done it. Because friends were worth more than a career any day. But Jake had seen to it that she didn't think about it for longer.

Vanessa remembered Maria's electrifying conversation with the dispatcher last night and laughed aloud. She would be glad of a friend like Maria.

"Don't tell Robert what I told you about Jake, and don't think about it too much," had been her last words to Vanessa through the car window as she drove off. But thinking wasn't so easy to command.

Yes. Of course he loved her. Maybe he didn't know it or couldn't admit it to himself, and maybe he was fighting it because of Jace and Larry and because of the nameless woman she knew was in his past, but Jake Conrad loved her.

She had to tell him the truth about Larry, help him put some of those ghosts to rest, so that he could stop being afraid of love. She had to help him disentangle his distrust of *her* because of what she had done to Jace from his distrust of that other woman she knew had hurt him, and then he would recognize that what was between them was safe and sure....

Everything she placed and polished that day was placed and polished with love. The kind of love that says, *I am building a nest for you and me, a place where we can be safe and protected—a home.*

She thought of the impersonal hotel luxury of his penthouse suite and promised herself that this apartment would feel like home to Jake Conrad.

THAT WEEK VANESSA moved office, too, from the pristine box at Concorp to the large high-ceilinged second floor of what they had begun to call "Number 24"—that being the number of the building's street address.

Here her office was more like what she had been used to—if much cleaner. All trace of the bankrupt company had been cleared away, the cutters were already at work on the production prototypes of the wool-polyester slacks and the shipper receiver was organizing his work space to his liking while the first fabric shipments trickled in.

Vanessa stood in the center of the big bright room that with luck would be her working home for years to come and felt the hum of a working enterprise all around her. This was it. She had begun.

There was a knock on the door, and Robert walked in carrying a bottle of champagne and two glasses. He held them up. "From Maria," he said. "For luck."

He popped the cork and filled their glasses and they drank to their own success.

"And to a spring line that'll knock 'em dead," Robert finished, and for the first time Vanessa felt the full strange weight of creative responsibility. There was no more Philistine, no more Tom Marx to pick through her design offerings and modify and cast out. That was *her* job now. She would be deciding—and very soon—which of the designs in her case would be turned into prototypes and become part of the new spring line and which would not.

It was at least equal parts frightening and exciting.

VANESSA HAD NOT REALIZED what an enormous act of faith the simple placing of an order for fabric was. She had seen Tom dither over his choices time and again, working out mixes and matches in a dozen different ways, trying to find the surefire guaranteed seller, and she had watched often with a faint distant contempt. *Then* she had made her fabric choices unhesitatingly: "This with this for the 458 group, Tom, and that with that for the 417s."

Now she understood the difference between drawing a salary and staking your heart and your business on the line with every decision. Now it was she who dithered: if this fabric was so popular with manufacturers this season, did that mean there would be a glut on the market come April? If that one was a little less popular, was that because it was higher in price or because Canadian women wouldn't like the "hand" of the fabric?

"What's the 'hand'?" asked Robert, who had strong ideas on cost and sat in on most of her meetings with fabric salesmen.

"It's like saying the touch or the feel," said Vanessa, and watched him make a mental note. She had to hand it to Robert: he might be here because Jake had called in a favor, but he was going to make the best of the experience. He could have stayed strictly on the accounting side and left all this to her. But Robert was learning everything he could about the "rag trade," as he now called it, including the small idiosyncratic vocabulary the industry used.

Sometimes she placed an order with her heart in her mouth, as though truly her life was on the line. "At this rate I'll have an ulcer by next week," she muttered after a particularly harrowing day, and Robert smiled.

"You'll feel better once all the decisions are made. Then it's just do or die, and you're good at that."

"Am I?" she asked.

"Yup," he said comfortably. "You've got a great capacity for hard work—and for putting the possible consequences out of your mind and just going full stretch."

She was certainly going full stretch after that, as she and Ilona, her young assistant, set to work making the sample models of the new spring line of "Number 24."

Vanessa had pondered and dithered over the name of the company and the line for days, until Robert had said, "Choose the name later. I've already incorporated you under 'Vanessa Standish Fashions, Inc.' We can register the 'style' later—if we can ever decide on one." He had laughed when he said it; he knew the name was important.

It was after they had begun referring to the factory by its street address, "Number 24," that she had been listening to a radio discussion in the design office one day. She was trying to follow the ins and outs of a political controversy that was being explained by a couple of commentators. It was complicated, and her background in Canadian history, she was deciding, was too sketchy to allow her to make sense of the debate that was raging across the nation. And then one of the voices said, "So what's going to happen, Bill, when the P.M. gets back to Number 24?"

Vanessa, on her knees beside a size-nine dummy, looked up and muttered through the pins in her mouth, "What's the P.M.?"

"The prime minister," replied Ilona on the other side of the dummy. "I don't think that's hanging right yet, do you? Do we need a larger tuck here, do you think?"

Vanessa, feeling an interesting prickle in the back of her brain, took the pins out of her mouth. "Then what's Number 24?" she asked slowly.

Ilona was concentrating on a pucker in the pinned garment. "It's the prime minister's official residence in Ottawa—Number 24 Sussex Drive," she said.

"What?" breathed Vanessa.

"Yeah. That's why this place is such a good joke. You know—'I was over at Number 24 yesterday.'" She flicked her long braid over her shoulder and turned her attention back to the dummy. Ilona Silverleaf was one-quarter native Canadian, her grandfather being of the Tlingit tribe in northern British Columbia. From him she had inherited her thick black hair, a fact she underlined by braiding it and wearing a small beaded headband.

"You're kidding," said Vanessa, thunderstruck.

"Nope," said Ilona. "There, that's got it! If we just shave this by an eighth of an inch right along the—"

"I don't believe it! That's wonderful! That's what we'll call ourselves!"

At last she had Ilona's full attention. "What's what we'll call ourselves?" she asked, her eyes round with surprise.

" 'Number 24,' " said Vanessa with a smile. "It's different, it's Canadian, it's—why didn't you tell me what it meant before?"

"Thought you knew," Ilona shrugged.

So Robert registered the styles "Number 24" and "Number 24 Fashions" and "24, Inc." and Vanessa crossed her fingers and ordered her first supply of stitch-in labels to be made up to her own design.

After that it all suddenly pulled together. It became real. She was responsible for a business not by a blind stroke of fate but because she was competent to do it. Because with hard work, she had the brains and talent to make it a success.

Things gained their own momentum. By the third week in August the factory was working full out on the first of the slacks orders, and production prototypes for the spring line were in the works.

It seemed to Vanessa that she was busier than ever, though now she worked fewer twelve-hour days, and she was calmer in the midst of all the activity.

Calmer, and lonelier. She returned to her beautiful apartment earlier these nights, long before the sun went down. So she had time for long walks along the beach and through Stanley Park, and time to play tennis with Ilona at the club she had joined there, and time for entertaining Robert, Maria, Ilona and one or two other people she had begun to make friends with.

But most of all, she had time to notice the gaping hole in her life, the hole that hard work only partially disguised.

The hole in her life left by Jake Conrad. She wanted him back now with an intensity that was like a fever.

CHAPTER TWELVE

HE CAME HOME on the nineteenth of August, looking as dark as a sheikh and very fit. Vanessa herself was darker than when she had left New York, but she had certainly not had time to devote herself to the sun, and next to Jake she looked like a moon maiden.

"Were you working or playing?" she asked him enviously that afternoon after he had arrived unannounced at Number 24 and thrown her into a barely concealed tizzy of excitement.

"Doing anything at all in that damned hot desert is work," Jake answered.

"Was the trip a success?" she asked, trying not to smile too much and too foolishly, trying to hide the sparkle he brought to her eyes.

"So-so," said Jake. "How about you, or don't I need to ask? This place is a hive of activity."

"Yes," she agreed. "Things look good."

Jake moved across her office to the racks by the wall. "What are these?" he asked, lifting a hanger to eye level and examining the soft green pleated skirt with interest.

"The spring line," she said, amazed to feel pride beating in her throat with an intensity she hadn't felt since she stood first in her class in grade six.

"Very classical?" he asked with a slow smile over his shoulder that turned her bones to water.

"Very classical," she agreed, suddenly shy of meeting his eyes for long.

"Very conservative?" he pressed.

"Well—relatively conservative," she said.

"Oh, ho," he said with another smile. "Only *relatively*!" He replaced the skirt and picked up the delicate feminine matching jacket, which was ruffled prettily around the neck and ruched in at the waist. "Pleased with yourself?"

"More than I would have thought possible," Vanessa replied softly. "Thank you, Jake."

He laughed. "Don't thank me yet." He hung the jacket back on the rack, thrust his hands in the pockets of his beige pants and turned. "Shall I pick you up for dinner tonight?"

She felt her heart stop. "Yes, please," she said simply.

Jake crossed to the door. "Good. Eight o'clock?"

"Yes," she said again. "I'm not in the hotel anymore, I'm—"

"I know where you are," Jake said, and then with a wave he was gone.

It was only after the door had closed behind him that Vanessa realized what she had just seen: the sparkle of sunlight she had noticed when Jake waved was the sparkle of six diamonds on the ring he was wearing.

SHE DRESSED AS CAREFULLY as a bride, and she dressed in white. The silk shirt had a high stiff collar cut low to a buttoned front and full sleeves with tiny cuffs; the matching dirndl skirt had pockets in the side seams. Her small delicate shoes had open toes and sling backs, and her evening bag hung over her shoulder on a thin gold chain.

Her hair curled thick and loose to her shoulders, caught up on one side with a white comb.

She looked younger than she had looked for years; young, pretty and soft, as though the long years of marriage to Larry had never happened. She looked nineteen. Except for the hollows under her cheekbones and the womanly fullness of her wide mouth, she looked like the girl who had fallen in love with Jace. It was because she was in love again, she knew, because love sparkled in her eyes.

Jake saw it the moment he stepped into the room, and he didn't like it. She knew by the way his lips tightened when he looked at her.

"It's hard to believe you're still on the market after six weeks," he said softly. "What do you do, beat them off with a broom?"

"I've been too busy for—" she began, then stopped and said, "Anyway, there was no one to beat off."

"Good," he said. "Nothing like blind stupidity for keeping the field clear. Shall we go?"

He took her to Skookum Chuck's, which was only a few minutes away from her apartment, and they walked the distance. The evening was pleasantly cool, with a fat-bellied sun low on the horizon casting a golden glow over the world and sparkling so brilliantly on the water of the bay that it hurt the eyes.

Jake wore sunglasses, and now, with his skin so darkly tanned, for the first time Vanessa saw the fine white line of a scar on his jaw—the scar that caused that crooked smile of his.

They sat at a secluded table for two in a nook by the window and ordered the poached salmon again. The meal was delicious, and they talked over it like old friends. Or new lovers, with a depth of communication that she had been waiting for for a long time. When the coffee arrived she turned back from the view of the bay and gazed at him. Then, almost involuntarily she reached out to touch a soft finger along the length of the fine white scar she had seen earlier, but which was invisible again in the soft lighting.

"How did you get that?" she asked quietly.

Jake jerked his head as if her touch burned him, and his dark eyes caught and held hers.

"It's a long story," he said.

"Was it caused by a woman, Jake?" she asked quietly.

"No," he said.

"But there was a woman who scarred you, isn't there? There is a woman you still hate?" *Please let me be able to help him,* she was praying into the silence, *please let him tell me.*

His face looked like brown paper stretched over a skull. She heard the harsh intake of a breath.

"Is there?" he countered.

"Please tell me, Jake," she whispered. "What did she do to you?"

He laughed. "She married another man, what else?" he said harshly.

There it was. The reason for his anguish, for his hatred of her—what she had done to Jace, his woman had done to him.

"Jake," she said. "I love you."

"You do not love me," he replied flatly. She wasn't going to get through to him, she knew it. But she had to keep trying.

"And you love me," she persisted, her heart suddenly beating as though she were risking her life.

He began to laugh. Softly, low, but with a quality that pinkened her cheeks.

"I do not love you, Vanessa, my dear," he said. "What is it you want to prove?"

The smell of coffee wafted under her nose and she jerked into startled awareness. A waiter refilled their cups, put the empty wine bottle into the ice bucket standing beside the table and pushed it away.

"Do you recognize the name Gilles Dufour?" Vanessa asked gently.

His hand gripped his cup so tightly all the tendons of his fingers stood out in relief, and inwardly she smiled.

"He's a salesman for Designwear." His voice was absolutely calm. "Why?"

"He was the top salesman for Designwear," Vanessa said. "But he's not anymore. He dropped them last month and took on our line."

Jake nodded to her over the rim of his cup, then took a sip of coffee. "Congratulations," he said.

"He brought a contract from a chain called Fairway with him," she went on softly, watching him as she spoke. "To supply women's slacks under the store label to the western region. Just the right size contract, too."

"Things are looking well for you, then." He wasn't moved in the least.

"Jake," she said in an urgent undertone. "There are a dozen other things—Robert, Number 24—Jake, why are you doing all that?"

His lean hand was very brown against the white china, but no tension showed in it now. She saw the ring, but now, suddenly, she was afraid to ask him why he wore it.

"Vanessa," he said silkily in a voice that made her shrink as though to ward off a blow, "if you find it impossible to make love with a man without convincing yourself that love is involved, please feel free to imagine anything you like about me. And tell me you love me if you must.

"But don't expect me to take part in your imaginings. You are a beautiful desirable woman, and I don't pass many moments in your company without thinking about making love to you. If you aren't adult enough to handle that fact, dress it up any way you like." His voice grew abruptly hoarse in his throat. "But come to some kind of terms with it, because I want you, and I intend to make sure that you want me."

THEY WALKED BACK to her home in silence. The ocean beat against the sandy beach in the darkness, its blackness silvered now with the light of stars.

"Good night, Jake," she said when she had unlocked the front door. For an answer there was only the soft wind in the trees and Jake's strong hand opening the door for her.

She felt like a fool. There was nothing to be frightened of. Vanessa walked through to unlock her own door at the foot of the stairs and led the way upstairs.

Inside her sitting room she flicked on a small lamp and then turned again, "Jake, I. . . I wish—"

But he was right beside her, and she turned almost into his arms. His breath fanned her temple. "Vanessa," he said softly, caressingly. "Don't be afraid. I'll make you want me."

But she already wanted him, desperately wanted him and loved him, whatever he thought. If he touched her now she knew she could not say no.

She was gazing fixedly at his crooked sensuous mouth, feeling hypnotized. When it moved nearer she remained still, waiting, unable to think or breathe, and when his lips brushed hers they parted involuntarily on a soft indrawn breath of anticipation.

The sound seemed to ignite him. His strong lean arms encircled her almost brutally then, and his mouth suddenly ravaged hers. Vanessa sagged against him. Everywhere he touched her, electric currents ran along her skin, shocking her into a need so desperate that reason was blotted out.

"Vanessa," he said in a deep tortured voice. "Vanessa, I need you." His mouth was pressing the hollows of her throat, the thin bones of her shoulders with a feverish intensity; as her head fell back she moaned and her arms reached up to hold him with a need that matched his, flame for flame.

His hands had pushed under her white shirt and his long fingers caressed the hungry skin of her shoulder and her long naked back under the fabric's soft folds. His touch was water in a desert: everywhere it ran her skin came gaspingly, electrifyingly alive, and it was never enough. Each tingle of his fingers against her made her understand her need for more.

When his hand moved upward from the hollow of her stomach, over her ribs and at last enclosed the full firm rise of her breast, she gasped out her breath on a pleading moan that Jake instantly smothered with a kiss. It was as though he wanted to take her cry into his body through his lips rather than his ears, as though the quality of that cry were meat and drink to him.

He slid the soft silk of her shirt from her body then and let it fall to the floor as she stood helpless in front of him, arms at her sides, like a small child being undressed for bed. But the look on her face was not like a child's, and when he pulled out the comb that held her loosely bound hair and its soft russet weight brushed down along her cheek she swayed against him. Her breasts pressed against the fabric of his shirt as her smooth naked arms wrapped tightly around his waist, and her head dropped involuntarily back to offer her mouth up for his kiss.

He breathed as though she had winded him, and his arms closed convulsively around her, but he did not kiss her. He stood looking down at her for a long moment of tortured stillness, and then his mouth began the long slow journey toward hers. Time stopped; it was as though a year of her life might pass before his mouth branded her.

She parted her lips for one pleading cry, "Jas. . . on." His mouth stilled his name on her lips, and as he bent to pick her up in his arms, his mouth still fastened to hers, she sensed a sound deep in him like tortured laughter.

As he carried her through a door into darkness he lifted his mouth. "That's right, my love," he whispered. "Jace."

But it wasn't Jace. It was Jake. And it was Jake she loved, even if he thought she needed the lie he had just given her.

"No," she whispered urgently as he set her down on her bed in the soft enclosing night. "I love *you*. I love you, Ja—"

This time his mouth covered hers with a ruthless suddenness that took her breath away. "Stop," he said.

As though afraid of losing her, he kissed her as he undressed, kissed her with sudden thrusts of passion that kept her breathless in the darkness as she listened to his clothes fall.

But he would not have lost her. She needed him, and she might have waited forever in that warm, soft, expectant darkness if he had asked her to.

He did not make her wait. A faint starlight lightened the gloom as the lean muscled shape of Jake Conrad bent over her, and his hands unerringly found her waist and the zipper hidden in the pocket of her skirt.

The touch of his fingers on her smoothly stockinged legs was like white heat, and when her breath hissed into the night he knew it and smiled. She reached for him, wanting the power to give him the same pleasure. In response to her touch he moved, and the rough warmth of his body covered hers.

There was nothing he did not know about her body. He touched her with an expert's touch, his hands and his mouth calculating each searing caress to push her closer and closer to mindlessness, his own desperateness held at bay with a tight, vibrating control that she wanted to break but could not. She cried out again and again as Jake watched her and touched her, and sometimes his teeth flashed in a smile.

But she could not move him.

"Jake," she whispered urgently, "Jake." His breath caressed her brow and his lips pressed against her temple.

"What is it?" he asked softly.

She could not see his eyes in the gloom. She said, "Jake, if you don't love me, why are you wearing the ring I gave you?"

He drew in his breath as though he were dying, and the hand that had been so tormentingly caressing closed like steel on the soft flesh of her upper arm. It was the reaction of a moment only; she felt him regaining control. But now she knew that her power lay in words.

"I love you, Jake," she began wildly, driven by a need she couldn't name, "I love you, I need you to touch me, I need your hands, I need your mouth kissing me, I need your body. I need you to love me; love me, Jake, please love me now, I love you...."

A groan ripped from his throat, and his mouth came down on hers with a violence of unleashed need that nearly destroyed her. His hand pressed her breast, her waist, her hip, no longer with the need to give pleasure, but to take it. His mouth left hers to find her breast, not now with the desire to arouse, but in the frantic need to taste her flesh.

It was this, at last, that swept her away. Vanessa gasped and moaned in passionate surprise, and then, as his body at last took hers, the darkness was inside her head and reason collapsed under the onslaught of need and pleasure.

He was the expert no longer. He was as lost as she, bones water, flesh fire, and his fingers gripped her with a fierce bruising need that he could not control as he demanded from her body everything she was able to give.

Without warning, then, she was frantic. The deep tumult began in her, and an ache so deep it seemed not to be a part of her but to spring from some rushing river between them, of which they both drank.

They reached the last frontier of joy and pleasure intermingled, and there were tears on her cheeks as, shuddering, his voice a deep rasping surrender, she heard Jake cry out her name.

SUNLIGHT ALWAYS WOKE HER. When Vanessa opened her eyes the bedroom was bright with it. The whole apartment was bright with it; that was one of the reasons she loved it so much.

Her head was in the hollow of his shoulder, her arm across Jake's suntanned muscled chest. She felt the black hair crinkling under her cheek and her breast and her soft underarm and sighed in deep content.

Vanessa tilted her head to look up at his face and was surprised to see that Jake was wide awake, one arm under his head, his eyes open and staring into the distance. The peace that she felt was not mirrored in his face.

The flowered cotton sheet slid down her back as Vanessa pushed herself up and sat sideways, gazing down at him. Her russet hair, glinting like fire in the sunlight, lay in a tousled cloud around her head and shoulders, and Jake moved a lazy arm to stroke it.

A smile touched her lips and her eyes as he looked at her. "Good morning," she whispered.

"Good morning." But there was no answering smile in Jake Conrad's eyes, not even the crooked cynical smile she knew so well.

She stroked his chest down to his flat stomach and watched his muscles rippling under his skin in response.

"You're beautiful," she whispered, meaning it, for the sight of his body pulled at her emotions in a way that was somehow disturbing.

"You made love to Jace last night." The words came out flat and cool, as though he were making a simple statement of fact.

She gasped, "No!"

There was a silence.

"Jake, I love you. And it was you who made love to me last night, and I always knew it. I never forgot it was you for one moment."

"Not even when you called his name?"

God, when would this demon stop torturing him?

What had she done to him, the woman who had married another man?

"I never called his name," she said.

"I think you did."

"No."

There was a closed cruel look on his face that disturbed her. "Jake," she whispered, her voice urgent with the knowledge that if only he would let her, she could heal his scars with love. "I love you. Please believe that. I love you."

A light of angry triumph kindled in his eyes as he looked at her, and he sat up and bent over her, forcing her to lie back against the pillows. He lifted a hand to catch a lock of her wild hair and stroked it between fingers and thumb with an odd sensual concentration.

"You don't love Jace anymore?" he asked, and his eyes were slitted and his crooked mouth was twisted in a smile.

"No," she said as calmly as she could. "Except as a memory. Jace is dead."

"And he's dead to you?"

"Jake—"

"He's dead to you?" Jake persisted. "You aren't in love with him anymore?"

"I told you, no."

"If he walked into this room now you'd feel nothing for him?"

"I...." How could she answer that? If Jace walked into this room now she might go mad, she supposed. "Jake, why is this so important? It was all over ten years ago. I don't feel anything for Jace except—" Except memory, the memory of first love? Except a tiny regret? But how could she regret anything in a life that had led her, at last, to Jake? She shook her head helplessly. "I don't feel anything for him, can't you accept that?"

"Nothing?"

How could she explain about the small corner of her heart that might, perhaps, always belong to Jace? He was waiting to pounce on every word. Yet there was no threat to Jake in that tiny tenderness; it simply was there.

"Jake, he's dead. He's been dead nearly ten years. I love you more than I ever loved him. Please forget about Jace."

A black flame leaped up behind his eyes, and his crooked smile became more cruel than ever. "Well, that's not easy," he said softly, his voice tight with the effort to remain steady. "That's not easy. Because I've been lying to you, my love. There is no cousin with the same name, Vanessa. There has only ever been one Jason Conrad, and that's me. I am Jace, Vanessa."

CHAPTER THIRTEEN

"JACE?" SHE WHISPERED softly, uncomprehendingly. Her eyes grew wide as she gazed at him. "Jace?"

He nodded. There was a strange smile on his face; he said nothing.

"Oh, my God! Oh, my God! *Jace!*" Vanessa exclaimed, tears starting in her eyes. She reached her arms around his warm naked chest and clung as the sobs shook her body. "Jace, Jace, Jace! Oh, I don't believe it! It's too—oh, God!" She lay back, wiping the tears from her cheeks, smiling tremulously up at him. "Why didn't you tell me before?" she laughed as another sob caught her throat, feeling as though her heart were going to explode. She forgot where she was, she forgot the past, the present; she forgot time. She only knew that the man leaning over her was miraculously and unquestionably both her men, both her deepest loves in one, that Jace and Jake were the same man—a man who belonged to her now as irrevocably as the rising sun belonged to morning.

She wrapped her arms around his chest again, pressing her face against the springing black hair with a joy that welled up from somewhere deep inside her. "I love you," she said, almost incoherent with joy and tears. "I love you so much! I ought to have known, I should have recognized your body if not your face, shouldn't I? Oh, your poor, scarred, battered face—and it's so beautiful now, but I should have known you, you—"

"Yes, I made a lot of slips." His voice was cool, and Vanessa was abruptly aware that he had not moved. She was clinging to him, but he was not holding her or touching her. . . nor was he smiling. When she drew back slowly and looked up at him, his face looked like a death's head.

"Jake!" she whispered, shocked. "What is it? What's the matter?"

Now he smiled, the kind of smile that made her wish he hadn't.

"You really are a most accomplished hypocrite," he said.

It was like a slap across the face, like ice water thrown across her heart. Vanessa shrank back into the pillow.

"Hypocrite!" she whispered. "Why do. . . what do you mean?"

"God," he breathed. "You're wasted. You should be on the stage."

"Jace—Jake, I. . . ."

"My name is Jake," he said roughly. "Jace may not be dead, but he hasn't been around for a long time."

Suddenly she felt nakedly vulnerable and as though she were in danger of her life. Trembling, she reached to pull the sheet up over her breasts.

"You don't love me, do you?" she said in a low

even voice, building frantic barriers to ward off the blow that was coming.

"I'm afraid not."

"You...it's hate, isn't it? You hate me." A little voice inside screamed that it wasn't true, that it was impossible that he should hate her, because if he hated her she would die. But the rest of her was numb, the rest of her could accept what he was saying with only the dullest, most distant sense of being bludgeoned.

"That's what it is," agreed Jake.

She closed her eyes and put a hand up over her mouth to contain a sob.

"Oh, God!" she whimpered, choking.

Jake rolled away from her, stood up and began to dress. With a tortured fascination Vanessa watched him.

"Is this it, then?" she cried, her voice cracking in disbelief. "I'm never going to see you again?"

"No," he said, turning to face her as he buckled his belt. "This is by no means it. I'm not finished with you yet—I've barely begun."

Hope fluttered frantically outside her heart, begging to be let in. "Begun what?" she faltered, but the look in his eyes killed the hope.

"Begun to make you pay."

"Pay? Pay for *what*?" she whispered with a dull terror starting to throb in her. My God, how could he hate her so much when all she felt was love?

"What do you think?"

"My God, for—but that was *ten years ago*, Jake," she begged him, her voice hoarse with protest.

"It was ten years," he stated grimly, and it took her a moment to realize what he meant.

She said in disbelief, "You've remembered and hated me for ten years?"

"Not remembered," he corrected her again. "I didn't remember you for ten years. But you shouldn't have come back, Vanessa."

Suddenly she was cold, icy cold all over. A woman would have to be a masochistic fool to love a man who hated her as much as this. Anyway, she had no feelings left: she was pure, detached, as cold as an angel.

Vanessa flung back the sheet and crossed the room to pull blue jeans from the closet. Ignoring Jake's presence she thrust her long legs into them and zipped them up. "So now you want your revenge, is that it?" she said in a choking voice. "You're going to take the opportunity of my being in Vancouver and being in love with you to make me pay for what I did ten years ago?"

"I didn't *take* the opportunity," he said, laughing suddenly. "Haven't you understood? I *made* it."

"You *made* it!" Vanessa pressed her hand to her mouth. "You mean all this—everything—" she waved her hand vaguely "—it was all for this? The business, bringing me here—just so you could have me under your thumb?" Her voice was high and cracking, almost unrecognizable. The pain was threatening to break through the frail icy barrier she had set up against it, and it was sharp, stabbing and a thousand times worse than the pain of losing him the first time.

"Why?" she cried on a long howling note of uncomprehending agony.

"Why did you marry Larry?" he asked abruptly.

"Why didn't you tell me not to? Why didn't you write to me?" she cried angrily and she knew that it was a hurting anger that had lived inside her all these years and that *this* was why she had planned on looking up Jace, to ask him this.

"Tell me," he said as though she hadn't spoken.

She slapped him. Slapped him with all the strength in her slim body, all the anguish in her heart. Jake twisted with the force of it; and then he was swinging around, his hands raised, and he caught her with a force that sent her sprawling across the bed. Before she could catch her breath he had flung himself on top of her and pinioned her wrists.

"Tell me why you married Larry."

"Why?" she demanded, and her anger filled her with a wonderful pulsing strength. "So you can decide whether your hatred is justified? So you can plan just the right degree of revenge?"

He shook her wrists a little. "Tell me," he repeated. "Vanessa, I want to know."

"Do you! Well, you had your chance to ask me that question ten years ago and to raise your objections then, and I didn't hear you doing it. My reasons are none of your business. You were satisfied to hate me without knowing the reason; you can just go on hating me."

He began to kiss her, his lips running across her cheeks and lips, throat and breast, knowing she would hate it, knowing she would flinch from that burning touch.

"Vanessa," he said softly, threateningly, "tell me."

If that meant he would take her against her will if she didn't tell him, Vanessa thought, blind with rage, then he deserved whatever he got. And he would get what he deserved. She would make sure of that.

She laughed lightly, and it was a sound that chilled even her blood. "Can't you guess?" she asked in a high voice. "Can't you really guess? Or perhaps you don't want to know as badly as you say!" She smiled and opened her eyes at him. "Larry was such an exciting lover, Jake," she said, the words almost surprising her as they came from her mouth. Maybe Jake was right, she should have gone on the stage. "You...Jace was a lovely person, but...." Her voice trailed gently away. "I think I knew it that night Jace...you made love to me, but I didn't want to admit it to myself: I couldn't have lived without Larry. I couldn't have given *that* up."

Jake's face was wiped clean of all expression, but behind his tan he was white to the lips. His hands clenched her wrists so tightly she felt her bones would snap. Vanessa opened her eyes wide at him, still distantly amazed at the ease with which the lies came to her, at how deep and powerfully her unleashed anger burned.

"Larry found out about you and me," she said. "He told me I was a fool, that I couldn't live without him and that I knew it. I did know it, but Larry said he would prove it to me. That night he—" Vanessa's voice deepened as though with pleasure at the memory "—oh, he was wonderful, Jake. He showed me what I'd be giving up if I left him. Afterward...

he said I'd have to marry him immediately or not at all. We were married two weeks later."

He was like a stone statue, remote and unseeing, a man she could no longer reach. Vanessa felt as though it were all new, the terrible helpless regret of ten years ago, when, after the bright fires of self-sacrifice had burned low, she had seen the ashes she had made of her life.

She had been too young, at nineteen, to know what she was doing on the day she had given in to the soft pleadings, the gentle tears of Larry's mother. Too young to know that what she had been asked should never have been asked of anyone.

But when Jace had not answered her letter, she had imagined that the sacrifice and the pain were hers alone. Now she knew better, now she knew what she ought to have known ten years ago, what she would have known if she had had faith in this love. Jace's life, too, had gone up in flames the day she had married Larry, and the heat of those flames had bent his ferocious passion toward revenge, had twisted his enormous capacity for love into this black self-destructive power to hate. And was still at work, destroying her own love for the man who looked into hell when he looked at her.

Well, it was all too late now. With a floating detachment Vanessa watched Jake get up off the bed and bend to pick up his jacket, watched him put it on. He would leave her now, but it hardly mattered: he was already as far away from her as he would ever be.

When he turned to face her the flesh of his face

was drawn tight, the shadow of the faint fine scar she had seen last night pulling the left side of his face. Vanessa sat up, unconsciously straightening her shoulders, like someone in the presence of a judge.

"I haven't finished making you pay," Jake said, in a voice so strained it was unrecognizable, and when his eyes met hers they were haunted. "If you thought you had made up for ten years in one night, Vanessa, you were wrong. You owe me, and you're going to pay."

VANESSA STOOD UNDER THE SHOWER till it ran cold, trying to numb her brain, trying to wash away the memory of the past hour.

But it did not wash away. She scraped her wet hair back into a ponytail and pushed her sore body into her blue jeans and a T-shirt without knowing or caring what she was doing and slammed out of her apartment without a backward glance.

"Holy cow, what happened to you? You get locked out in the storm?" Ilona exclaimed when she arrived at Number 24. She had never arrived at work before without makeup, without being smartly put together.

Funny, thought Vanessa. *That's exactly how I feel. As though I've been locked out in the storm.*

"I woke up late," she said briefly, and Ilona glanced at her closed face and held her peace.

They were hard at work all day. Duplicate models of the entire line had to be made for all the salesmen to use as samples. Although so far Number 24 had only one salesman, Gilles Dufour, they would have to take on at least four more across the country if they were going to be any kind of success. With any luck Robert would hire them during the next month, and by then the samples would be ready to send off to them. All this wasn't what Vanessa was used to, of course, and it was rather fascinating to think that the clothes she had designed and made in Vancouver might be worn by women an entire continent away in St. John's.

She worked at speed all day, cutting and pinning and marking and giving orders with an almost desperate precision.

"Death watching you or something?" Ilona asked finally.

Vanessa jumped. "Pardon me?"

"Death. My grandfather says your own death is always watching you, just waiting for the time. Some days he watches a little more closely, so you feel his shadow, and those are the days when you feel driven: you know death is nearby, and you're afraid he might reach out and touch you before you're ready, before you've finished what you have to do. People who are always driven, he says, are people who feel, inside, that death is watching them very closely."

"Well, he's watching me today," said Vanessa.

But it wasn't Death. It was Jake. And the shadow he had cast over her would darken all the years of her life.

SHE WAS GLAD the designing part of the job was over for the moment, because the creative spark in her had died. In the days that followed that terrible morning with Jake the pleasure seeped out of her work until finally she moved through her working day like an automaton. She performed mechanically, if expertly. She perfected the sizes and the fit for the production prototypes, putting in tucks and altering the cut till the perfectionist inside her was satisfied.

"Your cost per item is going to be too high," Robert said one day, showing her the figures. "You're including too much detail work."

"The detail work is what makes the garment," Vanessa said flatly. "I told you there'd be detail work."

Robert looked as though he didn't know how to deal with this new cold businesslike Vanessa. "Well, there's too much. This isn't New York, Vanessa. Ted can't set up a production line of detail workers; we don't have a large enough run. He tells me all this has got to be done by the ordinary sewers."

Vanessa rooted through the papers on her desk, absentmindedly wondering if a design she had rejected for spring could be used in the summer line.

"Well, let it be done by the ordinary sewers. What's wrong with that?" she said.

"It costs the bloody earth, that's what's wrong with it!" said Robert. "You're putting yourself into another price bracket, Vanessa, and it won't work."

Where the devil was that folder of discarded designs? When she thought that soon she would have to start designing the summer line, Vanessa's forehead grew damp. There was nothing flirting in the corner of her mind's eye this time, waiting to be fleshed out, waiting to become.

She said, "Didn't you tell me we had an extra hundred thousand so I could keep quality up and prices down my first season?"

"Yes. Or use it for advertising. We agreed to spend it on advertising in the trade journals, Vanessa. It's already earmarked—"

"Well, let's not. Let's use it on producing a better product." She found her folder of designs and opened it. She had been feeling very creative while she designed these; some of them, with a little adjustment for a lighter fabric, might—

"Vanessa, we are committed. There's only one way to get this work done and that's to use subcontractors."

She looked at him calmly. "Well, fine, Robert, that sounds fine."

"Vanessa, subcontractors use home sewers. Are you aware of what that means?"

It meant slavery, or little better. It meant mothers on social welfare working long hours to eke out the hopelessly insufficient welfare check or non-English-speaking immigrants being taken advantage of.

"Oh, well, it's not so bad in Canada, is it?" she said.

"Vanessa, where the hell do you think you are, the Garden of Eden?" Robert asked with a cool laugh. "Exploitation is exploitation, no matter where it is."

Funny, she had used the exact same phrase to Tom once, over the very same issue. "Damn it, Vanessa, they don't even speak English!" Tom had exploded, as though that somehow made it all right. Funny how much she was learning about life, having to run things.

"Robert, nobody has to accept the work," she pointed out in the same voice that a million had used before and a million would use after her. "I'd rather pull the money off the advertising budget, but if you don't want to, what's our alternative?"

"The alternative is to kill some of that detail work you're insisting on," Robert said reasonably.

"Robert, this is Number 24's first season. It's important that we don't cut any corners now; we've got to make a splash. I'll have less detail work in the summer line, and even less for next fall. By next Christmas we'll have phased out the home sewers completely, okay?"

"Okay," said Robert, getting to his feet. He gathered his papers together and left her alone, staring down at her folder designs.

A drop of water fell onto the sketch of a yellow pencil skirt with a pretty fan of kick pleats over the left knee and Vanessa watched the yellow ink blotch and run onto the white background. The pipes are leaking, she thought stupidly, looking up, but there were no pipes overhead, and no condensation that she could see on the ceiling. As she looked down again, another drop landed, and then she understood. With a laugh that shook and turned into a sob she wiped her cheeks, and then, abruptly, she was facedown on her desk, head in her arms, sobbing. Her whole body shook with the force of her weeping. The sounds must have been audible in the other offices, but no one came to investigate. She was utterly alone.

SEPTEMBER THIRTEENTH WAS DECLARED Terry Fox Day in Canada, and his great Marathon of Hope was to be commemorated by small marathons in cities and towns across the nation. It seemed that everyone she talked to either planned to "run for Terry" or had pledged money to someone who did.

She felt a deep personal connection with the young man who had died before she had even come to hear of him, and now, in moments of a despair so dark she sometimes thought she could not survive, sometimes she remembered that gentle, open, ordinary face and wondered what depths of darkness he had run through to reach the light.

"I'm running in the Marathon of Hope," she said suddenly to Ilona one afternoon, surprising herself. "Will you give me a pledge?"

"I'll pledge you if you'll pledge me," Ilona said. "I'm running, too." They both laughed, caught up in the secret shared by an entire nation, and offered each other ten dollars a kilometer over the ten-kilometer run. By the time Terry Fox Day arrived, Vanessa was running for twenty-three dollars a kilometer, and Ilona for forty. They ran the course together, smiling at the dozens of other joggers wearing Terry Fox T-shirts and at the people waving as they went by, and feeling very strongly their kinship with the family of man.

A few days later Vanessa collected checks for the Terry Fox Fund totaling two hundred and thirty dollars and listened with a bubble of pride when she heard that the fund had gone over the twenty-seven-million-dollar mark.

"Terry suggested a dollar for every man, woman and child in Canada," Celeste Boyd said as she smilingly passed over her check, "and he has certainly made it."

Jake's secretary had pledged ten dollars, which gave Vanessa an excuse to go upstairs. "Is Jake in?" she asked casually as the check was being written.

"No, he isn't. Why, did he pledge, too?" asked Jean with a flicker of hastily smothered surprise, and Vanessa knew with a sickening wrench that Jean had been instructed to keep Vanessa away from this office.

"Not me," she said gaily. "But he must have pledged someone, don't you think?" A number of Concorp employees had run in the Marathon of Hope and Jake certainly could have pledged them all without feeling the pinch.

"I don't know," said Jean. "I don't think anyone asked him."

"Didn't ask Jake Conrad?" Vanessa demanded unbelievingly. "If I'd known that I'd have asked him for a hundred dollars a kilometer!" If she could have got near him, she amended mentally. And if she could have got a word out in his presence without begging for something very different from a donation....

"Good afternoon, Mr. Conrad," Jean chirruped in a panicky voice, and Vanessa whipped around and her eyes locked with the cold angry gaze of Jake Conrad.

"Good afternoon, Jean. Good afternoon...Vanessa," he said, and she knew he had almost said, "Mrs. Standish."

Vanessa had an insane desire to run, but she stood her ground. In a bright brittle voice that fooled no one, she said, "Jean says she doesn't think you pledged anyone in the Terry Fox run, Jake! Did you?"

"I pledged Marigold," he said, his eyes steady. He had a briefcase in his hand; he looked as though he would open it and start to work the instant he got behind his desk. He looked busy and important.

"And how much did that cost you?" Vanessa demanded.

"Nothing. Marigold didn't run."

Jean tittered and choked herself off, and there was a short silence.

"Well, I ran," offered Vanessa. "I'm just collecting my pledge from Jean." That let Jean off the hook for allowing Vanessa in the vicinity, she hoped. "How would you like to make a retroactive pledge?"

"For how much?" he said, as though it would be too much trouble to argue with her.

"A hundred dollars a kilometer?" Vanessa hazarded, her eyes wide as she gazed into his.

"How far did you run?"

"Ten kilometers."

"Fine." He looked over her shoulder. "Jean, would you make out a check to the cancer society for Mrs. Standish for one thousand dollars?" He moved toward his office door.

"Not a *company* pledge!" Vanessa said. "The company should pledge much more than that! That's your *personal* pledge! You should give me the check from your personal account."

He held her gaze for a long moment, his hand on the doorknob. Abruptly he opened the door and held it for her. "Come in," he said.

Her heart in her mouth, Vanessa crossed the threshold and felt him follow her in and close the door.

As she hesitated, he strode across to his desk and, laying his briefcase on it, flicked the snaps open.

"What do you want, Vanessa?" he asked.

"A thousand dollars for the Terry Fox fund," she quavered.

He sank down in his stuffed black leather chair, threw some files out of his case onto the desk, snapped the case closed and set it on the floor. He opened a drawer in his desk, pulled out a flat maroon checkbook, dropped it with a little slap on the desk top. Without taking his eyes from her, he pulled a pen out of his inner breast pocket and unscrewed the lid.

He wrote the details on the check smoothly, without pausing, signing his name the same way he wrote the rest, without a flourish. Vanessa had sat down in the chair in front of his desk, and he ripped the paper from the book and flicked it casually across the desk. Then he sat looking at her.

Vanessa picked up the check with a hand that nearly trembled. "Thank you," she said, staring unseeingly down at it, unable to meet his eyes. His silence terrified her; at any moment he might break it to tell her to go.

"Jake, how do you want me to pay?" she blurted in a sudden rush of courage.

He knew what she meant; his hand was in her line of vision and she saw it tense on the pen he was holding. Her ring was gone, a white mark against his tan showing where it had been.

"Why, are you going to offer some sort of voluntary payment?" he asked dryly.

"Could I?" she asked, her head still bent.

"What, for example? Crawling to Calgary in sackcloth and ashes?" The sarcasm in his voice drummed against the top of her head. "Or were you thinking of something a little more personal, like becoming my mistress till I tired of you?"

Her head snapped up. "Is that what you want?" she began. Is that what he had meant—that he would destroy her emotionally the way she had destroyed him emotionally?

"No, that's not what I had in mind," he interrupted roughly. "For one thing, I am already tired of you. And for another, a voluntary payment won't be nearly so satisfying as one extracted under protest."

She shivered at the coldness in his voice. "Oh God, Jake," she protested. "You don't want to *rape* me?"

His face became a frozen mask of distaste. "My God, women!" he exploded with a mirthless laugh. "No, I do not want to rape you," he said precisely. "For one thing, I don't want you sexually. For another, since I understand these days that rape isn't sexual but political, I would consider the animal bludgeoning of the body and the spirit an extremely unimaginative method of revenge, either against society or against an individual. To say the least of it."

Vanessa shivered again. "Who was your mentor, Machiavelli?"

Jake smiled his crooked smile. "No," he said softly. "You were. And I think I learned my lessons well. Someday I'll ask you whether you think I did."

"Jake," she begged, "if it's my heartbreak you want, you've already had it. I fell in love with you thinking I had a chance to make you love me, and found out you hated me. Isn't that enough? What else is there?"

He shook his head. "If I thought you had a heart that was worth it, that might have been enough, Vanessa. But your kind of heart, if it does in fact break, heals too quickly for what I want. When you do pay me, it's going to be payment in full. I'm going to break you another way. I'm going to ruin you, Vanessa."

She gasped. It sounded like a line from a melodrama, except that it was delivered in such a matter-of-fact voice.

"Ruin me, how?" she demanded with a nervous laugh.

He looked at her. "Professionally, how else?" he demanded. "I am going to let you go on building up Number 24 for as long or as short a time as the mood takes me, and then I am, one way or another—and I have my choice of several—going to bring it crashing down around your ears so loudly you'll never have the courage to start up in business again."

For one appalling second she was shaken to the roots, then she bit her lip and made an effort at recovery.

"How are you going to do that?" she demanded coolly. "You're bluffing. You have no control over Number 24."

Jake raised his eyebrows. "You're more naive than I thought. I can pull the plug on you in that company from so many different directions it would make your head spin."

"What?" she gasped.

"Did you really believe that that quarter-million-dollar contract had you safe?" He shook his head and laughed softly but said no more, and Vanessa took courage. He *was* bluffing, trying to scare her.

"Of course it does," she said. "Unless you think giving me a quarter of a million dollars is making me pay." His smile was crookedly arrogant, and she snapped, "Then tell me, if you're so sure of yourself!"

"It'll be a pleasure," Jake said softly. He reached down to pull open a drawer and after a moment pulled out a file. He laid it flat on the desk.

"First," he said, "there's the little matter of the debenture that financed Number 24. If your lawyer had checked the agreement carefully, he might have noticed that the debenture can be called at any time. If the debenture were called, Number 24 would have no choice but to go bankrupt. Bankruptcy of the company is deemed in your management contract to be sufficient cause for the termination of the contract without compensation." He paused. "That's one way.

"Then there's Gilles Dufour. If Gilles and one or two—or all—of your other salesmen were suddenly to abandon your line in the middle of a season or even show very poor orders in one or two seasons running, you'd have a big deficit to catch up. I don't think you'd recover in this economic climate."

He smiled. "Then, Vanessa, there's that nice little ongoing contract to supply slacks to Fairway. It's just possible that one season the store might say you hadn't made the slacks to their specifications. It might take a costly lawsuit to prove otherwise. Or the unshipped portion of a large order might be suddenly canceled one day for reasons beyond anyone's control."

He paused and looked at her as though expecting her to speak, but Vanessa was beyond speech.

"Still not enough? Well, then, consider this: it won't be long now before you have to go down to the Canadian embassy in Seattle to renew your temporary visa to allow you to go on working in Canada. At that time you will need a statement from your employer showing good reason for your visa extension. You'll need the same kind of statement if you apply for a permanent visa. Suppose that due to reasons beyond anyone's control that statement wasn't forthcoming?"

He looked at her stricken face, white and wide-eyed in the afternoon light.

"Enough? There's more, Vanessa. There's the building 'ease at Number 24 that allows Concorp to give you immediate notice to vacate under certain conditions that Robert would never have let go by if he didn't know so well that I want your business to be a success.

"Or there's Robert himself, whom I might suddenly need back at Concorp with only a few hours' notice. Think you could manage losing him without warning?"

Jake sat back. He smiled. "There are one or two other ways, of course, the best of all—" his hand moved unconsciously on the file folder beneath his hands "—a very unexpected one that you presented me with yourself, like a gift. But I think you see the point. You are about as invulnerable at Number 24 as a frangipani on a polar icecap. It might survive the few warm days of summer. But not the winter. And winter is coming, Vanessa. You just won't know when."

Vanessa stood up, distantly surprised to find that her knees held. She said, "You must be mad if you think that after being told all that I'll continue putting all that effort into something you're going to wreck. I quit, Jake. You'll have my resignation first thing in the morning."

He laughed at her. "Good!" he said levelly. "Just what I wanted you to feel! But you can't get out so easily, Vanessa. In fact, you can't get out at all."

His hand moved to the edge of the file folder and he opened it. It was moderately thick with documents and papers, and the top one she recognized as a photostatic copy of her management contract.

"You aren't the only one protected by this contract," Jake smiled. He looked down. "Do I need to read you the clause regarding any untimely resignation, or do you remember it?"

She was silent, and after a moment Jake began. "Seventeen. In the event that the—"

"Shut up!" she snapped. "I remember it well enough!"

"Good," Jake's voice was as flat and cool as stone. "Don't make the mistake of thinking I wouldn't take you to court, Vanessa. I would. I'd also take any potential employer to court. It just won't be worth anyone's while to try to hire you as a designer. If you resign tomorrow, or anytime before this contract allows—" he tapped it lightly, almost caressingly "—you can say goodbye to any career in fashion design for at least five years."

She was frozen, staring at him. "What do you want, Jake? What do you want?" she whispered hoarsely.

He looked calmly up at her. "I want you to put your heart and soul into something, Vanessa, and then I want to take it away from you, piece by piece, while you fight desperately to hang on to it."

She laughed. "After this, you expect me to put heart and soul into Number 24? You must be mad! I'll run it into the ground and make sure you lose as much money as possible while I'm doing it!"

"Maybe," agreed Jake. "Maybe you will, in spite of the clause in your contract that allows me to sue you personally for recovery of funds if wanton disregard for the good of the business can be proved. You could do it in a way that would make that hard to prove; you're more than intelligent enough for that. You'd have a chance to show how intelligent in a court of law.

"But I don't think you'll do that, Vanessa. I think you'll work twice as hard at Number 24 after this. I think your soul is invested in Number 24, and I think you'll spend your energy trying to make it such a profitable undertaking that you could refinance it with a bank, for example, when I tried to pull the plug on you. I think you'll work like a demon trying to plug every leak I've told you about and trying to find the ones I haven't. And with every day's work, I think you'll get more and more committed to Number 24, more and more convinced you can save it.

"You might even try to convince me that it's so profitable and prestigious a company for me to own that I'd be a fool to pull the plug. And it might work. You see, I haven't decided how much revenge I want. Maybe it'll be enough seeing you constantly insecure. Maybe I'll never pull the plug, Vanessa," he said softly, insinuatingly. "Maybe you can convince me, when the time comes, not to do it. There may be a way out. There are lots of possibilities. Maybe you can beat me at my own game. You'll never know unless you try."

It seemed as though she were looking down at him from a great height, as though she were floating up near the ceiling. She couldn't feel her body.

"You're evil," she thought, and heard the words being said aloud, as though her mouth had somehow produced the sounds of its own accord. "You're worse than Machiavelli, Jake, you're in a class by yourself. I think what you told me the other day is right, even if you don't know it. You aren't Jace, not the Jace I remember. Jace is dead; your soul is dead. Jake is just a distant cousin, an empty shell pretending to be a human being.

"I was wrong when I thought I loved you, Jake. There's nobody in there to love."

Somehow she had turned and was moving to the door, so her legs must be carrying her, Vanessa thought dimly. She opened the door and walked out without another word, without a backward glance, as though she were leaving an empty room.

CHAPTER FOURTEEN

"HELLO, DARLING," said the voice over the phone at nine o'clock the next morning. "How is life in the backwoods treating you?"

"Colin!" Vanessa exclaimed. "How are you?"

"I'm fine, of course," he said blithely. "I'm here in New York, where the action is. You're the one who's consigned herself to the frozen wastes of Canada. How *is* the weather, by the way?"

"A bit rainy, right at the moment. As it happens, however, Vancouver has a milder climate than New Yo—"

"Oh, please, no gushing travelogue, darling," he interrupted. "As long as you aren't stuck in a snowbank, I'm happy."

"You can be happy, Colin: no snowbank," she said with an irritated laugh. "How is business?"

"Isn't it funny you should mention," Colin said. "That's what this call is about: business. I want to drum some up."

"From me?"

"No one else, love. Now listen: I've designed you a signature fabric and some Number 24 motifs in my spare time. It's a summer design, very cool and light, Vanessa, and I've sent off the sketch by courier. If you like it and order immediately I can deliver by Christmas."

If I'm still here by Christmas, Vanessa thought involuntarily, feeling a sudden sharp pang at the thought that her future might not include Number 24.

But as long as her present did, she was going to run it the best way she knew how. As far as she knew, no ready-to-wear manufacturer in Canada had anything like a signature fabric, and although a few might have monograms, they were mostly done in imitation of the designer ready-to-wear fashions like Pierre Cardin's.

A thing like this could succeed wildly or fail wildly, and what did she have to lose? Nothing that she wouldn't be losing in the end, anyway.

"Colin," she laughed, "that's the best idea I've heard all month!"

When she had put the phone down on Colin she went next door to Robert's office. "T-shirt manufacturers, Robert," she announced. "Anybody around who'd supply T-shirts to our design and with our label?"

"I can have a look," said Robert. "What's in the works?"

She kept her explanation brief, not mentioning Colin at all, not letting him see the scope of what she was considering. Robert looked as though he were both dubious and willing to be convinced but trying hard to look more willing than dubious.

"It's pretty ambitious for your second season," he said. "But I'll look into the cost and possibilities if you want."

Vanessa thanked him and turned to go. "Oh, by the

way," she said as an afterthought. "Do we have a copy of our lease around anywhere? I'd like to have a look at it."

"Sure," he said. "I'll ask Roberta to run off a copy for you today."

She had thought it just possible that Jake had been lying in order to frighten her, but when she examined the photostatic copy that Roberta dropped on her desk later that day, there it was, in clause thirteen. "If, in the best estimate of the lessor, the said premises are being used by the lessee in a manner or for a purpose other than that defined in the lease, and if, in the best estimate of the lessor, the said uses are deemed to be detrimental to the property or to the best interests of the lessor or of the other tenants of the building, together or severally...or if the lessee is convicted in a court of law of violating any federal, provincial or municipal statute on the said premises, whether in the course of the business being carried on on the said premises as defined in the lease or otherwise...then the lessee may be given thirty days' notice to quit the premises...."

Vanessa leaned back and rubbed her eyes, wondering how many of the myriad laws of the land Jake could be certain of their breaking one way or another in the course of a business day and which function of the business had inadvertently not been defined in the lease.

Her eyes dropped back to the document.

"Fourteen. If the business of the lessee should suffer a labor dispute...." Vanessa wrinkled her forehead. What was this? Then she sat forward with a snap. "That the said premises should be picketed... to the detriment of the reasonable function of the business of the lessor or of the other tenants together or severally...for more than thirty days, then the lessee may be given notice of the termination of the lease...."

Vanessa felt an insane desire to laugh. Jake Conrad was right: he had her coming and going. A strike! She couldn't believe it: all he had to do was engineer a strike and he could put her out of business!

Suddenly she thought about Ted Loomis and how quickly he had found the labor force she had needed. To whom would all those people feel they owed their loyalty? To the man who'd hired them, who controlled their working conditions, or to herself and the company that paid their wages? And to whom did Ted owe his loyalty—to her or to Jake Conrad?

Vanessa breathed slowly as a new thought assailed her: how had Robert ever let a clause like this slip by him? Or did Robert, too, feel more of a loyalty for Jake than he did for Number 24? Was Robert, in fact, here only to serve Jake's purpose, to set up the methods for him to destroy her?

Vanessa shook her head. She was getting paranoid, which was just what Jake wanted. If she kept this up, soon she would be examining Ilona's friendship and wondering if Roberta sent Jake a photocopy of all the mail every day....

Vanessa opened a drawer and blindly threw in the lease. She would look at it later. Jake wasn't likely to start a strike today, and right now she had work to do.

She also had a dinner date this evening, with a man she had met at the tennis club she had joined. With any luck he would take her mind off her troubles and Jake Conrad.

But it wasn't to be. "This is the best place to eat on English Bay, if not in the whole of Vancouver," David said as he parked the car, and with a strong sense of impending doom she looked through the windshield and saw Skookum Chuck's.

She could hardly cry, "Not here, anywhere but here!" without having him think her a lunatic, and she could think of no reasonable excuse for asking him to take her elsewhere. But she was absolutely convinced that Jake was going to walk in with Marigold on his arm and spoil her evening, and she couldn't keep her eyes off the door all evening.

Her obvious jitters and preoccupation made conversation strained, though David did his best. Eventually he began to talk about his ex-wife, who had divorced him unexpectedly a year ago, and Vanessa encouraged him because it meant she could listen with half an ear.

But Jake did not come to Skookum Chuck's that night, and by the time David pulled up in front of her house again she felt she owed him some explanation for her distracted behavior.

"David, I'm awfully sorry I've been such lousy company. I've got too much on my mind at the moment."

"That's okay," he said. "Problems?"

She nodded.

"Legal or emotional?"

And he really was a kindly person, and she laughed and said, "Are those the only choices I get?"

He laughed with her. "I find that most people's most worrisome problems usually fall into one or the other, or both."

He seemed to be speaking from a professional point of view, and she suddenly remembered. "Of course. You're a lawyer."

"Yes, ma'am," he said. "You need a lawyer?"

"I might, David," she said thoughtfully. It couldn't hurt to have a Canadian lawyer go over the contract and the debenture agreement and even the lease. "I just might."

David pulled open a wallet. "Here's my business card. I'll write my home phone on it for you," he said as he did so. "Give me a call, Vanessa."

She let herself into the house feeling more secure than she had all day. She wasn't just going to sit around waiting for the ax to fall, as though it were inevitable. Jake Conrad wasn't infallible, he wasn't God. He must have made a mistake, left a loophole. If he had she would find it and use it. If he hadn't—well, she would have to try something else. But she was going to fight Jake Conrad—every way she knew how.

ON SATURDAY SHE DID SOMETHING she had been promising herself she would do for a long time: she walked the sea-wall promenade the whole distance around Stanley Park. It was a walk of several miles, and the sky and the sea were gray with the light continuous drizzle that was Vancouver's trademark.

But Vanessa wore her new bright yellow sailor's mac and hat over a thick sweater, breathed in the fresh damp air and let the soft wind carry off her worries and the sight of mountains and the threatening sea soothe her.

That night she slept soundly, and she dreamed of Jake Conrad and knew in the dream that she had dreamed of him often without remembering. He was holding a letter, and he opened it and a snake curled up out of the letter, a beautiful snake that fascinated her. When she put her hand out to it, it sank its fangs into her arm, and its body writhed suddenly and grew large and immensely powerful; she could feel its terrifying power all around her. It was wrapping its body around her waist, and Vanessa knew there were words she could say to stop the snake from hurting her, but she couldn't remember them. They were in the letter, and she looked at Jake and saw a look of helpless surprise in his face. He set the letter down on a desk and it was a file folder, thick with documents, the words "PACKAGE DEAL" written across it. "It's in there," she said urgently to Jake.

She awoke with the words on her lips and terror in her heart and sat up in the gray light of another wet day.

The file folder. There was something in the file Jake had showed her, something he hadn't told her about. "The best one of all," he had called it, and Vanessa knew that Jake would not have told her about all those vulnerable areas if he had intended to attack her there. If she plugged those leaks it wouldn't matter. The real danger lay somewhere else.

Jake wouldn't tell her about that one. There would be only one way to find out what it was: get her hands on that file in his desk, and do it soon.

THE ENVELOPE FROM COLIN arrived by courier and was waiting on her desk Monday afternoon when she returned from lunch. Resolutely pushing aside all the thoughts of Jake and the file in his desk, which, up to now, had been consuming her, Vanessa turned to the envelope gratefully, knowing the contents would absorb her.

The fabric sketch was in watercolor: a pale soft green with a textured-weave pattern of swirls. After a moment she realized that the swirls read "number twenty-four" over and over. "It will look a bit like watered silk," read the note in Colin's handwriting that was attached to the sketch. "The pattern comes out when it catches the light—otherwise it looks absolutely plain. Other colors, of course, but green should be your trademark."

That was an interesting idea. Vanessa laid down the board and picked up the one beneath, flicking back the protective onionskin to examine Colin's design for a logo.

He offered several. A green cat lying on its back, playing with a ball that was inscribed with the number 24; a house with a lighted window and 24 on the door; "number twenty-four" written in words, both in a straight line and in a horseshoe; and several others; always in green, picked out with white and red.

She liked them all, for different reasons. The

horseshoe shape would go on the back pocket of casual pants, and for skirts and blouses...not in the traditional breast-pocket position, perhaps, but... on the cuff? Yes, perhaps, on the left sleeve cuff—the cat, the house? She had liked the house best at first, but somehow the horseshoe began to look better and better....

Did she want a green horseshoe for a trademark? Did she want a trademark emblem at all? A horseshoe was a western, a country symbol, and most of her clients would be city-bred women.... Suddenly she had a vision of a black silky cocktail dress with long full sleeves and delicate cuffs, and on the left cuff, a small, diamanté horseshoe. Her heart beat a little more quickly, and she knew she was onto something. The horseshoe would not always have to say "number twenty-four," of course. Sometimes it could be stitchwork, sometimes an appliqué... sometimes you'd have to look hard to see it, sometimes there'd be a row of them down the sleeves—down the left sleeve....

And in the fabric. Colin should redesign the fabric pattern with horseshoes.

Abruptly Vanessa picked up the intercom and buzzed Robert's office.

"Are you busy?" she asked. "There's something I'd like you to see."

"Be right there," said Robert's voice, and within thirty seconds he was walking through her door.

"Is this going to cost me?" he asked cheerfully, and she smiled. She and Robert had a lot of arguments over the running of the business, but they never descended to the level of the arguments she had had with Tom Marx, and neither she nor Robert carried a grudge, regardless of who won.

"Yes," Vanessa said now, "but it's worth it."

"It always is," Robert sighed resignedly.

She showed him the sketches and began to outline what she had in mind. As she talked she became more and more enthused, and picking up one of the sketchbooks that was always handy she quickly sketched out a few of her ideas for him.

"Once we have the fabric design I want, we can do it in a hundred different ways—in contrasting colors for sportswear, in gold thread for dressy blouses, canvas tote bags later on, some just stylized horseshoes, some reading 'number twenty-four'—"

Robert interrupted. "Vanessa, this is a pretty expensive idea."

"Robert, we can start small. I could use the fabric for only shorts, for example, and put the logo on them; and if we can get those T-shirts with the logo on the sleeve...we can go small or big with it depending on what the reaction is. I want the logo. The logo isn't the expensive part; it's the fabric that's expensive, and we can try that out slowly."

"The logo may not be expensive, Vanessa, but it's one more step in the production process to get it on the garment, and that is going to cost. You've got to make up your mind what kind of operation you've got here and what kind of prices you're going to charge."

The argument was familiar to both of them. It waged good-naturedly but seriously for half an hour and then finished without a decision having been made.

Robert promised to have a look at the figures, and Vanessa promised to hold off asking Colin for a modification of his fabric design for a while.

As a distraction from what was most pressing on her mind, Colin's envelope had been everything she could have wished, Vanessa thought. She was flushed and excited and filled with ideas for the summer line now.

The moment she thought that, of course, all her worries roared back like a flash flood, and she found herself saying suddenly, "Robert, why is there a clause in the lease allowing Concorp to terminate the lease if we're picketed by strikers?"

Robert leaned back. "That was Jake's idea, and I must say I thought it a good one. What it means, in practical terms, is that if we *are* struck, we've got one extra bargaining tool against the union."

"We'll be forced out of business if they don't settle quickly?" She made it a question.

"Something like that. It could work."

"It could backfire, too. Especially if Jake were bought out or something," Vanessa suggested gently.

Robert blinked. "True," he said. "But it's a five-year lease, and that's not likely to happen in the next five years. If it hasn't proved to be of any value, get it taken out when you renew."

The switch from "we" to "you" reminded her that Robert wasn't going to be at Number 24 over the long haul, and she felt a tiny pang. She enjoyed working with Robert: she understood Robert and he understood her.

That his understanding didn't extend to Jake and his motives in this business wasn't really surprising: in his dealings with her it seemed that Jake was acting entirely out of character.

THAT EVENING, ODDLY, she suffered reaction for the first time. Vanessa walked home from the bus stop under the bright green umbrella she had learned to carry with her every day, possessed of the calm confidence she was used to. Her thoughts were on her determination to win every battle with Jake Conrad, to beat him at his own game. She felt no hint of any approach of melancholy.

But inexplicably during that short walk her resolve began to slip away from her, as though the wind were pulling off a protective cloak or the rain dissolving the marrow of her bones. By the time she had mounted the suddenly endless stairs and gained the comfort of her home, Vanessa felt sodden, sick, empty—and helpless. What was the use? Why bother to try to fight, to care about anything? Jake had the upper hand. She was a fool if she thought anything else.

Everything that she had not allowed herself to feel after the numbing blows of the past days swamped her now. Vanessa sank down on the couch more hurt and discouraged than she had ever felt in all her life.

She had never before, not once, been able to understand the tragic despair that drove people to suicide. Even in her lowest moments, even when life was at its rottenest, something inside her had been unquenchable, had made her think, *but life isn't real-*

ly like this; life is good, it's just my *life that's bad for the moment, and my life will get better.*

Always before, there had been hope, and she understood now with an absolute clarity that it was hope that gave one courage to face life's horrors. If you looked around the globe, life itself was *not* always good. For some people—for lots of people—it must seem more of a burden than a gift.

It was hope that made life seem good even through the bad patches. Hope that tomorrow would be better.

But tomorrow would never be better for Vanessa. Not anymore. Not. . .not in a world where Jake did not love her.

"It's hate, isn't it? You hate me," she heard herself saying; and Jake's answer, "That's what it is." And then suddenly her head and her ears were full of every ugly, brutal, hating thing Jake had said to her, a cacophony of torment. "You really are an accomplished hypocrite," "I am already tired of you," "You owe me and you're going to pay," "I pledged Marigold—" oh, God, how that one ripped, though she had scarcely heard it at the time "—I want to take it away from you, piece by piece," "You shouldn't have come back, Vanessa," "It's hate, isn't it? That's what it is. . .that's what it is. . .that's what it is. . . ."

She screamed aloud in protest, plugging her ears to make the voices stop; and abruptly, as though a television set had been shut off, there was a deafening silence all around her. In the gray gloom of her sitting room, as the soft rain, falling harder now, was whipped against the windows, Vanessa let the tears come.

She was appalled at herself. She was a cheerful, intelligent, hard-working person. She couldn't believe that the lack of one person's love—that one man's hatred could take all the joy out of life, could rob her of her reason for living. It simply wasn't possible. But it *felt* possible, and her tears did not stop.

Eventually she knew that this was more than just the pain of a few days or weeks: these were the tears of ten long years, and the hope that was dying now was the hope that had sustained her during all that time.

She had lied to herself. She had never forgotten Jace. She hadn't wanted him to be happily married and proud of her success in a brotherly way, the way she had let herself believe.

My God, he was right, she was a hypocrite! If he had let her, she would have ripped Jace Conrad away from anyone or anything that held him.

Vanessa shuddered, looking into the blackest parts of her heart for the first time in her life. She would not have been sweet and understanding with whatever spineless creature she had found clinging to Jace. She would have destroyed the world if it meant she could have him, and smiled at him in its smoking ruins.

CHAPTER FIFTEEN

On a Friday evening late in September Vanessa made sure her makeup and clothes were perfect, brushed her shining just-washed russet hair out over her shoulders and left Number 24 early. By four-fifteen she was ensconced in the lobby of Jake's hotel in a comfortable stuffed chair that had a good view of the front door and, through the large windows, of the wide driveway.

Vanessa held an open copy of the national edition of *The Globe and Mail*, but she didn't even pretend to read it. She simply sat there, watching for Jake Conrad.

Her watch said five past six when she saw him arrive. He came through the door, around to the little nook where she was sitting and right up to her chair without any break in his stride, as though he had known she was there. Vanessa was so surprised she hardly had time to blink.

A curl of dark hair was falling forward over his brow, and his eyes looked distant, black and hooded as he stood over her.

"What do you want?" he demanded in a brusque emotionless voice.

She had been depending on taking him by surprise—following him to his suite and pushing her way through the door before he knew what was happening. Now he would probably throw her out.

"How did you *see* me?" she demanded, unaccountably assailed by a desire to hit him.

"Don't be a fool," he said, as if everybody knew he had second sight. "Answer my question."

Vanessa stood up. In her high heels her eyes were not so far below his, and she suddenly remembered that ten years ago she had been wearing the then-fashionable platform shoes, which had made her almost as tall as Jace. That was why Jake had seemed taller than the Jace she remembered. She wondered how much that small detail had thrown her off the scent, because she ought to have known. She was a fool not to have known. If nothing else, she ought to have known him by the urgency deep inside herself, as though there was a line attached to the deepest part of her being and he was always pulling on it.

"I want to talk to you," she said, her voice hoarse, almost inaudible with the tension of her frightened need.

He turned without a word, was halfway across the lobby to the elevators before she knew it. Her heels clicking on the marble flooring with an urgency that made heads turn, Vanessa ran after him. He did not speak to her, did not look at her again as they waited by the elevators, as they took the long journey upward together.

Inside his penthouse suite, she sank into one of the chairs by the window, her body trembling.

"Drink?" Jake asked brusquely, and she could use some Dutch courage right now.

"Brandy, please, Jake," she said softly; and he silently reached and poured.

"Please sit down," she said nervously to his back a few moments later as he handed her a glass and went and stood looking out the window. "You make me nervous like that."

"If you have something to say, say it," he said tiredly, not moving even to look at her.

"Jake." She swallowed some of the brandy, suddenly frightened that she would cry. "Please, can I tell you why I married Larry?"

His body became, if possible, more still. "You've already told me, I believe," he said in an expressionless voice.

"No, that...that wasn't the real reason. I was lying, you must have known I was lying."

"Must I?"

She began quickly before he could say no, "Jake, I don't know if I ever told you about the Standishes. They—my father went to work for them when I was ten. They were always good to us. Mrs. Standish was—was like a mother to me. Mommy died when I was only three and—she helped me, growing up. She didn't have any daughters, and she told me all the things I always imagined that a mother does tell a daughter....

"When Daddy died I was only sixteen, and then they really adopted me, right into the family. And Larry was the first boy I dated and everybody was so happy and thought it was so right."

There were tears trickling down her cheeks, but she ignored them, trying to keep the sound of them out of her voice. "I spent Christmases with them; after you left on Christmas Eve that's where I went, that's where I always went for Christmas. And that night when the men were all in the next room playing cards or some game or something...Daniella—Mrs. Standish—told me that...that Larry had cancer of the spinal column and the doctors had said he could only live for six to eight months."

Jake did not move, but Vanessa had almost forgotten his presence. Her eyes were not seeing the room in front of her. "I looked through the French doors at all the Standish men around a table, laughing and squabbling like children, and Larry's eyes were so bright and full of life I just couldn't believe it. He didn't know, Daniella said. The doctor was a family friend. Everybody but Larry knew....

"She told me she knew about you. Told me they'd all noticed, except Larry; they'd guessed I was in love with someone else. And she asked me about you and I told her—told her you...you wanted me to go at Easter....

"She said Larry would be dead by the summer, that if we could just wait a couple of months, you and I, I could...I could marry Larry and make the last months of his life happy, that he'd told her he was going to propose to me over Christmas, that he loved me very much. And if I turned him down it would destroy him, and it was only for a few months, and if you loved me you'd understand."

Vanessa closed her eyes, remembering that tortured terrible moment, remembering those soft pleading eyes, asking for her whole happiness and making it seem such a little thing to ask....

"Larry asked me to marry him at midnight. I was so confused I couldn't think, I felt...I'd wanted to speak to you, ask you about it.... I was going to try to phone you the next day; she didn't tell me he would ask me that night...and I had to say yes or no.... Afterward I wanted to change my mind. Lou—Larry's brother—got mad at his mother, told her she didn't have the right, and then suddenly I was siding against Lou, I was saying I did love Larry, and it was true, I was fond of Larry, in a warm way, like a boy. I suppose I'd have been happy with that, too, if you hadn't taught me...taught me the difference...." She broke off, because that made the tears stronger so they threatened to choke her.

"They announced the engagement at a big New Year's Eve party. Everyone was there, and everyone was so happy for us, said it was so right. And Larry was...so happy and laughing. He'd pleased everyone at once, even himself. He always wanted to please.

"That was the night I wrote you, when I knew it was too late to ask you anymore. Mrs. Standish surprised us by saying the wedding would be in two weeks, and I knew I couldn't do it myself, stop all those preparations, kill everyone's happiness, and it was only for six months and I could make him happy before he died."

"But he didn't die."

He still had his back to her, unmoving, and his

voice sounded hoarse and strained, breaking into the flow of her memory.

"No, he didn't die." Vanessa took a deep breath, feeling as though it was the first oxygen she'd had since she began this story. "He...he didn't have cancer of the spinal column after all. He had a disease called neurofibromatosis. It's a different kind of disease, it causes a slow breakdown.... We didn't find out about it till two years later, and that's when Larry learned his mother had had the cancer diagnosis two years before but that we'd all kept it from him.

"That's when he understood why I had refused to leave college, had insisted on working after we were married. And why I refused to have a baby. He wanted children so badly, but I—I'd kept saying no.

"He knew then why I'd married him. He knew I'd known, that I'd done it out of pity." Vanessa bowed her head and felt the tears come rushing down her cheeks. "He...he looked at me as if he hated me. He said if I'd left him alone he might have found a woman who really loved him, who'd have wanted his baby even though he was going to die—*because* he was going to die.

"I offered to have his baby then. There was no telling then how long he would live, how long it would be before he became physically disabled. He could have had a child then and watched it grow...but he refused to let me. He...he made sure I couldn't. He said I'd already given up too much for him. After that he never asked me to quit work. He knew why I wouldn't want to live on Standish money afterward, why I had to have a career. He was very understanding after that. He never complained when...it got bad.

"But his soul was gone. He was just nothing. He hated his mother, and if he didn't hate me, he...he despised himself for loving me. I knew he wanted to make me leave him, but he couldn't make himself do it. He needed me, you see. And that...that destroyed him. He despised himself.

"At the end he needed me more than ever. He forgot what he knew about why I'd married him. He'd never known about you, you see. He never knew what I'd given up. If he'd known he *would* have made me leave him, but I never told him. I knew it was too late for you and me; I'd known that when you didn't answer my letter."

She was crying openly now, her head bowed, her hair hiding her face. But Jake wasn't looking at her. He was still there, staring out the window at the mountains. Vanessa swallowed and breathed deeply to calm herself.

She said, "I just wanted you to know," and got up and walked to the door and slipped quietly from the room. Imprinted on her mind was the sight of the tall still figure by the window, unrelenting, unforgiving, and she thought she would carry that image to her grave.

THERE WAS A LETTER from Lou Standish on the mat when she got home, a friendly, brotherly letter asking how she was and if she needed any help, legal or otherwise. Vanessa felt a pang of guilt, realizing that she hadn't once written the Standish family since leaving New York.

But now her heart rebelled against the instinctive feeling of guilt, and what she felt was, *they've had me for ten years, but now I belong to me.* She missed her other close friends in New York, but oddly, she never consciously missed the Standishes. Perhaps, when she put her life right—*if* she put her life right—it might be safe for her to speak to Daniella Standish again.

She put the letter away. In any case, she couldn't answer it this weekend. She would be too busy this weekend.

She would be busy waiting for Jake to call, or to come. When he had absorbed what she had told him, he would have to begin to forgive. And if he could forgive her, then he must stop hating her.

Then, perhaps, she could start again with him. She had no real competition: the only women she had ever seen him with or heard him mention were Marigold and Louisa Hayward, and they were no competition. Louisa was the sort of woman a man kept around because there would be no danger of becoming involved with her in any way other than sexually, and judging by what Jake had said about diamond bracelets, Marigold was the same.

Her worst enemy was her own past. It might take him a while to absorb what she had told him, till he could see her again clearly, without all those bitter memories clouding his vision. But he had to do it, he had to.

Somewhere inside her Vanessa knew that if there

was going to be any hope for her, Jake would, in some way, come to her this weekend. Even if only to ask her a question or to rail at her for her submissive stupidity.

She must be here when he reached for her, because Jake Conrad wasn't the sort of man to reach a second time.

There was plenty to keep her busy inside for a weekend. Vanessa pottered and cleaned and polished, and painted the bathroom a lighter shade than the landlord had put on the walls, because dark rooms depressed her.

Her confident anticipation peaked late Saturday afternoon and began a slow decline. By Sunday afternoon she had lost hope.

He was not going to come to her.

MONDAY MORNING SHE WAS LATE leaving the house for work, and the mail had arrived by the time she got downstairs.

There was an official-looking letter from a development company: her former landlord had sold the property and her rent was now payable to the new owners. From October first, would she please make her checks payable to Conrad Property Development Limited and send them to the above address?

Blackness pressed in on Vanessa for a moment and she clutched the wall for support: Conrad Property Development was a name she had seen many times on Concorp letterhead. It was part of Conrad Corporation.

Jake had not forgiven her, hadn't come to terms

with what she had told him. He was still out for revenge, and she felt the net of his power drawing tighter and tighter around her.

AT FIVE PAST ONE on an October afternoon Vanessa walked off the elevator at the floor that held the Concorp executive offices, said an unremarkable hello to one or two people and moved straight to Jean's unoccupied post outside Jake's office.

Glancing around with a little flutter of fear, she moved with outward assurance to tap on Jake's office door. If he were inside she would say she was looking for Jean; but there was no one inside. Vanessa slipped silently in and shut the door, then glanced around the room to be sure there was no one lurking in the corners. Then she moved to the desk, pulled open the right-hand lower drawer she was sure was the one from which she had seen him take that file.

There was a number of file folders, all neatly inside green hanging files; her eye was drawn immediately to the only one with a blank label. Her heart beating wildly, Vanessa pulled out the buff folder and dropped it on the desk.

The first item was the photostat of the management contract. She shut the drawer with a bang, pushed the file into her big leather design portfolio and crossed to the door in a space of seconds. In another few seconds she was in the elevator; minutes later she was in the street. She took a deep shuddering breath and hugged the portfolio case tightly under her arm.

Every way she turned, she was fighting for her life.

VANESSA PULLED THE sitting-room draperies against the twilight and closed the door. She felt threatened and insecure, like a criminal who doesn't know whether or not the police are chasing him.

Her soft green leather portfolio case lay beside her on the couch, and Vanessa was as frightened of it as if it did contain the snake of her dream.

She suddenly desperately wanted a cup of coffee, but she pushed the need impatiently aside, recognizing it as her mind's delaying tactic. She didn't want to know what it was that Jake had thought so important; she would have liked nothing better than to bury her head and forget it.

But now it was more than business ruin that threatened her: if Jake drove Number 24 into bankruptcy she would be forced to leave the country, for all the reasons he had mentioned.

Leaving the country meant not getting another chance with Jake. Her entire happiness now hinged on whether she could make Number 24 a success. She had only one tiny slim chance with Jake now: that time would heal.

She could buy time with Number 24. Vanessa zipped open the portfolio and reached through sheaves of sketches of the summer line down to the thick file deep inside. Please, God, let it be something she could fight....

He had photostatic copies not only of her management contract but also of the debenture agreement and the lease of the premises at Number 24. Vanessa turned them all over. There was nothing to be gained from reading them again, though she might take them to David and see if he could find some other danger she wasn't aware of or some loophole that would save her....

Next came the letter that had been written by Conrad Corporation to the Canadian consulate in New York, asking that she be granted an immediate temporary visa in Canada. Almost unconsciously she noted the date: June twenty-fifth. She had been granted her six-month temporary visa on June twenty-ninth. Within about two months she would have to fly down to Seattle to apply for a permanent one.

Vanessa bit her lip. Time was so short. She did not believe that Jake meant to let her go on and build Number 24 into a real success before he destroyed her. He had the power to do it at anytime. He hated her. Why would he wait?

I'll write my own letter from Number 24, she resolved now. *Or I'll get Robert to write it. And I'll go down to Seattle this month, before Jake expects me to go....*

A copy of the letter she had received on Monday, informing her that the house she lived in and loved so much now belonged to Jake...there was nothing new in all this. Had the dream been wrong? She laughed a little, feeling foolish. Since when had her dreams been oracles?

A list of names and addresses, many of them looking Chinese, all in Vancouver. Vanessa wrinkled her forehead in perplexity. None of the names meant a thing to her. She couldn't recall ever having heard them before. She turned the page. On the next sheet were only two names and addresses: Ronnie Pardeh and Mrs. V. Spears, both in Vancouver.

These names seemed familiar, but where. . . ? Vanessa's eyes flew open in startled surprise. Of course! Ronnie and Mrs. Spears were the subcontractors who did outside work for Number 24! Then what were the other names? The home sewers they used?

What on earth was this?

Vanessa's heart was beating now in loud urgent thumps as she turned to the next sheet of paper. It was covered with typing. At the top of the page a line of capitals read, "TRANSCRIPT OF A CONVERSATION WITH MRS. WAN CHU. . . ."

A hand seemed to close on her throat, cutting off breath. Vanessa closed her eyes for a moment, not wanting to read. But she had to read, and she forced her eyes open and onto the page: "I make lining for inside skirt. . .they bring me pieces all cut out, I sew here, and here, then I turn this like this. . .I start work eight o'clock, I work to late, very late at night, sometimes ten-twelve hour a day. . .that's right, that's right, about forty cent an hour. . .I can't get other work. I got children at home, I don't speak good enough English. . .I don't tell anybody I work like this, they find out they take away welfare money. . . ."

There were four statements in all, and they all said almost the same thing. One woman had her three children help her with the pinning and folding and counting. One still had not paid for the sewing machine she had bought on time in order to get the work, and the money she earned wasn't enough to cover the monthly payments on the machine. All the women were supplementing either welfare money or income from part-time work that wasn't sufficient to live on.

Doggedly Vanessa read the statements through and turned the last page. Underneath were several photostated pages that seemed to be an excerpt from the federal statute governing minimum wage in Canada.

After that there was only one more page, and it was almost blank. First there was a person's name, and then, "c/o the fifth estate," with a post-office-box number in Toronto.

The person's name meant nothing to her, although after the impact of what she had just read Vanessa felt wooden, as though her brain were hardly functioning. And what was the fifth estate? The fourth estate, she knew, was journalism, but she always forgot what the first three were—law and the clergy and the landed gentry, perhaps? Or was politics in there somewhere?

But she had never heard of a fifth estate. Vanessa looked at the printed letters on the page. They were beginning to swim before her eyes. Maybe it was a secret society, like the Freemasons or the Rosicrucians. Maybe they were putting vengeful curses on her every night in a secret ritual, at the behest of brother Jake Conrad.

Or maybe this was a secret pipeline to the government for anonymous tip-offs about lawbreakers. She could imagine thousands of dirty little white envelopes, and inside each the scrawled name of someone who wasn't paying his or her fair share of income tax. . . and on one of them her own name, but her name wouldn't be scrawled, it would be written in Jake Conrad's sharp clear handwriting, and underneath, "Violating federal wage statutes."

She began to see how love could turn to hatred. That primal force in her that would have destroyed the world for Jake Conrad might easily turn its dark necessity toward rage. She began to see how Jake had ended up hating her. . . by how easily she might end up hating him.

She had to think. She had to think what to do. Leaving the file on the sofa, Vanessa got up and went to the kitchen. It was dark now; she had been reading by the light of one small lamp, and she turned the lights on as she went.

In the kitchen she filled the electric kettle and plugged it in. She was still not used to the appliance; she marveled every time she used it. The first one she had seen had been Maria's, the day she moved into this apartment. Maria's emergency moving supplies had included mugs, coffee and an electric kettle.

"Never seen one before?" Maria had repeated. "What do you boil water in, then?"

"In a kettle on the stove top," Vanessa had replied, and after she had finally convinced Maria that most Americans did the same, Maria had laughed incredulously. "You mean to tell me that there is a great untapped market of 100 million American households, none of which has an electric kettle? My gosh, someone should tell Jake. He'd make a fortune!"

Vanessa hadn't told Jake; she'd supposed he

knew. Anyway, somebody, somewhere, surely, had already tried to sell electric kettles in the United States on a large scale.

Or maybe that was the difference between millionaires and ordinary people: perhaps millionaires tried the ideas that ordinary people assumed had already been tried.

Vanessa unplugged the kettle and made coffee, adding larger amounts of sugar and milk than usual, as a form of comfort. Then she went to the bedroom and undressed, slipping on her black robe. She couldn't get her brain to function. She kept thinking that she had to think, but her mind was like a mule: no matter how she whipped it, it couldn't be forced toward that dark abyss.

Child labor. Slave labor. She was exploiting the weakest of society in order to make money, like any nineteenth-century capitalist. "Well, that's three quarts of milk I wouldn't be able to give my kids otherwise, isn't it?" one of the women had said, in response to the interviewer's comment that the young single mother of two worked all day for enough money to buy three quarts of milk. She wondered if the interviewer had been Jake.

Vanessa's mind balked again, and numbly she carried her cup back into the sitting room and sat down on the sofa.

She stared at the papers. She was a criminal, wasn't she? Was she? Morally she was a criminal, but legally? God, what were the penalties for being in contravention of the minimum-wage laws? Was it a criminal or a civil offense? A slow prickling fear began to creep over her. What had Jake said? "The laws are there. . . half the population could be in prison if they were enforced."

He would want that, wouldn't he, she thought grimly. That would be the ultimate revenge: have her locked up in prison. Yes, that would be the kind of thing Jake would think of. That would be why he called this "the best of all." She would be condemned to hell by her own actions. She would not even be able to blame him. That would make the revenge perfect.

My God, she thought, *prison.* Suppose it really came to that? How could she bear that? How did anyone bear it? Her heart began to thump frighteningly. She squeezed her eyes shut.

Or maybe they would simply deport her as an undesirable. Then, if Canada's laws were anything like the States', she would never be allowed back into the country. That would suit Jake just as well, she supposed: either way he wouldn't be seeing her again unless he came to her. . . .

He had told her he hated her, but somehow she hadn't believed him. She had believed him angry, believed she had hurt him unbearably, believed he had long ago stopped loving her. But even though she had thought she was accepting that he hated her, even though intellectually she had accepted it, emotionally she had refused to believe it, had rejected the reality of it.

Now she had to believe it. Vanessa looked down at the proof of his hatred, the trap so delicately baited, so carefully laid, the evidence so painstakingly gathered, lethal.

A kind of blackness was filling her, a hurting horrid blackness that she couldn't remember ever feeling before. Jake hated her. She couldn't evade the realization any longer. He hated her, wanted to hurt her, wanted her to suffer the worst human-devised torment possible in the so-called civilized western world. He wanted her to be branded a criminal, to go to prison. He wanted her to be beaten and spat on and maltreated and shackled whenever a tormentor felt the whim. He wanted her life to be permanently blighted, wanted her scarred. *Believe it,* she told herself, forcing herself to accept it. *He wants this.*

Lou Standish had told her about prisons once, when she had asked him why he had abandoned criminal law and moved into corporate. He had told her of the hopeless waste of humanity, the irreversible personality damage that such degradation caused. He had discovered that he could do nothing to change it, and he was, he had said, too much of a coward to face that information day after day.

After that Vanessa had never again hoped anyone would go to prison. She knew it was a nearly insoluble problem. She knew that there were some people who couldn't be left free in society, but she could not be vengeful enough to wish to subject a human being to that.

But Jake Conrad was wishing that on her. He had not engineered it—she had given him the opportunity on a plate—but he was prepared to make use of it.

Every time she thought of it, it was as though a bludgeon fell on her heart. Nothing had ever hurt her like this, not the death of her mother or her father, not the pain of her wedding day, nor anything in the long years since. Not even the moment when she had heard that Jace was dead.

There was a sudden knock at the door at the bottom of the stairs, and Vanessa made a quick instinctive move toward the incriminating papers beside her, her heart beating in her mouth. Then she laughed and forced herself to relax. It could only be the downstairs tenant, since anyone else—even the police—would have had to ring the outside doorbell.

She didn't know her neighbor downstairs very well, except to know that he had two beautiful pedigreed cats named Barney and Jezebel and that he was a private person and did something bookish for a living. She had spoken to him briefly once, on a day when Barney had come up for a visit and stayed the whole day.

Vanessa jumped up, pulling her black terry robe more snugly around her. She glanced around the room, wondering if Barney had come up without her noticing, then padded barefoot down the stairs.

The door opened rather awkwardly outward, and Vanessa pushed it slowly, in case she caught her visitor behind it.

But she needn't have worried: her visitor knew enough to stand to one side, and his dark overpowering shape filled the opening immediately.

Jake.

CHAPTER SIXTEEN

VANESSA TRIED TO PULL the door shut, but Jake slipped his shoulder inside with a violent move that made the handle fly out of her grasp. The door hit the wall with a loud bang, and Jake started up the steps toward her.

She flew at him like a wild animal whose lair is invaded, feeling as though she must protect her home from him at all costs. The force and unexpectedness of her attack drove him across the small foyer and up against the entrance door, but she was hampered by the full sleeves and long skirt of her robe, and he was stronger.

They fought, extraordinarily, in a grunting silence, neither of them saying a word until, having forced her back up the stairs, he held her heaving body at the top.

"Get out of my house!" she wailed, her voice a long high animal cry interrupted by a sobbing gasp for the air she needed. "Get out."

"No," he said flatly, his breathing just as erratic, and then he loosened his clasp to let her go. Without a second's hesitation she raised both arms and thudded them against his chest to push him downstairs. Jake caught the railing to regain his balance, then lurched forward, grabbing her angrily and forcing her around the gallery and into the sitting room, where a push sent her headlong onto the sofa.

It was insane, the rage they ignited in each other. Vanessa glared up at him through the tangle of hair spilling over her face, aware but uncaring that her robe had pulled open over her breasts and that her long legs were uncovered. She clawed her hair savagely off her face, her burning stare not leaving his. "I'd like to kill you!" she rasped.

"I'd like to kill you, too," said Jake, breathing with exertion and glaring down at her. "Little hellcat."

There was tension humming in the air between them, as though that violent confrontation had turned on a distant power source that now gripped them both in its heavy field. With trembling, clumsy fingers Vanessa pulled the black robe over her breasts and legs, helplessly watching his eyes watching her every move.

"What do you want?" she demanded angrily, but her tongue felt thick in her mouth.

Jake's glance broke away from hers to take in the papers from the file she had stolen from his desk. She had landed on the sofa among them, and they lay littered all around her now, on the sofa and floor. "You're a thief, too," he observed flatly, cruelly, but she saw that he had to swallow before he spoke.

"And who are you?" she demanded contemptuously. "The angel Gabriel? Nobody makes a million dollars these days without stepping on a few toes, do they?" A lock of hair fell over her eye and with an impatient jerk of her head she tossed it back. "Is this how you deal with your business rivals? Get them thrown into prison for doing the same kind of thing you do yourself?" She felt a paper under her hand on the sofa, and slowly closed her fist on it. "Is this what you came for?" she demanded, holding the wrinkled page up to him. "This nasty, spying little bunch of documents that's going to cause my final downfall? Take it!" She threw it violently toward him, but the paper floated ineffectually down to the floor. Vanessa jumped up, grabbing other papers as she did so.

"You hate me!" she exclaimed, ripping, crumpling, tearing the papers between her hands and throwing them wildly at his dark angular face. "I didn't believe it before, but I believe it now! I know it now! I've seen this, and this, and this—" she threw the torn pages at him "—and nobody could do what you're going to do unless they were filled with hate!

"Well, all right, here's your revenge! Take it! Make me a criminal, get me sent to prison! No matter what happens to me there, I still couldn't become a worse animal than you are right now, Jake! Because I loved you—in spite of everything, I *loved* you—right up to this moment! And you've let life poison you—you're full of hate, and that makes you the lowest form of life there is! I look at you now and I can't imagine how I ever loved you."

She stood straight, the shredded papers between them on the floor. Jake was unmoving, watching her. "You're contemptible. You haven't the faintest idea about life or love. And when I think I let you touch me, let you make love to me, *wanted* you to—" she shuddered "—it makes me cringe. It makes me feel as though I'd let spiders and snakes crawl over my body and—"

He reached out and jerked her against him, the look on his face almost a snarl. "That's enough," he said. His hand touched her throat. "Shut up."

The electric humming in the air was suddenly so strongly powerful it deafened her. Vanessa felt panic hit her in a giant slapping wave that nearly carried her way. "I won't shut up!" she shrilled. "Let me go!"

The look in his dark eyes changed as he stared at her, and his arm around her back tightened its hold. "My God, Vanessa," he whispered, and bent and kissed her.

She wanted to scream. She felt as though a trap had suddenly closed around her, the trap of his arms and his mouth, making it impossible for her to move.

She had to force herself into action, lifting her arms to fight him, jerking her face away from the hungry pressure of his mouth. She dragged in a ragged gasp of air, pressing away from him. "Let go of me!" she cried, and with her free hand she slapped his face.

Jake let her go so suddenly that she fell backward to the floor. She lay there in momentary shock, then was suddenly seething, as angry as she had ever been in her life. Jake's eyes were black as he stared down at her, and he hadn't moved even to touch a hand to his flushed cheek. He stood like a street fighter, his arms loose at his sides, waiting.

"Get up," he commanded. His lips hardly moved, but a pulse was beating in his throat, and suddenly Vanessa's stomach was a swirl of confusion. Slowly she got to her feet a short distance away from him, facing him and watching his eyes take in the flash of her flesh in the black robe's opening.

"You—" she began when she was on her feet, but he reached out roughly and pulled her to him with such unexpected violence that it took her breath away. His kiss was angry, harsh, and his strong hands gripped her forcefully as his tongue thrust deeper into the softness of her mouth.

She went up in flame all at once, like an explosion; the hot roar of her own burning deafened her. She forgot everything then, was aware only of the most immediate messages of her body and brain: there was a hand on her breast; it was Jake's hand.

Under the fierce pressure of his lips she moaned, half in pain, half in ecstasy, but his angry intensity only burned higher so that his touch seared her.

He broke off the kiss when he was ready and stared into her eyes as one hand moved to stroke the thick russet tumble of her hair. The intensity of that touch, too, was nearly painful, and the passionate response of her own body to it terrified her.

"Stop," she whispered.

Every muscle in his face was pulled taut; he looked like a granite carving of himself. His dark eyes devoured her. As though she had not spoken he pushed her away from him.

"Go into the bedroom," he said in flat command. "Take off your robe."

She closed her eyes, silently fighting against the effect that his voice had on her, fighting not to obey. He understood that. With a brief crooked smile he pulled her back to him then and held her tight while one dark hand found her breast. He rasped the nipple gently with his thumb, his eyes harshly, cruelly watching her face.

Electricity flowed from his fingers through her breast and arm, down across her stomach and along her legs, so that she could hardly stand. She moaned and bit her lip and opened her eyes to see him staring into her face as though he needed the sight of her roused desire to stay alive.

The look on his face was like a blow to the stomach, and she heard the little grunting cry she made with distant surprise.

"Jake," she pleaded, but there was no shaking his angry control.

"Go into the bedroom," he commanded again.

She felt stunned, not under her own control. She wanted to yield to him, but his cold control frightened her. He let her go and stood rigid and unmoved, waiting. In the jumble of emotion and passion he had stirred in her she wanted to soften his anger, to appease him. And it somehow seemed to her as though he would not touch her again unless she obeyed him—and she needed him to touch her....

Vanessa licked her lips, opened her mouth to speak, but the look in his eyes stopped her. She was powerless. She could not exert her own will. She had no will. Her body's dictates controlled her now, and her body wanted Jake.

Vanessa stepped back one and then two paces and then, as though under compulsion, turned and walked through the door to the bedroom.

He followed her. The sound of each step behind her rippled along her spine as though the vibration were his mouth. At the foot of the bed she turned and stopped. Jake stopped, too, and blinked once, slowly, his heavy lids briefly hiding his dark eyes from her.

"Take off your robe," he said again, and obediently she did so, letting the rough cloth of the robe slither off her shoulders and down her curving body to her feet.

She saw a flicker of fire behind his eyes then, and not taking his eyes from her he shrugged off the soft tweed jacket he was wearing and his hands dropped to his waist.

"Lie down," he said, and then he fell on her, and took her; and every touch of his body and his clothing seared her skin, and every flicker of his anger made her gasp.

"Don't ever hit me again," he said, his voice rasping in his throat, while she clenched her teeth to keep back the moan that was ripping its way through her throat. "I don't like it when women hit me. Do you hear?" He waited, wanting an answer. "Do you hear?"

"Yes, *yes*!" she gasped wildly, not knowing how she formed the word.

"Good," he said with a crooked smile. "Now—" he bent his head and she felt the heat of his mouth against her throat and cried out the response of her body "—tell me again that you don't like it," he said, his mouth moving down to the white rise of her breast. "Tell me this is spiders and snakes crawling over your skin. Tell me you hate it, Vanessa." His body, his voice, his mouth were urgent against her, demanding, and she was helpless under the onslaught of pleasure that assailed her.

"Jake," she begged, and he looked into her dark eyes and knew she could not say it. Suddenly his anger swelled in him, and his black eyes narrowed and his scar pulled the muscles of his face.

"Don't ever tell me not to touch you," he said, slowly and harshly and spacing his words. His hands jerked her arms above her head and closed tightly on her wrists, and she felt the wild climb of passion begin in her body as his anger beat against her. "Don't ever tell me you don't like the touch of my body or my hands. I know what you like better than any man living or dead—don't I?"

It was drowning her, crashing her over and over like a huge wave, smashing her with sensation.

"Jake!" she cried.

"That's right," said his voice softly in her ear. "Jake. Don't you forget it. And don't you ever tell me any different."

She screamed then, as sensation billowed up in her in a sweep of bright blackness that enclosed her brain in a smothering blinding swirl. Through the swirling blackness then, she felt his hands clench convulsively on her wrists, heard his shuddering voice call her name in a moaning helplessness, and his body against hers at last was out of control.

REASON RETURNED SLOWLY. To Vanessa, her head in the hollow of his shoulder and the cloth of his shirt under her cheek, it was like waking up from a drugged sleep, a deep, deep dream.

She sat up slowly, looking down at him, and slowly, slowly remembered. She felt appalled, sick at what had happened. What had he done to her to make her submit like that, when she knew he hated her, wanted to destroy her?

Jake's hand moved against her back, stirred in her long tangled hair, and she felt rather than saw his eyes open. With a sudden shudder Vanessa pushed her way down to the end of the bed and bent to pick up her robe.

In front of the sofa the carpet was littered with torn crumpled papers, mute evidence of everything she had forgotten, everything she now remembered. Tying the belt of her robe with a little snap Vanessa moved across to the sofa and gazed helplessly around. Then she bent to pick up the buff unlabeled folder and knelt on the floor.

She picked up every scrap of paper, smoothing and straightening each one and placing it in the file folder. After a few minutes she became aware that Jake was in the doorway watching her, but she didn't hesitate in what she was doing, didn't indicate by the flicker of an eyelash that she was aware of his presence—until she had collected and meticulously smoothed every piece of paper.

Then she stood up and faced him. "There you are," she said coldly, dropping the folder onto the coffee table with a small slap. "That's what you came for—all your precious evidence that's going to put me in prison—take it. Take it and get out."

"Vanessa." His voice was a flat command, and it enraged her. She gritted her teeth.

"My fingerprints are all over it, if you want evidence that I'm a thief, too, and all over your desk drawer as well, I'm sure. A criminal breaking into an office to remove evidence of her crime: the police will like that, won't they? And you will, too," she said sneeringly. "It'll make you feel how pure and upright you are by comparison, won't it, Mr. Angel Gabriel?" She drew her lips into a tight smile. "But before you get completely carried away with your own integrity, let me remind you that you aren't so far above rape as you thought!"

Jake threw up his head. It was the first indication she had had that he could hear what she said. "I didn't rape you," he said in a gravel voice.

"What was it you called it?" she asked brightly. "The animal bludgeoning of body and spirit? Unimaginative, you said, and I have to concur. I only hope you found it as unsatisfactory as it was unimaginative."

She didn't know where the words were coming from. She had a bitch living inside her whom she had never met before. Now she laughed mirthlessly and pointed at the folder on the table beside her.

"Please take your evidence and go. If you need more revenge, send me to prison. But—" she stared coldly into his eyes, "—do—not—ever—touch—me—again," she said, giving each word equal space and emphasis.

"Damn it, Vanessa—" he began, and with a wild oath she picked up the folder and strode across the room to thrust it into his arms.

"Get out of my house!" she growled in a raw animal voice, feeling that if he did not leave, her mind would snap. Her voice rose to panic. *"Get out!"*

He swore, a steady impatient stream of curses, and left her, walking out to the hallway and down the stairs without another word or look. Vanessa waited at the top of the stairs until she heard the outside door slam. Then she ran down to the foyer to make sure he had left.

His car was at the curb. She saw the interior light come on, saw him throw the file folder into the passenger seat as he got in. Then there was blackness again, till the engine roared into life and the bright headlights reached out into the night.

Vanessa made sure both doors were locked and ran upstairs. But the apartment no longer seemed her safe haven from the world.

VANESSA HAD DISCOVERED that running her own business meant she simply couldn't work a forty-hour week like everyone else. She worked late at Number 24 during the week, almost always the last person to leave at night, and when there was extra pressure on—as now, when she was designing the summer line—she frequently worked on Saturday.

Today, striding through the streets of Vancouver in jeans, sneakers and a heavy sweater, her long hair swinging in a ponytail, her portfolio under her arm, she was glad to be going to Number 24. Work meant she would have to concentrate, and that meant there would be no room to be thinking of other things.

It was a chilly, beautiful, sunshiny day. From her home to Number 24 was a walk of about twenty-five minutes, and she had got into the habit of walking every day unless it was particularly wet. October *was* wet in Vancouver, and it felt wonderful to be walking again under clear skies.

A blue-and-white police car drove past, and Vanessa shuddered inwardly. It was an unfamiliar feeling: she had never been afraid of the police in her life. But supposing Jake had gone to them last night? Suppose there was a warrant out for her arrest?

Vanessa looked up at the clear open sky and felt her own freedom. She could go anywhere, do anything... especially in this wonderful mad city where even the most eccentric behavior and dress were greeted with an easy benign tolerance by the people at large.

Jake wanted to take this away from her. Or perhaps all he wanted was to feel that he could: to make her live with this tormenting feeling of being under threat. That she didn't know was the torture.

She unlocked the door of Number 24 with a sudden sense of the futility of what she was doing: working so hard to make a success of something that would be snatched away from her the moment she succeeded. But she couldn't have done anything else. She was committed to Number 24, as Jake had predicted. She wanted to make it successful.

She worked all morning on the summer line, incorporating appliqués in both the horseshoe emblem and a large 24 in figures with a small written "number" over the two. She had decided not to restrict herself to one single emblem: Number 24 was quite unique as a name; she could use it in any way without its losing its distinctiveness.

After several hours, for relaxation, she sat at the sewing machine and began to stitch the black velvet costume she was making for a masquerade party Robert and Maria had invited her to on Halloween.

"Come as Someone," she had been instructed, and Robert had told her that the party was an annual event and that people were usually pretty imaginative with their costumes. Vanessa had decided to go as the Cavalier poet Richard Lovelace. Using a sketch in a large costume book that had been her constant companion since her second year of college, she had designed knee breeches and a jacket in black velvet with a collar and cuffs that would require several yards of lace. She hadn't bought that yet and might go hunting through the stores for it this afternoon.

But after an hour of sewing and pinning, and without conscious decision, she suddenly found herself rooting through her big shoulder bag for David Latham's business card.

"David Latham, Q.C.," it read, and she wondered what the letters meant. He had written his home number on the back of the card; he answered on the second ring.

"Vanessa!" he exclaimed rather breathlessly, as though he were in the middle of some heavy exercise. "No tennis this morning? I was sure we'd see you at the club."

She explained about working, and he clucked his tongue and berated her gently for the waste of a perfect Saturday. Finally she said, "David, I need some legal advice, and I think I need it urgently. If you're free for lunch, would you mind eating with me?"

They decided on a restaurant named Victoria Station that had some quiet corners, David said, and Vanessa put down the phone with a sudden relief that told her how unconsciously tense she had been.

Victoria Station was named and decorated after the railway station of that name in London. Vanessa had never been to England, and she supposed the decor was more like something from 1890 than modern-day England, but she liked the atmosphere, the sense of foreignness. And, as David had promised, the restaurant had some quiet corners.

"David, have you ever heard of the fifth estate?" she asked, when they were settled in one of the corners and had ordered their meal, and he was looking expectantly at her.

David wrinkled his forehead. "You mean the TV program?"

"The TV program! I don't—is *that* what it is?"

David shrugged. "There's a program called 'the fifth estate' on CBC. Where did you hear the name?"

"I read it—written down with an address. Could that be it?"

"I don't see what else it could be. The address can always be checked out."

This was too confusing, Vanessa thought. What on earth would a TV program have to do with her?

Abruptly her eyes were wide with a sudden thought. "What kind of a show is it?" she asked, but the answer was already forming inside her own brain.

"Oh, an investigative-journalism, public-crucifixion kind of thing," David replied. "I suppose you could call it Canada's answer to '60 Minutes.' "

Vanessa blinked. "Public crucifixion," she repeated softly. "I wonder what's worse—being accused and getting your day in court or just being accused?"

"As a lawyer," David smiled, "I naturally want everyone to have their day in court. Either way, however, a little mud sticks a long time. Is someone siccing 'the fifth estate' onto you?"

"I think so," said Vanessa. "Or the police, I'm not sure which." She paused as the waiter brought their salads and then told David about the subcontractors and the home sewers. She didn't tell him about the file from Jake's desk or all the other ways in which he was threatening her livelihood. She would have to later, if she wanted his advice on the contract and the lease, but just now it was unnecessary. This was much more urgent.

When she was through, David shook his head. "All right," he said, "first things first: you aren't in contravention of the minimum-wage laws. You contract the work out, Vanessa. The subcontractors are self-employed, not your employees, and legally, what you pay them isn't a wage. Even if your subcontractor were stupid enough to hire the home sewers as his employees, which I can guarantee you he is not, they would still be *his* employees, not yours. But you can take it as read that he contracts the work out to them, and if they disclose that income on their income-tax forms—which again is highly unlikely, especially if, as you say, most are on welfare—if they do, it's as self-employed income. So you aren't doing anything illegal."

Vanessa was suddenly a lot hungrier than she had been a few minutes ago. She attacked her salad with a smile of relief.

"However," David went on after a moment, "'the fifth estate' is another matter. They deal in ethics and public morals as much as in legality. But you're pretty small potatoes, it seems to me, to make an interesting story: one little manufacturer doing the kind of thing everyone does to survive. I imagine 'the fifth estate' would want to go after someone much bigger than you in a story like that: they'd want evidence that the government or a crown corporation or a big well-known business was knowingly involved in this sort of stuff.

"Where it seems to me that you might be vulnerable—and I'm getting out of my field here—is with your union. Are your plant workers unionized?"

Vanessa nodded.

"Yeah," said David. "Well, one thing that unions don't like is nonunionized home labor. It threatens their jobs. Am I right?"

He was right, though this aspect of the affair had not struck her before. She, Robert and Ted had certainly not advertised the fact that they were subcontracting, either to the plant workers or to the union representative, who called so frequently at Number

24 that Robert complained she thought it was her home. If the union found out....

"If your union finds out about it," David said aloud in nearly perfect time with her thoughts, "you could have troubles."

"Yeah," breathed Vanessa.

"It sounds to me," said David, "as though this didn't just happen. It sounds as though you've got an enemy around stirring up trouble. Otherwise, why 'the fifth estate'? Why not merely come to you and demand changes?"

She was glad he was so quick to pick up on that; she wouldn't feel so embarrassed, perhaps, when she had to tell him the whole story of the enemy who wanted to destroy her.

"Yes," she said quietly. "I have an enemy. I'm trying to figure out what weak spot he'll attack next."

"Who is it, the competition?"

Well, not exactly. Vanessa gave a little laugh. "David, the...I don't...I'd like to discuss the rest of it with you soon, but it's not necessary right now. This was urgent. I was afraid I was going to be arrested right away. Could I call you at the office for an appointment?"

"Sure," said David. "Give me a call first thing Monday morning."

They slipped into light conversation with the arrival of the main course. David had an afternoon engagement, so after Vanessa had paid the check, he drove her down to the Granville Mall and dropped her. "Thanks for lunch," he said, pulling away. "I'll call you if you don't call me."

The sight of blue-and-white police cars no longer made her jump as Vanessa wandered lazily through the specialty shops looking for buttons and lace. The relief of knowing she couldn't be arrested at any moment lightened her spirit so much she felt she could fly. Anything else was a molehill compared to that. Union troubles, investigative journalists—she could take on the world as long as the police weren't after her.

She found a beautiful gold lace for the neck and cuffs of the costume, which even Richard Lovelace would have loved, and chose antique gold buttons to go on the jacket front and gold lacing for the knee cuffs, with the satisfaction of knowing the costume would be very striking against her russet hair.

At four o'clock she caught the bus home. Walking from the bus stop, her ponytail swinging jauntily from shoulder to shoulder, Vanessa felt full of energy and vitality. She was free. No one was going to take that from her. As Barney ran across the lawn toward her, mewing a welcome, she ran up the front steps and inside the house.

Barney raced up the stairs ahead of her, but Vanessa wasn't far behind. At the top of the stairs she flung her shoulder bag and packages onto the small hall table and spread out her arms.

"Home!" she exclaimed happily, and it was her safe haven again.

CHAPTER SEVENTEEN

"ALL RIGHT." DAVID LATHAM leaned back in his spring-mounted stuffed leather chair and patted the flat of one hand on the desk. "Some of what Jake Conrad is threatening you with is bluff, and some of it has real teeth in it."

David's office was only moderately luxurious, but he was a partner in what she had learned was one of the most prestigious legal firms in Vancouver. She had also learned, by asking Ilona, that Q.C. meant Queen's Counsel, which was a crown appointment in Canada, as in England, and meant that David had both impressive talents and contacts. Lou Standish would have been proud of her: this was no "hole-in-the-wall kid." David Latham was a real legal eagle.

"Let's deal with the simple things first," said David. "You can stop worrying about your lease. If you're given notice under the provisions of clause thirteen or fourteen, you just sit tight. If Conrad wants to evict you, he can take you to court. Any strike would be over before it got before a judge. If necessary, we can tie it up in court forever. He won't get you out against your will."

Vanessa's eyes sparkled. "Really?" she demanded. "But Jake would be bound to know that—why would he bother?"

"From what you've told me, I would say in the interests of simple harassment. He can cause you discomfort pretty effectively—but we'll just cause him a little more, make him think twice about what he's doing." He smiled. Every time David used the word "we" Vanessa felt a perceptible lightening of her spirits.

"The same thing is true of the Fairway contract. They could try to pull something of the sort Conrad outlined to you—if someone in there is stupid enough to get the company tied up in a legal battle merely as a favor to Jake Conrad, but I doubt very much if anyone is. Your contract with Fairway is cut and dried. The worst thing you have to worry about is that they might not renew the order with you when this one is filled. You know better than I do what effect that will have on Number 24."

"We can do without them," said Vanessa, thanking God she had stuck to her guns so that that statement was true.

"Fine. Now about 'the fifth estate': on thinking it over, I thought you should bear in mind the possibility that you might be included in a broader sweeping investigation, say, of the garment industry as a whole. So if you do get a call, you stonewall it. Refuse to comment—if that doesn't work, refer them to me."

"Thank you, David," she said, wanting to laugh triumphantly in Jake's face.

"In the meantime, can you stop using subcontractors?"

Vanessa shook her head. Her discussion with Robert on the subject had been their first really vituperative argument since they had started working together. "We're into it now, Vanessa," he had said. "Against my advice, let me remind you, but it's too late now. It boils down to this," he had said finally. "Do you want to survive or not?" And that had clinched the argument: they were tied into subcontracting for two seasons at least.

"All right," said David easily, dismissing it. "Now, your visa: as you've realized yourself, it's no problem. You're your own employer. The laws are there to prevent foreigners from taking jobs away from Canadians. *You* are creating fifty or sixty jobs. The government isn't going to push those fifty or sixty Canadians into the ranks of the unemployed to please Jake Conrad, believe me. Just go down and get a permanent visa at your leisure."

There was a pause then, and Vanessa took a deep breath. "What's the bad news, David?"

He told her that Jake was in a position to call the debenture at any time and that the only way she could avoid bankruptcy if he did so would be to refinance the company. Because it was a very young company with no track record, in David's opinion there would be almost no chance of her finding a bank willing to undertake the refinancing. Did she have any financial backing of her own, anyone who might lend her the money to buy up the debenture?

There was one, of course. There had always been one.

"Well, there's a possibility," she said. As long as it

was a loan, a business loan that would earn them interest like any other investment, that would be different, wouldn't it? "More than a possibility," she amended. "Almost a certainty, if I want to ask."

David said bluntly, "I advise you to ask. Having your own backing would put you out of reach of Conrad's power, Vanessa—the other things he's threatened, such as picking off your salesmen, you'll be able to ride through if you have the backing."

She said, "I've got to think about it. Is there any other alternative?"

"There's doing what you're doing now—wondering when, where and if the ax is going to fall."

She picked that up. "Where else can it fall?"

"I'm afraid this is where you start to feel the teeth. In your management contract you agreed to a restraint of trade for five years in any area where you'd be in direct competition with the company you've built. He can probably hold you to that."

Vanessa blanched. "When I signed it I thought I'd be marketing only in Vancouver. Does that mean I couldn't sell anywhere in Canada?"

"There's been legal controversy lately about whether anyone can be prevented from pursuing their gainful occupation, but the chances are Conrad could get an injunction to prevent your working anywhere in Canada."

Vanessa took a deep breath. Where it really counted, it seemed, Jake had the power. "What about in the States?" she asked, brushing a tendril of hair from her forehead with fingertips that felt cool.

"That depends on a lot of things." David sat forward and tapped his fingers on the desk. "If the U.S. manufacturer who hires you has a sizable market anywhere in Canada where he'd be in competition with Number 24, at the very least Conrad could take it to court. If you wanted to start up your own business, he'd probably get an injunction preventing you from entering the Canadian market. In any case, Vanessa, he has the power to make your life miserable if you abandon Number 24 now. Unless, of course, you also abandon the design of ladies' wear and go into a different branch of the field."

"Such as children's wear," Vanessa said, noticing the odd fact that being cornered was a real physical feeling, as though there were walls all around her. Could Jake Conrad really destroy her career like this, with one powerful stroke?

"What if I just wreck the company, force it into bankruptcy through bad management?" she asked at length.

"I'd go very carefully on that one," David said. "It might be difficult to prove, depending on how careful you were, but he could certainly tie you up in some very ugly litigation. It wouldn't do your future job prospects much good, I imagine."

No. "So my only hope is to get the new backing," she said slowly.

"Unless you want to stay where you are and call Conrad's bluff," David pointed out. "Once he forced you into bankruptcy, of course, he'd have no more power over you."

"Of course," she agreed distantly. *Funny,* she thought, *he's got power over my integrity, too. I al-*

ways thought no one could touch that except myself, but he's going to force me to do the one thing I've always refused to do. I've got to ask the Standishes for money. I wonder if he knew that?

IT HAD BECOME OBVIOUS that Barney had decided to adopt Vanessa. He waited on the front step almost every day now for her to come home from work; and her bookish neighbor, coming in at the same time as she did one evening and watching Barney tear up the stairs when she unlocked her door, remarked with calm humor that he would be suing her for alienation of affection.

Vanessa was glad of the cat. She had never owned one, and she found that she had been missing something quite wonderful in her life. A cat was good company, and a soft purring body in your lap could be a great comfort.

The October days were growing shorter, she was thinking, coming home one evening to find Barney splayed out lazily on the wide top step to catch the last rays of the sun. She laughed at him, bending to caress his stomach as she mounted the front steps and then unlocking the door. Barney, wise in the ways of creative leisure, didn't move from his position until the door was open. Then, without even a glance to orient himself, he leaped up and dashed inside with her.

Immediately he was impatient for the second door to be opened, and he mewed demandingly for her to hurry with the key.

"You're a dreadful beast," Vanessa said caressingly as she followed his lithe body up the stairs. "Did anyone ever tell you you're a dreadful selfish beast?"

"Once or twice," said a voice above and behind her as she reached the top, making her gasp and whirl, nearly losing her footing. A male figure stepped forward from the sitting-room door.

"How did you know I was here?" asked Jake Conrad.

"You!" Vanessa said harshly in a voice too loud. "What do *you* want?"

She was poised, ready for flight. Barney wreathed around her ankles on his tiptoes, head up, tail up, back arched, at his most appealing.

"What do you think I want?" Jake asked, his voice sounding very quiet compared to her own.

In the silence Barney's purr sounded like a truck motor with one piston missing. Vanessa glanced down and tried to push his furry body away with her foot, because if she had to start running she didn't want to be tripped up by him. But Barney was feeling friendly as well as hungry; and he knew that once he had made it clear to the human's inferior intelligence that he would actually deign to be patted, she would be thrilled by the honor. Humans always were. So he came back and flung himself against her instep and gave one or two ecstatic little cries to encourage her.

"I really could not say," Vanessa said levelly. "Suppose you tell me."

"What would you say if I told you I...wanted to make an apology?" he asked in a matter-of-fact voice, and Vanessa's face became expressionless. She stared at him, her eyes cold, and almost eerily there was utter silence for a moment as Barney stopped purring.

"Get out," she said, contempt threading her cool low voice. What kind of a fool did the man take her for? "Get out of here."

His face darkened, and he shrugged. "I can oblige," he said, his voice going up on a warning note, "but it would be better for you to listen to what I have to say."

"Yes?" she said brightly. "Why?" Barney, purring again, was making encouraging little forays toward the kitchen and back again, trying to make her understand. He gazed up at her, radiating lovableness.

"Because you are in a vulnerable position and I hold all the cards."

"I don't think so," Vanessa replied coolly. She didn't move from her strategic position at the top of the stairs.

"Vanessa, I want to talk to you," Jake said doggedly. "If you'll listen to me now I won't bother you again."

"You don't bother me now," she said in level scornful tones. "Please get out of my house." It wasn't true that he didn't bother her. Her heart was beating in her ears like a drum. She realized that she was afraid of Jake.

He was wearing blue jeans and the same navy bomber jacket he had loaned her the day he took her to the top of Grouse Mountain; the thought crossed her mind that that had been in the spring and now it was fall. How much had happened in between. She had lived a lifetime in four and a half months.

Taking his hands out of the pockets in a movement that caused her heart to thud with fear, Jake said evenly, "If you don't listen to me, I'll phone the police."

"And tell them what?" she demanded. "I've had legal advice, Jake. I am not the employer of all those people you so painstakingly interviewed! So what are you planning on charging me with?"

He took that without a blink and said carelessly, "It might cause you inconvenience, nonetheless, to have the charges investigated."

She thought of David saying, "No one would be bothered with small potatoes like you," and smiled.

"However," said Jake, "there's also a charge of illegal entry and theft—"

"There is, if you want to risk a countercharge of blackmail!" Vanessa shot back triumphantly.

His eyebrows snapped together. "What?"

"You'll have to show them the file I stole, won't you? I'll tell the police you were using the contents of that file to get sexual favors from me, that you were blackmailing me with the fear of criminal prosecution! How will you like that?"

She couldn't imagine what corner of her mind that had surfaced from, but she felt exactly the same exhilaration that she sometimes felt when she came up with a new design. She began to laugh. "But don't stop there, Jake! You've got lots more threats you can use against me, haven't you?" She sobered, and her face was suddenly grim. "Why don't you threaten to call the debenture tomorrow? That's what you want to do, isn't it? Or to crook your finger to bring Robert back to Concorp? Only I don't think that would work, Jake! I think Robert likes working with me. I think if I told him what you're doing he'd stay at Number 24 with me!"

Unexpectedly her voice cracked, and blinking, she dropped her eyes. Barney was on his hind legs, pawing delicately at her thigh.

Jake's voice was wooden. "I wouldn't be at all surprised," he said, and Barney started in surprise as a tear fell on his handsome chest. "Don't forget, in your triumph, that Robert is a Catholic. He might not leave Maria for you as readily as he'd leave me!"

She gasped, the tears drying instantly. "How dare you!" she snapped, fiery outrage blazing at him from her eyes. "Get out of here before I call the police and charge *you* with breaking and entering!"

"I didn't break anything," replied Jake. "I own this building. I came in with a key."

"Well, it's my home!" Vanessa shrilled. "I doubt very much if the laws of the land allow you to walk in at any time!" She turned and marched down the stairs to fling the door open. "Now get out!" she commanded him. "Get out of my house!"

Barney thought she might be talking to him, but he had no intention of going anywhere. He sat down firmly at the top of the stairs and began to wash a paw.

Jake stepped over him to walk down the stairs toward her. His eyes were blazing with fury, but she was too angry to be frightened. He reached past her and his hand closed over hers on the knob as he pulled the door shut. Then he put both hands on her shoulders and pulled her to face him.

"You goad me beyond endurance," he said roughly. "But this is the last time. There's nothing I want from you anymore—except for you to keep away from me. Do you hear what I'm saying? I don't want to see you in future. Do you understand that?"

His hands burned her shoulders with a melting fire. In spite of all her anger his touch softened her. Vanessa bit her lip.

"That's fine with me!" she blazed, wishing that he would either take his hands away or—she put a brake on her thoughts. "Do I take it this is goodbye?"

"This is goodbye," repeated Jake grimly. She wondered if she should talk to a bankruptcy lawyer in the morning, and she stared up into his eyes for a long silent moment. She knew suddenly that she would have no heart to continue the company; if Jake wanted to put her into bankruptcy, she would let it happen and go home.

"Then kiss me goodbye, Jake," she begged involuntarily in a voice suddenly grown hoarse, and behind his eyes she saw the empty future that would be hers. "Kiss me goodbye."

He went white to the lips. "My God," he exclaimed hoarsely. "You never stop, do you?"

He brushed by her and was through the door in a moment. Vanessa stood motionless on the staircase, listening to him go, and the sound of each step was an agony that stabbed her heart.

It was over. Vanessa sank down on the steps, her

face white, her eyes wide and unblinking. She gave a small incredulous laugh. All his machinations had been unnecessary after all. If he had only known it, Jake Conrad had got his revenge in one tiny moment.

She didn't care if Number 24 was blown into sawdust in the night, she saw with wonder. That had been nothing but a blind. It was Jake she wanted, nothing else. And Jake did not want her.

CHAPTER EIGHTEEN

DURING THE NEXT FEW DAYS Vanessa worked as though Death were watching her again, making decisions, giving orders and executing designs with a speed and precision that seemed to be beyond her conscious control. She did not know where her energy came from.

In the evenings, it left her. When Vanessa walked out of the door of Number 24 at night she walked straight into an emotional and intellectual no-man's-land. To think or to feel would be to remember that Jake Conrad did not love her, that from now on she walked in darkness.

It was a blessing that she had her work to keep her going, she knew; otherwise she might have crawled into bed and stayed there. She seemed suddenly to have a dozen different things to do with her time, a dozen irons in the fire—all keeping her from the occupation of thinking.

Her summer designs were well in hand, and the round of fabric salesmen was just beginning. This time, she noticed, she felt calmer, more confident about her choices, more decided about what she wanted.

She fought long and hard with Robert over the designs for the signature fabric and emblem that Colin had sent her. In the end they both compromised—Vanessa agreeing to give up on using the fabric for the summer line and Robert agreeing that they would launch the new appliqué on several items and commission another company to manufacture a T-shirt under the Number 24 label.

For a while she had been seeing David Latham socially, but now she stopped. He was very intelligent, a nice man, and she enjoyed his company, but he was starting to wonder why she would not go to bed with him. She would have liked to be able to go to bed with him and forget Jake, but she remembered her years in Larry's bed while she was trying to forget Jace, and she knew it would be no good.

There might never be another man for her, she knew. The fact that she had destroyed his love for her didn't mean she could also destroy her own love for him, no matter how much she wished to.

In spite of her resolve to bankrupt Number 24 if Jake called the debenture, she hadn't, in the end, been able to face the possibility. So she had called Lou Standish. She had told him she wanted to buy up the debenture so she could own the company outright, nothing more; and she had asked him if the family would lend her the money. He had agreed to it instantly, without consulting them, and the Standishes were using this as an excuse to keep in touch with her: Lou phoned her often with family news and messages while he was working out the details with David Latham. She wondered, not for the first time, how much of the family's fondness for her was guilt.

One night, about ten days after Jake's visit, Vanessa got home after a late dinner with friends she had met through Robert and Maria to find a large bulky envelope lying on the mat—bearing the distinctive navy-and-gold Concorp logo. She caught her breath, unable to do more than stare down at it for a long moment while Barney blinked at her curiously from his station by her door.

She carried the envelope upstairs, her chest contracting in pain as though she had been stabbed. *I can't face it,* she thought. *I can't face actually seeing it.* She couldn't bear to open the envelope here by herself, alone. She needed a friend by her, someone who would understand, someone whose presence would prevent her from crying herself sick. She would take it to the office tomorrow, open it with Ilona in the room, she decided. Ilona didn't know anything about what was going on, but she would certainly understand what it meant when Jake called the debenture to bankrupt Number 24...or better still, she would take it to David Latham and ask him, as her lawyer, to open it for her.

The envelope lay on the coffee table all evening while she pottered and fed Barney and washed and blow-dried her hair. When she went to bed it was still there, radiating its cruel energy into the room. Vanessa tossed and turned until three, unable to sleep. Then, finally, she got up, put on the light and her black robe and went back to the sitting room. She sat on the sofa and stared at her doom.

This is the worst possible time to open it, she thought suddenly. *I should have opened it earlier.*

Three o'clock in the morning is when most suicides occur, and I know why. It's because this is the time when there's no hope in the world.

She slit open the envelope and shook the contents out onto the table. She wrinkled her forehead. She had expected one enormous document, somehow, but what appeared was a whole host of smaller documents and contracts and single pieces of paper.

On the very top was a tiny slip of paper from a memo pad. "From the desk of Howard Spiegel," it read across the top, and scrawled across it, in writing she had seen many times since she had joined Concorp, she read, "Vanessa—please sign and return one copy of each to me." It was signed, "Howie."

Underneath, the first paper was a document entitled "Addendum." Vanessa skimmed the first few lines in growing disbelief: it seemed to be an addendum to her management contract. God in Heaven, what was this? "Clause seventeen. . .agree that the restraint of trade. . .shall be reduced from a period of five years. . .to a period of three months. . . ." And at the bottom, Jake's black full-looped signature.

Her hand shook as she picked up the next document, also labeled "Addendum"—to the debenture agreement: "That. . .except in the case of the insolvency of the said company. . .there shall be no demand made. . .for a period of five years from the date of the original agreement."

She rooted wildly through the remaining papers. There was a new lease on the premises at Number 24, backdated, which altered clause thirteen and deleted clause fourteen altogether; a backdated letter guaranteeing Robert Dawe's job at Concorp for a period of one year....

Jake Conrad had painstakingly dismantled every single trap he had laid for her. Vanessa sat stunned amid the bits of paper, half still unread, and tried to assimilate it. He was giving up all his power over her. Even, at the bottom of the envelope, she found four tiny cassette tapes, one labeled "Wan Chu" and the others the three names she recognized from the typed transcripts she had read.

Why had he done all this? What was the point? The traps that he had set for her could only have been sprung by Jake himself. If he had changed his mind about revenge, he didn't have to do anything. She had been in danger only from *him*.

There could be only two reasons for what he had done, she thought finally: to give her peace of mind, and to protect her from his whim if in the future he should change his mind. But peace of mind was exactly what he did not want her to have. "Maybe I'll never pull the plug," Jake had said. "Maybe it'll be enough seeing you constantly insecure...."

Vanessa sat still for a long time, lost in thought. For the first time in days thinking was not an agony.

"WHO ARE YOU bringing to our masquerade party?" Robert asked idly a day or two later. "Or are you and Jake coming together?"

Vanessa was working out some figures with him; her pencil stopped on the page. "Is Jake going to the party?" she asked casually.

"Far as I know," said Robert, looking back to his figures. "I make that fifteen-eighteen with a three percent—"

"Does he know I've been invited?" Vanessa interrupted.

Robert shook his head, whether in answer or because the numbers weren't working out she couldn't tell. He dropped his hand back on the keys for a rapid calculation, then looked up. "Well, he might assume it. You've been to most of our parties since you got here." It was true; Vanessa had been adopted by Robert's and Maria's crowd since the night of that first dinner party.

"Yes, but Jake hasn't," Vanessa reminded him. "He was there the first time you invited me, but then he went out of town, remember?"

"Did he?" asked Robert abstractedly, keying in more figures. "Yeah, I guess you're right. Well, then, I guess he doesn't know. Damnation, have I put that three percent in or not? Anyway, do I take it you're bringing someone else? Maria needs to know."

"No, I'll be alone," Vanessa decided suddenly, though up to now she had been toying with the idea of asking David. "What are you using three percent here for, anyway, Robert? It doesn't look right to me."

She could do that, she had discovered—force her mind onto the work at hand when all she really wanted to do was think about her personal life. If she hadn't been able to do that, she wouldn't have survived.

Robert was swearing mildly, looking through the papers on his desk for validation of the three percent. "Robert," she said abruptly, unaware of having come to any decision. The tone of her voice made him look up more sharply than she had intended. "Robert, if Jake asks, please don't tell him I'm coming to your party."

Right from the beginning she and Robert had had an understanding—the kind that grows up between similarly forthright open personalities.

Robert made a calculation. "Sure," he said absently. "You're right about that three percent—it's wrong."

VANESSA LIKED COSTUME. She had always liked to design clothes for herself that, without being of any discernible period, had the flavor of a costume. The chance to design a full-fledged period costume for the masquerade party had delighted her, and the finished outfit—in black velvet and antique gold—was very beautiful.

But on the night of the party she stood at her open closet door for a long moment with the black velvet suit in her hand, then hung it up again and took out her green silk-taffeta dress.

She had mended it; under Jake's hands the material had ripped along the ruffle seam to the hem, and it had been a simple matter to repair it and move the ruffle slightly to hide the evidence. When she put it on, it looked as good as new.

She swept her hair tight against one side of her head to fall in a cloud against the other shoulder and cheek, and fastened on dangling diamanté earrings and a bracelet. Wearing a huge crinoline under the skirt, a glittering net stole, bright lipstick and nail polish and, under the ruffled black eye mask she had made, a dramatic makeup that made her brown eyes even darker, she looked vaguely Hollywood Fifties. People at the party might consider her a little unimaginative, but she wasn't dressing for the people at the party.

"Rita Hayworth," she introduced herself to Maria and Robert at the door, and Robert announced her in a formal voice, "Miss Rita Hayworth."

The room was filled with a collection of the famous and the infamous through the millennia, from Confucius and Cleopatra down to Queen Victoria and Captain Kirk. It seemed a very large party, especially as Vanessa was used to the Dawes' more intimate dinner parties, and many of the masqueraders were completely unrecognizable. If Jake was in the room Vanessa couldn't see him. She moved through the main room slowly, talking to people she knew, and was directed through to the adjoining room, where a bearded prophet was serving drinks behind a long makeshift bar.

"Rita!" he greeted her enthusiastically.

She replied, "Moish!"

"What are you drinking?" asked Moses, who was otherwise known as Howard Spiegel, the Concorp lawyer.

She wanted to be just light-headed enough to do what she had to do but not in any danger of losing control. A vodka martini, though she wanted one, would be too potent.

"Dry sherry, please," she said. She fell into conversation with a hard-drinking white-haired man in a Victorian suit and a blond Yasser Arafat and watched the room for Jake. She was on her second sherry and was wishing she had asked for a vodka martini after all when Robert's stentorian voice announced, "Madame du Barry," and then, "Sergeant Preston of the Yukon and his dog, King!"

There were shouts of laughter in the other room as Jake came through the door, masked and wearing a red jacket and a fur hat, and after a moment Vanessa saw why. Behind him, on wheels, he was pulling along the most disreputable, moth-eaten, bedraggled stuffed toy dog Vanessa had ever seen. From several holes in its nearly hairless pelt it trailed sawdust and straw stuffing, and one sorry ear hung over its only surviving glass eye.

Everyone was shrieking with laughter. Howie, behind her, asked Vanessa, "Who the hell is that?"

"It's Jake," Vanessa told him, hiccuping on a giggle.

As though he heard his name through all the noise Jake looked toward her through the doorway. Then he froze, his jaw clenching, and behind the black eye mask his eyes burned into hers, brilliant with anger.

It could have lasted only a second, but to Vanessa the look seemed to go on for an age before Jake turned back to the very sexy Madame du Barry, all in spangled turquoise and gold with pale blond hair, who was hurrying up to take possession of his arm.

People were still laughing as Jake's progress through the room brought the mangy dog to their better view, so Vanessa's delighted laugh of discovery was lost in the room to all ears, perhaps, but Jake's.

His angry look had proved the one thing she had wanted to know—whatever he had said, whatever he thought, Jake Conrad was not indifferent to her.

Madame du Barry didn't realize what she was doing when, a few minutes later, she insisted on moving over to the bar for a drink, but Jake could hardly protest, and so he ended up there beside Vanessa, where he poured himself a whiskey.

"Good God, Jake, is that you?" asked Howard, laughing loudly. "You look like a cocktail waiter with a head cold!"

Jake laughed and looked down at his red jacket. "Could be because I borrowed this from one of the hotel bartenders, I suppose."

Pretty Madame du Barry gushed, "Isn't that just typical? I go to all kinds of trouble to try to look authentic and plan my costume for *weeks* in advance, and Jake forgot all about it till this afternoon—and he's the one who gets all the compliments!"

"Not all of them, I assure you," said a man dressed as Julius Caesar from her other side, gazing appreciatively at her invitingly low neckline. Caesar was a little drunk. "You are due for quite a few yourself, *madame*, and to prove I'm right I'll start...."

"Where'd you round up King?" Vanessa asked Jake in an undertone while Caesar carried on over the Rubicon. She forced herself to sound light and friendly. "He looks a little the worse for wear."

"In a friend's garage," Jake answered shortly, but he was looking at her dress and she knew he remembered.

"He looks sort of an indeterminate breed," she commented with a smile. "Not to say mongrel. Didn't you tell me King was a husky?"

"Did I?" Jake asked briefly.

"Sure you did," Vanessa said. "You remember—that night we went walking in Stanley Park and you nearly made love to me beside Lost Lagoon."

He sucked in his breath as though he had been stung, and Vanessa smiled at him in blatant seduction. Dancing had started in the other room, and at that moment the white-haired man in the Victorian suit asked Vanessa to dance. As she moved off on his arm she felt rather than saw Jake's instinctive movement to detain her, instantly controlled.

"Who are you?" she asked the man as they moved onto the dance floor.

"You mean you don't recognize the red nose?" he asked. "I'm Sir John A., my dear."

Vanessa laughed in delight. "Sir John Eh?" She'd never danced with a title before. "How do you do? But I meant, what character are you dressed as?"

He stopped dancing and looked at her. "That is my character!" he exclaimed. "Good God, what is education in this country coming to? Don't tell me they didn't teach you about Sir John A. Macdonald at school?"

"No, but I'm an American," Vanessa confessed as he guided her into dance again. "I've only been in Canada four months."

"Ah, that explains it!" exclaimed the man, who really seemed quite gentlemanly and dignified enough for an earlier century. "I shouldn't think you'd ever heard the name of Canada's first prime minister."

"No," agreed Vanessa. "Is that who you are?"

He nodded. "What did you mean about the red nose?"

"Our beloved Sir John A., as he is affectionately known, had a marked propensity toward the imbibing of spirituous liquors," he said with a twinkle. "I do not myself have a disinclination for the bottle, as you may have noticed. Nevertheless, a spot of my wife's rouge, judiciously applied, was required to provide the necessary roseate hue."

Vanessa laughed delightedly just as their movement turned her toward the door. Over Sir John A. Macdonald's shoulder she saw Jake and Madame du Barry walking into the room. She let her eyes lock with Jake's and stared at him till she felt light- headed.

"Are you by any chance a teacher?" she asked Sir John, when his guiding hand moved her into a turn that removed Jake from her line of vision. Her heart was beating as though she had run a mile.

"Retired, my dear," he said. "Retired. I taught English and history for some thirty-four years."

"And how do you know Robert and Maria?" she asked.

He told her that he was Robert's father and that his name was Harold; and they talked until the music stopped. Vanessa looked around to see a rather unwilling Madame du Barry being claimed by Julius Caesar for the next dance, and she thanked Sir John A. Macdonald and excused herself.

"Dance, Jake?" she asked softly as the music started again, and slipped into his arms. He could not push her away without turning this into a scene, and Madame du Barry, who had been expecting Jake to tell Caesar to push off, was incensed.

"Well!" she snorted indignantly as Caesar triumphantly bore her away.

Jake's hands were like steel at her waist. "What the hell do you want, Vanessa?" he grated softly, and she laughed.

"I want to dance with you, Jake," she said, her body swaying with the soft music. "We've never danced, have we? But we should dance well together, Jake," she said huskily. "They say when people are good together in bed it shows on the dance floor."

He clenched his jaw and swore, then deliberately reached to take her hand in a painfully strong grip. His other arm tightened around her waist as he pulled her against him. The touch of his body went to her head like wine; as he began to move her in dance her head dropped helplessly back.

Vanessa clung to sanity. She must maintain control, she mustn't let Jake get the upper hand. Not tonight.

"You think we're good together in bed?" Jake asked coldly. She laughed and did not answer. "Hmm?" he prompted, and it seemed as if he wanted to know almost against his will.

"Would you like it if I said yes?" she asked softly.

"Do you want to have been a good lover for me, Jake? I wonder why, when you never want to see me again?"

He said nothing.

"Or is it just that you want me to admit that for me it was good so you can have the pleasure of telling me that for you it was nothing, that Madame du Barry over there excites you far more than I ever did?" She smiled seductively at him through her mask. "But I don't believe that, Jake. You couldn't make me believe it. You forget she's around half the time. You don't forget I'm around, do you, Jake? Any more than I can forget you."

"Shut up," he muttered, and she hoped she wasn't imagining the sound of strain in his voice.

"That's why you don't want to see me ever again," she continued. "Because when you look at me you remember what effect you have on me, you remember what you can do to me. You know you can make me faint with a word, a touch. You know that sexually you're the man I can't say no to, and you like that too much."

Jake grunted as though his muscles had clenched involuntarily. His hand holding hers was almost unbearable and his arm around her waist was an iron band. Vanessa smiled against the pain.

"You like it so much you lose control, don't you, Jake? And you don't like to be out of control, do you? You don't like to want something so badly it makes you shake, makes you wild. I haven't forgotten that this is the dress you ripped off me to make love to me one night." She looked at him. "You haven't forgotten, either, have you, Jake?"

He was staring down at her with the blackest eyes she had ever seen in her life, and she wished suddenly that this could have been simpler, that she could have gone to him and said, "Jake, you love me, but you don't want to admit it to yourself. I love you, too. Please admit it." She could hear his breathing, feel the labored rise and fall of his chest against her. They had stopped moving. In the dim-lit room the other dancers swayed around them.

"What the hell do you want, Vanessa?" he demanded hoarsely. The music went silent except for one haunting horn that tugged at her reason, invited her away.

Her hand clung around his neck and she leaned back against the pressure of his arm to look up at him. His eyes were glittering through his mask with an expression that made her hiss her breath in through her teeth. "I want you to kiss me," she whispered. "Kiss me one last time for goodbye."

She felt the tidal wave in him and knew with a triumphant joy that he could not refuse. His hand pressed against her back, forcing her face up to his, and then Vanessa closed her eyes and felt his mouth find hers blindly, hungrily. He freed her other hand and she wrapped it around his neck and clung to him as his arm encircled her and held her as though he wanted the kiss to destroy them both.

When he lifted his mouth the blackness was swirling around her and the music had stopped. "Thank you," she whispered drunkenly against his neck, unable to stop clinging to him. She felt his hand on her arm, and with a sudden fear that he was going to force her to let go of him, she released him and stepped back out of his arms. She took a deep breath and smiled.

She looked him in the eyes. "That story you told me about coming to New York later and dancing with me—was it true, Jake?"

His hands had reached for her, but now they dropped to his sides. "We didn't dance," he said in a low voice. "I watched you from a distance."

Oh, God, when would he crack? When would she get through to him? She said, "I couldn't believe I wouldn't have recognized your touch. I feel as though I'd have known you blindfold. If I had recognized you then, I'd have asked you to take me with you, Jake." A pleading note escaped into her voice. "Would you have wanted me?"

Just for a moment there was a stillness about him that was frightening. "Yes," he said. "I would have wanted you." He coughed to clear the hoarseness in his voice. She felt as though she were in a battle for her life where there was no scoreboard, no way to tell if she was winning. She tried desperately to read him. "I nearly took you anyway," he said.

"I can just imagine that," she smiled. Being dragged out to a car by a dark stranger who suddenly turned out to be Jace. "Nine unnecessary years," she said softly as another record started, and she watched Madame du Barry's determined approach behind Jake's shoulder. "And you still can't forgive me. Nine years is nothing, though, compared to forever. Is it, Jake?"

She knew that he would push her aside now and

take Madame du Barry in his arms, and she couldn't bear that. Vanessa stepped away from him then and moved through the dancers to the doorway. When she turned to look for the sight of them dancing together what she saw instead was Madame du Barry alone in the middle of the room, her mouth an oh of angry surprise...and Jake, not a foot away, Jake within reach as Vanessa turned, Jake putting out a hand to grasp her arm. Vanessa bit her lip and caught her breath on a sob.

"Come with me now," he said softly, his eyes burning into hers, and suddenly it hurt her heart to beat.

CHAPTER NINETEEN

THEY DROVE IN SILENCE for a long time, headlights cutting through the darkness of the long road on the north shore of English Bay, the engine a quiet hum in the night. Finally Jake pulled off the road onto a small promontory above the water and shut off the engine. Vanessa's heart was thumping so that she could hardly breathe. After a moment she wound down her window to let in the sound of the sea and the gulls.

Jake said quietly, "My mother and father had a lousy marriage from the beginning. A lot of it my mother took out on me. Long before you happened on the scene I'd learned that a woman who said she loved me one day wasn't going to love me the next.

"She finally left when I was eight years old. I never let another woman get close to me—housekeepers, my father's girl friends; some of them were kind, some of them might have genuinely cared, I guess—I never let them in. Not until you."

Vanessa looked at him, shadowed in moonlight, and remembered Jace's wonder, long ago, at how deeply it was possible to love. "In all my life," he had said once, clinging to her, "I've never loved anyone the way I love you!" If she had believed that, truly believed it. . . .

"I used to wonder, afterward, why you? I finally decided it was because I'd been so helpless in that damned hospital, helpless and scared, and it left me vulnerable. It just happened to be you who walked in. I figured that any woman would have had the same effect. That's what I told myself for nine years." He was gazing straight ahead, out over the ocean, his eyes unblinking.

"In nine and a half years there hasn't been another woman who got to me, and when I saw you at that cocktail party last June I was sure I was cured of everything except a strong taste for giving you your own back.

"But you're the woman who can always get to me. Only by the time I realized that, it was too late. Too late to ignore you, too late to send you away. It became a battle with me, trying to get my revenge before you got to me again, trying to destroy you before you destroyed me." Still he did not look at her, and Vanessa, torn between joy and pain, felt tears burn her eyes.

"Jake—" she whispered hoarsely, but he interrupted.

"Let me finish," he said. "I'm aware that I'm not telling you anything you don't know. When I walked in tonight and saw you in that dress I knew you knew, and I knew what you were going to do. I brought you out here to tell you you can do it, Vanessa. There's no question that you can put me through hell. You were doing it tonight, you're doing it now, just sitting there. You've got me so blind I can't see my hand in front of my face. If you tell me you want me I'll believe you—right up to the moment you tell me you don't. You said, do I like to know that my touch arouses you. My God, I dream about it." He passed his hand over his eyes. "I dream about seeing that look on your face, hearing you call my name. . . ."

She couldn't speak. She sat in frozen horrified silence, listening to this recital of what he thought she was, unable to protest, unable to open her mouth on a word.

"Whatever you want me to admit—" his voice hardened "—I admit it." For the first time in the faint light of the stars he looked over at her. "I admit it because I want this to stop. If you want the satisfaction of hearing me admit I still love you, you hear it now. If you want to know that it's all I can do to keep my hands off you, you know it. I'm telling you this so you won't have to come hunting for proof of your conquest, Vanessa. Because after this I want you to keep away from me. If what you want is the pleasure of seeing me constantly wanting you, *that* you are not going to get. It ends here. Take whatever satisfaction you can from this, because it's all you're going to get."

A tear burned its way down her face, and then suddenly there was a flood, and she felt them like rain on her hands clenched in her lap. "Oh, Jake," she whispered brokenly.

He jerked his head to look at her. "Why are you crying?" he asked in surprise, as though in all his life no woman had cried for his pain, as though he did not understand that such a thing was possible. All the pain of a lifetime was in his voice, but he truly did not know why she was crying. Vanessa thought of how she had added to that pain, and understood dimly that if she told him now that she loved him, he would not be able to believe it. He could not bear to believe it.

"I'm sorry," she said softly. "I'm so sorry, Jake. Please, would you take me home?"

His jaw tightened and without a word he reached to turn the key. The car roared to life under his hand. They drove again in silence, and then at last she recognized the approach to the bridge over the narrows and knew that she would soon be home.

"Jake," she said as the metal bridgework flipped past the windows and the darkness of Stanley Park loomed up ahead, "will you come in with me? I've got—I want to tell you something."

She looked down and saw her green dress with a stab of pain. What a fool she had been, thinking to force him to realize he loved her by reminding him of his sexual need of her. She should have known that a man like Jake could not have deluded himself so long. He knew he loved her, and he knew that she was a source of pain to him. God, what he must have thought of her when he walked into Robert's tonight! How he must despise her, thinking that she wanted to use that powerful all-consuming love to torture him.

What imp had made her wear this dress tonight, had brought her so far along a road that would be so difficult to retrace?

He had not answered her request but when he pulled up in front of her house he shut off the car engine and got out with her, and she sent up a prayer of thanks.

Upstairs she said, "I'll put on the kettle. Would you like a cup of coffee?" He nodded and moved into the sitting room, taking off his jacket.

Vanessa went to the kitchen, filled the kettle and then walked through to the bedroom. As quickly as she could she got out of the green dress and slipped on blue jeans and a loose shirt, then combed her hair loose and removed her jewelry and all her makeup.

Back in the kitchen she made coffee, laid a tray and carried it back to the sitting room. Jake was standing at the window, shirt sleeves rolled up, hands in his pockets, staring out to the water of the bay in the distance.

She set down the tray and called his name softly, and he turned. "Come and sit down," she said, nodding at the sofa; but she remained where she was, kneeling on the other side of the coffee table, facing him. When he sat, she poured two cups of coffee.

"Jake," she said quietly, looking at him. "I love you."

He smiled a crooked half-smile. "Of course you do," he said, leaning forward to take the cup as casually as if they had just agreed on the likelihood of rain.

"You...you know?" she faltered. Jake shrugged lightly, as though his knowing or not knowing was of no consequence. Vanessa was bewildered. "Don't you care?" she asked, breathless with a sudden fear.

Had he lied to her? Had he, after all, lied about loving her?

"Not much," said Jake, taking a sip of coffee.

She had expected anger, or disbelief, perhaps, or, if she were lucky, guarded joy. She could not understand this. "Why?" she breathed, feeling tears press up behind her eyes again.

He said coolly, "Because whether you love me or you don't makes no difference. I can't afford your kind of love, Vanessa."

"Can't *afford* it?" she repeated stupidly, and he smiled.

"Can't afford it emotionally. If I tried to live with the love you're capable of it would kill me."

She gasped, "What do you mean?" But somehow, inside, she knew what he was going to say. He was going to say that she had lost him.

He said, as though he were reciting facts at a business meeting, "I mean it would never be enough and I'd always be trying to pretend it was more than it was. Your feelings are shallow, Vanessa. One day you'd find your love had died altogether, and on that day you'd walk out of my life. I don't want to spend my days living in fear of that moment. I'd rather take what's inevitable now and get back in control of my life."

She thought of her discovery of her own love, how she would destroy the world to get him. She said, "You don't know about my love. I love you, I always have, I always will. It's nothing shallow."

"Yes," he said, "I know. I've heard it before." And she knew she could not reach him.

"Jake," she said, "there's always a risk to loving and being loved. Trusting anyone is a risk. But if you don't take the risk, we both walk alone forever. And that's like being half-dead, Jake.

"I've seen the way you deal with your women—with anybody. You don't let anyone touch you You're afraid to live. I love you, Jake. Don't shut me out forever because I made a terrible mistake once. You love me. We have a chance to make up for everything together. But you have to let me love you. You don't know how much I love you because you've never let me show you, let me tell you. You say it's because you think I won't love you enough, but I don't believe that. It's because you're afraid I *do* love you enough, that I love you too much. You've learned to live without love, Jake. You know how to do that. That's not what you're afraid of. You're afraid of learning to live with love. You were afraid ten years ago, too. That's why you didn't propose then, that's why you didn't ask me to go with you then—you were afraid to believe in my love, just as I was afraid to believe in yours."

She had to stop because he had set down his cup and stood, and she was crying. She had known from the beginning she would lose. She jumped up.

Dispassionately he looked down at her, wiped a tear from her cheek. "You're wrong," he said. "I know exactly how much you love me. If I let myself love you I'm still alone."

He turned to reach for his jacket and she flung herself at him and clung to him. One chance, she had one last chance.

"Jake," she begged. "Come to bed with me. Love me one last time for goodbye." She wrapped her arms up around his neck and pressed her mouth, wet with tears, against his.

His arms wrapped tightly around her and he kissed her with a slowly increasing need, searching and tasting till she was nearly drunk with the mixture of joy and need that flooded her. When he released her lips she was crying more fiercely than ever.

"Love me," she sobbed in relief. "Please love me."

He kissed each wet eyelid and set her away from him. She knew then. "No!" she cried wildly, and it was a scream of pain; and she ran to him and clutched at him. "You want me, Jake! I know you want to love me!" She reached for him, desperation tearing her reason to ribbons, trying to hold him, to touch him; but he held her away and picked up his jacket.

"I love you!" she cried again.

"You'll get over it," said Jake. He walked out to the staircase, and blinded by tears, she followed.

"It's fear, Jake," she said. "You're not winning now; fear is winning. You're afraid to love." She gulped and her voice dropped to a whisper. "Jake, I love you. Please don't be afraid."

He was gone. She heard the doors close below, and sank to her knees and held the banister. "Please, God, bring him back," she said, and when she realized she was praying aloud another flood of tears was released. "Make him come back," she sobbed over and over, but in the darkest part of her heart she knew there was no one to hear.

IT SEEMED A LONG TIME LATER that she struggled to her feet and went in to run a bath. Afterward she didn't bother to dry herself, just wrapped up in the black terry robe and went into the kitchen to make fresh coffee.

She wouldn't give up. Tomorrow she would find the energy and determination to start again with Jake, she knew. But tonight she didn't feel anything but exhausted pain. Tomorrow there would be hope, but tonight she felt only a bleak empty hopelessness.

She took her coffee into the sitting room and sat there, not thinking, not feeling, letting the time go by. At two she heard the beginnings of a cold driving rain against the windows. At three it stopped.

In the silence of the street then, she heard the slam of a car door, then the front door, then her own door downstairs. She heard the sound of a footfall on a step in unbelieving wonder, set down her cold cup and stood.

Jake was in the doorway then, damp and dark, his eyes haunted, his wet hair plastered blackly to his head.

"You were right. I was wrong," he said simply. "I'll take whatever love you have to give, for as long as you want to give it."

She flew to him across the room.

JAKE LEANED OVER HER, his strong hands encircling her head as though he would crush her with love. "I love you," he said in a voice made harsh by emotion.

He ran his hand through the tangled russet curls spread out on the pillow. "Just looking at your hair like that twists my heart," he whispered, as though every word were a torment, and Vanessa felt the answering twist in her own heart. His lovemaking had been fierce and tender, knowing and loving all at once, and if she lived forever she knew she would never be free of him. He had touched a deep stormy need in her that made her feel like a child with only one light in the universe to guide her.

"I love you," she said desperately. "How could I have done it? How could I do that to us, knowing what we had?"

Jake closed his eyes. "Don't regret it," he said softly. "Don't regret anything. We're here now, that's all that matters."

"You didn't lie to me, did you?" she said, for now he was the Jace she remembered. For the first time in ten years he had made love to her not in anger but in love, and this man she would have recognized blindfold. "You really did die, in a way, when you got my letter."

He looked at her. "It felt like dying," he admitted. "I came out of surgery and I felt like someone else. I knew that no one could ever hurt me again."

Vanessa breathed sharply. "And no one has?" she asked, horrified, for if no one had had the power to hurt him no one had had the power to make him happy, either.

"No one did," he agreed.

She said, "You had a far worse ten years than I did." At least she hadn't been so completely alone inside.

"I thought I was happy," he said in faint surprise now to see that he was wrong. "I thought I was in control, and I liked that. I thought I'd got over you, and if no woman ever made me feel more than a detached desire I told myself I was lucky." He laughed self-mockingly. "I told myself that all I wanted to do was make money—and never let myself see that that was only in order to prove something to you. It wasn't till I saw you again and felt that if I wasn't as rich as the Standishes, at least I could dazzle most women with my wealth, that I began to understand I had been driven to make money for the day when I could stand in front of you and say, 'You chose wealth over me, look what a mistake you made.' "

She shook her head helplessly. "I'm sorry," she whispered.

"My heart nearly kicked me to death when I saw you across the room—in *my* hotel, and all I could think of was taking you to bed in my hotel and reminding you of what you'd given up...and when I saw that you didn't even remember me, I—"

She put her hand to his lips. "What are you saying? I remembered you—I just didn't recognize you. You were changed, so cold and cynical. The Jace I remembered was—"

"Yes," he said. "I know. I realized that almost at once. And suddenly I was no longer sure who would be in control when you found out who I was...and before I knew what I was doing I was killing off Jace Conrad."

"And nearly killing me off in the process," she said.

"Afterward I felt like a fool—I kept making mistakes—but I wanted you so badly I'd have.... I was stuck with the role I'd given myself—Jake might not have a very good chance with you, but it was better than Jace's chances, once you knew how I'd been lying. I made so many mistakes I was sure you'd guess."

"Inside, I did," she said. "I dreamed the truth once. But consciously I never had the least suspicion. Anyway, how did you come to have another name so handy?"

"I'd always been called both Jake and Jace—my family called me Jace, friends Jake. My mother had always called me Jace. After the operation I used Jake all the time."

There was too much there to reply to. Vanessa looked at him helplessly, and he smiled at her and kissed her, no longer blaming her for his pain. "But it didn't work anyway. As Jake or as Jace, I couldn't make you want me," he said, his jaw clenching momentarily. He stroked the long line of her naked back as though to reassure himself that she was really there. "I couldn't get you to stay...and then I realized that the way to you was through your work, that you cared about that."

She remembered him saying, "Everybody has a weak spot," and smiled down at him. "If you'd only known," she said. "I thought that was the way to *you*." For part of her determination to accept the job had always been the need to get to know Jake.

He said, "I thought I'd stopped hating you long ago, but suddenly I was acting like a crazy man—I no longer knew whether I wanted you. . .or revenge on you. But when you accepted the job, there was no going back. I was out of control."

His face was dark against the pillow slip, his eyes haunted with memory. "I wanted you to know what I'd felt, but I knew I couldn't break your heart. I thought your feelings were—" He broke off. "I thought business was your soft spot, that that would hurt you worse than anything."

He didn't think she loved him deeply, he meant, and Vanessa realized with a pang that in a way he still could not believe in her love. *"No,"* she whispered urgently, wrapping her arms around his chest and pressing her face into his neck.

"The night we first made love I was horrified by the strength of my own need," he said. "Part of me wanted to end the game there, to tell you everything. But then how would I have kept you here? I had no hold over you till the company was producing and your designs were acutally in the marketplace."

"So you ran away to Saudi Arabia."

He lifted a strand of her hair. "You called it charity," he said. "And I knew you were right. I was as close to begging as I'd ever been in my life."

Vanessa blinked against the sudden hot prickle of tears. "You don't ever have to beg for me," she said. "I'm the one who's begging—I have been since the first day."

There was silence as Jake stroked her head. "Yes," he said. "You knew from the first what was important, but I was too pig-headed to listen. I wanted to hurt you the way I'd been hurt. How can I blame you for ten years after the unnecessary hell I've made out of the past few months?" he whispered hoarsely. "After the way I nearly turned ten years into forever?"

Vanessa closed her eyes. "Thank God you didn't," she said softly, and it was a prayer. There was a bird singing in the tree outside her window; it was morning.

"I stayed away till I knew you were firmly settled in the business," Jake resumed after a moment, "and I could start to turn the screws. I was going to tell you who I was, what I meant to do—and you won after all. All you had to do was tell me Larry was the lover of your choice, and I was destroyed all over again."

"I wasn't winning," she protested. "When you told me what you planned to do to me, how much you wanted to destroy me—you nearly did. I loved you, remember, and you hated me worse than anyone living."

There was a long pause then; she wondered how much of that he could accept. "It's morning already," she said, her head on his chest, where she could hear the strong reassuring thud of his heartbeat and the resonance of his deep voice. "We've been awake all night."

His hand stroked her head. "Your hair is beautiful in the morning sun," he said. "Like a forest fire."

She tickled her hand through the crinkling dark hairs of his chest. "Would you like some coffee?" she asked. "Breakfast?"

"All right," he agreed. They sat up slowly and

looked into each other's eyes, and Jake rubbed his hand over his rough chin.

Vanessa unearthed an old baggy bathrobe that she had inherited years ago from Colin. It had once been a chocolate terry cloth but was now so faded and worn that both color and material seemed indeterminate.

"Is this the best you do for your men?" Jake teased her as they walked to the kitchen, and he caught a flicker of gold from her dark eyes.

"Nobody's ever objected," she told him demurely, and he caught her by the shoulders and kissed her.

"Witch," he said.

"When you accused me of wanting to take Robert away from Maria," she asked, "did you really believe that?"

Jake smiled ruefully. He said, "I wanted to tell you I loved you, and suddenly you were flinging another man in my face. I didn't believe it before or afterward, but I guess right in that moment I was so crazy I'd have believed anything."

Vanessa smiled, shaking her head, then filled the kettle and plugged it in. "Did you know that Americans in general don't use electric kettles?" she asked suddenly. "Do you think that's a market worth tapping?"

Jake sat at the kitchen table, reaching for a peach from the bowl of fruit in the center. He raised a curious eyebrow. "Is that so?" he asked interestedly. He bit into the flesh of the peach and the juice sprayed his mouth. He looked at her. "I like your business head," he said. "If you ever decide to give up design I'll give you a job at Concorp."

She smiled at him, pouring boiling water over the instant coffee in two white mugs. The delicious scent of it filled the air, and she wanted to laugh in her delight at the morning. "I'm not giving up Number 24," she said, shaking her head. "I promised to make you a profit, and I'm going to."

Jake finished off the peach and spooned sugar into his coffee. "Not much doubt of that," he said. He smiled and leaned back into his chair, and he was as relaxed here in her home as she had always imagined him. Already, she could see, this was more comfortable to him than the penthouse suite.

"You know," he said, as though the comfort he felt had impinged on his consciousness, "your neighbor downstairs has given notice." He looked around appreciatively. "Would you like to renovate the place, turn it back into a single-family home?"

"And live here?" Vanessa breathed. "I'd love it, Jake. I want to make a home for you that's really home.... I could do it, here."

He looked at her for a long silent moment, absorbing that.

"When I told you why I married Larry," she asked later, over the breakfast they had made together, "didn't that change anything for you?"

"For some reason it made me angrier," Jake answered, frowning in thought. "I don't know why. I was angry at everybody then—the Standishes, you, myself...."

"I waited for you all that weekend," she remembered with a shiver. "That's when I started to realize you really meant it, and I knew I had to get that file from you to protect myself. And then I really knew how much you hated me. You wanted to send me to prison." Jake leaned across the table to lift her chin up and kissed her lightly. "You wouldn't have sent me to prison, would you?" she whispered then. She raised her eyes and looked at him.

He said, "There never was any question that I could. Nothing that you were doing was illegal. I hadn't even thought of threatening you with prison—that was your own inspiration. But when you were shouting about prison I thought that that would scare you more than the threat of bad publicity."

She closed her eyes. "It did that."

"It did more than that—it made you hate me," he said, and she heard in his voice that her sudden turn from love to anger had been no more than he'd expected.

"No," she said deliberately, looking into his eyes again. "I never hated you. I have never hated you even when I felt as though I did."

Jake smiled a half-smile. "It wasn't till I'd finally succeeded in what I set out to do that I realized it wasn't what I wanted. I didn't want you hating me, I wanted you to love me." His hold on her tightened. "I wanted you to want my touch, my lovemaking, the way you had before. . . I had to make you say my lovemaking wasn't repulsive to you. . . afterward, lying there, I finally accepted that I loved you, that I'd never stopped loving you—when it was too late."

Vanessa sucked in her breath. "Was that when?"

"That's when," he said, his eyes darkening. "I was lying there thinking things out, and then suddenly you were up collecting all those papers you'd torn up. And I thought, that's fair, I'm learning I love her just when I've finally turned whatever love she had for me into hate."

"No," was all she could say, thinking of how she had screamed at him, while he had been understanding that.... "Not hate," she whispered softly. "I never hated you."

He laced his fingers through her hair. "Yes, you did," he said calmly.

Tears spangled her lashes. How much more easily he could accept hate than love. "But you came back," she remembered suddenly. "After all that, you came back."

"I wanted to tell you I was giving up, that I wasn't going to use any of the control I had over you and Number 24. I was going to say I loved you, see what you would say—but you couldn't even bear to listen to me, and I heard myself threatening you with arrest to make you listen—and that's when I knew how hopeless it was. I was so obsessed with you I couldn't act rationally. I hadn't from day one. And I'd lost you again, this time by my own actions."

A tear fell on his hand and he jerked in surprise. "Are you crying?" he asked, a note of pain in his voice. "Oh, my God, my darling, don't cry." He stood then and pulled her in to his warm broad chest. "I'm sorry I hurt you, don't cry...."

She said very softly, "I'm not crying for me, Jake, I'm crying for you."

His chest heaved in a shaken laugh that might have been almost a sob. "For me? My darling, why are you crying for me?" as though he could never need anyone's tears.

"Because you've been so hurt," she said gently, her arms going around him, her face burying itself in his neck, and for an unguarded moment he went still. "But I'll make it all right," she promised in a shaky voice. "I love you. I'll never hurt you again. I'll love you forever."

His arms enclosed her in warmth. "No," he said. "I'll love you forever. You'll love me for as long or as short a time as you can, my love. It doesn't matter. Don't shed any tears for me, Vanessa. I'm happier than I know what to do with if I only have this for a month."

Vanessa drew a shaky breath, understanding for the first time the nature of the decision he had come to out there in the cold rain. He had not come back because he could believe in her love, but because he had decided to accept whatever happiness was offered him. And he was prepared to open himself to her, to run the risk, when he had nothing more to trust in than his need of her. She pushed back against his arms and looked up lovingly into his eyes.

"You have me forever," she said tenderly. "I'll spend my life making you believe that, but you may as well begin believing in it now. I love you, and I'll go on loving you, and I'll still be loving you when you tell me to stop."

Jake's hold on her tightened and he lifted a gentle hand to her chin. His slow crooked smile spread over his face, the look in his eyes making her heart beat faster.

He was beginning to believe.

"I'll never tell you to stop loving me," he said, and bent to give her the promise with his lips.

Epilogue

IT WAS SNOWING in New York, a softly whirling snow that disappeared as soon as it touched the pavement. Vanessa snuggled down into the warmth of her fur coat, a wild mink that Jake had insisted on because it matched her hair. She was clinging to his arm, laughing up into his face, as he stopped and reached to open a famous door.

"Is this where we're going?" she asked, her voice climbing in surprise. "Cartier's?"

"This is where we're going," said Jake. And suddenly she remembered that long-ago promise, and she laughed lovingly up into his face. "Hello," she smiled winningly at the impeccably dressed man who approached them.

"Good afternoon, *madame*. Good afternoon, Mr. Conrad. May I wish you a merry Christmas?" he said, returning Vanessa's smile. "Is there something we can show you?"

They wished him a merry Christmas, and Jake said, "It's our tenth anniversary. We're looking for something very special." Expressing his congratulations, the man led them to a counter where a salesman was lovingly altering a display of sparkling diamond jewelry.

"Ten years," repeated the salesman when he had been informed of their errand. "Not many marriages last such a long time these days, do they? You must feel very lucky." Discreetly he laid a tray on the glass counter in front of them.

Jake was smiling down into her eyes. "Very lucky," he said softly. "Take off your gloves, darling." He picked up a ring on which a large diamond was flanked by emeralds.

Her left hand already sparkled with the diamonds and warm gold of her six-week-old engagement and wedding rings, and Jake caught it in his as she pulled off the glove, and he dropped a kiss in her palm. "These were for the first ten years," he reminded her softly, then picked up her right hand and slipped the emerald ring down over her knuckle. "This one is for forever."

"Forever," she echoed, smiling up into the dark eyes that held no trace of remembered pain; and she knew that he believed it, and happiness exploded in her heart and sang through her blood in a deafening triumphant chorus.

Forever.